CRITICAL ACCLA

'A million readers can't be wrong!
day, sit back and enjoy a bloody good read' **Howard Linskey**

'Taut and compelling' **Peter James**

'Leigh Russell is one to watch' **Lee Child**

'Leigh Russell has become one of the most impressively dependable purveyors of the English police procedural' ***Times***

'DI Geraldine Steel is one of the most authoritative female coppers in a crowded field' ***Financial Times***

'A brilliant talent in the thriller field' **Jeffery Deaver**

'Brilliant and chilling, Leigh Russell delivers a cracker of a read!' **Martina Cole**

'A great plot that keeps you guessing right until the very end, some subtle subplots, brilliant characters both old and new and as ever a completely gripping read' ***Life of Crime***

'The latest police procedural from prolific novelist Leigh Russell is as good and gripping as anything she has published' ***Times & Sunday Times Crime Club***

'A fascinating gripping read. The many twists kept me on my toes and second guessing myself' ***Over The Rainbow Book Blog***

'Well-paced with marvellously well-rounded characters and a clever plot that make this another thriller of a read from Leigh Russell' ***Orlando Books***

'A well-written, fast-paced and very enjoyable thriller'
The Book Lovers Boudoir

'An edge-of-your-seat thriller that will keep you guessing'
Honest Mam Reader

'Well-paced, has red herrings and twists galore, keeps your attention and sucks you right into its pages' ***Books by Bindu***

'5 stars!! Another super addition to one of my favourite series, which remains as engrossing and fresh as ever!'
The Word is Out

'A nerve-twisting tour de force that will leave readers on the edge of their seats, Leigh Russell's latest Detective Geraldine Steel thriller is a terrifying page-turner by this superb crime writer' ***Bookish Jottings***

'An absolute delight' ***The Literary Shed***

'I simply couldn't put it down' **Shell Baker,**
Chelle's Book Reviews

'If you love a good action-packed crime novel, full of complex characters and unexpected twists, this is one for you'
Rachel Emms, *Chillers, Killers and Thrillers*

'All the things a mystery should be: intriguing, enthralling, tense and utterly absorbing' ***Best Crime Books***

'A series that can rival other major crime writers out there...'
Best Books to Read

'Sharp, intelligent and well-plotted' ***Crime Fiction Lover***

'Another corker of a book from Leigh Russell... Russell's talent for writing top-quality crime fiction just keeps on growing' ***Euro Crime***

'A definite must-read for crime thriller fans everywhere'
Newbooks Magazine

'Russell's strength as a writer is her ability to portray believable characters' ***Crime Squad***

'A well-written, well-plotted crime novel with fantastic pace and lots of intrigue' ***Bookersatz***

'An encounter that will take readers into the darkest recesses of the human psyche' ***Crime Time***

'Well-written and chock full of surprises, this hard-hitting, edge-of-the-seat instalment is yet another treat... Geraldine Steel looks set to become a household name. Highly recommended' ***Euro Crime***

'Good, old-fashioned, heart-hammering police thriller... a no-frills delivery of pure excitement' ***SAGA Magazine***

'A gritty and totally addictive novel'
New York Journal of Books

ALSO BY LEIGH RUSSELL

Geraldine Steel Mysteries
Cut Short
Road Closed
Dead End
Death Bed
Stop Dead
Fatal Act
Killer Plan
Murder Ring
Deadly Alibi
Class Murder
Death Rope
Rogue Killer
Deathly Affair
Deadly Revenge
Evil Impulse
Deep Cover
Guilt Edged
Fake Alibi
Final Term
Without Trace

Ian Peterson Murder Investigations
Cold Sacrifice
Race to Death
Blood Axe

Poppy Mystery Tales
Barking Up the Right Tree
Barking Mad
Poppy Takes the Lead

Lucy Hall Mysteries
Journey to Death
Girl in Danger
The Wrong Suspect

Leigh Russell

SERVING COLD A

REVENGE KILLING

NO EXIT PRESS

First published in the UK in 2024 by No Exit Press,
an imprint of Bedford Square Publishers Ltd,
London, UK

noexit.co.uk
@noexitpress

A CIP catalogue record for this book is available from the British Library.

ISBN
978-1-83501-045-7 (Paperback)
978-1-83501-046-4 (eBook)

2 4 6 8 10 9 7 5 3 1

Typeset in 11 on 13.75pt Times New Roman
by Avocet Typeset, Bideford, Devon, EX39 2BP
Printed and bound in Great Britain by
CPI Group (UK) Ltd, Croydon CR0 4YY

To Michael, Joanna, Phillipa, Phil, Rian and Kezia.
With my love.

Glossary of Acronyms

DCI – Detective Chief Inspector (senior officer on case)
DI – Detective Inspector
DS – Detective Sergeant
SOCO – scene of crime officer (collects forensic evidence at scene)
PM – Post Mortem or Autopsy (examination of dead body to establish cause of death)
CCTV – Closed Circuit Television (security cameras)
VIIDO – Visual Images, Identification and Detections Office
MIT – Murder Investigation Team

1

LAUREN WAS ON HER way out to buy cigarettes when the tenant who lived on the ground floor peered out and beckoned her with a gnarled finger. Mentally rehearsing her refusal to help the old woman with her shopping, Lauren hesitated at the foot of the steep staircase.

'You must be hearing things,' she replied, when the old woman paused to take in a wheezy breath. 'Probably the TV.'

'Don't give me that. I may be getting on, but I'm no fool. She's up there every week. I've seen her on the stairs, always the same one. She stays all night, and I know what she's doing up there. They think I don't hear them fornicating.' The old woman's eyes gleamed with malice as she spat the word. 'You tell him I know what he's doing up there with his drug peddling and his women. The Lord will mete out His punishment. And you're no better.'

Lauren turned her back on the old crone and clattered upstairs to confront Jay.

'I knew it! You're seeing another woman!' she screeched, without even stopping to take off her coat. 'Who is she? Don't lie to me! The old bag downstairs just told me about her, so you can't deny it. As soon as my back's turned, you've got someone else up here. And don't tell me this was just one of your mates scoring some dope, because I know she stays here all night.'

'You listened to that old fishwife?' Jay replied, raising his eyebrows in surprise. 'You can't believe a word she says. She's batty as a fruitcake. Are you telling me you trust her word against mine?' He spoke lightly, but his eyes blazed with fury. 'That old bitch has got it in for me. She goes out of her way to stir up trouble for me. I've warned her before to stop all this spiteful nonsense. Why on earth would you listen to her?'

Lauren wasn't convinced by his protestations. 'Why would she lie about it?'

Jay turned away, dismissing the accusation with a casual shrug. 'How should I know? She makes shit up. I've told her what I'll do to her if she carries on causing me problems.'

It really was the final straw as far as Lauren was concerned. Six months had passed since she and Jay first got together, and she was keen to move in with him. Apart from any other consideration, it was unnecessary for them both to be paying rent. Although she liked living with her flatmate, Natalie, she only had a small room to herself in their shared flat, while Jay had a self-contained apartment all to himself on the first floor of a house. There was easily enough room there for two people, so it was obvious she should move in with him, but he seemed content to live on his own, paying his rent all by himself. As long as he had enough left over for food, beer, cigarettes and drugs, he had told her that was all he needed. Much as he loved having her stay with him every Saturday, he said that during the week it suited him for her to sleep at her own place.

'You're missing the point,' she had protested. 'We could be together every night. Then she wouldn't be able to make stuff up about other women.'

Monday to Friday she was up and out before he needed to wake up, he had told her, and in any case, some of his punters didn't want to be seen by anyone else. It made them twitchy, and that was bad for business. She knew Jay faced increasing competition from the growing number of drug dealers in the city, so had decided not to insist, telling herself he would come round eventually if she was patient. She had been prepared to wait, but now his neighbour had put her straight about the other woman who regularly spent the night with him during the week.

'Stop going on about it,' Jay snapped, waving his hand around. 'And where are my cigarettes?' A scowl twisted his good-looking features. Then his expression softened, and he spoke in a wheedling tone. 'You can see for yourself there's no one else here. You know I have people coming and going all the time, but no one else stays here, only you.'

'No one in their right mind would *want* to spend time in this stinking dump,' she retorted under her breath.

Vexed, she pushed a dirty plate off the arm of the sofa. It landed upside down, scattering greasy crumbs on the carpet. She should have noticed the signs: a red flush spreading across his cheeks, the flaring of his nostrils, but she was too upset to hold back.

'I'm sick of the way you treat me,' she snapped. 'You can sit there feeling smug, thinking you're getting away with it, but I won't put up with it any more. I won't be cheated on, and I won't be treated like one of your whores. You need to start treating me with respect, or…'

'Or what?' he asked her, leaning back in his chair.

His lips curled, but he clenched his right fist and started beating a tattoo on the arm of his chair with the fingers of his other hand, while his gaze never left her face.

'Or you can sling your hook,' she replied, daring him to retaliate.

'What are you talking about? You can't throw me out of my own flat.' His bark of laughter further infuriated her.

'Very well then, I'll leave, shall I? You think I'm joking? Well, I've got news for you, because I'm not staying here another minute.' She bit her lip, realising she was breaking up with him, but she was too angry to stop. 'I don't know whatever made me think you were worth it. You're just a jumped up pathetic little backstreet drug pusher. You think you're some big shot drug baron but you're nothing. Even the police can't be bothered to arrest you. That's how insignificant you are.'

He had never raised his hand against her before, and she had refused to believe he ever would. His muckraking neighbour had passed on a rumour that Jay had put his last girlfriend in hospital; had she not been too scared to press charges, he would probably have served time. But Jay had persuaded Lauren that he had never really cared about his former girlfriend, who had been shallow and self-centred. He had painted so monstrous a picture of her that Lauren had ended up convinced that, far from being abusive, Jay was a saint for having put up with her for so long.

'It wasn't entirely her fault,' he had explained, with a sad smile that made him look positively cherubic, with his blue eyes and turned-up nose. 'She couldn't help herself. She was insanely jealous. It's completely different this time. With you, it feels right.'

To begin with, Lauren had loved him for the understanding he had shown his neurotic ex-girlfriend. Only gradually had she had come to suspect that he was not as thoughtful as he claimed. Still, there had probably been some truth in what he told her. It might have been drugs that had made his ex so dependent on him, and dope could make people paranoid. She wondered if that was happening to her. Her flatmate had formed a different opinion of Jay. As soon as she met him, she had told Lauren in no uncertain terms that Jay was a narcissist.

'You don't even know him,' Lauren had protested. 'You've only met him once.'

'Once was enough to see what he's like,' Natalie had replied. 'He's bad news.'

Lauren had ignored Natalie, defending Jay until her flatmate gave up and stopped talking about him. Now, with her cheek stinging from Jay's slap, Lauren realised she had been naïve to dismiss her friend's warning so hastily. Seeing his expression, she felt faintly sick. Far from apologetic, Jay seemed excited, as though he found hitting her exhilarating.

'I'm leaving,' she said, forcing herself to speak calmly.

Her words sounded oddly hollow, as though someone else was speaking, and she realised her legs were trembling. Before she could move, Jay pushed past her and went to stand in the doorway, blocking her exit.

'Get out of my way, right now. I mean it.' In spite of her determination to retain control of the situation, her voice rose as fear overwhelmed her anger.

Stepping forward, she attempted to squeeze past him. Suddenly, she was spinning round, his arm pressing against her throat. Choking, she lashed out in a panic, kicking at his legs and scrabbling to grab hold of his arm, desperate to force him to relax his grip, but he was too strong for her. After a moment, she hung limp in his grasp, waiting for an opportunity to free herself.

'You think you can walk out on me, you tramp?' he muttered between clenched teeth. 'You think you can just walk away? No one does that to me. No one.' With each iteration he jerked his arm viciously, ramming it against her throat, making her gag.

The edge of his other palm struck her chin as he clamped a hand across her mouth. She couldn't see him, but she could hear him panting, his fury almost palpable.

'How about if I throw *you* out, see how you like that,' he hissed in her ear.

He dragged her through the door. She began kicking and scratching at his arms again, although she could hardly breathe, while his hand muffled her screams of protest. She was still struggling, afraid he was going to choke her to death, when they reached the top of the stairs. Frantic with terror, she deliberately stamped her pointed heel down on his foot. He let out a yelp of pain and released his hold on her neck, losing his balance. He reached for the banister with one flailing hand, enabling her to squirm out of his violent embrace. She fell face down on the floor. The carpet felt scratchy against her cheek, and it stank of cigarettes and stale beer.

As if from a vast distance, she heard him cry out several times as he tumbled down the stairs. Before he reached the bottom, there was a horrible thump and then he was silent. Shocked, she scrambled to her feet and staggered back to the flat to grab her coat and bag, before stumbling after him, clinging to the banister, her legs shaking. He was lying motionless at the foot of the stairs. As if in a dream, she leaned over the mound of his body, terrified he would reach out and grab her. Breath rasped in his throat, but he didn't move. All she could think was that she had to get away from there. As she stepped over him, his eyelids flickered and his hand twitched. Stifling a scream, she staggered away down the hall. Just before she slammed the front door behind her, she thought she heard his voice call out her name.

She stepped out into an overcast world of grey rain. A car sped past, drenching her legs with the splash from a large puddle at the kerbside. Without looking back, she made her way to the bus stop. A large woman waiting there gave her a wary smile. Lauren turned away. A man strode past, his coat collar turned up against the rain. Still in a daze, she gazed back along the glistening street, wondering if Jay had recovered from his fall, and whether he would come after her. She began to cry, but no one noticed her tears mingling with the rain on her cheeks. If anyone had realised she was crying, they would probably have assumed she was pissed.

Hours seemed to pass before the bus drew up. Even though it was stationary when she boarded, she clung to the rail and the backs of the seats, afraid her legs would give way. The large woman from the bus stop nodded at her with a cheery grin as she passed. Lauren whipped her gaze away as though she had been stung. Staring at rain sliding down the window she shuddered. In her mind she could hear Jay's voice calling out to her from the foot of the stairs and wondered if he would remember how she had fled, leaving him lying there alone. But it was too late to go back and, in any case, she reminded herself fiercely that she never wanted to see him again.

2

WORN OUT AND READY to put her feet up, Ariadne pulled into her drive. Although it was technically still autumn, the evenings were drawing in and there was a feeling of approaching winter in the air, heralded by more than just a drop in temperature. The sky was tinged with grey, and recent heavy showers had aided the gusty weather in stripping the trees of their last lingering leaves. Regretting having left her gloves at home that morning, she hurried from the car to the house. She was ravenous, and hoped her husband would have dinner in the oven. All she wanted to do was eat, slump in front of the telly for a couple of hours, and fall into bed.

As she was hanging up her jacket, she heard voices in the living room. Having released her shoulder-length black hair from its elasticated band, she glanced in the mirror before going in to find Nico talking to a man he introduced as Yiannis. Even before she heard his name, Ariadne guessed their guest was Greek, like her husband. With the same black hair and olive complexion, seeing them from behind the two men could have been brothers. Only when they stood up and turned to face her, did she see how different they were. While Nico was slender with delicate features, the stranger had thick, tufty brows which overhung his dark eyes set in a fleshy countenance and, although short, he was stocky. He looked older than Nico, who was forty. Stifling a yawn, she greeted the stranger politely.

'Yiannis needs some help,' Nico said as he gestured at their visitor to sit down again. 'It's more your area than mine,' he added apologetically.

Ariadne hesitated. She guessed Yiannis wanted her advice in her professional capacity, but if this was a matter for the police, he should really be following official procedure, not approaching her privately. That her husband expected her to help his friend was typical of Nico. His reluctance to turn down a request for assistance had landed him in trouble more than once. It both irritated her and, at the same time, was one of the reasons she loved him. As a detective inspector working in serious crime, she spent her working life investigating the consequences of the darker side of human nature. If only more people shared her husband's generosity of spirit towards his fellow man, the world would be a better place.

With a sigh, she settled on the sofa, and asked Yiannis what she could do for him. At least she would hear him out before sending him to the police station or, if necessary, escorting him there herself. Nico left the room to make coffee, and she heard him tinkering about in the kitchen.

'I own a house in Penley's Grove Street,' Yiannis began, leaning forward in his chair and gazing earnestly at her. 'This house is divided into two maisonettes, and both are let to tenants. This morning I received a call from one of my tenants, an elderly lady who lives on the ground floor. She said she had heard a noise outside her door, and when she opened it she saw her neighbour lying in the hall. She didn't know what to do, and so she called me.'

He paused and Ariadne waited, stifling a yawn. This sounded like the preamble to a dispute between neighbours. She began mentally rehearsing how to extricate herself from Yiannis's problem as courteously as possible.

'She complained that he wasn't moving, and she was afraid to go out,' Yiannis explained earnestly.

'I understand that's a problem,' Ariadne said. 'But I'm not sure what you want me to do about it. Had her neighbour fallen down the stairs?'

Yiannis paused as Nico entered the room carrying a tray of coffee. Nico raised his eyebrows in silent enquiry.

'I'm getting to it,' Yiannis said, before turning to face Ariadne again. 'I went there straightaway to see what the problem was. And there was a body.'

Ariadne wasn't sure she understood. Too tired to remonstrate, she accepted a cup of strong Greek coffee even though it was early evening and she knew it would probably keep her awake that night. Biting back the temptation to say she had no idea what Yiannis was talking about, she asked him to be more specific about what he had found.

'There was a body,' Yiannis repeated, and she noticed his voice trembled slightly. 'It was my other tenant, who lived on the first floor. He was lying at the foot of the stairs.'

Ariadne took a gulp of coffee which burned her tongue. 'You said "a body"… '

'I called for an ambulance at once,' Yiannis continued, speaking rapidly now, as though keen to reach the end of his account. 'He never stirred, and when the paramedics arrived, they told me he was dead. I was worried he could have been saved, if I'd known what to do, but I was afraid to touch him in case I injured him further. But they told me my tenant had been dead for some time. Before I arrived he was dead. He had – how do you say it? – mortis of the body. There was no doubt about it. He was dead.' He shuddered. 'The paramedics called the police, who took the body away. But now I have to go to the police station even though I have done nothing wrong. Nothing! So I came straight here to ask Nico if you would help me. He told me once that you have influence at the police station. He is so proud of you.' He hesitated, his face suddenly pale, before adding in a low voice, 'I do not want to go to the police station.'

Ariadne had only recently been promoted to the rank of acting detective inspector, and was gratified to hear that Nico was proud of her work. But she couldn't assist Nico's friend in an independent capacity.

'Yiannis, I'm afraid you have no choice. You will need to present yourself at the police station to make a statement. There's no need to worry,' she added kindly, seeing his stricken expression, 'you're a witness, that's all. The likelihood is that your tenant collapsed and died from natural causes – a heart attack or a stroke, something like that. Was he elderly?'

'He was a young man, a man in his prime,' Yiannis replied miserably. He hesitated before adding, 'I was told he took drugs, but I had no way of knowing if that was true. I saw no sign of it myself. If I had known, I would have thrown him out. I don't want any trouble.'

'What made you think he was taking drugs?' Ariadne asked.

'Not serious drugs,' he replied quickly, with an anxious grimace. 'There was no mention of serious drugs. And it probably wasn't true. The old woman on the ground floor told me he was selling drugs. She said disreputable visitors came and went at all hours, disturbing her. But she was always complaining to me, about many things, and I took no notice of her. As far as I was concerned he was a good tenant. He paid his rent, and what he did in private was not my business. If he was doing anything illegal, I knew nothing about it. I only heard rumours from a confused old woman. It had nothing to do with me. I don't want any trouble,' he repeated.

'I'm sure you won't be convicted for running a drug ring,' Nico said, smiling. 'You can't know everything your tenant was doing.' He nodded at Ariadne, asking her to confirm that was the case.

'But why must I go to the police station?' Yiannis cried out, his composure breaking down. 'What do they want with me?'

'Presumably they just want a statement confirming he fell down the stairs,' Nico replied. 'It sounds like his death was an accident. You've got nothing to worry about.'

Ariadne acknowledged her husband's words with a smile of her own. 'I'm very sorry about the circumstances,' she went on, 'but there's really nothing to be afraid of.'

As she spoke, her phone buzzed. Glancing at the screen, she saw that her former colleague, Geraldine, was calling. Making a mental note to call her back once Yiannis had gone, she ended the call.

'I do not want to talk the police,' Yiannis muttered.

Questioning him, Ariadne learned that he had left an unpaid debt behind when he left Greece, some years earlier. Wary of running into his creditor, he had not been back since. She assured him the detectives investigating a possibly suspicious death would not be interested in his bad debts. But she had a feeling he might be concealing the true reason he had left Greece all those years ago, and had never been back. It wasn't until she was setting her alarm for the morning that she noticed the missed call from her friend, and remembered she had forgotten to call Geraldine back. Resolved to contact her the next day, she went to bed and fell into an uneasy dream where she fled Greece after being chased by a white rabbit called Geraldine. 'You could have waited for me,' the rabbit grumbled, crouching in her boat as she rowed towards the open sea.

'Don't let me drink coffee in the evening again,' she complained to Nico the next morning.

He smiled and kissed her on the nose. 'When have I ever been able to stop you doing anything?' he asked.

3

THE BABY WAS CRYING again. Reluctantly, Geraldine hauled herself off the sofa where she had been dozing and made her way into the bedroom. Tom lay in his cot, his face red with the effort of yelling, his fat little arms reaching up with clenched fists, as though ready to take a swipe at whoever answered his imperious summons. The strength of his anger was almost palpable, giving her a faint sense of dread that she would be unable to calm him, but he settled down to feed almost at once. She savoured her relief, resigned to the fact that the anticipated rush of maternal rapture had so far seemed to elude her. She had tried to explain to her sister that her enjoyment of motherhood was still tentative.

'I'm sure your maternal feelings will come,' Celia had assured her, complacent in her own mothering skills. 'Just be patient. You're probably still exhausted.'

Geraldine had felt relatively confident when Celia had visited her, but now she was alone again with a tiny creature utterly dependent on her for his survival. At times she was afraid the magnitude of her new responsibility would overwhelm her. Never before had she concealed her feelings from her life partner, but she had been unable to share her struggle with anyone, least of all with Ian who wanted only to hear that she loved being at home with Tom. She couldn't bear to disappoint him. Working as a detective inspector in serious crime, Geraldine had never before experienced this constant nagging self-doubt. A murder investigation gave her defined goals and objectives, and required a logical thought process in which emotion played no part.

She was not used to feeling helpless with a dizzying love that seemed to tear her away from her own personality. Added to her emotional turmoil was her piercing guilt at feeling bored, spending her waking hours with one tiny person who did nothing but cry and feed.

There had been heavy showers on and off all the previous day. Every time she had decided to go out for a walk to clear her head, there had been another downpour, and now it was raining again. Had she had only herself to think about, she would have put on a waterproof coat and gone out without hesitation. Tom had been grizzly all day and she knew they would probably both feel better for a change of scene, but somehow she didn't have the energy to get herself and the baby dressed to brave the rain. She could take the car, but where was there to go? Her sisters both lived miles away, and her local friends had all been colleagues at the police station in York. Ian had urged her to take Tom along to the police station to show everyone, but really, what was the point? Under pressure at work, they would have no time to socialise. They would tell her what a fine-looking baby Tom was, before turning back to their work, leaving her excluded from the camaraderie of the police team. She missed that aspect of her work so much it was like a physical pain in her guts. Never alone now, day or night, she had never felt more isolated.

Ian was home late. Unapologetic, he told her that he had stopped for a beer with a few of his colleagues.

'You know how it is,' he said cheerily. 'One thing leads to another. I kept meaning to leave and then someone else got in a round.' He laughed, a man at ease with life.

Geraldine smiled, genuinely happy for him. Just because she was stuck at home with a baby was no reason for Ian to feel similarly trapped.

'How was your day?' he asked, peering at her.

'Oh, fine,' she lied. 'He's growing all the time,' she added, more for something to say than because she actually thought the baby was significantly bigger than he had been the previous day, or the day before that.

'Yes, he looks healthy,' Ian agreed.

He took Tom from her and the baby gurgled with pleasure as Ian swung him up in the air. Geraldine remonstrated feebly to him to be careful, trying not to feel peeved that Tom seemed so much happier when Ian took him than he ever was when she picked him up. At the same time, she was relieved to hand the baby over. Perhaps for an hour or two she might be able to forget about her responsibilities and relax. Running a team of fellow detectives investigating a murder had never seemed as challenging as taking care of one tiny, helpless human being.

'So, what's to eat?' Ian asked.

With a sinking feeling, Geraldine realised she hadn't prepared anything for supper.

'I'm sorry,' she mumbled. 'I fell asleep this afternoon. I've been so tired today. I completely forgot, and then I didn't want to take Tom out in the rain, and then he fell asleep,' she added, feeling as though she was back at school, offering a string of excuses for failing to hand in her homework.

Humiliated and confused, she felt tears gather in her eyes, but Ian was looking at Tom and didn't notice.

'Not to worry,' he said breezily. 'I'll get us a takeaway. What do you fancy?'

She shrugged without looking up, unable to trust herself to speak in case her voice betrayed her emotion. She had been at home all day, with nothing to do but feed and change the baby, and she hadn't even thought to prepare dinner for Ian when he arrived home after a day at work. Tom was over five months old and sleeping through the night so she could no longer claim she was recuperating from the birth, difficult though that had been. Meanwhile Ian insisted on telling her what a wonderful job she was doing as a mother. She wanted to shout at him that she wasn't a wonderful mother at all, that she hated being stuck at home with the baby, and all she wanted to do was return to work and have her old life back. But Tom had come along, and her identity had changed into something glorious and terrifying. She was a mother and would be for the rest of her life. There was no going back. Geraldine had long ago come to terms with her own biological mother giving her up for adoption. A dysfunctional alcoholic who had given birth to twins, it was understandable that she had been unable to cope. Geraldine's own situation was completely different. But in her darkest moments, she wondered whether she had inherited some flaw that would make her an unsuitable mother.

'How about fish and chips?' Ian asked.

Geraldine nodded. 'That would be lovely,' she muttered, grateful that he hadn't seemed to mind her thoughtlessness, yet irrationally annoyed by his carefree attitude.

Although she wasn't hungry, she knew it was important to eat sensibly. If she wasn't overwhelmed by maternal love for her baby, at least she could behave like a responsible mother and do her best to serve her baby's needs. Allowing herself to weaken wouldn't help either of them. She told herself love would grow and smiled, watching the way Tom's eyes followed Ian around.

'I'm sorry,' she whispered.

Ian looked at her in surprise. 'Are you crying?'

'It's my hormones,' she said, wiping her eyes.

'As long as that's all it is,' he replied, before turning his attention back to the gurgling baby.

'That's all it is,' she murmured. She hoped it was true.

4

In her early forties, Ariadne had been pleased to be asked to cover her colleague's role as a detective inspector, while Geraldine was taking maternity leave. There was a chance the promotion to acting DI might become a permanent appointment. Their young colleague, Naomi Arnold, had moved up through the ranks relatively quickly and was already a detective sergeant.

'You'll be a DCI before long.' Ariadne said, half joking, but Naomi took the comment seriously.

'I certainly hope so. That's what I'm working towards, but who knows?'

'You're ambitious,' Ariadne replied, a little wistfully. 'And that's not a bad thing,' she added quickly, seeing her colleague scowl.

'Why shouldn't I be ambitious?' Naomi asked. 'There's nothing wrong with trying to get on in life, is there?'

'Nothing wrong with that at all.'

Listening to Naomi made Ariadne feel rather old and staid. Pretty, with blonde hair, fair complexion, and pale blue eyes, Naomi looked delicate and dippy, but she was focused on her work and it looked as though she had an impressive future ahead of her. Ariadne wondered how much more successful her own career might have been, had she been less content to simply accept her situation in life, but it was pointless to regret what might have been. With an interesting and challenging job and a happy marriage, she had plenty of reasons to be content and was generally very satisfied with her life. Only occasionally did she question whether she might have pushed herself to achieve more.

'Have you spoken to Geraldine at all?' Naomi asked.

With a pang of guilt, Ariadne remembered the call she had missed from their former colleague.

'Actually, she called me yesterday, but I didn't get to my phone in time, and then I was busy and forgot to return her call. I'll speak to her this evening.'

Naomi was surprised Geraldine hadn't yet brought her baby in to the police station, and said as much, but before Ariadne could respond, they were summoned to a briefing.

'I hope she and the baby are all right,' Naomi said, as they walked towards the major incident room together. 'I mean, I thought she would have been in to see us by now. It must be getting on for six months since she left.'

'I'm sure everything's fine,' Ariadne reassured her. 'Ian would have told us if there was anything wrong, wouldn't he?'

Naomi nodded. 'Yes, Ian seems happy, doesn't he? You're right. We'd know if anything was wrong, wouldn't we?'

Detective Chief Inspector Binita Hewitt was waiting impatiently for the team to assemble. With her slender figure, trim dark bob and penetrating stare, her neat jacket seemed to reflect the precision she demonstrated in her work. Ariadne admired her senior officer's meticulous approach to investigations, but she worried that at times Binita paid too much attention to detail, for all that she liked to urge her team to look at the 'bigger picture'. Her collaborative approach made her seem indecisive at times, but she had proved successful in leading murder investigations before, and Ariadne had confidence in her leadership.

'It'll be interesting to see how well Binita does without Geraldine, if we've got a murder on our hands,' Naomi murmured.

'We all miss her, but I'm sure we'll manage,' Ariadne replied, a trifle tersely.

She did her best to overlook the implication that she might not prove capable of taking over in Geraldine's absence, and sighed. Already she was beginning to feel the pressure of her additional responsibility and, as far as she knew, they didn't even have a case to investigate. She wondered if anyone else was doubting her competence, but was quick to dismiss such pointless speculation. When she had discussed the situation with Nico, he had expressed absolute confidence in her and, as he had pointed out, he knew her better than anyone. Besides, she wouldn't have been offered the promotion, even temporarily, if her work record hadn't demonstrated that she was up to the job.

While Geraldine had been Ariadne's best friend on the team, she was aware that a close bond had developed between Geraldine and Naomi, after Geraldine had saved her younger colleague's life. Remembering what had happened, Ariadne resolved to look out for Naomi. She knew how much the young officer had relied on Geraldine, and regretted having spoken to her so brusquely. But there was no time to say anything more to her now as everyone was in place, and the detective chief inspector began. A man had been discovered in a property in Penley's Grove. The death could have been accidental, as the victim appeared to have fallen down a flight of stairs. With a shock, Ariadne realised Binita might be talking about Yiannis's tenant. She listened with growing alarm as Binita described how paramedics who attended the scene had felt there was something strange about the death. Binita paused for breath, and Ariadne blurted out, 'Strange in what way?'

'I'm coming to that,' Binita replied sharply and Ariadne looked down at the floor. 'The issue was that the body was found lying at an unnatural angle,' Binita went on. 'It's possible the injured man shifted himself into an awkward position before he died, but the paramedics thought it looked as though the body might have been moved post mortem. There was sufficient doubt for them to contact us, and the officers who attended the scene reported that something didn't look right. We have no details yet, and in any case we won't know for certain until after the post mortem, but in the meantime we're treating the death as suspicious. So let's see what we can find out about the dead man. We need to be ready to investigate if it turns out there was something unlawful about this death, as it seems might be the case. Nothing has yet been confirmed, but the consensus so far from those at the scene is that we need to look into this.'

Binita told them the dead man's name was Jay Roper, and he was known to the police as a small-time local drug dealer. His body had been discovered by an elderly neighbour who had contacted his landlord. Ariadne hesitated, but there was no point in admitting she had already met the dead man's landlord. She might be wrong and, in any case, if Yiannis had any involvement in the death, the investigation would uncover it.

'Come on,' she now exhorted the team. 'Let's get going and make short work of this.'

She was rewarded with a palpable lift in the atmosphere, as her colleagues smiled in appreciation of her positivity. Maybe being a detective inspector leading a murder investigation wasn't going to prove so hard after all.

5

BEFORE QUESTIONING YIANNIS, ARIADNE drove to Penley's Grove to question Mary Jones, the tenant who had called the landlord to tell him about the body. There were no parking spaces outside the house, and she had to draw up a few doors along. Pulling up the hood of her jacket, she hurried through a fine rain to the terraced house where Jay had lived. A cordon was already in place, with a uniformed constable posted by the front door. A couple of rubbish bins occupied most of the narrow paved yard, with an empty milk bottle and some rotting vegetables lying on the ground between them. No attempt had been made to brighten up the yard with flowers, or to sweep up the discarded rubbish. Ariadne logged her arrival and pulled on a protective suit and shoe coverings before negotiating the common approach path up the steps to the front door.

In the entry hall, a black and white floor covering cleverly designed to look like tiles had lifted in one corner to reveal that it was actually linoleum. At the far end of the hall, a steep staircase led up to the first floor. A painted wooden banister ran up one wall, but it was feasible that someone could have lost their footing and fallen headlong down the stairs. Carefully following a route indicated that skirted the hall, Ariadne reached Mary's front door and knocked. Mary didn't come to the door straightaway. After waiting a few moments, Ariadne knocked again and at last the door opened. The reason for the delayed response was immediately apparent. Mary stood bent over a walking stick which she was clutching with one hand, while the other rested on the door. She was wheezing, possibly from the effort of walking to the door, but her eyes were bright as she peered up at Ariadne.

'Yes?' Her voice was thin with age. 'What do you people want from me now?' she asked, taking in Ariadne's protective outfit.

Ariadne introduced herself.

'What do you want with me?'

'I'm here to ask you a few questions.'

'You'll have to come in then. I can't stand for long. It's my legs.' As if to emphasise her point, the old woman tapped her walking stick on the floor. 'Have you brought me my milk? They won't let me go anywhere. They're saying I can't even step out of my own apartment. And they're telling me I have to move out,' she grumbled.

'I'm sorry for causing you more inconvenience. I won't keep you long. But I do need to ask you a few questions about your neighbour.'

'Oh dear. Do we have to go over it all again? It was a terrible business. Terrible. He was a horrible man, you know, always disturbing me with his racket, and the street door opening and closing all day long. He had them coming to see him at all hours of the day and night.'

'Who came to see him?'

Mary shrugged and peered at Ariadne, her shrewd eyes glinting with malice as she mumbled darkly about the fires of hell. 'I don't know who they were,' she said at last. 'But he was up and down the stairs at all hours, answering the door. Are you going to come in or not? Only I can't stand here all day.'

She turned unsteadily and shuffled along a narrow hall, leaning heavily on her stick. Ariadne followed her past a raincoat hanging from a row of hooks on the wall above a worn pair of fur-lined ankle boots and a shopping trolley. Mary led her into a living room where two faded chintz-covered armchairs and a matching sofa were arranged in a semi-circle on a threadbare red patterned carpet. On a low table in front of a grimy fireplace, a large television screen dominated the room. The room looked old-fashioned but cosy, with cushions on every seat, lace-edged antimacassars, and a knitted blanket thrown over the back of the settee. A faint smell of soap and lavender failed to mask a stale body odour that greeted Ariadne as she entered the room. With a breathy grunt, Mary lowered herself slowly on to a chair, leaning on the arms as she manoeuvred herself into a sitting position.

'Can you describe what happened when you discovered the body?' Ariadne asked, shifting a plump corduroy cushion from an armchair and sitting down.

'I already told the constable what happened,' the old lady quavered irritably. 'My memory's not what it was.' She sighed. 'Anyway, I didn't know he was dead, not at first. No, it was Mr Yiannis who found out he was dead, not me. I thought he had passed out from all the drugs he took.'

'What was he doing in the hall?'

Mary shut her eyes and, for a second, Ariadne was afraid she had dozed off. 'I was just back from doing my shopping, and I was in the hall when I heard her upstairs, yelling.'

'Who was yelling?'

'I don't know which of them it was, do I?' The old woman's lips moved silently for a second. 'I knew what he was up to. I was a bit racy myself back in the day.' She cackled unexpectedly. 'You wouldn't think it to look at me now. But that was before I was saved,' she added, sombre once more.

'Before you were saved?'

'God forgives all who truly repent.'

'Who was yelling upstairs?' Ariadne steered the conversation back to her question.

Mary leaned forward in her chair, and a dry cough shook her narrow frame. She held out two gnarled fingers. 'He had two women. I heard them shouting, him and one of his women. I can't tell you who they were. He might have had more than two of them, visiting him up there,' she added thoughtfully. 'He had people coming and going at all hours, disturbing me. I hurried inside and shut the door, but I could still hear them shouting. Don't think I couldn't hear what went on up there.'

'You didn't mention this shouting before?'

The old woman dismissed the question with a flutter of her veiny hand. 'You can't expect me to remember everything that happens, at my age.'

'Did you hear what they were shouting?'

'He shouted, "No one! No one!" That's all I remember. Other than that it was all just raised voices, making a terrible din. No thought for me. No consideration.' She paused and her rheumy eyes grew sharp with alarm. 'Next thing, there was a lot of noise, like someone pulling luggage down the stairs, bump, bump, bump, and more yelling and groaning, and then it all went quiet. "Someone's moving out," I thought, "and good riddance."' She mumbled something about fallen women and their sinful ways. 'I put the kettle on, and then I listened through the door, just to make sure the noise had stopped.' She closed her eyes again. 'And I heard something.'

'What did you hear?' Ariadne prompted her.

'It sounded like a kind of moaning. I opened my door a crack to see what was happening out there, but I kept the chain on the door, just in case. You can't be too careful, can you, especially these days. And he was lying there, on the floor, at the bottom of the stairs!' Her eyes were wide open now, and she gripped the armrest of her chair, looking scared. 'I shut my door straight away to stop him coming in. As I told the other policewoman, I was too frightened to go out.' She put one wrinkled hand over her mouth and closed her eyes.

Afraid she was going to cry, Ariadne made a reassuring comment, before urging the old woman to continue with her story.

'There I was, trapped in my own flat!' she repeated. 'So I kept calling the landlord and eventually he answered, which was a blessing, because sometimes it takes days to get hold of him. And that's all I can tell you. After a while I heard a ruckus but I still had no idea what was happening. Then someone knocked at my door and, this time, when I opened it, I saw the hall was full of people all talking at once, and there was my neighbour from upstairs lying on his back, surrounded by police and doctors and I don't know who else. They told me he was stone cold dead. But there was no sign of his trollop. What I'd taken for a suitcase being dragged down the stairs had been my neighbour. Before I could set foot outside my flat to ask how long they intended to be there, blocking the hall, a very polite young policewoman stopped me. She wanted to know if I had seen anyone entering or leaving the building that morning, which I hadn't. Then she told me I wasn't to go out into the hall until they'd finished, and asked me if I needed anything. As it turned out, I didn't need much because I'd already been to the shops that week, but I asked her to get me some milk.' Her face relaxed in a smile. 'The Lord takes care of us all.'

It seemed an odd expression, given that her neighbour had just fallen to his death.

6

Lauren had been too scared to go back and check that Jay was all right. Telling herself he would be fine, she tried to act as though nothing unusual had happened, and they hadn't rowed at all. But she had seen him hurtling down the stairs and was convinced he must have injured himself, perhaps seriously. Just thinking about it made her feel sick. She kept wondering whether she could have done anything to stop him from falling, but she had been knocked over as they struggled. By the time she had clambered to her feet he was already halfway down the stairs.

Everything had happened so quickly she had scarcely had time to take in what was going on. One minute she had been threatening to leave him, and then he was looming over her, pressing his hand against her mouth, dragging her out of his flat. All she could remember after that was how she had fought against his vice-like grip on her wrists. She had kicked him as hard as she could. If she had been wearing her canvas trainers, she would probably have bruised herself. As it was, the pointed metal toecaps on her black patent shoes were sharp and unyielding and must have hurt his shins. She vaguely remembered stamping on his foot with her heel, and that was what had startled him into releasing his hold on her. The next minute, he was gone. It had all been over in a flash. She had seen his hands flapping around in a vain attempt to hold on to something as he fell, and then he was lying in a heap at the bottom of the stairs.

Some spirit of self-preservation had sent her racing back into his flat to seize her bag so she could flee before he recovered.

She had no recollection of rushing down the stairs to the street door, but she must have clambered across his body, or perhaps leapt over it, because somehow she had found herself outside on the pavement. She had a hazy memory of making her way to the bus stop, rain mingling with her tears. On the bus, damp and wretched, she had stared resolutely out of the window, avoiding looking at other passengers, as the bus carried her away from his flat and his inert body lying at the foot of the stairs. Not until she was nearly home had it occurred to her that he might be dead.

Her flatmate, Natalie, was away visiting her parents for a week. Arriving home to silence, Lauren had gone straight to bed, shivering. She didn't know whether her relationship with Jay was over, or if he was even still alive. Nearly delirious with grief, she lay in bed, crying and aching for what felt like hours. At last, she hauled herself her out of bed to make herself a mug of tea. Having drunk it, she felt a lot better and went back to bed where, at last, she fell asleep. Having slept fitfully through the rest of the night, she woke up with a pounding headache. Seeing herself in the bathroom mirror, she was startled by her appearance, her face pasty and her eyes red and blotchy as though she had been rubbing them for hours. After phoning her manager to say she had flu, and would probably be off work for a few days, she had some breakfast and then slunk back to bed and tried to sleep.

After a few days, she was feeling a little better, and able to think about Jay without bursting into tears. Luckily her flatmate was still away, so she didn't have to face any awkward questions, but she had decided to tell Natalie that she and Jay had split up. For all she knew, it was true. In any event, it would account for her crying and would give her a plausible reason for refusing to talk about him. Turning on the television, and waiting for the weather forecast before her soap, she was shocked to see him mentioned on the local news. The police were investigating the death of a man who had died after a fall down some stairs. She had a horrible feeling she was responsible for the accident. The horror of what had happened came flooding back, and she felt faint. Jay was dead and she would never see him again, never feel his arms around her or his lips on hers. As if to confirm her suspicion, the face of the old woman who rented the apartment below Jay's flashed up on the screen. Her wrinkled lips moved and she announced that she had heard her neighbour fall down the stairs. Bursting into tears, Lauren wept hysterically for a few moments.

Only when she calmed down a little did she register the significance of what she had heard. The news report had said the police were investigating the circumstances of Jay's death. That must mean they suspected he had been murdered. She trembled, wishing she could remember exactly what had happened when he had fallen. She wondered if the police could prove she had been there, watching. As it turned out, she had witnessed more than an accidental tumble. She had been watching her boyfriend die. Given that she had not called for an ambulance, but instead had fled the scene, it was almost inevitable the police would conclude she had deliberately pushed him down the stairs.

Forensic evidence of her DNA would be all over his flat, and they could probably prove she had been present when he fell. Appearances were against her. Her memory of the incident was confused, but she did recall struggling with him. Perhaps she had pushed him, but if so, she had acted in self-defence. *He* was the one who had dragged *her* along the landing, seemingly intending to push her down the stairs. In any case, it was the fall that had killed him, and that had been an accident. She hadn't even known he was dying. She was almost sure she had heard him moaning as she reached the front door and ran out into the street. Taking in a few deep shuddering breaths, she tried to think clearly. If she went to the police and told them exactly what had happened, they couldn't possibly suspect her of murder.

'*I had no idea he was so badly hurt*,' she muttered to herself, rehearsing what she would say to the police when they questioned her, as they were bound to do.

'*Why did you run off and leave him if his fall was accidental, as you claim?*' she imagined a stern-faced policeman demanding. '*Why didn't you call an ambulance when you saw he was hurt? You say you heard him moaning when you were leaving, so you must have realised he was injured. You knew he was alive, yet you left him to die.*' At her side, a grim lawyer would sigh and shake his head, and advise her to confess to the murder of her boyfriend.

'*You had a row,*' the policeman would press on, ignoring her denials. '*You discovered he was cheating on you with another woman, so you killed him. Confess! Confess! Confess!*' she imagined the policeman shouting at her. She could picture the scene. In her imagination, the policeman looked just like her headmaster at school. The longer she thought about it, the more hazardous her position seemed. It was true she had accused Jay of two-timing her and they had argued about it. The nosy old cow from the downstairs flat had doubtless been eavesdropping, and would be only too eager to come forward to accuse her.

From watching crime dramas on television, Lauren knew exactly what the police would be looking for, and was aware that she had an obvious motive for wanting to lash out at her cheating boyfriend. Added to that, she alone had had the opportunity to attack him, and the means had presented themselves right in front of her. She might attempt to convince a jury that his death hadn't been planned, but the fact that she hadn't summoned help when Jay had his accident would confirm her guilt. She wasn't even sure any longer that it had been an accident. In the terror of the struggle, had she deliberately pushed him to his death?

There was no time to beat herself up about what had happened. She would have to worry about it later. For now, she needed to focus on evading arrest. The police were probably already looking for her. She had to get away without delay. Dashing to her room, she packed her rucksack. She had no idea where to go; she knew only that she had to hide somewhere the police wouldn't find her. Once they caught her, it would all be over. No one would pay any attention to her protestations of innocence. She would be convicted of murder and given a long prison sentence. What kind of defence could she put up when she herself wasn't convinced she was innocent? Tears streamed down her face as she crammed clothes and a random hand towel into her bag, her thoughts spinning wildly. She wondered whether to leave a note for her flatmate. Her best option would be to hurry to the station and jump on a train, any train, and get as far away from York as possible. Her mother lived in Leeds, but the police would probably be looking for her there. She had to move fast, and find a place where she could never be found.

As soon as she saw a car cruising along Gillygate, Lauren was afraid the police had come looking for her. When her doorbell rang a few minutes later, she knew it was them. She struggled to control her panic, but it was hard to think clearly. One thing was obvious: they were bound to suspect she had killed Jay. She couldn't stay where she was, waiting for them to find her. On the other hand, she wondered whether it would be an overreaction to run away. After all, she had done nothing wrong and there was no reason why she shouldn't talk to the police. It wasn't her fault Jay had tripped and fallen down the stairs. For a couple of days she hadn't even realised what had happened to him. It wasn't until she had gone back to see him, and had seen the police activity at his lodgings, that she had believed he was dead. Now the police were ringing her doorbell while she sat on the floor, hiding her face in her hands and trembling, waiting for them to go away.

The ringing on her bell seemed to go on forever, but at last it stopped. Doing her best not to move the curtain, she peered down into the street. The police had gone, for now, but they would be back. Before they returned, she had to act quickly. The easiest response would be to simply wait where she was, open the door to them and face their questions, but there was no guarantee they would believe she had done nothing wrong. Jay had assaulted her, and there were bruises on her neck to prove it. Even so, the police might not believe she was innocent. They might twist her statement and say she had attacked him, and he had grabbed at her in self-defence when she had pushed him down the stairs. She had seen too many crime dramas on television to trust them. On balance, she decided it would be too risky to wait for them to come back and arrest her. Once she made her escape, she would be free.

Just before she left, it occurred to her that her flatmate might report her missing if she returned to find the place empty. Lauren couldn't risk drawing attention to her flight. Rummaging around for paper, she wasted precious time fiddling around to remove a sheet from the printer. 'Had to go away for a few days,' she wrote and then tore the sheet in tiny pieces and started again. It was best not to be too specific. 'Gone away for a while,' she wrote and added, 'Met someone,' as a vague explanation. Leaving the note under a mug beside the kettle, she pulled on her winter fleece and jacket, hoisted her bag on to her back, and left, hoping Natalie wouldn't notice she had raided their joint kitty. As she pulled the door closed behind her, she wondered if she would ever see her flatmate again. It started to rain as she reached the street, and she began to cry silently. Since her argument with Jay, everything in her life had gone wrong, and it was all his fault.

7

Avril, the young blonde anatomical technology assistant at the mortuary, greeted Ariadne like a long-lost friend. Recently married, Avril was bursting to talk about her wedding. Before Ariadne had a chance to speak, the pathologist's assistant launched into a detailed account of the event.

'Sorry I've not been around for the past month. We both took time off for the wedding, of course, but then, seeing as we were travelling so far, we had an extended honeymoon. It was fabulous. I want to show you some photos of where we were staying, but first, here's the wedding.' She took out her phone and began scrolling through her photos, without pausing in her commentary to allow Ariadne to respond. 'We were lucky, it was a glorious day. We took a chance on the weather being fine, because it can rain, even in August. That would have been a nightmare. Can you imagine?'

Ariadne extricated herself with difficulty, but not before she had commented that Avril's wedding dress was beautiful, and she looked lovely, and the wedding looked wonderful, and the honeymoon must have been brilliant. Her comments were sincere in that she was genuinely pleased for Avril, but she was only really interested in the results of the post mortem she was there to hear about.

The pathologist, Jonah, looked up as Ariadne joined him. Ugly in repose, his pug-like face lit up when he smiled, making him seem surprisingly attractive.

'I take it you've heard about the wedding of the decade?' he whispered, winking and gesturing towards the office where Avril worked. 'Or perhaps that should be the wedding of the century? Dear Avril. She does get overexcited. Still, better to have joyous occasions to celebrate than cause for grieving.' He lowered his eyes to gaze at the corpse lying on the slab between them and sighed. 'Goodness knows, we see enough of that here.'

'Can you shed any light on the reason for my visit?' Ariadne asked, nodding at the body.

Jonah heaved a theatrical sigh. 'And there I was, thinking you had come here to see me. It says a lot when a woman is more interested in a dead man than in me.' He clutched his chest. 'You've broken my heart, inspector.'

Ariadne chuckled. 'Well, I won't tell your wife if you don't. So, have you got anything you can tell us?'

'Oh very well then, seeing as you're determined to talk about him, I'll have to swallow my disappointment. Come on then, let's get on with it,' he replied, with another exaggerated sigh. 'My rival was a well-fed chap, in his mid to late thirties, fond of his drink if the state of his liver's anything to go by.' He gave a wry smile. 'He was in surprisingly good health, given that he was a heavy smoker, but that would have caught up with him eventually. When will people learn to avoid what's bad for them? It's possible he had a few other unhealthy substances in his system, but we'll have to wait for the tox report to be sure about that. He had good muscle tone, so he probably worked out or did exercise of some description.'

'What did he die of? The team at the scene were suspicious, based on the position the body was lying in, but we're going to need more than that. As soon as you can let us have your report—'

Jonah nodded. 'You'll have my official report as soon as I've finished examining him.'

'Is there anything you can tell me now?' Ariadne hesitated before adding that Geraldine had told her Jonah used to share his initial impressions with her, in confidence. 'Of course, I may have misunderstood,' she added quickly. 'If you're not happy to speak off the record, that's fine. Far be it from me to push my luck, especially with a man who's brandishing a bloody scalpel.'

Jonah nodded easily. 'As long as we're off the record, I can say whatever I like.' He gave an impish grin. 'So, what would you like to hear? I'll happily share my darkest fantasies with you. Or if you prefer to hear something truly appalling, I can tell you one of my jokes. They're guaranteed to make your toes curl, although you probably won't laugh.'

Ariadne smiled. 'Why don't you start by telling me about him?' She looked down at the dead body lying between them.

'Ah, my rival for your attention – of course. Well, he sustained a few bruises before he died.' He pointed to a black smudge on the dead man's knee, and another on one of his elbows. 'He probably picked these up when he fell down the stairs.'

Ariadne nodded. 'Yes, a witness heard the accident.'

'If it *was* an accident?' Jonah murmured.

'You mean you think he was pushed down the stairs?'

Jonah shrugged. 'Unless your witness saw what happened, I'd say it's impossible to be certain one way or the other.'

'The witness heard the body falling, but before that she also claims she heard shouting. Are you saying you think his fall could have been caused deliberately?'

'Given what happened to him, I wouldn't be surprised. But don't quote me on that. It's just speculation.'

'What do you mean, "what happened to him"?'

'You'll be interested to hear that he appears to have been in a fight before he fell down the stairs.' He indicated several welts on the dead man's shins, as well as a small dark lump on the side of his head. 'Some of these he could have picked up on his descent, but look at this.' He pointed to a small round bruise on the dead man's ankle. 'This one clearly appears to have been made by a fairly sharp object. I'm not sure a fall down some stairs could have caused it.'

'On his ankle?'

'He might possibly have bumped into something, but it was more likely made by someone kicking him with a pointed toecap. And this definitely doesn't look as though it was caused by him falling down the stairs.' He indicated a small round bruise on the top of the victim's right foot. 'It appears his foot was stamped on by someone wearing high heels. Don't quote me on any of this, but it's hard to see what else could have left that particular bruise. And look here.' He pointed at a series of small black marks on the victim's upper arm. 'These were made by fingers. Someone grasped him by the arm, none too gently, while he was still alive.'

'So he was in a fight before he fell down stairs, which suggests he might have been pushed,' Ariadne said. 'What was the cause of death? You said he hit his head. Could that have killed him?'

'He banged his head a few times, but only enough for him to be dazed, and possibly even knocked out temporarily. But contrary to what you might think, the fall wasn't fatal. It might have been, if he'd been left unattended for long enough without recovering consciousness, but he was dead before that could happen.'

'Surely you can't know that? He was dead when he was discovered not long after he was heard falling down the stairs.'

'After his tumble, he was still alive when someone suffocated him.'

Ariadne made no attempt to conceal her surprise. 'You're saying he was suffocated?' she repeated. 'Are you sure?'

Jonah smiled sadly. 'This may not be a particularly endearing party trick, but I can tell when someone has been suffocated.'

'How did that happen?'

'The way it usually happens, by his airways being blocked,' Jonah replied with a faint grimace. 'It certainly wasn't what I was expecting to find,' he admitted. 'But there's no doubt he was suffocated, and that's what killed him. And I'd say that was definitely deliberate.'

He pointed to the dead man's mouth and nose. 'Can you see the faint bruising there? There are signs of congestion via dilation of the blood vessels along with tiny haemorrhages, and blood engorgement of the viscera, and the spleen is affected. And look at this.' Using a delicate implement, he lifted one of the dead man's eyelids. 'The bloodshot eyes are another indication, and that's what first alerted me to the possibility that he'd been suffocated. Unless someone sat on his face by accident, then I'd say he was almost certainly murdered. But, of course, that's not for me to say. I'm not the detective here.'

Ariadne stood for a moment, processing what Jonah had told her, before she asked about the time frame.

'I can't say how soon after he fell down the stairs the suffocation occurred, but I'd guess it happened almost at once. We're moving further into the realms of supposition now, so you mustn't quote me on this, but I don't think he was sufficiently injured in the fall to have lost consciousness for long. It's likely he was stunned, and so didn't realise what was happening until it was too late to resist. Like I said, this is all just speculation on my part. But it's what the evidence leads me to suggest, off the record.'

'So you think he was murdered,' Ariadne muttered. 'Your examination of the body supports what the officers at the scene reported.'

'I'm speculating based on the evidence in front of us,' Jonah said. 'What I'm telling you appears likely, but is as yet uncorroborated.'

He was an experienced pathologist, and Geraldine had advised Ariadne she could trust his opinion, even when his findings were not yet confirmed.

'Based on your findings, can I report that you believe he was murdered?'

'You need to check whether anything might have been obstructing his breathing, before you reach that conclusion. As I intimated, it's possible something like a heavy coat landed across his face when he fell, and he was too dazed to free himself. It's very hard to see how that could have exerted sufficient pressure to suffocate him, but we have to acknowledge it as a possibility.'

Ariadne checked the images taken at what was looking increasingly like a crime scene. Nothing was covering the victim's face in any of the pictures, and now she knew what to look for, she could detect a very faint discolouring of the flesh around his nose and mouth. Under magnification, two very faint indentations were visible, forming two parallel lines across the bruising on the dead man's nose. She wondered what they were. Jonah merely shrugged when she asked his opinion.

'From where I'm standing, all I can say is that you would be well-advised to open a murder investigation,' he said.

'And you'll be putting that in your report?'

'Yes. It's not an absolute, but weighing up the balance of probabilities, I don't think anyone could have covered his face and prevented him from breathing by accident, do you?'

Ariadne thanked Jonah for his help and hurried back to the police station to log her report and speak to Binita.

8

Ariadne summoned the team so she could ensure everyone was up to speed with the results of the post mortem. It was the work of a moment to confirm that nothing had been covering the dead man's face when the paramedics had arrived, so someone had removed whatever had been used to suffocate him after he was killed and before Mary looked out into the hall and called her landlord.

'It was probably drug-related,' a constable said, and a number of officers murmured in agreement.

'Yes, that could be the case,' Ariadne concurred. 'But there's no point in speculating at this stage, without any evidence that anyone else was involved.'

'It's a pity there's no ring bell or security camera at the property,' Naomi said.

'That would have been helpful,' Ariadne agreed. 'But we need to focus our attention on what we know, and not worry about what we don't have. Jay was a drug dealer, so a team is asking around that community to see whether anyone has any leads. Jay's neighbour reported that two women regularly visited him. There seems no reason for his neighbour to lie, so for now we'll accept that as a working hypothesis. If two women were visiting him, that raises various possibilities. Our priority is to find them.'

As the team dispersed to follow up any potential leads, Ariadne felt pleased with herself for keeping the investigation tightly on track. While she was focused on the practical questions raised by the case, she found it relatively easy to maintain control. Only when she thought about it did she feel slightly nervous about the responsibility she had taken on in accepting promotion to acting detective inspector while Geraldine was on maternity leave. Ariadne knew that if she did well, her new appointment might become permanent, and that added to the pressure she was already feeling. Her husband, Nico, had been guardedly encouraging about her promotion.

'If that's what you want, then go for it,' he had said.

'What do you think I should do?'

'That's not for me to say,' he had replied, smiling. 'I can't make decisions about your career. I'm not even a police officer. But you know I'll support you whatever you do.'

Faintly shocked to realise that part of her had actually wanted Nico to make the decision for her, she had answered almost without thinking.

'I'll do it.'

Her husband's smile had seemed a little wistful. She wondered whether a part of him had regretted her reaching a decision that would mean her taking on more responsibility and probably working longer hours, but she knew she would regret it if she turned down the opportunity to step up and run an investigation.

'I can do this,' she had told Nico, aware that she was saying that for herself.

If anything, a quick check of the contact list on the dead man's phone created more problems than it solved. Not only did he have a long list of names, but he had been contacted by numerous anonymous callers. It was going to take time to trace all of them, and initial reports were not positive. Many of the unknown calls had come from burner phones. And in the meantime, they were no closer to finding his two girlfriends, if they even existed. DNA from two women was discovered in Jay's bed, at which point Ariadne applied for more officers to help in the hunt for the women Mary had mentioned. At last, CCTV near Jay's flat revealed a young woman arriving at a bus stop very shortly after

Mary's call to her landlord. It was difficult to be sure, but close study of the film recorded on the bus itself showed the woman appearing to look around wildly with a hysterical air.

'Right,' Ariadne said, when she was shown the footage. 'Let's find her.'

While security film taken near Jay's flat on the night he died was being gathered and scrutinised, another team had been trawling through the contacts on Jay's phone and social media platforms. They struck lucky very quickly. A woman who resembled the passenger on the bus had phoned Jay on numerous occasions, sometimes several times in one day. It was noted that she had never called him on a Saturday.

Lauren Shaw lived above a hardware shop in Gillygate and worked in a florist in Goodramgate. As far as the police knew, only Mary and Yiannis, and now possibly Lauren, had gone near the body before the paramedics arrived. Naomi and Ariadne went to question Lauren first, as she was the most likely suspect, having been overheard quarrelling with him shortly before he died. There was no answer at her flat, so they drove to the florist where she worked. Sandwiched between two larger shops, the florist's was barely wide enough for two people to stand side by side between buckets of flowers and bouquets that lined the walls, so Ariadne went in alone. A sullen girl in a green overall was fiddling with one of the displays. When Ariadne approached her and asked to speak to Lauren, the girl shook her head.

'Don't know anyone called Lauren,' she replied and turned away.

When Ariadne introduced herself, the girl scowled and told her she would have to speak to the manager. Just then, a stout middle-aged woman came bustling through an internal door. Throwing a vexed glance at the girl, the woman asked if she could help Ariadne.

'I'm looking for Lauren.'

'Well, you've come to the wrong place.'

'I understand she works here.'

'She did, but she hasn't shown her face here all week and hasn't been in touch since Monday, when she called to say she had the flu. I've had to ask my daughter to help out in the shop, and she's got her studies to think about. It's been very difficult. Young people these days are so unreliable. You wouldn't have caught me not turning up to work without so much as a word, when I was her age. I understand people fall ill, but how ill do you have to be to not even pick up the phone? Don't tell me she's been incapable of getting to a phone for four days!' A red tinge coloured her cheeks as she spoke. 'I don't even know if she's got the flu.'

'We need to talk to Lauren urgently,' Ariadne replied. 'If she contacts you, please tell her she's not in trouble, but she needs to come to the police station to help us with an enquiry.'

While Ariadne was speaking, the manager's flush faded and she looked grave. Her daughter was listening closely.

'Is she a wanted criminal?' the girl asked, jigging from one foot to another with excitement.

'Be quiet, Daisy,' her mother muttered. 'You heard what the inspector said. Lauren's not in trouble, they just need her help. You'll probably find her at home,' she added.

Ariadne didn't reveal that they had already been to Lauren's flat and no one was there. Instead, she enquired whether the manager had found Lauren unreliable in the past.

'She's been working here for nearly a year and she's never been a problem until now. But you never can tell what's going on with young people. You think you know them and then—' She glanced anxiously at her daughter.

'Well, if you see her, don't forget to give her the message. We'd like to speak to her as soon as possible.'

'What did she do? Is she a fugitive from the law?' Daisy asked, her eyes shining with curiosity.

Ariadne gave what she hoped was a reassuring smile. 'It's nothing like that,' she fibbed. 'Please tell her we're concerned about her,' she added. The last thing she wanted to do was scare Lauren off, but she suspected the damage had already been done. If Lauren did turn up at the florist's, there was no knowing what spin the shop manager's daughter might put on the police visit.

Next, Ariadne and Naomi drove to the small hotel where Mary was being accommodated. The old woman didn't seem surprised to see them.

'Have you come to move me somewhere nicer?' she asked, displaying an incomplete set of yellowing teeth in a leer that might have been intended as a smile or a grimace. 'I'm not one to complain, but this place is damp. It stinks of mould. It's no good for my chest.' She gave a cough that sounded forced.

'We're sorry to bother you again. We just need to ask you a few more questions,' Ariadne said. 'May we come in?'

Mary's eyes narrowed. 'You said it was just a few questions, so why don't you ask me and get it over with? They've only given me one chair, and I dare say we can be done in the time it would take me to hobble back to it. You must be busy,' she added sourly. 'You young people always are.'

It was true they were in a hurry to move on and question Yiannis again. All the same, Ariadne insisted they go in so Mary could sit down.

'Do you remember if there was anything covering your neighbour's face when the landlord opened your door?' she asked, getting straight to the reason for their visit.

'Covering his face?' Mary repeated, frowning. She appeared to be thinking. 'Well,' she said at last, 'I didn't see anything. But something could have fallen off. I really couldn't say.' She scrunched up her face until her eyes were swallowed by wrinkles. 'Now you mention it, there could have been a coat over Yiannis's arm.'

'Are you sure?'

'At my age I can't be sure of anything. Can I lie down now? I can't sit for long. It gives me a backache.'

'One more thing before we go,' Ariadne said. 'You mentioned overhearing your neighbour having an argument with someone shortly before he fell down the stairs.'

She paused and Mary nodded, scowling and mumbling under her breath.

'What did you say?'

'I heard them arguing all the time.'

'Can you tell us anything about his visitors?'

'There were two women who went upstairs, never at the same time. I think he was having carnal relations with them both.' Her voice tailed off into a wheezy cough that sounded genuine.

'What can you tell us about these two women?'

Mary shook her head. 'I never saw them, not close up, not so as I'd recognise them if I saw them again. But I heard them running up and down the stairs. One every weekend, the other only in the week, both thumping up and down as though the devil was at their backs.' She shook her head, mumbling that he probably was.

'How do you know there were two of them, if you didn't see them?' Naomi asked.

'I saw their feet on the stairs,' Mary answered sharply. 'And sometimes I saw their legs. But I never looked out until they were halfway up. I didn't want him yelling at me for spying on him. Horrible man. No manners, and no respect.'

'Can you describe the shoes of the woman who was there on day he fell?' Ariadne asked, although she had all but given up on getting anything useful out of the old crone.

Mary screwed up her eyes until they disappeared again.

'She was in a hurry,' the old woman replied. 'Always in a hurry, that one. Her shoes were black and shiny with sparkly toes, like a fairy. She flew up the stairs.' Her eyes glittered mischievously.

'Can you describe the other woman who visited him regularly?'

'High heels,' Mary replied promptly. 'High heels and black stockings, and a skirt that barely covered anything. I saw more of her backside than her face.' She let out a wheezy cough that could have been laughter, and muttered something about the visitor 'showing her cheeks'.

Ariadne thanked the old woman for her help and they left, assuring her there was no need for her to get up. The mention of a coat over Yiannis's arm was significant, but the prosecution was unlikely to be able to call Mary as a witness if Yiannis were to be arrested.

'Batty as a fruitcake,' Ariadne muttered.

'I think you mean nutty as a fruitcake,' Naomi said. 'Why would a fruitcake be batty?'

Ariadne grunted, remembering what Jonah had said about the bruising on Jay's shins and foot, which seemed to tie in with both sparkly toes and high heels. It was a pity the witness was so doddery, but at least they could find her when they wanted to question her, and the suggestion that Yiannis might have been carrying a coat over his arm might be significant. On reflection, Ariadne wasn't sure if the old woman's account was actually very helpful. In some ways it seemed to make the situation even more complicated than before, as it seemed to implicate all three potential suspects: Yiannis and both the women who were regular visitors to Jay. The more information they discovered, the further they seemed to be from identifying the killer.

'Lauren never phoned him at the weekend,' Naomi said as they drove away. 'Is that because she was the woman who stayed with him every weekend?'

'It's looking as though she was there on Saturday night,' Ariadne replied. 'But all we know for certain right now is that we need to find her urgently.'

9

THE ROOM WAS STIFLING. The sound of grizzling infants and the squeaking and clattering of toys, against a background of murmured conversation, were as oppressive as the heat.

'It's stultifying in here, isn't it?' Geraldine murmured to Tom, who was squirming uncomfortably in her arms. He fixed his eyes on her as she was speaking and stopped wriggling for a few seconds before screwing up his face and letting out a squeal of protest.

Carefully she set him down on the floor before he could start yelling in earnest, and dismissed an irrational sensation that the other mothers were watching her. She felt awkward sitting among so many younger women, who all seemed familiar and easy in each other's company. They might have known one another at school, and perhaps now met regularly in Starbucks for coffee. Coming to the church hall toddler group would be only one in a series of social activities for them and their little ones. In a few years' time, their infants would probably attend the same school, while the mothers organised rotas for the school run, and play dates at the weekend. Some of them might go on holiday together. Geraldine suspected she was the oldest person in the room. She looked young for her age, but there was no denying that some of the other mothers might be young enough to be her daughter. She reached down to stop Tom from toppling over, and leaned him more securely against her legs. She had been sitting there for half an hour, and so far no one had spoken to her.

It had been Ian's idea that she visit a toddler group. He insisted that, even if Tom was too young to interact with other infants, he needed the experience of mingling with them. Ian was right, of course, and so Geraldine had looked online and found a toddler group that met only ten minutes' walk from their flat. This was her second visit. An exuberant young woman welcomed her warmly each week, and relieved her of a token fee to cover the cost of a rusk for Tom, and a cup of tea and a digestive biscuit for herself. The woman handing out tea took pains to point out that the biscuits were plain in case little fingers grabbed one and smeared chocolate on themselves and, presumably, everything else in the room. After that, Geraldine might as well have been invisible. Feeling sleepy, for a few seconds she didn't realise a woman beside her was addressing her.

'I'm sorry, what was that?' Geraldine said. 'I was miles away. I'm Geraldine,' she added, in a belated attempt to be friendly.

'I asked how old your grandson is,' the woman replied.

Geraldine hesitated. She didn't mind being mistaken for Tom's grandmother, but she wondered if the other woman would feel awkward being corrected.

She smiled as brightly as she could. 'Tom's six months,' she replied, 'and he's my son, actually.'

'Ah,' the other woman said. 'I'm sorry. I – I wasn't looking.'

'No need to apologise,' Geraldine hastened to reassure her. 'It's an understandable mistake. I'm not as young as some of the other mothers here.' She laughed, a little too loudly, and then wished she hadn't, because forcing an obviously fake laugh only made the exchange more embarrassing.

She had no opportunity to explain that she really didn't mind being a mature mother, because the other woman had already turned away to talk to someone else. Certainly Geraldine hadn't been ready for motherhood when she was in her early twenties, like some of the women in the room, although she suspected they might have preferred a few more years living a fun and carefree existence before taking on the responsibility of motherhood.

'How old is your little boy?' Geraldine asked, as the woman beside her stopped talking to someone else.

'She's a girl,' the woman replied shortly.

Geraldine shrugged. 'It's not always easy to tell,' she muttered, but the woman had turned away again.

Feeling dashed, Geraldine leaned down and scooped Tom up in her arms. 'We don't care, do we?' she whispered to him. 'We're happy just being here and watching, aren't we?'

As though in response to her question, Tom flung his head back and began to bawl. One or two women threw her sympathetic glances, but Geraldine had spent long enough sitting in a stuffy room, assailed by a cacophony of noises that would grate on her nerves if she heard them individually, and had combined to become almost unbearable. Tom might enjoy watching other children – although she had seen little evidence of that – but she derived no pleasure from sitting in the toddler group where she felt, if anything, more isolated than when she was at home with Tom. How was it possible she could feel intimidated by a roomful of mothers? She had faced life-threatening situations with less apprehension than she felt walking into the church hall, where all the other women seemed to deal with their infants as though it was the most natural thing in the world, which, of course, it was to most women. Perhaps Geraldine's nerves stemmed from an instinctive recognition that she had inherited an unnatural trait from her own dysfunctional mother.

'The problem is, you're used to your status at work,' Ian had told her when she had tried to explain how she had felt after her first visit to the toddler group. 'You're not used to having to start again and work your way up from the bottom.'

Geraldine had laughed at his analysis of her experience. 'What are you talking about?' she had replied. 'There's no hierarchy at the toddler group.'

But, of course, that was no more true than Ian's blundering misunderstanding. The brassy woman who collected money for refreshments was clearly the organiser, and the other women were drawn to her as though to an acknowledged leader. When she mentioned songs they could sing in their circle, the other women all joined in. When she asked for suggestions, they clamoured for her to choose their recommendations. Geraldine had named a song that Tom liked, but her voice had been ignored. She hadn't yet been accepted as one of the group.

'It's almost like a cult,' she had told Ian.

'You just said there's no hierarchy in the toddler group,' he pointed out, sounding amused and slightly dismissive.

He had told her to make an effort, and she had. But Ian had no idea how difficult the situation was for her, not knowing anyone, and having nothing in common with the other women, beyond the fact that they were all mothers.

'They're all younger than me,' she said, in an effort to explain how she was feeling.

'So what?' he replied. 'Some of the players in my football team are half my age, and many of my colleagues at work are younger than me. What difference does that make to anything? Listen, Geraldine,' he went on more kindly, 'if you don't like that toddler group, find another one. There must be loads of them in York. You've probably just hit on one that's a bit of a clique, that's all. But I do think it's good for Tom to learn to interact with other children.'

He didn't add that he thought it would be good for Geraldine too, but she suspected that was what he was thinking. To change the subject, she asked him about his work. It was hard for her to dismiss a flicker of envy as he began to talk about a case he was working on.

'At least you don't have to worry about any of that any more,' he said, smiling.

Geraldine looked down, afraid of betraying her feelings.

Before Tom was born, she and Ian had discussed her taking at least a year off before returning to work. She couldn't admit that the prospect of returning to work was all that kept her going from day to day.

10

OVER TWENTY-FOUR HOURS HAD elapsed since Jay's landlord had been asked to come to the police station to answer a few more questions. Recalling his reluctance to present himself at the police station, Ariadne decided to question him at home. Naomi drove Ariadne along Walmgate. They turned off into Hope Street and pulled up outside a neat semi-detached red brick house. Going through the wrought iron gate, they crossed a paved front yard enclosed by hedges still verdant even so late in the year, the leaves glossy and healthy. A woman answered the door. She was dressed all in black. Her narrow bowed shoulders made her look even shorter than the five feet or so she must have reached if she were standing upright. Her dark hair, streaked with white, was tied back in a bun at the nape of her neck and she wore no make-up. But her lined face was beautiful. It was difficult to gauge her age, but Ariadne judged she must be in her sixties, and possibly over seventy.

'Are you Mrs Karalis?' Ariadne enquired.

'Yes. I am Thalia Karalis.'

When Ariadne asked to speak to her husband, Thalia looked grave and shook her head.

'I am a widow.'

'I'm sorry.'

Thalia's shoulders rose in a slight shrug, and she smiled sadly. 'My husband died many years ago.'

'You have a brother called Yiannis?'

'No.' This time Thalia's smile was amused, yet cautious. 'Yiannis is my son. And who are you, please?'

Ariadne introduced herself and her colleague.

'You are here because his tenant died?' Thalia asked.

'Yes, that's right. We'd like to speak to Yiannis. Do you know where he is?'

'Yes, he is here.'

Thalia hesitated before inviting Ariadne and Naomi into the house. She ushered them into a small study off the hall, and asked them to wait. A solitary chair was set at a wooden desk under the window, opposite a fireplace surrounded by decorative blue and white tiles. A thick blue and white rug lay on the carpet in front of it. Ariadne wondered whether the rug had been placed there to conceal a worn patch in the carpet, which looked threadbare. Turning the chair to face into the room, Ariadne sat down to wait, with Naomi standing beside her. They heard Thalia padding up the stairs to fetch her son. Floorboards creaked overhead, and several minutes passed. Ariadne was growing concerned at the length of time it was taking for Yiannis to appear, and wondering whether he might have done a runner on learning the police had arrived to question him, when the door swung open and he appeared. He smiled wearily at Ariadne and greeted her in Greek.

'You were asked to come to the police station to answer a few questions. Why didn't you comply?' she demanded, answering him in English and rising to her feet.

Yiannis shrugged and was silent for a moment, as though he was weighing up his response. 'Well, you're here now,' he said at last, 'so you can ask your questions. What is it you want to know?'

Ariadne invited him to sit down but he said he preferred to stand. She felt awkward, facing him across the cramped study. She would have preferred to be seated in an interview room.

Irritated that Yiannis was dictating the circumstances for the meeting, she took a snap decision.

'I'd like you to accompany us to the police station now,' she barked, more brusquely than she had intended.

Yiannis's shoulders drooped and he gazed at her with a worried expression, but he didn't remonstrate. A light rain began to fall as the three of them hurried along the pavement to the car. Half an hour later, they were seated in an interview room. Yiannis had called an acquaintance of his, a dark-haired lawyer with glittering teeth and sharp eyes who arrived very soon after Yiannis contacted him. The lawyer began talking rapidly in Greek, but Yiannis stopped him with a raised hand, and warned him that Ariadne spoke Greek.

'She is the wife of Nico Moralis,' he added.

'We will talk later,' the lawyer murmured to Yiannis, this time speaking in English.

Ariadne announced for the tape that nothing of any consequence had passed between Yiannis and the lawyer. The latter had merely expressed dismay at the situation, asking Yiannis what trouble he had got himself into this time. Nothing more was said, but Ariadne was sure Naomi had registered the implication that Yiannis had been in trouble with the law before. Remembering his claim about owing money, she wondered once again if a bad debt was the only reason Yiannis had fled from Greece. On learning that Ariadne understood Greek, the lawyer fell silent and the two men sat gazing at her, waiting for the questions to begin.

'You haven't been arrested and are not suspected of breaking the law,' Ariadne assured Yiannis, 'so there's actually no need for a lawyer to be present. That said,' she went on quickly, before the lawyer could butt in, 'you are entitled to invite him here, if his presence makes you feel more comfortable.'

'If Yiannis is not under suspicion, please tell us what he is doing here,' the lawyer answered for his client. His words were courteous, but he glared at Ariadne with undisguised hostility as he spoke. 'You could easily have questioned him at his home.'

'Yiannis was first to arrive at the crime scene, so he is a key witness in our investigation into the murder of Jay Roper,' Ariadne replied promptly.

Yiannis frowned. 'Murder?' he repeated.

He turned to the lawyer and spoke rapidly in Greek, waving his hands frantically in the air as he spoke.

'He said he is horrified to learn that his tenant was murdered,' Ariadne translated for the tape. 'He believed Jay had died from falling down the stairs, and his death was an accident.'

Yiannis spoke in Greek again.

'He says he didn't know his tenant was murdered,' Ariadne translated again.

'I'm sorry,' Yiannis said. 'I forgot to speak in English. But what you said shocked me greatly. I had no idea he was murdered.'

Having confirmed that Jay's death was no accident, Ariadne asked him about Jay's girlfriends. Yiannis shook his head and said he knew nothing about the women who had visited his tenant at home. However hard Ariadne pressed him, he insisted he knew only what his other tenant had told him – that one of the women was thinner than the other, and wore shoes with fairy toes, whatever that meant. Yiannis was equally unforthcoming when Ariadne enquired whether he had been carrying a coat over his arm when he found the body.

'A coat?' Yiannis repeated. 'Why would I be carrying a coat instead of wearing it in this weather? Every day it rains.'

'If he did kill Jay, he's a bloody good actor,' Ariadne remarked, as they walked back to their workstations after the interview. 'He seemed genuinely taken aback to hear that Jay was murdered.'

'I couldn't understand what he was saying, but isn't it possible he was dismayed to discover we know Jay's death was no accident?' Naomi asked. 'He might have committed the murder, confident everyone would believe it was an accident. That wouldn't be a crazy assumption, given that the victim had just fallen down a steep flight of stairs. If Yiannis killed him and believed himself safe, it's understandable he would be upset to discover we're looking into Jay's death. But I agree, he certainly seemed shocked when you mentioned that Jay was murdered.'

'Well, either he's lying about carrying a coat that day, or else Mary was confused about what she saw, which isn't hard to believe,' Ariadne said. 'But if Jay's neighbour is telling the truth, then one of his girlfriends was there when he fell down the stairs. We need to speak to Lauren.'

11

Luckily it was relatively mild for late autumn, or Lauren might have struggled to cope with a single night out of doors. She had seen numerous weather forecasts on the television, but the inevitable drop in temperature overnight had never seemed particularly significant to her, until now. It was the contrast. During the day, while the sun was out, she had been warm enough in her coat, even when it was drizzling. But she had been completely unprepared for how cold it became after the sun set. She couldn't imagine surviving for long at such a low temperature. Once her ordeal was over, she resolved to start a campaign to raise awareness of the plight of the homeless people she passed on the street. She had never paid them any attention, although hurrying past with her eyes averted she had noticed they always had grubby-looking sleeping bags with them, even in the summer. Now she knew why.

Having spent a single night under a bridge, huddled inside all the sweatshirts and jumpers she had hurriedly stuffed in her backpack, she realised she had to find shelter for the coming night. She had hardly closed her eyes since leaving her flat. For hours she had slunk around side streets, afraid to go in shops where she could at least have passed the time, because she couldn't risk being spotted by a security camera. She had kept moving to avoid attracting attention, but with nowhere to go it had been an aimless and worrying time. She didn't know how long she could continue to live like that, buying food from a street stall, and scurrying through a pub to use the toilet and sneaking outside again before anyone spotted her. Even wearing sunglasses, she could be recognised if the police were out looking for her, and anyone she passed could be an officer in plain clothes.

She was convinced the police would be looking for her by now. Even if they hadn't wheedled it out of the old bitch on the ground floor, someone who knew Jay would have given them her name. In any case, she must have called him at least once a day since she had started seeing him and often more frequently than that. When he hadn't answered straightaway, she had sometimes called his number ten times before he finally spoke to her. The police were bound to have picked up on that, and would already have traced her from her phone number. She had had the foresight to leave her phone behind when she left home, so they wouldn't be able to trace her movements, but that meant she had no phone. Even Jay's death had not left her so alone, because at least she had been able to talk to her friends, and she could have gone to see her mother. Now she was cut adrift from everyone she knew, utterly isolated from the world.

She couldn't return to her flat. Her flatmate, Natalie, would be there, wondering what had happened to her. The police were probably waiting for her there by now. Nor could she risk going to her mother's house in Leeds because travelling on the train was too risky with the police looking for her. In any case, her mother's house was one of the first places they would look for her. Running away like this must have convinced them she was guilty, but at least she was free. Once the police found her, she would be locked up, perhaps for the rest of her life. She was a fugitive from the law, she told herself grimly. And it wasn't her fault. That is, she didn't think it was.

Her memory of what had happened to Jay was muddled. She knew he had fallen down the stairs and she had left him, moaning, in the hall. But the reason he had fallen was lost in a confused jumble of memories. She recalled their struggle on the landing, and her fleeting but very real terror of being sent hurtling down the stairs to her own death. At the time she had been convinced he intended to push her backwards over the edge. But how he had come to lose his footing and fall in her place remained a mystery. On reflection, she couldn't help wondering if she had misjudged the situation; it was hard to believe he had seriously wanted to harm her. Not only that, but she had an uneasy feeling she had blundered in running from the police. She had acted on impulse, without any long-term plan. Had she presented herself to the police and explained how Jay had attacked her, they might have accepted that she had been acting in self-defence. His death, while accidental, would have been attributed to his own violent behaviour. As it was, she had as good as signed a confession that what had happened was all her fault.

If she could revisit the past, she would behave differently and call an ambulance as soon as he tumbled down the stairs and knocked himself out. That was what an innocent person would have done. Her own response forced her to question whether she was in some way responsible for his death. On balance, she decided she had been wise to run rather than risk facing a murder charge. It was better to remain at liberty than trust the police would believe her story when she wasn't even sure she believed it herself. Had she deliberately sent Jay plummeting down the stairs? Although she didn't believe it, she wasn't sure she could prove her innocence. The police would be looking for a culprit and she would fit the requirement nicely: a jealous girlfriend attacking her two-timing boyfriend in a crime of passion. Because, if she knew Jay had been two-timing her, the police were bound to have found out too. There was no way of knowing for certain what the police were thinking, but she had a very bad feeling about it.

Her safest option was to try and get right away, and make a fresh start. Perhaps she could make her way to a tropical island where she could sleep on the beach and find herself a job in a taverna, like happened in films. But to do that, she would need her passport and more money than she could get her hands on. The money she had saved in her account would be impossible to access without revealing her whereabouts, and there wasn't much there anyway; however, she had nearly fifty pounds on her in cash, having brought all her week's spending money with her. In addition to that, she had raided the communal money tin in the kitchen. She and her flatmate contributed to the kitty each week, and used the proceeds for their joint food expenses like milk and tea and the electricity meter. They didn't dip into it every week, but Natalie insisted they keep the tin topped up, which was just as well, because Lauren had been able to take nearly twenty pounds from the kitty. She wasn't stealing; she fully intended to reimburse her flatmate. In the meantime, the money had kept her going so far, but it would soon run out. She had to find a way to gain access to her account and vanish before the police could arrive. She wondered how many times she would be able to get away with that, and how long it would be before she was broke as well as homeless.

Somehow she had to escape from York altogether and find a job far away, where no one would be looking for her. In the meantime, she had the approaching night to get through without freezing to death, and it would soon be dark. To compound her misery, a heavy rain began to fall. Before long, her coat was soaked through. Drops of water slid down her back, touching her skin like icy finger tips. She couldn't face the prospect of another night shivering under Lendal Bridge. A small B&B might suit her, if she could disguise her appearance. Wandering along Bootham, she turned left along Bootham Terrace, and walked past a long row of smart brick terraced properties. Tired and hungry, she was beginning to feel physically faint as well as dejected, when she noticed a small sign in a bay window: 'Vacancies'. It was only ten minutes' walk from her flat in Gillygate, but no one knew she was there. A hideout in Bootham Terrace might actually be a shrewd choice. The police wouldn't be looking for her so close to home. In any case, what other option did she have, with the night closing in on her? Even if the rain stopped, she would never dry out without shelter and warmth, and she was shivering uncontrollably.

Glancing around the deserted street, she climbed the few steps to the entrance and rang the bell. She waited, while damp seemed to seep through her skin and into her bones. The door was opened by a neat-looking woman in a fussy floral dress.

'I need a room for tonight,' Lauren blurted out through chattering teeth.

The landlady sniffed and studied her through narrowed eyes. Bedraggled and dirty, Lauren realised she must look disreputable after her night sleeping rough, and she crossed her fingers as the landlady hesitated.

'Payment in advance,' the woman snapped briskly.

Lauren agreed without even asking how much the room cost. Once inside, she breathed a sigh of relief, but her problems were not over yet. She tried not to flinch when the landlady asked for her full name and her permanent address. Wary of admitting that she was, effectively, homeless, Lauren thought quickly. If she gave her own address, the landlady might wonder why she needed somewhere else to stay in York, but she was reluctant to give her mother's address in Leeds in case the landlady decided to contact them. Meanwhile, the woman was waiting, pen in hand, staring suspiciously at her prospective guest. Quickly, she gave a random address in Leeds, in a road she was familiar with. She didn't know the exact postcode so she invented something that sounded plausible, hoping the landlady wouldn't discover her subterfuge until she had left York. Right now, all she wanted to do was lie down in a warm dry bed and sleep. In the morning she would set about finding a disguise so she could make her way out of York.

'Coat and shoes off,' the landlady barked. 'Breakfast at eight.'

12

JAY'S PARENTS LIVED IN Pocklington, half an hour's drive from York. Ariadne decided to speak to them at home. The news of Jay's death had been shared with them the day after what had appeared to be an accident. A few days had passed since then and the investigation had moved on. She now had to tell them their son had been murdered, and she was keen to speak to them before they could hear about it from an intrusive reporter. The roads were predictably snarled up around the narrow streets of York, but once she was out on the A1079 the traffic flowed more freely and she tried to relax. The rain stopped and the sun came out, and she would have bowled along quite cheerfully had she not faced the prospect of relaying distressing news when she arrived at her destination. She reached Pocklington in little over half an hour. It was a small market town, not too busy in the middle of the day, and she saved a few minutes by avoiding the town centre.

The Ropers lived in a terraced house in a row of red brick properties on the outskirts of the town. An occasional car drove past as Ariadne drew up and climbed out of her car. Relieved of the difficult task of revealing that their son was dead, she wondered how much difference the cause of his death would make to the bereaved parents, and could only hope her visit would not add to their suffering. She sometimes wondered about the psychological damage her work might have on her, but there was nothing to gain from maudlin introspection. It was better for everyone concerned if she focused on the practical demands of her job and did her best to wrap things up as swiftly as possible.

Before setting off, she had rung to check the Ropers would be at home to meet her. Even though they were expecting her, they took a long time to come to the front door which opened directly on to the narrow pavement. No one passed by as she stood outside, waiting, and a light rain began to fall. She was beginning to wonder if Mr and Mrs Roper had both gone out, when the door was opened by a short woman who gazed mournfully up at her. Her narrow pinched lips were twisted in a grimace, her eyelids were red and swollen and her lips trembled as she spoke.

'Are you from the undertakers?' she asked, in a voice that was little more than a whisper.

Ariadne held up her badge and murmured an apology for disturbing her grief. 'May I come in?'

'Oh yes, you rang earlier. You'd better come in.'

The front door led to a tiny hall with one door and a narrow staircase off it. Mrs Roper ushered her into a cramped reception room, with two slightly battered armchairs and a couple of upright chairs. The carpet and curtains were threadbare, but the furniture looked comfortable. A grey-haired man was sitting in one of the armchairs, distractedly stroking a black cat on his lap. Ariadne took one of the upright chairs, and Mrs Roper sank on to the second armchair with a faint sigh. The man barely glanced up at them. After expressing her condolences, Ariadne told them the police suspected that Jay's death had not been accidental. As if in response to the news, the cat sprang off Mr Roper's lap and stalked out of the room, its tail in the air.

'So are you telling us he was ill?' his mother asked. 'He never said anything to us, did he? Norman? Did you know about this? Was it – cancer? Or his heart? I know he smoked.'

Mr Roper didn't answer but gazed at Ariadne with a perplexed expression. She wondered if he had been prescribed medication to help him through the initial shock of his grief.

'No, he wasn't ill.' Ariadne took a deep breath. 'The

circumstances surrounding Jay's death are being investigated,' she said carefully.

'You're telling us he was murdered?' Mr Roper interrupted her, suddenly sitting forward and looking alert, dispelling Ariadne's first impression that he was befuddled. He turned to his wife. 'That's why they haven't let us collect his body. They think he was murdered.' He looked at Ariadne. 'That's it, isn't it? Didn't I tell you?' he added, turning back to his wife. 'What have I been saying to you?'

Mr Roper's voice shook with suppressed emotion as he went on to confide that their son had fallen in with a bad crowd.

'He started with the cannabis when he was still at school,' Mrs Roper said, shaking her head. 'He wasn't a bad boy, but he was easily led.'

The time had come to answer Mr Roper's question directly. 'I'm sorry to tell you we are looking into your son's death. There is evidence to suggest he was murdered.'

Mrs Roper dropped her head in her hands, but her husband merely nodded and asked quietly how it had happened.

'We were told he fell down the stairs,' he said woodenly.

'We were told he fell,' his wife mumbled from behind her hands. 'They said he fell. It was an accident. They said he wouldn't have known what was happening. They said he didn't suffer.'

'We're investigating all the circumstances surrounding his death, but the evidence suggests he wasn't alone when he fell.'

'Do you mean someone pushed him down the stairs?' Mr Roper demanded, growing more strident as Ariadne hesitated to divulge details.

There seemed little point in explaining that Jay had been suffocated. It was enough for them to know someone had been responsible for his death.

'It's looking possible,' she equivocated. 'Can you think of anyone who might have wanted to harm your son? Please think carefully.'

But both Jay's parents looked at her, pale and shocked, and shook their heads in unison.

'He was in with a bad crowd,' Mr Roper repeated wretchedly, as though that explained what had happened. 'It was the drugs. It was someone involved with those blasted drugs.'

But for all their talk about the 'bad crowd' their son mixed with, and their admission that he took and possibly sold unspecified drugs, neither of them knew the names of any of the people he had mixed with.

'It would help our investigation if you could identify any of his friends, or anyone he associated with,' Ariadne said.

'What about—' Mrs Roper began, and broke off, with a slight shake of her head.

Ariadne waited.

'He mentioned someone.' She frowned with the effort of remembering. 'Was it Turnip?'

'Turnip?'

'I think that's what he said.'

'Yes, you're right,' her husband agreed, suddenly animated again. 'He did talk about someone called Turnip, and it wasn't long ago that he mentioned him. Do you think this Turnip could be responsible for – for what happened? Jay said he was a mad fucker. His words, not mine,' he added apologetically. 'Was it Turnip? It was something like that.'

'Jay came here asking us for money,' Mrs Roper said miserably.

'He was always on at us for money,' her husband interjected, a hint of anger in his voice.

'This time he told us it wasn't for himself that he wanted it. He said he needed money to help out a friend of his, who'd been in hospital. I can't remember exactly what the story was this time. And, of course, he promised he'd pay us back.'

'Which he never did,' Mr Roper added bitterly.

Neither of them had met Jay's friend, Turnip, and they both admitted they saw very little of their son. On the rare occasions that he visited them, it was to ask them for money.

'It was the drugs,' his mother said sadly. 'He was never like that as a child.'

'Like what?' Ariadne asked.

'Mean and selfish,' she replied tearfully, clearly making an effort to control herself.

'What can you tell me about his girlfriend?' Ariadne asked them.

'His girlfriend?' Mrs Roper echoed, glancing at her husband. Her voice trembled. 'What girlfriend?'

Heaving a sigh, her husband reached out to pat her hand gently. 'What my wife means is that Jay liked to play the field, as they say. He had a series of girlfriends, none of whom lasted very long. We thought,' he glanced anxiously at his wife, 'we thought perhaps he was reluctant to commit to any one girl. Some young men are like that.'

'Until they meet the right girl,' his wife added, finally breaking down in tears. Years of disappointment lay behind her weeping.

'We always hoped he would meet someone and settle down, but that hadn't happened yet.'

'And now it never will,' his wife wailed, abandoning any attempt to control her grief.

'We thought he would grow up,' Mr Roper added bleakly. 'It's all right, Debbie. He's out of his turmoil now. He's at peace.'

The interview paused for a few moments while Mr Roper did his best to comfort his wife.

'I'll go and put the kettle on,' Mrs Roper hiccupped at last, clambering to her feet. 'You carry on.' And she scurried from the room, sniffling and wiping her eyes.

Ariadne continued to probe, and Mr Roper told her that Jay had brought one of his girlfriends to their house the previous summer. Her name was Carly, and he and his wife had been hoping Jay had finally embarked on a serious relationship, since he had brought the girl to Pocklington to meet them.

'Can you recall her second name?'

He shook his head. 'He only introduced her as Carly.'

'What can you tell me about her?'

Mr Roper described a pretty, slim brunette of about thirty, who had worked as a teaching assistant in a primary school. That was all he knew about her.

'She seemed to be besotted with him,' he added disconsolately.

'All the girls were keen on Jay,' Mrs Roper said, rejoining them and sitting down.

'He was a real charmer, full of beans,' Mr Roper added. 'He was the life and soul…' He broke off with a sigh. 'We did our best but… The truth is, we lost him a long time ago.'

Ariadne thought about the mound of dead white flesh lying on Jonah's slab at the mortuary and shivered. It was hard to imagine Jay, alive and exuberant, with a string of adoring girlfriends. He remained an enigmatic figure, a reliable tenant to Yiannis, a source of aggravation to his neighbour, and popular with women. It seemed that everyone who had known him presented a different picture of Jay, and the more they investigated his death, the further they seemed to be from discovering the truth. At least the Ropers had given her two names to follow up: Turnip and Carly. Before she drove off, she contacted Naomi.

'I'm afraid Carly's all I've got,' she said. 'We need to do another search of his list of contacts and his social media platforms, and we can also search for a teaching assistant in York with the first name Carly, or possibly Carla or Caroline. And I'll get on to the drug squad to see if they know someone called Turnip.'

She drove back towards York through intermittent rain, feeling more optimistic than she had been before her visit to Pocklington. Her windscreen wipers were poorly aligned and squeaked whenever the rain eased off. The noise was irritating, but at least she could see the road ahead, as long as she could tolerate the rasping sound. She gritted her teeth and put her foot down, squinting through a patch cleared by the wipers.

13

After driving back from Pocklington in a relatively positive frame of mind, Ariadne returned to a grey and wet city. Pulling up the hood of her light jacket, she hurried indoors. On her way she stepped in a large puddle, which turned out to be deeper than she had realised. One ankle drenched in freezing cold water, she stomped inside, feeling disgruntled.

'Cheer up, it may never happen,' the desk sergeant called out to her as she passed him.

It was a crass comment to make to someone working on a murder investigation, but she let that pass. It wasn't the desk sergeant's fault she was feeling prickly under the weight of her responsibility. The sergeant was the sort of affable colleague everyone appreciated having on their team, and he had only been trying to cheer her up, so she smiled and muttered something about the rain. Before agreeing to take on this case, she had been fairly easygoing herself.

'You have to learn to walk between the raindrops,' the sergeant replied with a wink.

Actually, Ariadne reflected as she walked along the corridor, he had a point, in a way. If she could make her way through all the information they were gathering and pick out what was crucial, she would discover the truth. But with no idea of what might be significant, every detail had to be considered from every possible angle. Most of the team were satisfied that Lauren was guilty, but Ariadne insisted they keep other possibilities in mind. She hadn't completely dismissed her suspicions of Yiannis, and they hadn't yet tracked down Jay's other alleged girlfriend, Carly.

Slipping off her shoe and wriggling her toes inside her cold, wet sock, Ariadne began typing her report. Once she finished, she would take a short break for a coffee and a doughnut, and re-energise herself with sugar and caffeine. She decided to stop off at the toilets and dry her sock under the hand dryer on her way to the canteen. With that cheering prospect to spur her on, she typed quickly. But no sooner had she finished writing up her report, than she received a message that required urgent action. With a rueful glance at her damp sock, she summoned the team to the incident room for an update. Dry socks and hot coffee would have to wait.

Ariadne held up her hand for silence. Outside, rain pattered steadily on the windows, obscuring their view of the grey sky. A faint mutter rippled around the assembled officers as she reminded them that DNA from two women had been found in Jay's flat. For a moment, no one seemed to grasp the significance of this information.

'Is there anything to indicate they were seeing him regularly?' Naomi asked.

A few other voices piped up, all talking at once, offering different opinions.

'We don't know they were his girlfriends.'

'He could have had someone go in to clean for him.'

Ariadne laughed at that suggestion. 'You've all seen the photos of his place. I hardly think anyone did any cleaning there.'

'Wasn't he a dealer?'

'We don't know they had anything to do with his death.'

'What about all the people who visited him to score?'

Ariadne interrupted the speculation. 'There was enough DNA on his sheets, in his bed, from two different women, to indicate he was having regular sexual relations with both of them. There's no room for doubt about this. It seems he didn't wash his bedding,' she added, with the faintest hint of distaste.

'Filthy animal,' a constable muttered.

Ariadne continued. 'We suspect Lauren was there on the day he died. She's our priority and we're focusing our attention on finding her. In addition, his parents told us about a girlfriend called Carly. According to the Ropers, she was working as a teaching assistant in a school in York last year when they met her. We need to track her down and find out if she was the other woman who shared Jay's bed.'

'Just because his parents thought she was his girlfriend doesn't mean it's true,' Naomi said. 'He didn't have a particularly close relationship with them.'

'No, but it gives us a lead to go on for the second woman; now we have confirmation there were two of them.' She looked around with an air of tentative optimism. 'So let's get going with searching for Lauren and Carly.'

'Given that he seems to have been cheating on them both, the chances are one of them might have pushed him down the stairs in a jealous rage,' Naomi added, her blue eyes animated. 'That seems like a motive.'

There followed a brief discussion about why Lauren had run off, and where she might have gone. Some of the officers thought Lauren's disappearance was a clear admission of guilt, but while they were searching for her, it was possible Jay's killer had already found her.

'Granted one of these women might have pushed him down the stairs in a fit of jealousy. Is it likely she would then deliberately suffocate him?' Naomi murmured as they left the room. 'That would be some temper! Does that sound like a crime of passion to you? She might have pushed him down the stairs in the heat of the moment, but suffocation strikes me as cold and deliberate. I mean, how long can a moment of absolute rage last, the sort of rage that drives out every sane thought and feeling, and leads to murder? It would have taken a few seconds, at least, for him to reach the bottom of the stairs. And how long would it have taken her to suffocate him? Wouldn't that have given her time to cool off a little, seeing him injured like that? Was she frightened he would accuse her of assault if he recovered? Or perhaps his killer was just insane, regardless of any fleeting passion.'

'All murder is insane,' Ariadne said. 'Anyhow, either way, he was murdered and Lauren might have been there, so we need to question her. It looks like one of those two women may have killed him.'

'It could have been a man,' Naomi said. 'Perhaps a rival for Lauren's affections. The killer had to be strong enough to overpower Jay and suffocate him.'

'Not if the fall had knocked him out.'

'True,' Naomi agreed. 'While he was lying at the foot of the stairs, stunned, it could have been the opportunity the killer had been waiting for.'

'And from what Mary told us, there was no one else there that day, apart from the woman Jay was arguing with,' Ariadne added.

'How reliable is Mary's account?'

Ariadne paused. 'I don't think she would deliberately mislead us. She's a religious woman and she seems to know the Ten Commandments, but she's old and weak and she could be confused.'

'What about Yiannis?' Naomi asked.

Ariadne shrugged, dismissing the thought of Nico's friendship with the landlord. While they were talking, they reached Ariadne's desk. It was time to stop speculating and start looking for Jay's girlfriends. In the meantime, she wanted to search for the man called Turnip while the hunt for the two women continued. With a wistful thought about coffee and a doughnut, she turned to her screen. At least her sock didn't feel so damp, and she was thankful for that small comfort. Things could be worse.

14

ARIADNE HAD WORKED CLOSELY with a colleague, Brett, who had contacts with the local drug scene. She needed to look for him but, before doing anything else, she finally succumbed to her hankering for coffee and a doughnut. Entering the canteen, as chance would have it, she spotted Brett sitting by himself, a mug of tea almost hidden in his huge hand. Postponing her coffee yet again, she made straight for him.

'Turnip?' he replied, screwing up his fleshy nose and gazing thoughtfully at her across the table. 'Are you talking about Turnpike?'

'Could be. The witness who gave me the name wasn't sure if they remembered it correctly. Did Turnpike know Jay Roper?'

'Your murder victim?' Brett's overhanging eyebrows shot up. 'I couldn't say for sure, but they certainly mixed in the same circles. It's a fairly safe bet they would have known one another.' He took a swig of his tea. 'To be straight with you, neither of them was on our radar any more. With all the reassignments, it's been hard for us to keep track of the low-level pushers and dealers.' He scowled. 'The small fry have been given free rein lately. It's completely misguided, if you ask me, but what policy from above isn't these days? We've had our orders. But,' he leaned forward, his expression sombre, 'once you let the seemingly trivial offences go unchecked, people think they can get away with anything, and before you know it we're up to our necks in all kinds of trouble.' He shook his head. 'These days we're sniffing around at the tip of the iceberg when we should be nipping it in the bud.'

Ariadne tried not to smile at her colleague's mixed metaphors, but she sympathised with his frustration. Top brass, who formulated policy, listened to their political masters rather than consulting officers dealing with the daily reality of policing the streets.

'It's shortsighted,' Ariadne agreed. 'But has it ever been any different? We have to work with what we're given. So, what can you tell me about Turnip or Turnpike or whatever he's called?'

Her colleague nodded briskly. 'Yes, Turnpike. He's relatively harmless, as they go. Innocuous little black guy, a small-time dealer, never been involved in any serious crime, as far as I know. He likes to keep himself out of trouble. We were keeping an eye on him at one point, hoping he'd lead us to bigger fish, but—' he shrugged. 'We just no longer have the resources for that kind of speculative surveillance. Not where drugs are concerned, anyway. It's all about weapons these days, and the drugs scene is no longer a priority. In the long term, it's all going to go tits up, but will anyone listen? Still, I'm just a foot soldier. What do I know?'

'How can I find out if Turnpike knew Jay?'

'We're aware of them both. Tell you what, I'd be very surprised if their paths never crossed. Might be worth your while having a word with Turnpike, if you can find him. You might do well to ask around the homeless shelters. People living on the streets tend to drift in and out of there, and some of them keep their ear to the ground. When they're sober, that is. You might manage to track him down. Small, cheerful guy, slippery as fuck. Good luck with finding him.'

Ariadne thanked Brett, and went to get herself a coffee. By the time she returned, he had gone.

At the second homeless shelter Ariadne visited, she struck lucky. The manager's features were as tired and faded as her clothes, but her careworn face creased in a smile when Ariadne asked for Turnpike.

'Well, you're in luck, inspector,' she said. 'He's here.'

She led Ariadne to a communal area where a few men in jeans and T-shirts were staring blankly at a small television screen. The manager pointed out a slim man with a bald head who was slumped in a high-backed chair, his legs resting on a foot stool. His appeared to be sleeping, and Ariadne saw that one of his legs was in a cast. He opened his eyes when she called his name.

'That's me. I'm Turnpike,' he said, raising a hand in greeting and speaking with a marked American twang. 'What's up, girl?' His eyes widened in surprise when he saw Ariadne's identity card. 'Whatever went down, I wasn't there.' He raised his injured leg, grunting with the effort. 'Broken in three places. "You sure don't do things by halves," my old ma used to say.' He sighed. 'She's been gone a long time.'

Ariadne showed him a picture of Jay and asked whether Turnpike recognised him.

The ceiling light glimmered on his head as he nodded. 'That's my man, Jay. I heard he was whacked.' He shrugged. 'What you gonna do?'

'How do you know what happened to him?'

'Shit, girl, everybody knows that. I may be a cripple right now, but I don't live under a rock. I got ears.' He snorted and slapped his good thigh. 'He was a good cat,' he added, suddenly solemn. 'I'm sorry he's gone. But we all gotta go some day, ain't that the truth?'

'What have you heard?' Ariadne asked.

'I heard he's gone.' Manoeuvring himself into an upright position, he enquired how Jay had died. 'Fell down some stairs, you say?' He whistled. 'And that's how he died?'

Ariadne nodded. She didn't add that Jay had been suffocated after his fall.

'He had some good shit. Always did.' He glanced at Ariadne and gave a little shrug. 'Doesn't much matter who knows it now, does it? And I never said I scored. I admit nothing.' He winked. 'But I'm sorry he caught one. He never did me any harm. Not like some,' he added darkly, tapping his cast.

'When did you last see Jay?'

'Three, four weeks ago, must've been, before I was laid up.' He tapped his cast again.

'Were you friends?'

'Friends?' Turnpike repeated. He shrugged and looked away, suddenly aloof, as though the word held no meaning for him beyond a distant memory.

'Do you know if he had any enemies?'

'When you got no home, the whole world's your enemy.'

'But he wasn't homeless.'

'Who?'

'Jay.'

Turnpike shrugged and closed his eyes. 'Dude's dead and nothing's gonna change that.'

'Did he argue with anyone?'

Turnpike shook his head. 'Maybe. We weren't tight. He was just some dude.'

'Do you know if he had a girlfriend?'

Turnpike opened his eyes. 'Now how would I know a thing like that? I'm sorry he's dead,' he added, closing his eyes again. 'You make damn sure you catch the bastard who whacked him.'

The manager confirmed that Turnpike had been staying at the shelter for over a fortnight, since breaking his leg. Apparently he had been attacked but his assailants had not been caught. 'He was lucky we were able to accommodate him,' the manager added. 'We can't always fit people in when they need shelter. And it's not getting any easier with the cutbacks and the rising cost of living and unemployment higher than ever.'

Ariadne nodded. It seemed that lately everyone she spoke to was suffering from increased expenses and dwindling funds. She thanked the manager for her help, and took her leave.

'He just happened to be here at the moment,' the manager replied. 'He'll be off again as soon as he's able to get around. If it wasn't for his broken leg, he'd never have stayed this long.'

Turnpike could barely walk with his broken leg, let alone make his way up and down a flight of stairs. Whatever the nature of his relationship with Jay, Turnpike hadn't killed him.

15

AS ARIADNE WAS LEAVING the homeless shelter, her phone buzzed. Glancing down, she saw Geraldine's name on the screen. Feeling guilty for having forgotten to return her friend's previous call, she answered straightaway.

'Ariadne!' Geraldine called from the phone, sounding both surprised and pleased. 'I thought you'd be too busy to talk. How are you?'

'I'm fine. How about you?'

'Are you too busy to meet for a chat later on?' Geraldine asked. 'Perhaps we could get together this evening, just for an hour or so, like we used to? If you're free, that is?'

Feeling guilty at having ignored her friend's earlier message, Ariadne agreed. If she was honest, she didn't really have the energy to socialise, but Geraldine had been almost pleading with her.

'I can't wait to see you again,' Geraldine said. 'I'm desperate for some normal adult conversation for a change.'

Ariadne said that she would check Nico hadn't made any plans, and it would be lovely to catch up. As soon as she had spoken to Nico, she phoned Geraldine back to confirm their arrangement for that evening. Geraldine's delight was infectious, and Ariadne felt her own spirits lift.

'It's been a while,' she agreed. 'I've been so bogged down at work, it'll do me good to get away from it for a while.'

They arranged to meet at their usual haunt, a Chinese restaurant with small intimate booths, where they used to appreciate being able to talk freely, confident no one could overhear them. They had chosen it on account of the private seating rather than the food, although the menu was varied and reasonably priced. But as she drove to the restaurant, Ariadne's excitement faded, and she wondered what they would find to talk about now their lives were following such different paths. Still, it would do her no harm to sit and listen to Geraldine chatting about her baby, and the break from thinking about the case might even help to clarify her thoughts. At the moment, she was floundering. Nico was understanding enough to leave her alone as far as possible, but he could never fully appreciate what she was going through. Geraldine, on the other hand, would empathise with her frustration, and Ariadne could rely on her discretion should the subject of the case crop up. The more she thought about it, the more pleased she was at the prospect of seeing her former colleague.

Geraldine was waiting for Ariadne when she arrived at the restaurant. For a few seconds Ariadne didn't recognise the woman smiling and waving at her across the room. After they had exchanged greetings, and agreed it was lovely to see one another again, and had each commented on how well the other was looking, she admitted that she hadn't recognised Geraldine straightaway.

'It's because of your hair,' she added.

When working, Geraldine had worn her hair short. Since she had been at home with the baby, she had left it to grow.

'I just haven't got round to getting it cut,' Geraldine admitted. 'I know it sounds daft, because I'm at home all the time now, but somehow I never seem to get anything done.'

'I think it suits you like that,' Ariadne assured her, privately taken aback by Geraldine's admission.

At the police station, Geraldine had a reputation for efficiency. If anything, some of their colleagues had criticised her for working too hard, making them appear slack by comparison.

But no one could fault her success in resolving the most challenging cases. Now she claimed she was struggling to stay on top of things. Ariadne smiled sympathetically and murmured reassurances. After they ordered their food, Ariadne enquired tentatively how motherhood was suiting her friend. Geraldine shrugged and looked away, no longer smiling, as she reiterated she was finding it hard.

'Is it the sleepless nights?' Ariadne asked, with genuine concern.

'It's not that. Tom's an easy baby, although he has his moments. But he's sleeping right through the night now.'

'And how's Ian taken to being a father?'

'Ian's loving it. I'm the one who's struggling to adjust.' Geraldine hesitated, as though she was about to say more, then seemed to change her mind.

'Are you okay?' Ariadne prompted her, sensing that Geraldine was keeping something back. 'I would have phoned you before now to suggest getting together, but I thought you'd want time to settle into your new routine,' she fibbed.

The truth was, she had scarcely thought about Geraldine, except to miss her insights into whatever she and her colleagues were working on. She had been so wrapped up in her own problems at work, she hadn't even thought about contacting her friend to enquire how she was. The team had clubbed together to send her flowers and a giant teddy bear, but that was it.

'I can't believe it's been so long,' she added.

Geraldine hesitated before adding that she was fine, really. She was just tired. Convinced Geraldine's smile was forced, Ariadne didn't press her friend with intrusive questions.

'Well, you know where I am if you ever need to talk,' she said gently.

They chatted about Ian and Nico, and Geraldine enquired after Naomi and their other colleagues.

'Now,' Geraldine went on brightly, 'that's enough about me

and my newfound domesticity. Tell me all about what you're up to.'

'Oh, you know, just the usual,' Ariadne said.

'So, are you working on a case at the moment?' Geraldine asked.

'You didn't come here to talk about my work,' Ariadne laughed.

'Please,' Geraldine urged her, with a curious touch of helplessness in her voice. 'Tell me what you're up to.'

'You don't really want to hear about it.'

'You have no idea how much I want to hear all about it.'

There was something desperate in Geraldine's insistence that surprised Ariadne.

'Well, if you're sure.'

'Honestly, Ariadne, I'm gagging to have something to think about other than nappies and baby toys and weaning and puréed vegetables and jars of baby food. It's an endless cycle, every day the same. I love Tom, of course I do, and Ian's been wonderful, but it's... I don't know how to describe my life now. It's all been so overwhelming. But in a good way,' she added quickly, and again Ariadne suspected she wasn't being entirely truthful. 'Now, that's more than enough about me. Tell me about your case, and don't leave anything out.'

So Ariadne described how Jay Roper had fallen down the stairs, and had somehow ended up being suffocated. She told Geraldine about the victim's girlfriend, Lauren, who had gone missing, the two different samples of DNA found in his bed, and the two witnesses, Yiannis and Mary.

'So either Yiannis was lying about carrying a coat, or Mary was mistaken about seeing it,' Ariadne concluded her account.

'In all the shock of finding his tenant dead, Yiannis could have forgotten that he had a coat with him,' Geraldine said, 'because why would Mary lie about what she saw?'

Ariadne stared at Geraldine. 'Maybe,' she admitted. 'Mary

seemed a bit confused, but I wasn't suggesting she might have deliberately lied to us.'

Geraldine shrugged. 'A fresh pair of eyes.'

'But why would Mary lie about something so unimportant?'

'It's hardly unimportant if it was used to suffocate the victim,' Geraldine remarked drily. 'But let's go over it all again. We need to consider every possibility. We know someone suffocated the victim by pressing something over his face. We don't know what was used, which means it could have been a coat. But before anything else, we have to track Lauren down and find out why she ran away.'

Ariadne noticed that Geraldine was discussing the case as though she was on the investigating team.

'It seems like an admission of guilt,' Ariadne replied, 'but she could be innocent and just have been frightened she might be a suspect.'

'Or perhaps she's afraid for her own life. Could Jay's killer be after her next?' Geraldine paused. 'I wonder what Lauren saw that day Jay was killed? Did she kill him, or was she a witness to murder?'

Ariadne nodded. 'That's just what we want to know.'

'Either way, finding Lauren is the key to solving the case.'

'We've set up a search but the trouble is we have no idea where she is.'

'If she did witness someone murder Jay, and was seen, let's hope you find her before the killer does,' Geraldine said, as she helped herself to some noodles.

16

THALIA TRIED TO FOCUS on the book she was reading, but her thoughts kept wandering to her son. Yiannis had been a problem ever since his brother had been killed in a fight. Yiannis had only been ten when that happened. He had been such a carefree child before tragedy had struck their family. The loss of Thalia's firstborn had caused her husband to waste away and die, and it had twisted Yiannis's mind, the violence he had witnessed as a child changing him forever. She would never forget the night they had fled their island home together. In darkness they had stolen out of their white house perched on a hill overlooking the sea. Silently they had made their way down the steep cobbled path to the beach, where her nephew was waiting to ferry them to the mainland. Abandoning the familiarity of sunshine and olive groves, the white house with its spreading fig tree, and the sound and smell of the sea, they reached the mainland and boarded a plane that had carried them far away from the only home she had ever known. So she had journeyed to England with Yiannis. He was her son and she couldn't lose him too.

They had melted unobtrusively into the Greek community in York, where a cousin of her husband had helped them find work. That was a long time ago, and their flight from their homeland now seemed like a half-remembered dream, her life in Greece a story she had read, long ago. Gradually, they settled into a dreary but comfortable existence, and if she missed the sunshine of her island home, she never complained. Knowing her only surviving son was safe made the sacrifice worthwhile. There were times when she was happy. In the summer, when the sun shone, she could close her eyes and imagine herself back in her beloved island home, reaching to pick a fig the size of her fist, soft and sweet as jam. She had endured grey skies and freezing winters, cold rain and noisy streets with traffic hurtling by, and she had done so gladly. Her only happiness was to live with her son and see him prosper. He was all that remained of her ruined life.

She no longer mourned her dreams of growing old with her beloved husband at her side, grandchildren shrieking with laughter as they chased each other beneath the ancient fig tree. All that was lost to her. But even after so many years, England was not home. If Yiannis was taken from her, she would have nothing. When he came home one day, his face rigid with fear, and told her a man had been murdered in his property, her terror had returned. Every time she heard a car she trembled in case it drew up outside and police officers knocked on the door, looking for her son. This was no sleepy Greek island where police arrived by ferry. Here in York there was a police station a short car ride away. Whenever Yiannis went out she was afraid, wondering if she would see him again. She tried to read, but thoughts lashed at her, like breakers on a stormy sea.

At last she heard the front door close and knew he was home.

'Dinner's in the oven,' she greeted him as he joined her in the living room.

Returning his smile, she went to the kitchen to dish up.

'Smells good,' he said, when she returned with his tray.

Since coming to England, they had given up sitting at the table to eat, instead dining off trays in front of the television. She cooked for her son every night, and she still felt a frisson of pride at her skills in the kitchen. She had once worked in a restaurant owned by her cousin back on the island, but she had left all that behind when they came to England. Now, watching Yiannis tucking into his food, she told herself there was nothing to worry about.

'Have the police found out what happened in Penley's Grove?' she asked, when he had finished.

Yiannis glanced up at her, his expression guarded and difficult to read. 'Not that they've told me. I hope they get it sorted out soon,' he added, exasperation breaking through his forced composure. 'I need to find another tenant as quickly as possible. I've got bills to pay. But I can't even get into the property to show anyone round because the police are treating it as a crime scene. They won't say when they'll be done with their forensic examination. How long can it take to check out the hall and stairs? I asked and they just say it'll take as long as it takes. What kind of an answer is that?'

Thalia studied her son's face covertly, wondering whether his crabbiness was masking fear, or something worse.

'You could speak to Nico's wife again?' she suggested.

Yiannis shook his head. 'She can't do anything for me. We're in England now,' he said, as though they had only recently arrived in the country. 'The police won't help me, and I can't risk drawing attention to myself.'

'Why not? We belong here now.' But she knew he was right.

They sat in silence for a moment, but she had to ask him. 'Did you kill that man?'

He turned to her. She knew his face so well and could tell his shock was genuine. 'How can you ask?'

'I'm just so frightened,' she blurted out. 'What if they take you away?'

'Well, they won't, so you don't need to worry.'

He didn't seem to share her fear, but what if his confidence was misplaced?

17

Lauren rented a shared flat above a hardware shop in Gillygate. A study of Lauren's social media posts had revealed that she had met her flatmate at school, and they had remained friends. Ariadne went back to Gillygate early on Saturday morning, hoping to find Lauren at home. It was possible she had returned and could give a simple explanation for her recent disappearance. It wasn't unheard of for a young woman to meet a man and decide to stay with him for a few nights. The fact that Jay was a drug dealer made it slightly more plausible that Lauren might be spending time getting stoned somewhere, without thinking to let her employer know. Ariadne didn't hold out much hope, since Lauren had been off work all that week without having contacted her employer, but there was a chance she had gone away and forgotten to tell the florist, or had simply not bothered, or she might have left her phone at home. Any of those scenarios was possible, and would explain her silence.

She rang the bell and this time the door was opened by a sturdily built girl with a long flaxen plait. Ariadne recognised Lauren's flatmate, Natalie, from Lauren's social media posts. She was wearing pastel pink pyjamas and fluffy pink slippers. Peering round the door, she looked startled to see Ariadne standing on the doorstep.

'Oh, I thought you were—' she stammered. 'Sorry, I thought you were someone else.'

Ariadne asked if Natalie was expecting her flatmate.

The girl nodded. 'Yes. That is, I hoped it was her.'

'Doesn't Lauren have a key?'

'Of course she's got a key, but when you rang the bell, I thought she might have left it here. But what's it to you? Who are you? And what are you doing here?'

Ariadne introduced herself.

'The police? Oh my goodness,' Natalie cried out, her eyes opening wide in surprise. 'Has something happened to Lauren? Is she all right?'

'Can I come in?'

'Well, yes, I suppose so. If you want to,' she added, as she opened the door to let Ariadne enter.

'What makes you think anything might have happened to Lauren?' Ariadne asked.

'Well, she's not here, and you are.'

Her plait swinging gently behind her, Natalie led Ariadne into a small living room where magazines and shoes were strewn around, with an assortment of towels and clothes draped carelessly over the furniture. At one end of the room, Ariadne saw a tiny kitchenette, the sink crammed with crockery and pans waiting to be washed up. Various items of stale food, including an open packet of cereal, a half-eaten slice of toast, two bananas turning brown, and a bag of rice, vied for space on a narrow work surface.

Sweeping an untidy pile of T-shirts on to the floor, Natalie invited Ariadne to take a seat, offering no apology for the mess.

'Do you know where Lauren is?' Ariadne enquired as she sat down. 'If you know, it's very important that you tell me.'

'I'm guessing she's with her boyfriend,' Natalie replied, frowning and clearing a second chair in an equally cavalier fashion, as though she habitually threw clothes on the floor whenever she wanted to sit down.

Natalie explained that she had been away for a few days, visiting her family. On her return to York, she had found the flat empty.

'Did Lauren often go away?' Ariadne asked. 'Could she have gone to see her mother? I'd like their address, please.'

Natalie hesitated before going to find it. 'Here you are. But I don't think she'll have gone to see them. She didn't get on that well with them. She's more likely to have gone to see her boyfriend. She stays with him every weekend, so I'm guessing that's where she is. But—' She hesitated.

'Her boyfriend? Do you mean Jay?'

'Yes.'

'Do you know him?'

Natalie shook her head. 'I only met him once, in the pub, and—' She broke off with an embarrassed moue. 'Well, I can't say I liked him very much.'

'Why not?'

She shrugged. 'He's too old for her, for a start, and he seems, well, full of himself, you know? To be honest, I found him quite obnoxious. But Lauren's besotted with him, and that doesn't strike me as great either, because he's – well, he isn't that into her, if you ask me. I mean, he virtually ignored everything she said and hardly looked at her. All he did was talk about himself.'

'What did he say?'

'I can't really remember. He kept telling us he was making pots of money, although he refused to say how, and I had a feeling it was something dodgy. And he was talking about this flash car he was going to buy. That was it, really. He went on and on about the car, and how he wasn't going to stay in his poky little flat for long – which sounded like a dig at us for living here.'

'Did he ever come here?'

'Not that I knew about. Like I said, I only met him once. And Lauren won't hear a word said against him, so in the end we stopped talking about him. She told me she thought I was jealous but, honestly, nothing could be further from the truth. I wouldn't go out with that creep if he was the last man alive.'

'When did you last see Lauren?'

'I was away this week. As far as I was aware, she was here all the time, but she wasn't here when I got home yesterday evening at about six. I'd thought we might get a takeaway, but she was out.' Natalie shrugged. 'I assumed she was at Jay's place, although she didn't usually stay there on Fridays. Anyway, she wasn't here and her note didn't say when she's coming back. Look, what's this about? Why have you come here, and why are you asking all these questions?'

'You just mentioned she left you a note,' Ariadne said, responding to Natalie's questions with one of her own. 'Have you still got it?'

Natalie clambered to her feet and shuffled over to the kitchen area, her fluffy slippers making a swishing noise on the cork floor. Ariadne stood up quickly and accompanied her.

'Don't touch it,' Ariadne called out, seeing Natalie reach for a torn scrap of paper lying beside the kettle, and held in place by a tea-stained mug.

Natalie stared open-mouthed as Ariadne pulled on her gloves, and picked up the note very delicately. 'Gone away for a while. Met someone', she read, before slipping the note into an evidence bag.

'Do you have any idea where Lauren might be?' she repeated her earlier question.

'All I know is what she wrote in her note,' Natalie replied, watching Ariadne put the evidence bag in her pocket. 'She's gone off somewhere with someone she met. But I don't really understand it. The note suggests she's met someone new, but that doesn't make sense.'

'What don't you understand?'

'She's mad about Jay. Why would she go off with anyone else? Although knowing Lauren, anything's possible.'

'What do you mean?'

Natalie shrugged. 'She's had a lot of boyfriends. She falls for them without stopping to think. It makes her vulnerable, you know?'

Ariadne phrased her next question carefully. 'Did she have an ex-boyfriend who might have been jealous of Jay, or who might have held a grudge against Lauren for leaving him?'

Natalie shook her head. 'No, nothing like that. Her relationships were usually very brief. She's been with Jay for longer than anyone else I can think of. But I wouldn't put it past her to have split up with Jay and found someone else straightaway. I don't understand why she hasn't been in touch. Do you think something's happened to her? That's why you're here, isn't it?'

Ariadne spoke quietly. 'Who was your flatmate going to meet?'

Natalie shook her head, looking flustered. 'I've no idea. You're here because something's happened to her, aren't you? Something terrible.'

Natalie burst into tears and it took Ariadne a few moments to calm her down. When Natalie had regained her composure, Ariadne said she needed a sample of Lauren's DNA.

Natalie leaned forward and let out a low wail, like an animal in pain. 'She's dead, isn't she? That's why you want her DNA, isn't it? So you can identify the body.'

Ariadne did her best to convince her that they hadn't found Lauren's body.

'We have no idea where Lauren is,' she said firmly. 'There is no reason to suspect she has come to any harm. But she has disappeared, and we think she may be frightened. We need to find her as soon as possible so we can question her in connection with something she may have witnessed.'

'Is she in danger?'

Ariadne sighed, wondering if it was callous to worry Natalie. 'It's unlikely,' she replied, 'but until we know she's safe it remains a possibility. That's why we need to find her urgently.'

Natalie nodded briskly, as though she had reached a decision. 'What can I do to help you find her?'

Ariadne asked Natalie to call her friend and urge her to come home, or at least say where she was. There was a chance Lauren would answer a call from Natalie. The girl nodded and pulled out her phone. A few seconds later they heard a faint ring tone which sounded as though it was coming from the next room. They followed the sound and found a phone ringing on a rumpled bed. Lauren hadn't taken her phone with her when she left, suggesting she had left in a hurry. The chances that she had witnessed the murder seemed increasingly likely, as did the possibility that her life was in danger.

Ignoring Natalie's objections, Ariadne dropped the phone into an evidence bag.

'You can't take it. What if she comes back and needs it?'

Ariadne gazed around at the chaos of clothes and make-up. Noticing a pair of black patent shoes with silver toecaps, she wondered if they could be the shoes Mary had described as having sparkly toes. She made a note to have measurements of the points compared with the bruises on Jay's shins.

'Is anything missing?'

'I don't know,' Natalie replied, also looking around. 'I don't know what she kept in here.' She opened the wardrobe and a few T-shirts tumbled out. 'I think she's taken her rucksack,' she added.

'Did she take her passport?'

Natalie shrugged and opened a drawer beside Lauren's bed. 'It's here.'

Ariadne held out her hand and Natalie reluctantly gave her the passport. 'I don't know if I should,' she muttered anxiously.

'What about a driving licence? Did she drive?'

'I don't think so. I mean, no, she hasn't passed her test. I'd know if she had.'

Ariadne picked up a laptop that was lying on the bed, half-hidden by a pair of jeans.

'Wait!' Natalie shrieked. 'You can't just take her laptop when she's not here.'

'It might help us to find her.'

There was no point in staying any longer. Ariadne gave Natalie instructions to contact her if she heard from her friend, and warned her to touch nothing in Lauren's room before a search team had been there.

'What are you looking for?'

Ariadne explained that Lauren must have gone away deliberately, because she had left a note for her flatmate. It was possible they would come across details that could lead them to whoever she was staying with. She didn't add that Lauren might not have forgotten to take her phone; she might have left it behind deliberately so there was no possibility she could be traced. But there was no way of knowing whether she was running from the police, or from a killer.

18

Determined to do everything possible to find Jay's missing girlfriend, Ariadne went back to the florist where Lauren had worked. Although Ariadne had been there only two days earlier, the display in the window had changed, and a different girl was standing beside the counter, counting stems of leaves into small bundles. She looked up at Ariadne with a smile and asked how she could help. When Ariadne held up her warrant card and explained she was looking for Lauren, the girl frowned and shook her head.

'I'm sorry,' she replied, 'there's no one here called Lauren.'

'I think you'll find she works here or, at least, she did until a few days ago,' Ariadne said.

'Ah,' the girl's puzzled frown cleared. 'Yes, you must be talking about that girl who left without giving notice.' She gave a lopsided smile. 'It's an ill wind. I was looking for a job and saw the notice in the window and—' She opened her arms in an expansive gesture, still smiling broadly. 'Here I am. Can I help you? What are you looking for today?'

Ariadne was about to reply that she was looking for Lauren, when the internal door swung open and the stout manageress emerged. Her cheeks reddened slightly when she saw who was in the shop.

'I still haven't heard from Lauren,' she announced, glaring at Ariadne as though she was personally responsible for her former employee's disappearance. 'When you find her, you can tell her from me that she no longer has a job here.' She glanced at Lauren's replacement and moved away from the counter, gesturing at Ariadne to follow her. 'She has no case for wrongful dismissal,' she went on, in a low voice, 'because she was the one who decided to take time off without getting in touch. I'm sorry if she's been ill,' she added, not looking at all sorry, 'but I've got a business to run and a shop to see to. A tiny business like mine is no place for anyone who fails to pull their weight. I'm afraid my hands are tied.'

'We don't know where Lauren is, but we need to talk to her urgently,' Ariadne replied quietly. 'If she contacts you, please tell her she's not in any trouble with us, but she does need to come to the police station to help us with an enquiry.'

The manager merely shook her head to indicate she still had no idea where Lauren was.

'Well, if you do hear from her, please don't forget to give her my message. We're expecting to see her at the police station, and she needs to present herself there as soon as possible. If she's not in York, she can report to any police station. Tell her the longer this goes on, the more difficult it's going to be for her when we do catch up with her, and she can rest assured that, sooner or later, we will.'

Ariadne wasn't sure if that was true. Lauren might already have met with an accident, or worse. Having learned nothing new from the florist, she decided to drive to Leeds to speak to Lauren's mother. She went back to the police station to collect Naomi as, on her own, she might not be able to prevent Lauren from slipping away, if she was hiding at her mother's house. With that possibility in mind, Ariadne decided not to call ahead and forewarn Mrs Shaw of their visit.

'You do realise this could be a wasted journey if we don't let her know we're coming,' Naomi protested, but Ariadne was prepared to take that risk.

'It's only half an hour,' she said.

'Half an hour each way, if we're lucky.'

'But this way, we'll find Lauren if she's there.'

'*If* she's there,' Naomi echoed.

'And if she's not, there's a chance her mother will be able to tell us where she is.'

'Not if her mother's out.'

The traffic moved slowly, and it was nearly an hour before they drew up outside Jennifer Shaw's house. A tousle-haired boy of about eleven opened the door as soon as they knocked. He looked at them inquisitively.

'Is your mother in?' Ariadne asked him.

The boy yelled, 'Mum!' without turning away or stepping back from the doorway.

A woman came down the hallway, wiping her hands on a tea towel. 'Yes?' she called out as she manoeuvred her way past a BMX bike that was leaning against the wall. 'What do you want? It's all right, Dylan.'

The boy stepped back and his mother came to the door and repeated her question.

Close to, Ariadne could see her dark hair was streaked with white, and her face, youthful from a distance, was criss-crossed with fine lines. Ariadne held up her identity card and spoke very quietly so the boy wouldn't hear her.

'We'd like to speak to your daughter.'

Lauren's mother shook her head. 'She hasn't lived here for over a year.'

From inside the house, they heard a dog bark, and Dylan's voice telling it to be quiet.

'She moved out – oh, it's getting on for two years now. She's living in York, with a friend. A girlfriend,' she added quickly. 'I can let you have you her address if you give me a moment.'

Ariadne shook her head. 'We know where she lives. She's not there and we wondered if she was visiting you?'

'I haven't seen her for a couple of months,' the woman replied. 'We speak on the phone. She calls me. And—' She hesitated.

'She's got a boyfriend. I'm not sure where he lives, but it's somewhere in York. That's where she'll be. Her flatmate would know the address. Why do you want to know? Is she in trouble?' She looked flustered, as though the significance of Ariadne's questions had only just struck her. 'Has something happened to her? What do you want with my daughter?'

'Nothing's happened to her, as far as we know,' Ariadne answered with a reassuring smile. 'But we need to speak to her urgently. We'd like to take a look at her room.'

'I told you, she doesn't live here any more.'

'We'd like to take a look anyway, now we're here.'

'I don't understand. What are you looking for?'

Her son rejoined them. Overhearing Ariadne's request, he interrupted his mother before Ariadne could respond.

'Have you got a search warrant?' he asked eagerly. 'Has Lauren been kidnapped?'

His mother hissed at him to be quiet. 'I'm sorry, inspector. He's a good boy, but he does let his imagination run away with him.'

Lauren's bedroom in her mother's house was evidently being used as a store room. Cardboard boxes were stacked on the floor, and there was a pile of coats and trousers on the bed. Unlike Lauren's flatmate, her mother was apologetic about the state of the room, mumbling that she had been having a clear-out. Having conducted a quick search, Ariadne concluded that the only item worth investigating was an old laptop. Ariadne picked it up in gloved hands.

'You can't take that,' Jennifer protested. 'We might want to use it. She left it here for my son.'

'So it belongs to Lauren?'

Jennifer blustered and insisted that Lauren no longer used it. 'She bought herself a new one as soon as she started earning her own money, and she said Dylan could have her old one. You can't take it away. It belongs to my son.'

It was Ariadne's turn to be apologetic as she handed the laptop to Naomi, assuring Jennifer that it would be returned as soon as the police had finished with it.

'Please ask Lauren to contact me if you hear from her,' she said, giving Jennifer a card before she left. 'We would like to speak to her as soon as possible. It really is very important.'

As they left the house, Ariadne glanced back and saw Dylan watching them through a downstairs window.

19

It was almost impossible to believe she would never see him again, but Lauren knew what had happened, and was only too well-aware that it was final. In a way it had been inevitable, like the cliché of a train crash waiting to happen. Whatever else followed the incident, she had to accept that he was never coming back. After a couple of sleepless nights, her grief turned to anger. It served him right. There was no reason why his death should ruin her life. When she thought about it, she could see it was obvious he had been cheating on her with another woman. Why else had he only been able to see her on certain nights? It was the one explanation that made sense of his behaviour. Perhaps she had been wrong to dismiss what his neighbour from the ground-floor flat had said.

The old woman had cornered her in the entrance hall one evening. 'Off to see that young man of yours, are you?' she had wheezed.

Barely listening, Lauren had merely nodded, her thoughts on what would follow once she was in his arms with her lips pressed against his.

'You're not the only one who goes up there to see him,' Mary had croaked, her words checked by a hacking cough.

'Yes, well, whatever,' she had replied curtly. 'I don't know why you're poking your nose into other people's business.'

But Mary had reached out and grabbed her arm with a strength surprising in someone so frail. 'Wait,' she had insisted. 'You need to hear this. I'm telling you what he gets up to, when you're not around.' She gesticulated at the ceiling with her free hand. 'You're not the only one who goes up those stairs, you know. You're too young to throw your life away on a man like that.' She turned her head to one side and spat. A round globule of phlegmy sputum settled on the dusty floor and stared up at Lauren, like an evil eye. 'You remind me of my daughter.' A fleeting smile softened her face before her expression darkened again. 'My girl was taken in by a false-hearted lecher like him.' She jerked her head in the direction of the stairs leading to Jay's flat. 'He led her on and broke her heart. Don't waste your time on a lying cheat like that. I know what men like him can do. Heartless. Heartless,' she mumbled under her breath. 'He'll tempt you with his lies, then discard you when he's ruined you, and leave you to burn for eternity. Listen to me,' she urged. 'It's not too late to save yourself before he leads you to eternal damnation. Leave your sinful ways. Trust in the Lord and He will give you strength.'

With an effort, Lauren had pulled herself away and hurried upstairs, where Jay was waiting for her. When she had challenged him about cheating on her, he burst out laughing. His blue eyes sparkling with amusement, he had dismissed what she had been told as foolish drivel.

'Who was it told you I was seeing someone else?' he had asked her. 'Did that piece of gossip come from a trustworthy source? Only it seems you know more about my private affairs than I do. Come on, you know we don't keep any secrets from each other. Who's been filling your head with this nonsense?'

She had brushed away the question, unwilling to name the old woman for fear of creating bad feeling between Jay and his neighbour, but he had guessed anyway.

'It was that stupid old cow downstairs, wasn't it? Yes, of course it was,' he had gone on, when she refused to answer his question. 'Who else could it be? She thinks she can get away with making up stories about me, but we both know it's all lies. Who are you going to believe? A man who worships you, or some vindictive old hag who lives alone and resents other people's happiness? Do you know what she said to me the other day?'

He had related a hilarious anecdote about something Mary had said to him. It had been so easy for him. He could have said anything, and she would have been persuaded that his neighbour was lying, because she had already made up her mind to believe him.

'You know I adore you, don't you?' he had murmured and she had melted into his arms, knowing there was nowhere else in the world she wanted to be. She had responded at once, longing to stay in the warmth of his embrace forever.

'Why can't I come and live here with you, all the time?' she had asked him.

'You know there's nothing I'd like better, but the landlord would throw me out, and then we'd both be homeless. It's in the terms of my lease. No subletting and no cohabiting.'

'That's ridiculous.'

'I agree, but he's the landlord and he makes the rules. '

'He couldn't refuse to let you live with your fiancée. What if we were getting married?'

'We'll talk about that as soon as my rental agreement runs out. I'm going to buy you any ring you want, and we'll find a place where we can live together.' He leaned down and kissed her.

She pulled away from his embrace. 'Shouldn't we start looking now?'

'Soon. We'll find somewhere soon, and then we can be together always. Just be patient and trust me. You do trust me, don't you? It won't be long now.'

'I don't understand. What are we waiting for?'

'Listen, I wanted to keep this as a surprise until the cash starts rolling in, but the fact is I've got a massive deal in the pipeline, one that will bring in more money than you've ever dreamed of. We won't be relying on chickenshit for much longer.' He pointed at himself and grinned. 'I've got big plans for us when this deal comes off. Trust me, we'll be made. And the beauty of it is, it won't be a one-off. No more scratching around for a few quid here and a few quid there. With these contacts I'm building, we're going to be raking it in. I'm reeling in some serious players.'

'It won't be dangerous, will it?' she recalled asking.

'Don't worry, it's easy money, and it's risk free. This is the break we've been waiting for.'

At first she had believed everything he told her, but as time went on, she had started to suspect he wasn't being entirely honest with her. There seemed to be one excuse after another as to why she couldn't move in with him permanently, and he flatly refused to consider moving in with her.

'Is your room actually big enough for two of us?' he had asked, and she had to concede that he had a point, since she had one small room to herself in a shared flat. 'I have a lot of stuff,' he had continued, apologetically hammering his point home. 'I just don't see how that could possibly work.'

'But if we were living together, we could afford somewhere bigger than either of us has at the moment.'

'And we will,' he had assured her, 'just as soon as my agreement is up here and this deal takes off. It won't be long now.'

Still, she had clung to her belief that he was impatient for them to live together, and had told herself it was only circumstances that were keeping them apart. She had steadfastly accepted his excuses, and dismissed his old neighbour's warnings. She had believed he loved her, right up until the moment he hit her and nearly choked her.

20

NATALIE STARED MISERABLY AROUND the flat after the police officer had gone. Despite all the clutter, the place felt empty without Lauren. She knew she was being irrational, because Lauren often went out, and she usually stayed overnight with her boyfriend at the weekend. Lauren kept dropping hints that she was going to move in with Jay permanently, which had annoyed Natalie. It would be a nuisance if she had to find another flatmate, but in the meantime nothing seemed to be happening and, with any luck, it would turn out to be just talk. Lauren had always been prone to fantasise about her boyfriends but so far none of her relationships had lasted very long.

'You can't possibly understand the way it is with me and Jay,' Lauren had told her complacently. 'You've never been in love.'

Lauren sounded very earnest, and perhaps she even believed what she was saying, but Natalie had heard it all before. She had lost count of the number of 'soulmates' Lauren had met.

'There's no such thing as a perfect partner,' Natalie had insisted firmly. 'It's unrealistic to think that. How old are you? Twelve?'

'Since when are you an expert on relationships? How many boyfriends have you had in the past year?'

'How can you not hear how stupid you sound?' Natalie had retorted, stung by the reminder that she had never had a serious boyfriend. 'You keep saying there's just one soulmate for you, when we both know you've already been out with at least four. For goodness' sake, Lauren, make it make sense.'

There was no question Lauren had been genuinely infatuated with Jay. Natalie knew how hard her friend had tried to convince him it would be a good idea for her to move in with him. Still, the chances were she would become besotted with someone else as soon as Jay dumped her. People were less cautious when they were on the rebound, and Lauren might already be burying the pain of her latest loss in a new relationship. That was the most likely explanation for her disappearance. All the same, it was disturbing to know the police were looking for her.

Natalie wandered disconsolately into Lauren's room, wishing her friend would walk back in as though nothing had happened. She imagined Lauren's astonishment on hearing the police were trying to find her. At first, Lauren would accuse Natalie of winding her up. She hoped it would all turn out to be a huge fuss over nothing, but the police didn't waste their time searching for people for no reason. Not until then did it occur to Natalie that Lauren might have been killed by a dangerous criminal. In an unguarded moment when they were both tipsy, Lauren had confided in Natalie that Jay was on the verge of joining a major drug distribution network.

'If they find out I've blabbed, they'll kill me,' Lauren had whispered dramatically.

'But who are "they"?'

'I don't know.'

At the time, Natalie had laughed at the claim as a grandiose exaggeration, typical of Lauren. Now she was afraid that her friend's indiscretion might indeed have proved fatal. Heedless of the clothes she was crushing, she flung herself down on Lauren's bed and began to sob.

The uncertainty surrounding Lauren's disappearance was harder to bear than anything else. Natalie regretted not having asked the police detective more questions about what had happened to her flatmate, but at the time she had been too disconcerted to think clearly. The rent was due soon. She had no idea what she would do if Lauren didn't show up in time to pay her share. Natalie couldn't afford to pay it all by herself. If she tried to explain that the police were looking into her flatmate's disappearance, the landlord might throw them both out. She didn't know what rights she would have in such circumstances, but she supposed she could be evicted if the rent wasn't paid in full. Even if she could find the money, being in trouble with the police might be sufficient grounds for eviction. It would probably be best to say nothing for now, and try to scrape the money together somehow. She went to check the kitty, and was dismayed to find the tin empty. She wondered whether she ought to tell the police as the discovery seemed to confirm that Lauren had planned her disappearance.

She was jolted out of her miserable reverie by a shrill ringtone. For a second she thought it was Lauren's phone, but then she remembered the detective had taken that with her when she left. Yanking her own phone out of her pocket, she felt a fleeting hope that Lauren was calling to tell her all about her latest soulmate.

She could almost hear Lauren's excited voice. '*I know I've said this before, but he really is The One.*'

'Is that Natalie?' a woman's voice said. 'It's Jennifer, Lauren's mother. Is Lauren there? Can you tell her I need to speak to her? She's not been answering her phone and the police have been here looking for her.'

Not knowing what to say, Natalie panicked and hung up.

21

On Saturday evening, Ian cooked supper. Geraldine had been avoiding spicy food for a while, so it was some time since he had made a curry, which he referred to laughingly as his signature dish. Usually his enthusiasm when cooking made Geraldine smile, but on this occasion she waited stony-faced for him to serve the dinner. Ian had been adamant they should sit at the table to eat. Tom was asleep, and Ian wanted them to spend time enjoying a romantic meal together. Geraldine tried to feel pleased, but she was tired and feeling out of sorts. It didn't help that it had rained every time she had decided to go out for a walk, and she had been stuck indoors all day with a fractious baby. Now all she wanted to do was lounge on the sofa with her supper on a tray in front of the television. She didn't care what they watched, as long as they avoided the need for conversation. But it would have been unkind not to pretend to be having a good time, once they were eating, after Ian had made so much effort in the kitchen.

As it turned out, they both enjoyed the supper.

'That was amazing,' she said as they finished. 'I can't tell you how much I've missed your curries.'

Ian grinned, gratified and seemingly relieved. 'That's more like it,' he said. 'There's plenty more.'

'Honestly, I couldn't manage another mouthful. I'm completely stuffed.'

Ian insisted that he clear the table while she went into the living room and put her feet up.

'Don't be silly,' she replied. 'I've been sitting around all day doing nothing, while you've been out working and shopping and then coming home to slave in the kitchen.'

'Hardly slaving,' he grinned. 'I find cooking relaxing. It helps to take my mind off things. And you can't say you've been doing nothing. You've been looking after Tom, and I'm sure that's exhausting in its own way.'

Geraldine wondered if that was a slightly barbed comment, but then decided she was being paranoid. Ian had always enjoyed cooking. Hearing him hum as he clattered about, clearing up, she wondered whether he was making an extra effort because she had been out the previous evening with Ariadne, but she dismissed the thought as unjust, and obediently went to put her feet up in the living room. When he had finished stacking the dishwasher, Ian joined her. He was smiling, but his blue eyes were sharp.

'I'm glad you're looking a bit more cheerful,' he said as he flopped down beside her on the sofa and put his arm round her. 'I've been concerned about you.'

She gave what she hoped was a reassuring smile. 'Oh, don't worry about me,' she said. 'I'm fine. Now Tom's sleeping through the night, I feel almost human again. Only almost, mind,' she added, laughing.

She was taken aback by his next remark.

'It's understandable that you would be unsettled by seeing Ariadne.'

'Unsettled? What are you talking about? Why would I feel unsettled after seeing a friend?'

She realised she was overreacting to a thoughtless comment that had probably meant nothing, but she had really appreciated the time she had spent with Ariadne, and was keen to see her again. Discussing the case her friend was working on had made her feel energised. She tried to explain, but Ian shook his head.

'You don't need to put yourself under any pressure to go back to work,' he said, completely missing her point.

'Ian,' she sighed, 'we've talked about this before and when I go back to work is my decision.'

'Of course, that's understood, but we should at least discuss it. Before Tom was born, neither of us knew how you were going to feel about going back to work. Now we know and it's time we talked about it.'

Ian suggested she might want to stay at home with the baby, at least until the end of his first year, but the thought of taking the rest of the year off filled Geraldine with a faint dread. After so long at home, she might never be able to return to her role as a detective inspector. A future without work seemed to her like a void, an endless tunnel of nappies and school journeys and mindless play. She accepted it was a flaw in her character, but she had never felt drawn to friendship and fun. She preferred to work. Nothing matched the satisfaction of knowing she had served justice, and helped to prevent further suffering by apprehending a killer. She could tell herself she needed to keep working so she could continue to support her sister, but that wasn't the real reason, because she had inherited money to fall back on. The truth was that investigating serious crime was like a drug for her. Even her baby, whom she loved, couldn't fill the gap in her life as she sat at home, shaking rattles and tickling him, all the while telling him what a good boy he was, as though repeating the words would make it come true.

'Yes, you are,' she would croon to him when they were alone at home, 'you're a good boy.'

Tom would gurgle in reply, and smile and hiccup, but he didn't understand a word she said.

'There's nothing to discuss,' she told Ian now. 'I'll go back when I'm ready, and that will be very soon,' she added. Ian had no right to express an opinion about her life choices, but somehow this felt like a confrontation. 'I've been meeting with childminders,' she added, struggling not to sound defiant.

'I just don't want to put you under any pressure,' Ian said, looking crestfallen. 'I knew seeing Ariadne would set you off,' he added in a low voice.

Just for a moment, Geraldine felt guilty. Ian was trying to be kind and supportive, but she was disappointed to realise that he didn't really understand her at all. Before she could reply, Tom started to cry, and she stood up, relieved that they had been interrupted.

'I don't want to talk about it any more,' she said as she went to tend to the baby.

Ian didn't say anything, but she suspected he realised she had made her decision.

22

His mother gazed anxiously at him as he tinkered with his food. Yiannis glanced up at her, noticing strands of white showing against her black hair which was pulled back in her customary bun at the back of her head. Although no longer young, she was still one of the most beautiful women he had ever seen. When he told her so, she would scold him and tell him she was too old to be beautiful.

'There was a time,' she would say, with a wistful expression, before she snapped back into the present and held up her hands as evidence he was deluded.

'Look at me,' she would say. 'I'm as wrinkled as a dried-up fig.'

'You can be old and beautiful,' he would tell her. 'Beauty comes from within. You just have to smile.'

She had laughed at his nonsense. But this was no time for idle chatter.

'What's the matter with you?' she asked. 'You've hardly touched your food again, and you're looking pale. Are you sick?'

Yiannis shook his head impatiently. 'I'm fine. Stop fussing.'

'You're not fine. I can tell there's something on your mind. You can't fool your mother, Yiannaki. Tell me what's wrong.'

'What do you think is on my mind?' His voice rose and his mother shrank back. 'You know one of my tenants is dead. Who's going to pay his rent now? I've got bills that are overdue. Where's the money going to come from?'

'You'll find another tenant,' she said. 'It's a nice flat, and York is a popular place to live.'

'That's as maybe, but the police are still hanging about and I've got no idea when I'll be able to find a replacement. And now the old woman who lives on the ground floor is making a fuss about paying *her* rent. And as if that's not bad enough, to top it all off, the police are still sniffing around asking questions. Of course, I'm worried. You think I don't have bills to pay? You think I rent out those apartments just for something to do?'

'So long as you've done nothing wrong, there's nothing for you to worry about,' she assured him. 'Now eat. Starving yourself won't make your problems go away. It'll only upset you.' She lowered her gaze, knowing better than to provoke his temper.

Yiannis sighed. He had seen his mother's apprehension and despised himself for venting his frustration on her. She had stood by him, regardless of the trouble he had caused her. She didn't deserve his anger. 'I'm going out,' he said, too uncomfortable with himself to remain in her company any longer.

'You haven't finished your lunch,' his mother protested. 'You're not going to do anything stupid, are you?'

He walked out without answering.

Returning from the hotel where she had been staying, while the property was being examined as a crime scene, Mary had contacted Yiannis to insist on a reduction in her rent. She claimed she had been unable to live in the flat for a week, even though it hadn't cost her a penny to stay elsewhere, since the police had paid for her temporary accommodation. The nerve of her demand riled him. Didn't she appreciate the financial straits he was in now the upstairs flat was empty? Breathing deeply to control his irritation, he drove to Penley's Grove, and scowled as he drew up outside the house, recalling the crime scene tape over the doorway and the uniformed officers posted outside.

He had arranged to call on Mary, but although she was expecting him, she kept him waiting in the hall for more than five minutes before she opened her door. Dispensing with greetings, he told her bluntly that her rent was overdue. She started whining that she had not been in her flat for a week so it was unfair to ask her to pay rent for the whole month.

'You wouldn't expect me to take money off if you were on holiday,' Yiannis protested, adding that the rental agreement made no mention of a reduction in rent if the tenant had to vacate the property for any reason at all.

'Holiday?' she squealed. 'At my age? It was no holiday, staying in that place. It was cold and damp and there was black mould in the toilet. Stinking black mould!'

It was pointless explaining that he had never said she had been on holiday, and he was not responsible for the mould at the hotel where the police had accommodated her. But he had to make it clear to her that the rent was due, in full, irrespective of whether she had been in the apartment for the full month or not. Either she paid up, or she would be in breach of the agreement she had signed.

'I don't want to evict you,' he concluded severely, 'but if you refuse to pay me what you owe, I'll be forced to set the process in motion to remove you, and find a tenant who's willing to honour the agreement and pay their rent.'

Mary made a spitting sound through her teeth. 'What kind of person would threaten to throw a poor old woman out on the street?' she hissed. 'May the Lord strike you down for a heartless sinner.'

With an impatient sigh, he reiterated his demand that she pay her overdue rent and repeated his warning. 'You have until the end of the week.' Reduced to issuing threats to a frail old woman, he turned on his heel and marched out of the building, filled with self-loathing.

'Shall I heat your lunch up for you, Yiannaki?' his mother asked, gazing at him solicitously, when he walked back in.

He shook his head, struggling to control his exasperation. It wasn't fair to vent his anger on her, but he was finding it difficult to stay calm. To placate her, he ate his lunch, and did feel less stressed. It was difficult to feel aggrieved with his belly full of good, hot food. Before long he would find another tenant, and then he could settle back into his comfortable routine. He would call the lettings agent that afternoon and set things in motion. He was leaning back in his chair, savouring a strong coffee, when the doorbell rang.

'It's someone for you,' his mother said.

A smart, young blonde woman followed his mother into the living room, and his revived spirits sank once again when she introduced herself.

'Detective Sergeant Naomi Arnold,' he repeated stupidly. 'What can I do for you?'

'I have a few questions for you,' she replied airily. 'I won't keep you long. We just need to tie up a few loose ends. There's nothing for you to be concerned about.'

Her encouraging smile failed to reassure him. Yiannis waved at his mother to go away and leave him alone with the detective who took a seat beside him without being invited to sit down. The young woman stared evenly at him across the space between their two chairs while his mother left the room, banging the door behind her to indicate her resentment at being summarily banished from her own living room. Under any other circumstances, Yiannis might have been happy to find himself sitting down with an attractive young woman. As it was, he struggled to control his nerves.

'Before you start, I have a question for you,' he said, attempting to take the initiative. 'It's a week since the tragic accident took place at my property. How much longer do I have to wait before I can look for another tenant? It could take a while to find someone suitable in the best of circumstances, and your investigation isn't helping. I don't wish to sound unfeeling, but the longer this goes on, the longer I'll be waiting, and I really do need that rent money. I still have bills to pay – tax, utilities, maintenance, they don't pay for themselves.'

'We'll be done as soon as possible,' the detective assured him blandly, before questioning him about Jay's girlfriend.

'I already told your colleague, I don't pry into my tenants' private lives,' he replied, struggling to control his frustration. 'Don't you people talk to each other? We're always hearing about how overworked you are, yet here you are, wasting your time and mine in repeating questions I've already answered.'

Unperturbed by his irritation, she continued. Although she had claimed she only wanted to ask him a few questions, it felt more like an interrogation.

'What can you tell me about your ground-floor tenant, Mary Jones?'

'What can I tell you? Only that she's old and she lives alone. Until now, she's always paid her rent on time, and she's never caused any trouble. Until the recent unfortunate accident, I would have said she was a good tenant, getting on a bit. But she's been kicking up a fuss about paying rent for a full month, because you forced her to vacate her apartment for a week. An old woman like that, having to leave home. It's a disgrace. I can't say I'm altogether surprised that she's complaining about having to pay rent for a week when she wasn't allowed into her own home.'

'We had to keep the hallway clear, while the area at the foot of the stairs was being examined as part of a crime scene,' the detective told him.

'Crime scene,' he scoffed. 'The man fell down the stairs. It's hardly a crime to lose your footing and fall.'

He drained his cup, but the coffee was cold. Something else the police had ruined for him. With an effort, he maintained his composure.

'Would you say she's reliable?' the detective asked.

'Who?'

'Mary Jones.'

'I told you, she always paid her rent on time until you people came along and interfered.'

'Do you feel you can you trust what she says? She's quite old. Would you say she gets confused?'

Yiannis had answered enough questions. 'I'm sorry,' he said, gritting his teeth, 'I don't know what you mean. She's sharp enough when it comes to demanding a reduction in her rent.'

'I understand your frustration, but would you say her memory is reliable?'

He shrugged. 'How the hell should I know? I don't socialise with my tenants. It's a business arrangement. I maintain the property and they pay me rent, and that's the beginning and the end of it. Now, if there's nothing else, I'd like you to leave. I'm not a suspect in your investigation into why someone fell down the stairs. The stair carpet was professionally fitted, and the handrail is sturdy. As the landlord, I took all the necessary precautions to make the property safe for my tenants, and the building has been checked by Energy Performance and Health and Safety inspectors and whoever else the council sent to look it over and take my money for a safety certificate. I'm a responsible landlord, and I took out the recommended insurance. You can't blame me if someone failed to look where they were going on the stairs. Now, I'm asking you again, very politely, to get out of my house and leave me alone.'

After the detective had gone, Yiannis's mother came creeping back into the living room. She gazed at him anxiously. 'You didn't lose your temper with that young woman, did you?'

'Like I'm about to lose it with you, if you don't shut up?'

His mother sighed. 'I'll make you some fresh coffee, Yiannaki.'

She turned away, mumbling that there was no call for him to disrespect her. She had done nothing to warrant such rudeness.

'I'm sorry,' he called out. 'You're right, and I'm sorry. You're a saint to put up with me.'

'One extreme to another,' she muttered with a sigh. 'If he's not yelling at me, he's grovelling.' She turned to face him. 'Why can't you be more even-tempered? You have to learn to take things in your stride.'

'I guess my stride isn't very long,' he replied sullenly, aware that he sounded like a ten-year-old schoolboy.

23

On Sunday, there was no time for Ian to raise the subject of Geraldine's maternity leave, because she had arranged to take Tom to London on the train to meet her twin sister.

'It's a miracle I never croaked the day we was born,' Helena had told Geraldine, with a laugh. 'The doctors thought I was too sickly to last the week out, but I'm tough, innit,' she wheezed. 'You did well to get whisked away and adopted right from the start, but now we've hooked up again, you ain't getting rid of me again.'

'I don't want to be rid of you,' Geraldine had replied, aware that she sounded awkward and prim.

'It's a joke, innit? For fuck's sake, lighten up, sis.'

Meeting for the first time as adults, their relationship had initially been strained. Although they had been born identical, there were marked differences in their appearance. Geraldine's clear complexion and bright eyes were framed by glossy black hair, while Helena's face was scored with deep lines, and her hair was shot through with white streaks. Helena looked considerably older than Geraldine, her lifestyle having taken its toll on her health. Yet despite their different paths in life, gradually they had reached an understanding perhaps deeper than either of them had experienced with anyone else.

'I know you, sis,' Helena had said, more than once. 'You can't pull the wool over my eyes, for all you're so brainy. We're the same, you an' me, even if you are a hoity-toity brilliant detective and I'm an ex-junkie.'

When Geraldine had pointed out that Helena no longer used illicit drugs, Helena had smiled sadly. 'One day at a time, sis.'

Of course, Geraldine had stepped up whenever her twin needed money, afraid that too much pressure would send Helena spiralling back into addiction. So far, thanks mainly to Geraldine's support, Helena had remained clean for several years, but Geraldine lived in fear of discovering that her twin had relapsed. She had long ago determined that she would do whatever she could to help her sister, paying her rent and taking her out, and generally being available to her should she need emotional or financial support. It tended to be the latter.

They met at a tapas bar in King's Cross where they could sit outside under an awning. The location was convenient for both of them, with Helena living on the outskirts of North London and Geraldine's train terminating at King's Cross station. Helena was already seated at a corner table when Geraldine arrived. As she scanned the tables, Geraldine saw her grinning and waving.

'Thought I'd better get in early and make sure we had a table outside,' Helena explained as Geraldine sat down. 'Them stupid bastards only take bookings for tables indoors and I thought you'd like it better out here. People are less likely to be upset if the baby cries.' She grinned. 'It's warm enough, innit, with that heater and the screens to keep out the wind. And here in the corner a crying baby will be less intrusive and you'll be able to feed him without anyone poking their nose in.'

'And you can smoke out here,' Geraldine added, citing the real reason Helena wanted to sit outside.

Helena pouted. 'That weren't it at all,' she protested. But they both knew she was lying. 'Can't put anything past you,' Helena grumbled as she stubbed out her cigarette and handed Geraldine a menu. 'And I suppose goody-two-shoes Mummy won't let bad Aunty smoke near the baby,' she added with a mock grimace of horror.

Geraldine laughed and thanked her for the menu, even though she knew she would be paying for both of them.

'So, seriously, how you been?' Helena asked. She studied Geraldine appraisingly. 'Your hair looks good. Makes you look softer. Less scary, innit. How are you finding motherhood and all that? How is it? I've got to say you coulda knocked me over with a feather when you said you was having a baby, of all things. At our age!' She laughed the throaty laugh of an inveterate smoker.

Geraldine sighed as Helena lit up another cigarette, thinking how much Helena's habit was costing. But at least she was spending Geraldine's money on tobacco not heroin. That was something to be grateful for.

'Well,' she replied, 'I can't pretend it's easy.'

'Looks easy enough to me,' Helena said, nodding at the sleeping baby. 'He's a love, sis, and he don't look like he's no trouble at all.' She smiled. 'I'm enough trouble for one family, and I'll be sure to tell him so when he's old enough to understand. He's going to stay on the straight and narrow, that's for sure. He don't want to end up like me. There ain't nothing glamorous about grovelling about for a fix. Fuck that. Even reality ain't as bad as using. I'll make sure he knows there ain't no mileage in falling off the wagon.' She nodded sagaciously. 'He's gonna make us both proud and he's not going to go to the bad, not with you there to guide him, and my fucked-up life as a warning.'

For a moment she fell silent, looking wistful. Geraldine knew without being told that Helena was thinking about their birth mother, and the way she had brought up the only child she had kept with her. If only their mother had given both of them up for adoption, Helena's life might have turned out very differently.

'Still,' Helena said, 'water under the bridge, innit. And my bad luck in having her for a mother has been cancelled out by having the best bloody sister in the world.'

Recalling Helena's antagonism towards her when they had first met, Geraldine smiled, feeling as though a weight had lifted from her shoulders. Perhaps Helena was right, and being a mother needn't be so hard. Relationships didn't always have to feel perfect right from the start, and if she sometimes struggled with Tom, that didn't make her inadequate as a mother. Looking down at the cherubic little face sleeping at her side, she was gripped by an unaccustomed, yet somehow familiar, wave of affection for her son. When Helena praised Tom for staying asleep until they had finished their lunch, Geraldine felt quietly proud of him, and of herself. She didn't admit that she was enjoying the opportunity to show Tom off. At the toddler group, everyone had a baby and no one treated Tom as special in any way. That was fine, and exactly as it should be, but it was still satisfying to hear Helena babble on about what a beautiful baby he was.

He woke up, grizzling, as the waitress was clearing their plates away, and Geraldine fed him quickly, while Helena looked on, smiling. Over coffee, she mentioned her intention of returning to work. Helena was effusive in her support.

'You should do it, sis. You got to get out, face the world, interact with people, be with people. You're a mother, not a fucking nun. You ain't taken no vow of silence. And your job matters, and I don't mean just to you. It matters,' she insisted, slightly wistfully.

As they stood up to leave, Tom's stroller caught the wheel of a shopping trolley.

'Watch where you're going,' the woman with the trolley cried out. She turned away, muttering that Geraldine was a clumsy cow.

'And you can watch your mouth,' Helena retorted shrilly. She leaned forward and thrust her face close to the woman, who pulled back with a startled gaze.

'It's all right,' Geraldine said, pulling the stroller back and weaving her way between the trolley and her chair. 'Just leave it. There's no harm done. But thank you for defending me,' she added, and Helena beamed.

24

On Monday morning, Ariadne summoned the team. Waiting for a file which was taking time to load, she was one of the last to arrive, and she slipped into the room as quietly as she could. Her colleagues were chatting in subdued tones about their weekends, or about the case. Everyone was frustrated that Lauren was still missing, although opinions were divided as to whether she had done a runner because she was guilty, or because she had witnessed the murder and was scared the killer would find her, or whether she had simply hooked up with a new boyfriend and gone on a bender. All seemed to be equally plausible explanations.

'Perhaps the killer has already found her and done away with her,' a constable suggested grimly, provoking a few comments.

'It's never a good idea to witness a murder.'

'Almost as bad as being the victim of one.'

'And it's not a great idea to commit one either.'

'Do you think Lauren killed him, then?'

'You mean as in a crime of passion?'

'He did have another woman on the go, according to a neighbour, so it's possible.'

'Anything's possible at this stage,' Naomi pointed out.

Ariadne moved to the front of the room and the muttered speculation died out. No one else spoke as she voiced her disappointment at the ineffective search for Lauren, the lack of information about Jay, and the incompetent questioning of his landlord. She was reluctant to say too much about Yiannis, aware that she had kept quiet about her husband's relationship with him. She told herself Nico barely knew Yiannis, and they were no more than acquaintances from the same community, but she was uncomfortable about having met him in her own home. She focused her attention on Jay and his girlfriends.

'We need to trace the second woman he was allegedly seeing,' she said. 'And we need to find Lauren.'

They had matched one sample of the DNA found in Jay's bed to Lauren, but they had no lead so far for the elusive girlfriend, Carly, mentioned by his parents.

'We've circulated Lauren's description to police stations around the country, and we've passed on her details to every airport, port, and mainline station. It's beginning to look as though she's holed up somewhere in York,' Naomi said.

'Then we need to redouble our search of the local area,' Ariadne said, 'as well as sending out information further afield. And we have to look into the landlord's background,' she added, hiding her unease. 'We don't know anything about him other than that he came to the UK twenty years ago. He hasn't been in any trouble that we know about since he arrived, but there could be more to his story, so let's start digging.'

They urgently needed to find information about the girlfriend mentioned by Jay's parents. All they knew about her so far was that she was supposedly working as a teaching assistant, probably in a primary school somewhere in York, and her first name was Carly. A search of Jay's social media sites had produced no results and his phone records had drawn a frustrating blank. He didn't appear to list his contacts by their names, but by epithets. Lauren was 'Airhead' and there were several other descriptions which appeared to refer to women, not all of them complimentary. 'Droopy' and 'Belly' were two of them. All of the numbers on his phone had been traced and contacted. None was named Carly. Wondering if the Ropers had been mistaken in giving them that name, Ariadne arranged to return to Pocklington later that afternoon to speak to Jay's parents again.

'My husband is at work,' Mrs Roper told her when she phoned in the morning.

If they did find Carly, there was only a slim chance that she would know where Lauren might be, but despite their efforts, they were still no closer to finding her. Even if Carly knew nothing about Lauren, she might have useful information to share about Jay. With a full hunt for Lauren in progress, Ariadne decided to visit Jay's former workplace. She took Sam with her.

Sam Cullen was a fairly new recruit, and he was clearly pleased at being invited to drive her to an assignment. Having completed his training, he had arrived in York, keen to go out into the community to engage in what he described as 'real' police work. His colleagues had been quick to disabuse him.

'To be honest,' he had complained in the pub one evening, 'I thought, when I started, the job would be a bit livelier. I know it's important to keep a record of everything we do, but we seem to spend more time writing up reports than actually doing anything to write about. Whatever we do manage to do just turns into an excuse to generate yet more paperwork.'

'Welcome to the exciting world of modern-day policing,' Naomi had told him. 'Recording your actions and decisions is what it's all about.'

'The more action you're involved in, the more reports you'll be writing, and the less time you'll have for any action,' an experienced constable had pointed out, and they had all laughed as Sam twisted his handsome features into a comical grimace.

'More action with *less* writing would be nice,' he had responded, reluctantly joining in the general laughter. 'In fact, right now I'd settle for any action at all.'

'If you're talking about getting your leg over, you're in the wrong job, lad,' an old sergeant grinned.

'I don't know,' another officer said. 'I heard some ladies like a man in uniform.'

'How about some action buying a round?' the old sergeant suggested, nodding at Sam.

Young, with fair hair and boyish good looks, Ariadne could see why Geraldine had said the new constable reminded her of Ian. Geraldine and Ian had first worked together nearly twenty years earlier, when Ian was still a detective sergeant. Now, with the vivacity of a man half his age, Ian was developing a paunch, his shoulders were becoming slightly bowed, and his hair was turning white above his temples. But he was still good-looking, and Ariadne could see why Geraldine found him attractive.

'So it's a case of *cherchez les femmes*,' Sam quipped as they walked to the car.

Jay had once worked answering the phone for an IT company, before the role had been outsourced. Sam drove Ariadne to the office on the outskirts of York, but the visit was disappointing. There were two young men and a middle-aged woman at the premises. The other three members of the team were working from home. Ariadne questioned the woman first, and was told that Jay had worked from home and had very rarely been seen in the office.

'No one has been taking calls here in the UK for over two years,' the woman said. 'Answering the phone can be done remotely, so there's no need for anyone to be here. We do take calls, but it's never been done on site. We just run a skeleton staff here, making sure the tech is functioning, and any face-to-face with the public is done by our travelling sales reps. I read about Jay's accident. It must have been a terrible shock for his family. Of course, he's sadly missed here,' she added quickly. She raised her painted eyebrows and shook her head in a gesture of despair.

Ariadne gave what she hoped was a sympathetic smile. 'What we're really interested in is tracing his girlfriend, Lauren,' she said. 'Do you have any idea where she might be?'

'No, I'm sorry. I'm afraid I can't help you. Have you asked his parents? Maybe they would know.'

'What about his friend, Carly?'

The woman frowned. 'I never met his girlfriend or any of his friends.' She spoke dismissively. 'We're not that kind of business environment. We come here to work. I'm sorry,' she added, unbending a little, 'but we don't mix socially.'

Her two colleagues were equally unable to help. No one there had met Lauren or Carly, and they hadn't heard Jay mention either of them. Neither of the men in the office had met Jay in person although they had communicated with him online.

'I'm not usually here,' one of them explained earnestly. 'You just happened to catch me on a rare day in. To be honest, if we weren't in such a mess with our systems, I'd be at home now, working remotely.'

Ariadne left with a list of Jay's other colleagues which she forwarded to Naomi so that they could each be contacted by phone. But the chance that any of them would have any clue about where to find either of Jay's recent girlfriends was extremely remote. While they had to follow up any possible lead, leaving no stone unturned in the hunt for Lauren and Carly, no one held out much hope that their enquiries would yield any useful information.

Later that afternoon, Ariadne returned to Jay's parents' house in Pocklington. This time she went alone. She couldn't justify taking Sam away from the police station for a second time that day on what was likely to be another wasted journey. Once again, Mrs Roper answered the door and led her to the cramped living room with its faded furniture. Mr Roper was sitting in an armchair, looking morose. But the Ropers were unable to tell her anything more than Carly's first name.

'Can you remember where she was teaching?'

'She was a teaching assistant,' Mrs Roper replied. 'She wasn't a proper teacher.'

Ariadne gathered that Jay's mother hadn't approved of Carly.

'She was a nice enough girl, and very pretty, in spite of all the muck on her face,' Mrs Roper went on. 'But she wasn't right for Jay. She was too young, for a start.'

'How old was she?'

Mrs Roper shrugged. 'I don't know, but she was younger than him by a good ten or fifteen years. I knew she was trouble the moment I set eyes on her. You can tell with some girls, can't you?'

Her husband shrugged and said gruffly that she looked like a whore with all her make-up and tight clothes. His wife sniffed disapprovingly. They had no idea which school Carly had worked in, although she had told them it was in York, which narrowed the search down. They didn't know where she lived, and they hadn't even heard of Lauren. Thanking them, Ariadne left. Her whole day had been a complete waste of time.

'Those girls must be somewhere,' she told Nico that evening. 'It must be possible to find them. We just don't know where to look. Do you have any idea how many young women called Carly are working in schools in York?'

'But how many are teaching assistants?' he replied.

'None that we've been able to find. It's hopeless. Another dead end.'

25

The following day, Ariadne joined Naomi in the canteen for an early lunch. She watched Naomi's pert features twist in a scowl as she poked at her sandwich miserably.

'Even if we find Carly, if that really is her name, there's nothing to say she'll be able to shed any light on the murder. Do you ever get the feeling we're running around chasing our tails?' Naomi sighed. 'Don't you wish Geraldine was back? Somehow she seemed to have an uncanny knack for knowing which leads to pursue.'

Ariadne gave a wry smile. Having struck up a friendship after admitting to each other how much they missed Geraldine, they had fallen into the habit of going to the canteen together when they were both free at the same time. While Ariadne had been good friends with Geraldine, Naomi had looked up to her as an unofficial mentor. Ariadne was doing her best to support Naomi, but she wondered if she could be doing a better job of filling the gap left by Geraldine's absence.

'She was the best,' Naomi added wistfully.

'She was my best friend on the force,' Ariadne replied.

'I hope she's okay. I thought she might have brought her baby to see us by now. Do you think she's okay?'

'Of course she's okay,' Ariadne reassured her younger colleague. If Geraldine had any issues, she hadn't considered them serious enough to talk about. 'She was fine when I saw her on Friday, and you only have to look at Ian to see that he's really happy. He wouldn't be so cheerful if there was anything wrong at home. I think Geraldine's loving her new life, and why wouldn't she?'

'Yes, I'm sure you're right. She's probably forgotten all about work, and us. But some women find the transition from career to motherhood difficult and can't wait to get back to work. I just thought Geraldine would be one of them, but I suppose that was just wishful thinking on my part.'

Ariadne shrugged. 'Well, there's nothing stopping her returning to work, if that's what she wants to do. I don't think any of us would be sorry to see her back. I'm planning to meet her next week and I'll tell her you were asking after her.'

'She would know if we should be searching for this Carly,' Naomi said.

Ariadne laughed. 'No, she wouldn't know any more than we do. She didn't have mystical powers.'

'No, you're right. I suppose she would have been just as frustrated as the rest of us.'

'There's no point in fretting. We'll get to the bottom of all this, sooner or later.'

'You're always so positive,' Naomi said. 'That's something I really admire about you.'

'Well, there's no point in wasting energy being negative, is there? You know it takes more effort to frown than to smile?'

In the meantime, until they found Carly, they had no idea whether she would have any helpful information to offer. After lunch, Ariadne continued searching. She was about to take a break, when she received a message that a woman who was possibly of interest to the investigation had come to the police station to report a crime.

'The woman says her friend has a violent boyfriend, but refuses to come forward to report him for physically abusing her,' the desk sergeant said.

'Has this got anything to do with Jay Roper's missing girlfriends?' Ariadne asked. 'Only I am rather busy at the moment, investigating a murder. Can't you find a constable to deal with her? What about Sam?'

'The thing is, she said the victim of the abuse she's come to report is called Carly,' the sergeant replied.

They couldn't assume this was the Carly who had been seeing Jay, but even so Ariadne felt a shiver of excitement. Closing her iPad, she hurried to question the woman, who was waiting for her in the entry hall. The desk sergeant nodded at a thin young woman with spiky pink hair and a tattoo on the side of her neck. She was wearing a pink puffa jacket over a short black dress. The sergeant's gesture was unnecessary as the pink-haired woman was the only person waiting. Ariadne introduced herself. At first, the young woman was reluctant to give her name and shook her head nervously when asked. Ariadne put the question again, as gently as she could, and finally the woman muttered that her name was Breed. Her breath smelled of bubble gum. Ariadne was almost certain that Breed wasn't her real name, but she decided not to press her for fear of frightening her away.

'Can't we talk here?' the woman who had given her name as Breed asked, when Ariadne offered to escort her to a small interview room.

Ariadne looked around. As luck would have it, a couple of youths came into the police station just then and went up to the desk, jostling and talking over each other.

'Be quiet, Josh,' one of them said. 'Let me do the talking.'

'It was my phone,' the other one said.

Ariadne suggested that Breed might be more comfortable in a room where they could talk freely, confident that no one could come in and interrupt them, or overhear what they said. This time, Breed nodded. 'Okay then,' she agreed. 'But I can't stay long.'

Looking anxious, she followed Ariadne along a corridor to a small empty room.

'I read about that guy,' Breed began, when they were both seated. 'The one who fell down the stairs. I don't know if it's the same Jay, but I know someone who was seeing a guy called Jay.'

'Do you know his second name?' Ariadne asked, hoping to confirm she was talking about Jay Roper.

She tried not to feel optimistic. Random information often turned out to be misguided at best, and many people who came forward were cranks. The woman claimed not to know a surname, and said she knew him only as Jay.

'What's your friend's name?'

Ariadne felt the hairs on the back of her neck prickle as the woman replied. 'Carly.'

Ariadne nodded, outwardly calm, knowing she couldn't afford to lose this possible lead.

'Where did your friend's boyfriend, Jay, live?' Ariadne asked.

'I don't know. Somewhere in York.' Breed glanced around, as though looking for an escape. Perhaps she was afraid she was being recorded.

'Can you tell me anything else about him? Do you have any pictures of him so we can establish his identity?'

Breed shook her head rapidly, and her pink hair jiggled.

'All I know is what I told you. He's called Jay. I don't know if that's his actual name or just an initial he was known by. I never met him, but I do know he's a monster. If he's dead, I hope he suffered. It would serve him right.'

'What makes you say that?' Ariadne enquired gently.

'He used to beat my friend up. Honestly, I don't know why she stayed with him for so long. She's a mug. He should be behind bars. Dying's too good for him.'

'Where can I find Carly?'

Breed clammed up, perhaps feeling she had said too much.

'We want to protect your friend, but we can't do anything unless we speak to her.'

'She doesn't need protecting, not any more, not if Jay's dead. Is it true he's dead?'

'Breed, unless you give us more information, there's nothing we can do to help Carly.'

But Breed shook her head. 'It was a mistake, coming here. If he's dead then she's safe now. Tell me he's dead.'

'If you don't give me any more information, how do I know we're talking about the same Jay?' Ariadne asked, not unreasonably.

Breed refused to tell Ariadne her friend's surname, claiming that she only knew her as Carly. By the time she left, all she had disclosed was that her friend Carly had been the victim of physical abuse at the hands of a man called Jay. But if she was talking about the Carly the police were looking for, that information might be enough for them to find her.

26

GERALDINE WAS PLEASED WHEN Ariadne called to find out how she was getting on. They chatted for a few moments, before making arrangements to go out for another Chinese meal the following week. Geraldine was happy to learn that Ariadne seemed as keen as she was to meet up.

'I've missed you at work,' Ariadne admitted. 'I mean, we all have, but – well, it's not the same without you. It's a lot harder, somehow. I miss our chats in the canteen. And I know Naomi misses you too. She was asking about you.'

Just for an instant, Geraldine was overwhelmed by a wild longing to be back with her team. 'Give Naomi my best,' she said, 'and tell her I'll see her soon.' Before Ariadne could ask whether that meant she was thinking of returning to work, Geraldine enquired how they were getting on with the search for Jay's girlfriend. She tried not to sound too eager, but the case had been on her mind ever since she had first heard about it. With nothing else to occupy her mind, she had been thinking about the murder and had a few theories she wanted to test. She caught herself scanning the local news websites, ostensibly to see what was happening in York, but furtively searching for any mention of the investigation.

Ariadne let out an audible sigh. 'We understand he was seeing two women, and we want to question them both, but I can't say we're making much progress with finding either of them. Lauren's in hiding somewhere, or dead, and all we've managed to find out about Carly is her first name. Until we find them, we can only speculate that there was some kind of love triangle, and we don't even know if that's true. Our only witness is a doddery old woman who doesn't seem to know what day of the week it is.'

'These two women must be somewhere, assuming they're still alive,' Geraldine said. 'And if they're both dead, where are the bodies?'

'Lauren, the one Mary claims was with him at the time of the accident, has vanished. All we know about Carly is that she worked as a teaching assistant in a school somewhere in York, but we have found no teaching assistants called Carly working anywhere in York. The only teaching assistant named Carly we managed to track down was a well-built married woman in her fifties, nothing like the description of the Carly we need to speak to.'

'What does the missing Carly look like?'

'She's young and attractive, according to Jay's parents, although they also said she looks like a call girl, plastered in make-up and wearing figure-hugging clothes that left nothing to the imagination. Obviously she wouldn't dress like that for work, but she doesn't sound much like a teaching assistant.'

'If that's really what she is,' Geraldine said. 'Maybe his parents don't know what she does. Even if they were told she worked in a school, it might not be true. What kind of job might a pretty young woman do that she'd want to conceal from her boyfriend's parents?'

'You're right. We might be wasting our time looking everywhere for a teaching assistant, past or present, in or outside York. Why didn't I think of that?'

'You would have,' Geraldine assured her. 'It's the next logical step.'

'We've also learned that she was possibly the victim of physical abuse,' Ariadne said, describing the anonymous tip-off they had received. 'We're doing a search of hospital records to try and track her down.'

'That might well come up with something,' Geraldine agreed. 'Here's hoping.'

Ian had been playing with Tom while Geraldine was on the phone. Bouncing the gurgling baby gently on his knee, he gazed at Geraldine after she hung up.

'Who was that?' he asked. 'Was it Ariadne?'

She nodded.

'And you were quizzing her about a case she's working on.'

'I wasn't quizzing her,' she replied. 'We were discussing it, that's all.'

'You shouldn't be interfering,' he said sternly. 'You don't know the details of the case and it's not for you to go voicing your opinion when you haven't got all the facts in front of you. I know your hunches always tended to work out, but that was when you were directly involved in investigations. As an outsider, you have no idea what's going on.'

Geraldine flinched, aware that Ian was right. She was an outsider. She didn't belong in Ariadne's world. It might still be Ian's world, but she was no longer part of it and had no business to be discussing Ariadne's case with her.

'You've got enough on your plate, looking after Tom,' Ian added, not unkindly. 'You don't want to be worrying about anything else.'

Tom was a miraculous accident, a gift Geraldine had never expected, but he couldn't fill her life. Besotted by their son, Ian would never understand that having Tom wasn't enough for her.

A few hours later, Ariadne called back. 'We've recovered an image that was deleted from Jay's phone of a woman who looks like she could be Carly. Of course, there's no name or tag or link or anything useful like that, so it might not be her at all. A man seeing two women could be seeing any number of other women. But we've sent the image to the IT team and are hoping their facial recognition software will come up with an identity.'

'That sounds interesting,' Geraldine said in a low voice. 'Keep me posted.'

'Who's that?' Ian asked.

She shook her head. 'It's no one. I've got to go,' she muttered into the phone, and hung up.

She hated herself for concealing her thoughts from Ian, and wondered how their relationship could have deteriorated so rapidly. They had both been so happy when Tom was born. But having devoted her adult life to the pursuit of criminals, she couldn't just walk away from her life and become someone else. She had tried. She had taken Tom back to a local toddler group, where the other mothers now greeted her and Tom like friends. But they weren't her friends. They were pleasant women and she liked them well enough, but they existed on the other side of a rift that separated her from civilians. Some of them no doubt watched crime dramas on the television, enjoying the excitement of the chase, with villains dodging the forces of law and order to provide viewing entertainment. There was nothing wrong with that. Geraldine enjoyed a well-written murder story as much as anyone.

But the other mothers at the toddler group had never dealt with murder investigations in the real world. None of them had watched a post mortem, knowing the cold flesh on the slab had once been a living breathing human being, whose life had been snatched away by someone in the grip of an evil passion. The other mothers had never learned to close their minds to the horrors of everyday human brutality, so shock couldn't prevent them from doing their job. Gazing at the cheerful faces around her, she regretted her choice of career and wished her life could be a simple as it was for the other women in the room. But her experience had cut her adrift from these chattering young women, with their sheltered upbringing and cosseted lives. They discussed their various tribulations as their infants crawled or toddled around the room, or sat propped up watching warily, like Tom.

'…a whole day without Wi-Fi. I nearly went insane! And you know what he said when he got home?'

'…a rat, right in the middle of the garden, just sitting there, bold as brass.'

'…he woke up three times last night.'

'…say it's colic but I know there's more to it.'

Geraldine was only half listening. She was wondering whether Ian would like to stay at home all day with the baby, while she went back to work.

'Let's see how you like that idea,' she muttered.

'Sorry, Geraldine,' the woman seated beside her replied. 'What was that?'

Geraldine hadn't realised she had spoken aloud. 'I just said, I'm lucky that Tom sleeps through the night.'

The other woman smiled. 'Wait till he starts teething.'

Geraldine smiled back. Soon she was going to tell Ian she had reached a decision.

27

LAUREN HAD BEEN DOING her best to make a good impression on the landlady in the vain hope that she might be able to stay on at the guest house after she could no longer afford to pay for a room. She had wondered if she might be allowed to work for her accommodation, helping to make the breakfast and washing up afterwards, changing the beds and doing the laundry, and cleaning the rooms, although realistically she knew that wasn't going to happen. The landlady carried out all the domestic chores herself, and clearly kept a tight rein on her spending. But the weather continued cold and wet, and the prospect of sleeping rough worried Lauren. Regardless of how respectfully she spoke to the landlady, and however tidy she kept her cramped room, the woman glared disapprovingly at her whenever she went down for breakfast. Given that the landlady was charging an extortionate amount for her accommodation, Lauren felt aggrieved by her thinly veiled hostility.

She was sleeping in a converted attic at the top of a narrow flight of stairs leading up from the first floor landing. The ceiling of her room sloped, and she hit her head several times. Apart from the bed, which had a hard mattress with springs that poked her through the sheet, there was an old wooden wardrobe that stank of mothballs, and a small hand basin. The shared bathroom was on the first floor, so she had to go back down the narrow staircase to use it. Still, she was confident no one there knew who she was, and the police wouldn't be able to find her. She felt safe, tucked away at the top of the house. She had taken the precaution of giving a false name when she arrived, and the landlady had taken her cash payment without asking any searching questions, but Lauren was sure the woman viewed her with suspicion.

Even though the place suited her, she had to prepare to leave once her money ran out. Since she had brought very few belongings with her, it would be easy to sneak out without attracting attention. Not knowing when she might eat again, she hid her rucksack at the bottom of the coat stand in the hall, and went into the dining room to order a full breakfast. She knew she was stealing, because she had no money to pay for what she was eating, but she had no choice if she didn't want to starve.

'Rent's due,' the landlady said as she brought Lauren's plate of eggs, sausages, beans and toast, along with a mug of good strong tea.

'I'll fetch it as soon as I've finished this,' Lauren replied airily.

The landlady sniffed and went back into the kitchen, where Lauren could hear her clattering about. After gobbling down everything on her plate, Lauren slipped into the hall and grabbed her rucksack from its hiding place. Without looking round, she hurried along the hall and through the front door, closing it softly behind her. Once out on the street, she ran. She paused at the end of the street, wondering whether to take a route away from the city centre, but she thought it might be easier to conceal herself in a crowd, so she headed along Bootham towards the Minster. She walked quickly, keeping her hood up, terrified of being recognised.

Even in late autumn, the streets around the cathedral were busy. Seeing a policeman, Lauren hovered at the edge of a group of sightseers, hoping he would assume she was one of their party. With her rucksack on her back, she was fairly confident her pretence would convince anyone watching that she was a tourist. The policeman appeared to be scanning the area and she wondered if he was searching for her. The thought gave her a shock. It was time to adopt a disguise but, without money, that was going to prove difficult. If she'd planned what to do, she would at least have bought some hair dye and turned herself into a brunette. She regretted having left her phone behind. If she had been able to make a call, her flatmate might have helped her. But Lauren wasn't sure she could trust Natalie to be discreet. She was as likely to blab to the police as to help.

'*I thought the police would keep you safe*,' she imagined her flatmate bleating as Lauren was hauled off to a cell.

The watching policeman continued looking around, paying no attention to her. She might be safe for now, but she was helpless without money. If she withdrew anything from her account, that would betray her location and the police would track her down, like a hunted animal. In the end, she decided she had to take the risk and withdrew two hundred pounds from a hole in the wall. It was all she had. She chose the busiest street she could find, hoping her transaction would not be noticed among all the others. As soon as the money was in her hand, she hurried away, stuffing the notes into her bag. She had no idea where to go, or what to do, but at least she was no longer penniless. She realised it might be wise to try and leave the city, but her instinct was to stay there and lie low. The less she moved around, the safer she would be. She wondered whether to return to the guest house where she had spent the last few nights. She could tell the landlady that she had gone out to get more money so she could pay her. But she couldn't continue like that indefinitely without arousing suspicion, and in any case, before long she would exhaust her funds again.

She sat on a low wall, trying to work out what to do. Now she was no longer starving, she had to think beyond the short term. As she was turning over ideas, a young man came and sat beside her. He looked scruffy, but not dirty. Under normal circumstances, she would have looked away without noticing him, but nothing about her life was normal at the moment.

'Hello,' he said, catching her watching him. 'I'm Bobby.'

He grinned at her, and she wondered if he might be willing to help her. She decided to pretend she was foreign, to cover her tracks.

'I Maria.'

'Where are you from?'

'You help me find place to live?' she asked, smiling hopefully at him. 'I refugee,' she added desperately. 'I need place to stay where no one find me. And I need job. I have escaped bad man. You help me?' She wondered if she should have tried to speak with a foreign accent.

'Oh heck,' the young man said, 'you need to get help from the authorities.'

'No, no,' she cried out in genuine alarm. 'I not be caught. I not be sent home. Please, I not safe.'

She hoped he was falling for her story, but the young man stood up, and shook his head apologetically. 'I'm sorry, but I can't help you. Maybe you could ask at the library. It's down there. Just keep going straight. It's less than five minutes' walk. They might be able to help you.'

'I have money,' she told him, but he just shook his head and backed away from her.

Lauren felt bereft. Even some bedraggled stranger had refused to help her. She wanted to remonstrate, but was afraid he would want to accompany her to the library, and she had a horrible feeling the policeman outside the cathedral was watching her. Muttering her thanks, she set off in the direction of the library but turned off before reaching it, afraid of leaving a trail that could be picked up. Glancing over her shoulder, she thought she saw a policeman behind her in Blake Street. Hoping he wasn't tailing her, she hurried down Stonegate, and slipped into Hornby's Passage. She was fairly sure no one had seen her enter the narrow snickelway. High red brick walls closed in around her, and the entrance was under cover. She wondered whether she might stay there until the morning. It would soon be dark, and she was nervous about wandering the streets at night.

A figure approached her from the shadows so rapidly she had no time to run before he reached out and grabbed her. His fingers felt like iron as he gripped her, pinching the soft flesh above her elbows. Even though she was wearing a coat, she was sure her upper arms would be bruised. She hoped that would be the worst of her injuries. The man put his face close to hers and she smelt a whiff of something rotten.

'What do you want?' she mumbled, almost gagging from the stench. 'Take whatever you want, but please don't hurt me.'

It struck her that she was going to be assaulted, and she was afraid her attacker had a weapon. Even if he was unarmed, he was strong and could easily overpower her if she tried to resist. An image of her boyfriend flashed across her mind, and she felt a stab of longing for him to appear. It was like a physical pain in her guts. But there was no one to help her, and she had no intention of arguing with her assailant. For an instant she was tempted to kick him, but she held back, aware that it might be a suicidal move.

'What do you want?' she repeated, scarcely able to force the words out.

For answer, the man turned to one side and spat on the ground. She registered only that he had a pointed nose and pockmarked skin, and his fingernails were filthy.

'Phone,' the man rasped.

Lauren shook her head, her fear increased by the realisation that he was going to take her two hundred pounds and she would be left with nothing.

'I haven't got a phone,' she stammered. 'I left it at home.'

'Money.' His cracked lips opened in a snarl. He didn't look very old, but one of his teeth was missing.

Lauren trembled as she nodded. 'There's money in my bag,' she muttered. 'I can't get it out until you let go of me.'

The man dropped her arms, snatched her bag off her shoulder, and was gone. For a few seconds she listened to the fading sound of his feet pounding on the ground, and then she collapsed in tears, shaking with fear and relief. She was alive and unharmed, and very cold. Sitting on the ground, she clutched her knees to her chest and shivered wretchedly, wondering what she could do to keep herself warm overnight.

28

NOT LONG AFTER ARIADNE arrived at her desk the next morning, she learned that facial recognition software had come up with an identity for a woman called Carly, whose picture had been discovered among the photographs on Jay's phone. Ariadne studied the image of Carly Taylor, a strikingly attractive girl with high cheekbones, a button nose, full lips and a square chin. Her large dark eyes were accentuated by heavy black eyeliner, and her eyelashes were false. The subject of Ariadne's scrutiny was employed as a dancer at The Blue Cat, described on its website as 'a gentleman's club offering adult entertainment'. The venue was known to be discreet and orderly, attracting no trouble beyond an occasional drunken altercation.

Ariadne decided not to spook the dancer by turning up at her home. If she was out when Ariadne called, and heard that the police wanted to talk to her, she might go to ground. One missing girlfriend of the murder victim was bad enough. In the words of Oscar Wilde, 'to lose both looks like carelessness'. While she waited for The Blue Cat to open that evening, she looked into Carly's history. Hospital records showed a young woman called Carly Taylor had been admitted a few times over the past two years. On one occasion she had a broken rib, another time she had a fractured arm, and a third time she had hobbled in with a broken toe. Whenever the medical team at the hospital had seen her, they had flagged her injuries as a possible cause for concern. Following the third incident, the police had been alerted. When questioned about her injuries, Carly had steadfastly denied that she had been abused.

At last it was time for the club to open, and Ariadne drove to Toft Green with a couple of uniformed constables following her. The premises had an unprepossessing brick exterior. It could have been an office had its business not been advertised by a small blue neon sign: Blue Cat. A pair of hefty bouncers were lounging outside the door, although they were unlikely to be needed until after the pubs closed, if at all. One of them eyed Ariadne suspiciously, but she decided to conceal her identity until she was inside. She didn't want news of her arrival to spread, and strode past the bouncers without a word. They watched her closely, but made no move to challenge her.

In a dimly lit foyer, she paid the entry fee, and walked past another bouncer, as thickset as his two colleagues outside. She supposed he was checking for weapons when he glanced in her bag, because so cursory a search wouldn't have discovered any drugs. Inside the club, where the lights were low, almost every table was empty so early in the evening. Muted music was beating out a rhythm that wasn't loud yet seemed to make the entire surroundings vibrate. On a raised stage in the centre of the room, a couple of nubile girls in thongs were gyrating around poles. A couple of middle-aged men in suits were seated near the stage, engrossed in conversation and paying no attention to the dancers. As Ariadne hovered near the door, a girl in a skimpy outfit approached her.

'Would you like a table?' she asked with a bright smile.

Ariadne beckoned the girl to come closer and pulled out her identity card.

'I'm looking for a dancer called Carly Taylor. Please tell her she's not in any trouble, I just want a word with her about something she may have witnessed. Is she here?'

'Carly? Yes, she's here.' The girl's smile didn't falter but her eyes were now wary.

'Does she know what it's about?'

'Please take me to her,' Ariadne said. 'I'll explain to her when I see her. It concerns someone she may know.'

'Wait here.'

The hostess strutted away, hips swaying beneath her short skirt. She vanished through a door at the back of the room and shortly afterwards Carly appeared and approached Ariadne.

'Shall we sit down?' Ariadne asked.

Carly frowned at her. 'My friend told me you're a police officer?'

'Yes. I'd like a word. Is there somewhere quiet we can talk?'

'It's never quiet here,' Carly replied with a shrug. 'Over there is furthest from the speakers.'

She led Ariadne to a small table in a corner of the room near the door. As soon as they sat down, another girl came over to take their drinks order, and Ariadne waved her away. Carly pouted and muttered something about her being a cheapskate. Even when she was looking sullen, she was even more striking than she appeared in her photo, but despite her good looks, there was something pathetic about her. With her fake scarlet nails and thick make-up, she seemed to be trying too hard to look seductive and succeeded only in looking cheap. Still, she was undeniably attractive, and a lot of men probably wouldn't be put off by her tackiness. They might even find it added to her allure.

'What's this about, then?' Carly asked. She seemed curious rather than concerned. 'I've never been in trouble with the police and, as far as I'm aware, I've never been involved in any crime, nor witnessed any crimes. I don't know what you want with me.'

'Do you know Jay Roper?'

'Jay? Yes. What of it?' Carly paused to examine the nails on her left hand. 'I know a lot of men. What's it to you?'

Ariadne watched Carly closely. 'I'm sorry. I'm afraid I have to tell you that Jay's dead.'

'That's hardly a secret, is it? It was all over the news… for about five minutes,' she added bitterly. Heaving a theatrical sigh, she half rose from her chair and then subsided again; she could have been blinking away tears. 'There was nothing wrong with him,' she went on, suddenly flushed with anger. 'It was the drugs, wasn't it? Stupid bugger. He told me he was dealing with new suppliers. They did this. They gave him dodgy gear and it killed him.'

'I'm afraid I can't disclose details of what happened. When did you last see him?'

A flicker of annoyance crossed Carly's face. 'A couple of weeks ago. Why? What's it to you?'

'Did you argue?'

Carly shrugged. 'We were always arguing.'

'What were you arguing about?'

'Not that it's any of your business, but where's the sense in both of us paying rent?' Carly asked, suddenly animated. 'It's money down the drain. The fact is, my place is a shithole. I'm living on a knife edge with my landlady constantly on at me, threatening to evict me. Not that I've done anything wrong, but she doesn't like the hours I keep. Like that's her concern. I could have saved a small fortune by moving in with Jay. His place was easily big enough for us both. Only he refused to see sense. That's what we argued about the last time I saw him. "What if you move in and then we fall out?" he wanted to know. So I told him, if we split up, we split up, and I'd move out. But he wouldn't listen.' She tossed her head. 'Anyway, I told him if he wouldn't let me move in with him, I'd find someone who's prepared to put me up. Why should I be paying my own rent? Believe me, there's no shortage of desperate men. So what's with all the questions? Why are you here? Tell me what happened.' Carly's voice trembled and she began tapping her long nails on the table as though impatient to end the encounter. 'It wasn't natural causes, was it? I mean, it wasn't a heart attack. He didn't just die. Someone did this to him. Someone's to blame.'

'I'm afraid he slipped and fell down the stairs,' Ariadne told her. That was true, although she didn't add that it wasn't the fall that killed him. 'It happened at his flat in Penley's Grove, where you were hoping to move in. Were you there on Saturday night, last week?'

Noting how swiftly Carly's expression switched from emotional to wary, Ariadne decided she would have to be cautious about believing anything Carly said.

'I just told you, I haven't seen him for a couple of weeks, and anyway, I only ever saw him during the week, and then not every week. We weren't together, not in that sense. We had an open relationship, you know? We were free to see other people. It suited us both. I have several clients. And Jay,' she gave a wry smile, 'Jay was a player. But I was never at his place on a Saturday night.'

Ariadne said quickly, 'If you *were* there, by some chance, he must have fallen after you left, but you might have seen something that would help us to understand what happened.'

Carly shook her head.

'What can you tell me about him?'

'Like what?'

'Did he drink a lot? What drugs did he take? Did he ever feel dizzy that you were aware of?'

Ariadne didn't want to appear to treating Carly as a suspect, but the damage had already been done; Carly was on her guard.

'I already told you, I never saw him at the weekend. And you know from the toxicology report whether Jay was high when he died,' she added sharply.

Silently cursing the television crime dramas that informed the general public about the procedure for a post mortem, Ariadne nodded.

'Those reports are not always reliable,' she fibbed.

'But is he really dead?' Carly asked. 'I mean, it was on the news and I know it's true, but it's hard to take in.'

'I'm sorry,' Ariadne said, and hesitated before adding, 'we're not convinced the fall was responsible for his death. There's a chance someone might have killed him deliberately.'

Carly's hands flew up to her face so suddenly, Ariadne was afraid she might scratch herself with her long nails. But her reaction struck Ariadne as too dramatic to be natural.

'You mean someone pushed him down the stairs?' Carly asked in a horrified whisper.

'I can't share the details of how he died. We're going to need to ask you a few more questions about Jay, and that means I have to ask you to accompany me to the police station.'

'I can't leave now,' Carly said, genuinely alarmed. 'I'm on in half an hour. It's more than my job's worth to miss my slot.'

'I can speak to your manager and explain,' Ariadne began but Carly shook her head vehemently.

'You can't do that. If he thinks I'm in trouble with the law, he'll send me packing. There's no way I'm going to take that risk. I need this job.' She was pleading now.

'Very well. But you need to come to the police station first thing tomorrow morning. Shall we say nine?'

'Nine?'

'Nine o'clock in the morning.'

'Nine o'clock in the morning?' Carly echoed sceptically.

She seemed to have recovered remarkably quickly from the discussion about her boyfriend's death, but Ariadne knew that grief could affect people in different ways. Perhaps she had not yet processed the reality of her loss, but it was also possible she had already known that Jay had been murdered.

Carly appeared to be struggling to find appropriate words to describe her feelings towards Jay. She squirmed in her chair as though she was uncomfortable talking about her emotions. 'I liked him. I liked him a lot, but no, I wasn't in love with him. Nothing like that. I was fond of him.'

'And you're sure you never visited him at the weekend?'

'I told you, I wasn't there at the weekend. Certainly not in the morning.' She gave a half-hearted laugh. 'I don't go anywhere in the morning. I need my beauty sleep.'

'And you didn't stay with him on Saturday night?'

Carly shrugged. 'You can ask me that until you're blue in the face, but my answer isn't going to change. I only ever stayed with him during the week and then not every week. We were both busy.'

'You mentioned that he was cheating.'

'Cheating?'

'He was seeing other women. That's what you told me.'

'Did I? I can't be expected to remember everything I said.'

'So was Jay seeing any other women, to your knowledge?'

'Sure he was. Like I said, we had an open relationship.'

'You didn't mind that?'

Carly raised one painted eyebrow. 'Are you seriously suggesting I pushed him down the stairs because I was jealous?' Her painted lips curled very slowly, and her smile turned into a laugh. 'No way. You've got that wrong. He was my friend. I would never have hurt him. I might have pushed *her* down the stairs if we'd ever met.' She laughed again, a little uneasily this time, and then fell silent, biting her lip.

'So you knew he was cheating on you, and that didn't bother you?'

'I already told you, we were both seeing other people. How could it be cheating if we both knew about it? Look, like I said, Jay was good to me, he was generous, but he wasn't the love of my life. Men come and go and that's just the way it is. You're even more naïve than you look, if you think one man is going to stick around for long.'

Ariadne wondered fleetingly whether she had been naïve to trust that Nico would always be there for her, but she dismissed the thought as irrelevant. Plenty of marriages lasted. There was no reason why hers should be any different. A thought occurred to her and, with a sudden quickening of her pulse, she took another tack.

'Who else were *you* seeing?'

Once again, Carly instantly grasped what lay behind the question, almost before Ariadne had thought it through. 'You think there's a possessive man who wanted to get rid of a rival for my attentions, and he threw Jay down the stairs so he could have me all to himself?' She laughed. 'You're a terrible romantic, inspector, and you really haven't got a clue about people, have you? No, none of the other men in my life would have done something so stupid and, anyway, Jay was never that important to me. If you want my advice, you won't ever let one man take over your life. No man's worth it. Unless he's minted,' she added with a grin.

When Ariadne asked for the names of any other men Carly was seeing, she became evasive and on being pressed recited a string of first names: Bobby, Len, Mike, Dave, Steve. Ariadne suspected she was making up the list as she went along. There were others, Carly said, but those were her regulars. She insisted she didn't know their second names, and said she met them in different places, never the same place twice. When pressed, she said she couldn't remember where she had seen any of them. She had no record of when or where any of these rendezvous had taken place. Ariadne took down the few details, although there wasn't much and it was all too vague to be helpful. Even if Carly was telling the truth, which seemed unlikely, the men she met would probably not have used their real names.

'You wouldn't tell me their names, even if you knew them, would you?' Ariadne asked her.

'They're married men,' Carly protested, with a tiny shrug of her shoulders. 'They trust me to be discreet. Can you imagine their reaction if you lot turned up and started asking them about me?' She made a faint hissing noise. 'You'd get nothing out of them, and I'd be screwed.'

Ariadne moved on to question Carly about her trips to hospital and she admitted she had suffered a few injuries, but she denied having been assaulted.

'It was Jay, wasn't it?'

'Bollocks. Whoever gave you that idea is talking out their arse.'

According to Carly, no one had been responsible for her hospital visits. 'I fell over at home rehearsing my dance routine,' she said.

'These weren't just a few minor accidents,' Ariadne replied. 'Someone broke your bones. They could've killed you.'

Carly just shrugged again. Eventually the interview drew to a close. There was no point in dragging it out any longer. Talking to Carly seemed to offer several possibilities, but in the end Ariadne was left with nothing more than speculation.

'What did you expect?' Naomi asked her when Ariadne voiced her frustration in the pub after work that evening. 'The woman's a professional tease.'

'And I'm just another mug to her,' Ariadne grumbled. 'Whatever else she is, Carly's not stupid.'

'Is she clever enough to murder one of her lovers and get away with it?' Naomi asked.

But it was hard to see what motive Carly could have had for murdering Jay.

'Is it possible she was lying when she said she didn't care about Jay? Perhaps she was actually really possessive over him?' Naomi suggested.

Ariadne shook her head. 'No. That doesn't ring true. He wasn't a good enough catch for her.'

30

When Ariadne arrived home that evening, she was happy to agree with Nico's suggestion that they order a takeaway. It was his turn to make dinner, but he didn't feel like cooking. They discussed various options, and in the end it came down to a choice between a Chinese takeaway or fish and chips. Since Ariadne had been out for a Chinese meal quite recently, Nico suggested they have fish and chips. Recalling Carly's claim that no one man was worth committing herself to long term, Ariadne thought how lucky she was to have married someone as considerate as Nico. When she thanked him, he shrugged, looking baffled.

'It's just fish and chips,' he said. 'And it's only because I can't be bothered to cook. I hardly deserve to be thanked.'

While they were waiting for the order to arrive, Ariadne's phone rang.

'It's not a bad time, is it? I mean, you're not eating, are you?' Geraldine asked. She sounded anxious.

'No, the timing's fine, and I don't mind at all. Quite the opposite, in fact. It's always nice to hear from you and, to be honest, I could do with the opportunity to talk things through. This case is going nowhere.'

'Hang on a second, Ian's just come in. I'm just going in the other room.' There was a sound of muffled voices and then Geraldine said, 'Right, I'm back. Go ahead. I'm really interested to hear how it's going. Have you settled on a suspect yet?'

Ariadne described her meeting with Carly. 'So she could be a suspect, or it could have been someone else she was seeing who was jealous and wanted to be rid of Jay. I honestly don't know what to think. But talking to Carly didn't help. If anything, it's made the case seem even more confusing.'

'What was your feeling about Carly? Do you think she was telling the truth?'

Ariadne drew in a deep breath. 'I think just about every word that came out of her mouth was calculated. What I mean is, I had the impression she was too interested in the effect her words would have to care about the truth. I could be misjudging her, but she seems to have a flexible approach to the truth, and that makes her a very slippery witness.'

'In other words, you think she lied to you.'

'Yes. That is, maybe. I'm not convinced she killed him, but I'm struggling to know what to make of her. If she's hiding the truth, then who knows what her reasons are. We have too many damn suspects, and we don't even know who half of them are.'

'You just haven't found right one yet,' Geraldine replied unhelpfully. 'You'll have to go back to the crime scene and start from there. Hypotheses are all well and good, but we both know they need to be based on hard evidence.' She paused. 'Is there any possibility a third person was present when the murder took place? Anyone other than Jay and Lauren?'

Ariadne considered the question. DNA in the hallway had revealed traces from numerous people apart from the two tenants, the landlord, and the two women who had shared Jay's bed. Only Yiannis and the two women had left evidence of their presence on the stairs.

'There's no evidence Mary ever made it up to the first floor,' Ariadne said. 'So she couldn't have pushed him down the stairs.'

'Okay. So let's go through this carefully,' Geraldine said. 'Does it make sense for the landlord to have murdered one of his tenants?'

They discussed Yiannis for a while, but agreed that he was an unlikely suspect. There was nothing to suggest he had fallen out with Jay, who had always paid his rent on time and had looked after his flat well enough. Mary had probably complained to the landlord about her neighbour and his succession of visitors, but if Yiannis had been dissatisfied with him, he could have taken steps to evict him. Far from benefiting Yiannis, having a murder in the property was likely to cost him several months' rent.

'It's looking like one of Jay's customers could have been responsible,' Ariadne said. 'We know he was a small time drug dealer, selling his wares from home, so the most likely scenario is that one of his customers grew violent. According to his neighbour, he had people coming and going all the time. But there's no evidence of anyone else going upstairs.'

'Tell me more about this old woman, Mary,' Geraldine said. 'She was in the ground-floor flat when it happened. Did she see or hear anything, or is she deaf?'

'She's not deaf. She heard raised voices because Jay was arguing with a woman upstairs, and then shortly after that she heard him falling down the stairs.'

'Didn't she go out to the hall to investigate what was happening?' Geraldine asked. 'She sounds like a nosy neighbour.'

'She thought it was a bag or suitcase falling down the stairs, and then she heard groaning after that, so she looked out and saw the body and called her landlord. But she's old and frail and quite doddery and confused. She struggles to walk more than a few steps.'

After eliminating Yiannis and Mary, they were left with Lauren, Carly, and Jay's customers as possible suspects. Lauren was the most likely, and her disappearance seemed to confirm her guilt. Before they could continue, the doorbell rang and Nico shouted to Ariadne to join him. Their dinner had arrived.

'Sorry, I've got to go,' she said. 'Let's speak again soon.'

'Who was that on the phone?' Nico asked.

Ariadne looked up from sliding her greasy fish on to a

plate as she told him she had been chatting to her former colleague.

'How's she getting on?' he asked, his attention on transferring his chips to his plate.

Ariadne sighed. 'I think she's missing work.'

'You'd think she'd be pleased to get away from all that,' Nico replied, with a hint of asperity.

Ariadne knew Nico wasn't happy about her choice of career. He had given up trying to persuade her to give up working on murder investigations, but his disapproval was still occasionally evident.

'I don't find it repulsive,' she had replied when he expressed his feelings about her viewing cadavers. Although her response had been mild, she had been deeply hurt by his attitude.

'It's not just that. You're dealing with dangerous criminals,' he had grumbled. 'What if a murderer takes it into his head to attack you?'

She had tried to explain that there were set procedures the police followed, all designed to protect officers and preserve life. 'My job's as safe as yours, in fact it's probably safer. What would you do if a disgruntled client decided to assault you? At least I'm trained to deal with violent situations.'

'Exactly,' Nico had replied. 'They wouldn't waste resources training you in self-defence if there wasn't a risk of you being attacked.'

While she appreciated his concern for her, he had been forced to accept that she wasn't going to quit her job, and there was nothing he could say that would change her mind. She had done her best to explain that, as a detective inspector working on solving serious crimes, she felt her life had a purpose. As she tucked into her fish and chips, she wondered whether Geraldine missed that feeling. She hoped her friend was finding fulfilment in being a mother, but somehow it didn't sound likely. Selfishly, she hoped Geraldine would return to work soon. It was a shame to lose such a talented colleague. In the meantime, Ariadne was determined to keep her friend interested in the current case, which was puzzling enough to challenge even Geraldine's brilliant mind.

31

NATALIE WAS ASLEEP IN front of the television when she was startled awake by a noise. Instantly on her guard, she leapt to her feet and was reaching for her phone when she heard it again. Someone was knocking at the front door. Phone in hand, she stole silently down the stairs and peered through the peephole. Her heart was pounding so loudly she was convinced the caller would be able to hear it. Through the door, she could see a figure that looked more like a scarecrow than a burglar.

'Who's there?' she shouted. 'What do you want? I've got the police on speed dial so you can get lost if you think you can barge in here again and—'

She was interrupted. 'Natalie! It's me! Stop dicking about and let me in.'

Natalie opened the door to reveal a filthy, dishevelled figure who gazed miserably at her with bleary eyes.

She gaped. 'Oh my God, Lauren, you look awful. I honestly didn't recognise you. Where the hell have you been? What are you playing at?'

'What do you mean?' Lauren's voice wobbled, but Natalie was too angry to feel sorry for her bedraggled flatmate.

'What I mean is, you just disappear for over a week, without a word—'

'Didn't you see my note?'

'Yes, but that didn't tell me anything.'

'Can't we talk upstairs? I'm freezing out here.'

Once they reached their own hallway, Natalie rounded on her

flatmate again. 'Are you going to tell me where you've been all this time? Have you been living in a field of cows? Honestly, you look disgusting and you stink.'

Lauren just shrugged and didn't answer.

'You look like you've been sleeping on the street. Don't sit down!' she added sharply, as Lauren was about to take a seat on the sofa. 'I'm sorry, but you really do smell. Where have you been? I think you owe me an explanation.'

'Can we not talk about this right now? I'm starving. I haven't eaten all day.'

'All right, but not until you've taken off those filthy clothes and had a shower. You haven't picked up head lice, have you? Or fleas?' Natalie shuddered.

While Lauren showered and changed her clothes, Natalie heated up a mug of soup and buttered some toast. She felt confused and more than a little frightened. She and Lauren had been close since they were eleven, but now Natalie felt she hardly knew her friend. Something had happened to turn them into strangers. Well, Natalie had a secret of her own; Lauren didn't know the police we're looking for her. Natalie intended to tell her, yet instead she heard herself saying that the rent was due.

Lauren merely nodded, as if to say she knew but wasn't going to do anything about it. 'I lost my job,' she said flatly. And then she burst into tears.

'If you're in trouble, perhaps you should go to the police?'

'Of course I'm in trouble. I'm broke. I was mugged.'

'Then you should definitely go to the police.'

'I can't.'

A cold chill seemed to seize hold of Natalie. 'Why ever not?' she asked. 'Lauren, what have you got yourself into?'

'Nothing. I can't explain, but trust me, I can't go to the police.'

'Lauren, tell me what's going on.'

Lauren shook her head.

'Tell me, and I'll cover your rent this month,' Natalie said in desperation.

Lauren nodded, seeming to accept the offer. 'And if you could lend me fifty quid,' she added, 'and some change? I'd do the same for you.'

Natalie rummaged in her purse and handed over a twenty and a ten. 'That's all I've got on me. Now, tell me what's going on.'

'Tomorrow,' Lauren promised. Muttering that she was exhausted, she went to her room and shut the door.

Once she had gone, Natalie looked for the card the detective had given her, but she couldn't find it. She went in the kitchen and shut the door before phoning the enquiry number for the police station. There was no answer. She wasn't sure whether she ought to call 999, but she phoned 101 instead and was eventually put through to the police station in York.

'I'm calling to tell you that Lauren Shaw has come home. I'm her flatmate. My name is Natalie. An inspector asked me to call and let you know if she returned.'

'Can you tell me what this is about?' a clipped voice said.

'I don't know but a detective asked me to call.'

'Who did you speak to?'

'I don't know,' Natalie repeated, with a mounting feeling of desperation. 'I've tried but I can't remember her name. All I know is she's a detective inspector, and she looked Spanish or Italian or something. But she was English.'

She hung up. She had done what she could. She just hoped she had done the right thing. But if Lauren was in trouble, as seemed to be the case, surely it was better for her if it was sorted out properly. In any case, if Lauren had told her the truth, Natalie might not have decided to call the police, but Lauren was hiding something. Natalie wondered if she had been roped into a drug ring. Her story about being mugged was plausible, but Natalie was sceptical. If there was something illegal going on, Lauren had no business involving her. The police might not believe Natalie when she insisted she knew nothing about the dodgy affair her flatmate was involved in, and they might suspect her of being an accessory in whatever was going on behind her back. Natalie had always thought they were best friends. If Lauren wanted to keep her dirty business a secret, then she didn't deserve Natalie's unquestioning loyalty.

That night, Natalie hardly slept. She lay awake, thinking about what had happened, and wishing she hadn't been so quick to call the police. She should have given Lauren a chance to explain. Probably once she was less tired, she would be more forthcoming. But Natalie had made the call and she couldn't unmake it. She considered waking Lauren up and confessing what she had done. She tried to tell herself it was Lauren's fault for keeping secrets, but she felt sick at the thought their friendship was probably over and it was her own fault for being impatient.

Lauren was asleep when the police arrived the following morning: two uniformed officers, a man and a woman.

'It's okay,' Natalie stammered, shocked by what she had set in motion, 'she's not missing any more. She's here.'

'Which is her room?'

The female officer went to wake Lauren up

'Is she being arrested?' Natalie asked.

'No,' the stocky policeman replied. 'We're just taking her to the police station to answer a few questions, that's all.'

Lauren came out with the policewoman in tow, as though they were afraid Lauren might escape if they weren't watching her.

'I knew they'd be along,' she said. 'I don't know how long I'll be gone, but at least you know where I am this time,' she added, with a wry smile.

Clearly Lauren hadn't realised that Natalie had reported her homecoming to the police. Swept along by a wave of relief, Natalie flung her arms around Lauren, sobbing.

'Come along, miss,' the stolid police officer said, nodding at Lauren.

32

LAUREN GAZED LEVELLY AT Ariadne across the table, but she was clearly nervous, and her voice shook as she demanded to know why she was being questioned. Although she had insisted on having a lawyer present to represent her, she was speaking up for herself, while the duty lawyer beside her kept silent. He looked young and inexperienced, but he had been the only one available or, at least, the only one willing to accept the request. He gave the impression that he was not particularly interested in his client. Lauren, by contrast, seemed agitated. Despite her scowl, it was easy to see why Jay had found her attractive.

'My client has not been charged with any offence,' the lawyer murmured tentatively.

'We only want to ask her a few questions,' Ariadne explained.

'Is that why you dragged me out of bed this morning?' Lauren protested.

'She isn't a suspect, yet,' Ariadne added, looking at the lawyer and ignoring Lauren's outburst.

'Yet? Yet? What's that supposed to mean?' Lauren asked. She sounded vexed, but her fists were clenched and she looked as though she might burst into tears at any moment. She was clearly very frightened.

'As my client isn't a suspect, she is free to go home,' the lawyer said.

'We're investigating the circumstances of her boyfriend's death,' Naomi said quietly. 'We're very surprised that she's unwilling to help us with our enquiries. Naturally it makes us speculate as to the reason for her being obstructive.'

'We thought you'd want to help us find out what happened to Jay,' Ariadne added, turning to Lauren. 'Don't you want to see his killer brought to justice for what was done?'

'Killer?' Lauren blurted out. 'He fell down the stairs.' She broke off, realising that she might have been indiscreet. 'At least, that's what I heard… what I saw on the news,' she corrected herself. 'I wasn't there when it happened.'

'We all know that's not true,' Ariadne said.

'How do you know if I was there or not?' Lauren countered. 'Were you there?'

'Were you present at the time?' Naomi quietly followed up Ariadne's point. 'Be careful how you answer. We have a witness who saw you going up the stairs shortly before the incident.'

Lauren gave a dismissive grunt. 'You mean that old cow who lives on the ground floor? You can't believe a word she says. Everyone knows she's round the bend. Jay couldn't stand the sight of her. She's malicious as well as mad. If that's all the "evidence" you've got, then good luck with making it stick is all I can say.' She sat back in her chair and folded her arms with a gesture of finality, but her expression remained fraught.

'We have DNA evidence that places you at the scene,' Naomi said.

'My client has never denied that she visited the victim in his home,' the solicitor cut in swiftly. 'Your evidence does not indicate she was present when he died.'

'Of course you found my DNA there,' Lauren blurted out. 'I visited him all the time. He was my boyfriend.' She became tearful. 'I would never have done anything to hurt him. I loved him. We were going to get married.' She hid her face in her hands and sobbed, her shoulders heaving.

Ariadne waited a moment

'Were you engaged?'

Lauren looked up, her eyes puffy and her cheeks red from crying. 'We talked about it,' she said.

Ariadne decided it was time to put a direct question. 'Are you aware that he was seeing other women, all the time you were in a relationship with him?'

'That's a lie!'

Lauren's passionate outburst was telling.

'Isn't it true that when you discovered he was seeing another woman, you lost your temper and pushed him down the stairs? Why don't you tell us exactly what happened, Lauren? If it was a momentary impulse, and not a premeditated assault, it will help your case if you tell us that now. But whatever happened that day, you do need to start talking. This isn't going to go away.' She glanced at the lawyer who nodded to show he had registered the significance of what Ariadne was saying. 'After you pushed him down the stairs, you panicked, didn't you?' she continued. 'You panicked because you realised the tenant downstairs had overheard you arguing with him. We know what happened. What we want to understand is why you suffocated him. Were you still angry with him, or was it so he couldn't tell anyone that you pushed him down the stairs? Lauren, you'll feel better if you confess what happened. It's understandable you would feel angry and let down when you learned about his infidelity and a court will hear your defence sympathetically, but only if you stop lying and tell us what happened.'

Lauren shook her head and broke down, sobbing noisily. 'No, no, that's not how it was at all,' she sobbed. 'He slipped and fell. I admit we were arguing, but it was an accident. It was an accident. I ran down after him but then I left, because I was scared about what he would do to me. He was alive when I left. I ran off because I was scared he was going to hit me. I never thought he could be dead. I thought he'd blame me for his accident, so I ran away.'

'Why would he blame you, if it was an accident?'

Lauren wiped her eyes and sniffed. 'We had a bit of a scuffle, and I was afraid that old woman from downstairs would hear us. But I never pushed him and I never did anything to hurt him. I loved him!' Her voice rose in a wail.

Mary reported having recognised Lauren's shoes on the stairs shortly before the murder took place, but the old woman could hardly be considered a trustworthy witness. With the solicitor insisting they release Lauren, Ariadne felt she had little choice but to defer making an arrest, at least until she had an opportunity to discuss the situation with the detective chief inspector.

'You can go home, but please don't leave York for now as we may have a few more questions for you.'

'What does that mean?' Lauren asked, fear making her belligerent.

'It means you can go home,' the lawyer told her. 'I suggest you do what the inspector is telling you to do.'

'Go home before I change my mind,' Ariadne added, although she knew she couldn't hold Lauren for long.

Ariadne discussed the situation with Naomi at the pub that evening where they had gone for a quick drink after work.

'I hope I did the right thing letting her go,' she added. 'Of course, appearances can be deceptive and all that, but Carly seems too dispassionate to lash out in the heat of the moment, and Lauren seems to have genuinely cared for Jay.'

'Doesn't that suggest she might have been distraught on learning he was seeing someone else?'

'True.'

Either way, they agreed that Lauren remained a possible suspect and she should be brought in for further questioning.

'Maybe I shouldn't have let her go home,' Ariadne said, with a growing feeling of unease.

'You can send someone to pick her up,' Naomi pointed out. 'She should be home by now.'

'You know what, I think I'll do that. It won't do her any harm to spend the night in a cell.'

Ariadne made the call and a patrol car was despatched to Gillygate to fetch Lauren. Her flatmate informed them that Lauren had gone out for the evening without saying where she was going. Hearing that Lauren had disappeared again, and would possibly be out all night, Ariadne decided to pick her up in the morning. In the meantime, all patrol vehicles were alerted to look out for her.

33

LAUREN HADN'T RECOVERED FROM her frightening ordeal, when she had thought she was going to be murdered on the street. As if that wasn't terrifying enough, she had been carted off to the police station to be interrogated, with the threat of being arrested. The pathetic lawyer who was supposed to defend her had been useless. He had just sat there, fidgeting nervously, and hardly said anything at all. He might as well not have bothered to turn up. But at least she was free now, no thanks to him, and she could stop worrying about the police coming after her. If they had wanted to arrest her, they would have done so when they had her in their clutches. Instead, they had let her go. Lightheaded with a combination of shock and relief, she stumbled out of the police station.

A light drizzle was falling as she waited in a daze for her bus back into town, but she didn't care. The police didn't suspect her after all, and she was free to go home to her own comfortable bed. She would find another boyfriend, and this time she would be more careful in her choice. She boarded the bus, feeling as though a huge weight had lifted from her shoulders. Jay was dead, and nothing could bring him back, but she was young, and alive, and there were plenty of other men she could meet now she was no longer tied to him. With a shock, she realised that he had actually been holding her back, with his refusal to commit to their relationship. How could she have been stupid enough to believe that Jay had deserved her undying devotion? Somewhere in the world her soulmate was waiting for her; all she had to do was find him.

There remained the problem that she was broke, but that was a practical difficulty with an array of possible solutions. The simplest of these would be to return to her old job, if they would have her back. At the very least, they might give her a reference. Hoping for the best, she tidied up her face and hair before returning to the florist. She arrived shortly before closing time. Her luck was in, because her replacement at work had walked out the previous day, claiming the work was too physical for her.

'It's lucky for you I'm in a forgiving mood,' the manager said, gazing at her critically.

'It's not my fault,' Lauren protested. 'I told you, my boyfriend died suddenly. I've been at home for a week, in shock.'

'You don't look great,' the manager conceded, not unkindly.

'So can I come back, then?'

'I could do with an extra pair of hands, it's true, but are you sure you're ready?'

'I'm still grieving but I'm definitely ready to come back to work. I think it'll help me.' She didn't add that it would certainly help her financial situation. The manageress must have understood she was talking about money anyway.

'If you're quite sure,' the manager agreed warily. 'You can start tomorrow. Same arrangement as before. Technically, you never actually left.'

Buoyed up by having her job back, Lauren decided to go out for a drink. She had no boyfriend any more, so what the hell. She'd met Jay in a bar, why not someone else? The memory of her first encounter with Jay made her eyes water. Resisting the urge to reminisce, she sniffed a line of coke she'd been holding on to, before making her way to a pub she knew in Micklegate and went to the toilet to check her make-up. She was shocked to see how sickly she looked. A pale face stared dolefully back at her, with hair straggling over her forehead, and smudged mascara which made her look as though she had two black eyes.

Carefully she fixed her appearance, sniffed another line of coke, and strode back to the bar to get a drink. Recklessly she ordered the most expensive cocktail on the list.

'Allow me to get that,' an unfamiliar voice said.

A dark-haired stranger was standing beside her, their arms nearly touching. Lauren flinched, recalling how Jay had made the same offer the first time they met. Fiercely dismissing all thoughts of him, she turned to see a tall man smiling down at her. He was young and good-looking, with slicked-back black hair and an attractive smile. Returning his smile, she nodded and accepted his offer. They sat down at a corner table where he told her he was a car salesman, recently 'back on the market for a girlfriend', as he put it.

'The job's not ideal, but it pays the bills,' he said, patting down his hair with an involuntary gesture. 'I earn good money, truth be told, so I'm not complaining. And I'm completely over my ex. She was a nice girl, but we just weren't a good match. If I'm honest, she was hard work. I'm looking for someone I can get along with. I'm a simple man and I can't be doing with endless drama in my life.'

Noticing how he spread his legs on his chair, Lauren was glad they weren't sitting side by side on a bench. The alcohol mixed with the drugs she had taken were making her lightheaded, and the man's face looked faintly fuzzy. By the time she finished her second cocktail, everything made her giggle.

'This is nice,' she told him, nodding her head and giggling. 'This is better than… that.'

'Now, what I want to know is, how come a beautiful girl like you is single? Tell me there isn't a jealous boyfriend waiting to deck me?' He laughed, confident in his own attractions.

Lauren told him about the florist where she worked, and then regretted her indiscretion, realising he would be able to find her if he wanted to pursue her. After another drink, he invited her to go home with him.

'My room's not far from here,' he said. His smile hadn't altered, but it now seemed lascivious. 'We could walk there. It's not raining.'

She shook her head, suddenly getting cold feet. Things were moving too fast. She didn't know anything about the stranger. He was good enough company, but he was too sure of himself and there was something off-putting about his self-assurance. For all she knew, he could be a psychopath wanting to lure her back to his flat.

When she declined, he told her he was disappointed. 'But will you let me take you out again tomorrow?' he added, leering at her.

Mumbling that she had just gone through a painful break-up, she refused to commit to meeting him again, and hurried out of the pub. It could have been the effect of the alcohol, but once she was outside her tension dissipated. The cool night air was invigorating, and she felt happier than she had been for a long time. Somehow she had always suspected Jay was two-timing her. At least now the truth was out in the open, and she was finally free of him. She really had loved him, and the pain of losing him was still raw, but it was already overshadowed by her anger at knowing he had never really been hers to lose.

It was a dark night, the moon and stars concealed behind clouds. With only the street lamps to light her way, she walked quickly along Micklegate, and then parallel to the river and across Lendal Bridge. The pavement there was busy, yet she had a troubling feeling that someone was following her. She looked around and, on the far side of a group of noisy women, she caught a glimpse of a hooded figure. As her eyes fell on him, he spun round hiding his face from her. Laughing at herself for being paranoid, she walked on. The hooded stranger had nothing to do with her. She was just unsettled by meeting someone new. But as she walked on past the theatre, she was disturbed again by the sensation that she was being followed.

Suspecting the creep she had just met was stalking her to find out where she lived, she was tempted to stop and confront him. But she was tired. All she wanted to do was go home and fall into bed. The walk seemed to take forever, and she was relieved to finally reach Gillygate. Approaching St Giles Court on her left, she turned to cross the road when she sensed, rather than heard, a movement. Turning to look, she saw the same hooded person she had spotted earlier. Whoever it was must have approached her swiftly and silently, because they were standing right beside her. Lauren barely had time to register the figure wasn't as tall as the man she had met in the pub. She was aware only of a raised arm, and eyes glaring at her from the shadows beneath the hood.

34

IAN HAD A DAY off at the weekend, and he suggested they go out for the day. Geraldine smiled at the idea of them spending time together, as they used to do before Tom was born.

'That would be great,' she said.

He grinned happily. 'Like the old days.'

'Like the old days,' she agreed.

She was about to suggest they look for a babysitter, when Ian said it would be good for Tom to go somewhere new. 'I was thinking we might take him to Scarborough, and give him his first sight of the sea. Even if he's not old enough to appreciate what he's looking at, I'm sure it'll be good for him to experience a new environment, with different sounds and smells.'

Geraldine sighed softly, keeping her feelings to herself. 'Yes, I'm sure he'll love it.'

'What have I said now?' he asked wearily, sensing her dejection.

'It's nothing.'

'If I've done something to upset you, please tell me,' he said. The words were conciliatory but he sounded vexed.

She couldn't reply that she was finding everything about her life upsetting. Feeling guilty for not showing Ian enough appreciation, she brushed his question away and forced a smile. Before they had the baby, they used to discuss their issues with work, or gossip about their colleagues. If they had nothing to talk about, they would sit together in companionable silence. Geraldine no longer had anything to say, and the silences between them had become uncomfortable. Tom's slow progress offered no startling insights on a daily basis, and Ian was reluctant to share any news from the police station, afraid that it unsettled her to hear about it.

'I guess your priorities change when you give birth,' he had concluded, completely misjudging how she was feeling. 'I'll stop mentioning work. Death must be the last thing you want to hear about when you're busy caring for a new life.'

She had wanted to scream at him that he was about as wrong as it was possible to be, but it was all too complicated. She couldn't make sense of what was happening to her, so how could she put her feelings into words that someone else might understand? She would only end up hurting Ian if she told him she was unhappy. Perhaps, after all, she had never been happy, and work had been nothing more than a constant distraction from her underlying misery. Meanwhile, Ian supported her and in return deserved some kindness. It was unfair to complain to him about how bored and wretched she was feeling. Far better to cheer herself up and forge ahead with her life in a positive frame of mind. She reminded herself that Tom wouldn't be a baby forever, and paradoxically the thought filled her with dread. Trapped though she sometimes felt, she couldn't bear the prospect of Tom growing up and leaving her sheltering protection.

'He'll be going to nursery soon,' she said, as though challenging herself to say the words without breaking down.

'He's not even six months old.'

'Some parents send babies off at three months, or earlier.'

'And some people give their babies up for adoption at birth,' he added unkindly, and she bristled.

She gazed at Tom, sleeping peacefully on his mat. When she reached out to stroke his soft hair, his little lips puckered and she smiled.

'Are you sure you're all right?' Ian asked. He hesitated. 'Post-natal depression isn't uncommon, and if you're unhappy it's no good bottling it up. You could talk to someone, if you don't feel you can talk to me.'

If he had encouraged her to share her feelings with him, right then, she might have surrendered her self-control and allowed her pent-up disappointment to pour out. She wanted to confess that she was struggling as a mother, and his insistence that she was doing well wasn't helping. But she held back. At least she could shield Ian from the painful truth. It was enough that she was wretched with the way things had turned out. It would be cruel to spoil Ian's joy too. It worried her to think how close she had come to ruining his happiness.

'I'm fine,' she lied. 'It's just a lot more tiring than I anticipated.'

'All the more reason to forget about going back to work just yet,' he replied, not unreasonably. 'You can't turn the clock back, and we're not getting any younger.'

Knowing Ian intended to be kind should have comforted Geraldine, but she only felt more abandoned. They seemed to be trying to communicate across a widening gulf, as though they no longer spoke the same language.

Despite the melancholy that dogged her, she enjoyed the excursion to Scarborough. It was a beautiful October day, cold but bright, and the beach was almost deserted. A few people walked past, most with dogs, and Tom crowed with excitement when a small black spaniel trotted over to nuzzle his feet. It scampered away at its owner's call, leaving a wet mark on one of Tom's tiny shoes. Geraldine and Ian nearly burned their fingers on chips as they sat looking out at waves which rolled relentlessly, the water black and menacing.

'It's good to blow the cobwebs away,' Ian said.

Geraldine agreed. She hadn't felt so alive in months, almost like her old self.

'I think I have been feeling a bit low,' she admitted on the journey home. 'Everyone goes on and on about motherhood being such a joyful experience, and it is. Don't get me wrong. Having

Tom means everything to me. But it's—' She struggled to put her feelings into words. 'It's just that it's all so overwhelming and – it's so final. I mean, there's no going back, is there? Not that I'd want to go back,' she added quickly.

'You're doing a great job,' Ian assured her when they were home.

'But that's just it. Am I? I mean, it's kind of you to be so supportive, but how do you know I'm doing a good job? In an investigation you can see actual results and you know what's working and what isn't going anywhere, but this… How do I know if I'm giving him what he needs?'

She broke off, unable to articulate her deep fear that one day her son might grow up to reject her. Ian would dismiss her fears as irrational, and she knew he would be right. But she couldn't help how she felt.

'Sometimes he seems so frantic, I can't bear it.'

'All babies cry,' Ian replied gently. 'It's the only way they can make their feelings known when they're feeling frustrated. It's normal and healthy. It doesn't mean they're unhappy.' He smiled at her. 'You just wait. He's not even teething yet.' He reached out and put his arms round her. 'You have to stop being so hard on yourself. No one else is perfect either.'

After dropping Geraldine and Tom home, Ian popped out to the supermarket. She was pleased he was out when Ariadne phoned to discuss the latest development in the investigation she was working on. Her friend's calls helped to make Geraldine feel less cut off from the world.

'So you're thinking it was Lauren?' she asked Ariadne.

'Yes. When you think about it, why would she have run off like that unless she was guilty?'

'You know there could be a number of reasons. Maybe she witnessed the murder and was afraid the killer would come after her and silence her. Or she could be innocent but frightened of being suspected.'

'There's no reason why she would be frightened of being treated as a suspect if she's innocent,' Ariadne pointed out.

'You know that's not true. Innocent people have been suspected before now, and convicted too.'

Glancing down at Tom, who was peacefully sleeping on a blanket on the floor, she felt a surge of optimism.

'We're going to be all right,' she whispered gently.

'What's that?' Ariadne's voice reached her from her phone. 'I didn't catch what you said.'

She sounded a long way away.

'I think it's understandable for an innocent person to feel frightened,' Geraldine replied. 'However hard we try, we're none of us perfect.' She knelt down and gently kissed the top of Tom's head.

'That's very philosophical,' Ariadne laughed, 'but it's hardly helpful.'

'I'm not so sure,' Geraldine replied, but she was no longer talking to Ariadne.

35

AFTER CHATTING WITH GERALDINE, Ariadne left the police station. On her way home, she went to call on Yiannis. There were a couple of details from his statement that she needed to check, and she would tell him she preferred to talk face to face. The real reason for her visit was that she was hoping to have an opportunity to take a look at his coat and eliminate the possibility that the fabric might match the markings detected on Jay's dead face. With luck, she would be able to rule Yiannis out of the investigation altogether. Arriving at his home, she was disappointed to discover that he was out.

'I am sorry, but he is not here,' his mother said in answer to Ariadne's enquiry. 'You came to see him last week,' she added, looking apprehensive.

Ariadne nodded.

'Inspector Moralis,' Thalia read aloud, squinting at the card in Ariadne's hand. 'Ah, that's a Greek name. Are you from Greece?' She studied Ariadne's face. 'Or maybe you have a Greek husband?'

'I'm half Greek,' Ariadne replied. 'My mother's from Athens. And my husband is Greek.'

Thalia's eyes widened in recognition. 'Your husband is Nico Moralis,' she said, her face relaxing in a smile. 'Yiannis has told me about you, and Nico too. Your husband is a good man. Please, please, come in.'

Ariadne accepted the invitation, hoping to catch sight of Yiannis's coat, and to speak to him when he arrived. His mother said she thought he would be home soon, although she admitted she never knew exactly when he would walk through the door. As Thalia was pouring coffee, Ariadne asked to see Yiannis's coat.

Thalia shook her head. 'He would not leave his coat at home in this weather.' As if to illustrate her point, she shivered and pulled her shawl more tightly around her thin shoulders. 'It is very cold.'

'Yes,' Ariadne agreed, with a smile intended to put Thalia at her ease. 'I did wonder what on earth you're doing here in England, when you could be back on a beautiful warm Greek island, enjoying the sunshine.'

'And fresh peaches,' Thalia said, with a wistful smile.

'And olives.'

'And figs on the tree.'

'You must miss it,' Ariadne prompted her, wondering if she could persuade Thalia to open up about the reason she and her son had left Greece. 'And you must miss your family,' she added, when Thalia didn't respond.

Thalia stiffened and Ariadne lowered her eyes and took a sip of coffee, strong and black and sweet, as she waited for Thalia to reply.

'I have no other family now, only my son, Yiannis,' Thalia said at last. Her voice taut with repressed emotion, she described how her beloved husband had lost his will to live after the death of their firstborn son.

'My husband grew so thin, he faded before my eyes. He did not eat. He did not sleep. The doctors tried, but they could not save him. No one could. There was nothing I could do to comfort him. What consolation could there be for such a loss? He wanted to follow our beloved son. It is thirty years since he died, and I still love him as if he was at my side yesterday.'

'That's so sad,' Ariadne sympathised. 'I'm sorry for your loss.'

Thalia nodded. 'Yiannis was only eighteen when he was killed.'

Ariadne frowned. 'You're saying Yiannis was eighteen when his brother died?'

Thalia started and looked at Ariadne. 'No, no,' she cried out anxiously. 'Yiannis, my Yiannis, was ten when his brother was killed.'

Surprised by Thalia confusing her sons' names, Ariadne pressed her for information. In a low voice, Thalia described how her older son had been knifed on his island home of Skyros.

She was sitting on a low wooden chair. All around her the white walls of the houses seemed to glow in the light of the setting sun. The fierce heat of the day had eased off, although her next-door neighbours' air-conditioning units still whirred and creaked on the back of their houses. Round the corner, the town was poised to come to life, with shops preparing to display their wares: peaches as large as a man's fist; green and yellow and scarlet salads; and clothes and beads and souvenirs for the tourists. The sound of an engine cut through the air. Mopeds had only recently arrived on the island streets, which were too narrow and steep for cars. Thalia sighed. The older residents missed the quiet of their youth, when the only means of transport to disturb the peace was the occasional braying of a donkey as it carried supplies or materials up the hill from the coast. Now all the youths hankered after wheels, fast and noisy.

Her sons had gone out to stroll around the square. Her firstborn would be eyeing up local girls, while his younger brother tagged along, wide-eyed, impatient to grow up. She sighed. Not long ago, he had been content to stay at home with her, playing in the dusty street with the other small children. Now he only wanted to be with his brother. Her husband would be back from Athens soon. It was nearly time for her to start preparing dinner. But she would sit for another ten minutes, breathing in the scent of bougainvillea carried on the early evening breeze.

The rumour reached her before she heard it clearly: a faint hint of far-off screaming, a distant clamour of voices, footsteps running. Oblivious to what was happening down in the town square, she closed her eyes, relaxing before her evening chores. She dozed off for a moment...

A voice was calling her name, a hand clutching her shoulder, shaking her.

'It's your son.'

Her neighbour was shouting his name, tears streaming down her brown cheeks, while her eyes glared at Thalia in horror.

'What? What?' she stammered, not fully awake. 'Has there been an accident? Is he hurt?'

'Your son – your son is dead.'

He had been unarmed, Thalia explained, and there had been nowhere to hide. Trapped on a narrow cobbled street, he had been stabbed to death by a rival for a girl's attention. It had happened right in front of his brother.

'Who was only ten,' Ariadne murmured softly.

'It was terrible. They were very close, my two boys. Yiannis adored his older brother. He was a hero to him. Everyone loved my son.'

'What was his name?'

Thalia hesitated, and in that instant, Ariadne glimpsed a truth too startling to acknowledge.

'Georgios,' Thalia said, her voice low and tremulous. 'My firstborn son's name was Georgios. First my son was taken from me, and then my husband. It was more terrible than you can imagine. We suffered then, and we suffer now. He was my firstborn, his father's hope for the future.' Thalia began to cry quietly.

'But you had another son,' Ariadne said. 'You still had Yiannis.'

'My younger son, my Yiannis, yes, Yiannis, Yiannis is all

I have left. Do you understand? Everything else has gone: my family, my home, everything that once made life beautiful.'

Ariadne drained her cup of coffee, leaving the dregs, before enquiring whether the man who had killed Georgios had been tried and convicted. Thalia shook her head, unable to answer for a moment. At last she muttered that the man been punished.

'Everyone on Skyros knew it was murder,' she said sourly. 'Everyone knew my son was innocent. But the police arrived too late. They said it was not murder. They said my son was stabbed in a brawl. But that was a lie. My son did nothing. He walked in the street and was killed. What do *Astynomia* care about a street fight on Skyros? *Batsi*,' she spat the insulting term for the police. 'By the time they arrived from Athens, my son was already laid out in the church and neighbours had long ago finished washing his blood from the street.' She shuddered and swore under her breath. 'We did not leave my son's blood to dry on the street, like an animal.'

Ariadne leaned forward and took Thalia's hand in her own. The older woman's skin felt dry and chapped, and her hand was cold. Having grown up in a milder climate, no doubt she suffered in the English winters.

'You and your younger son must have been disappointed in the police, the *Astynomia*,' Ariadne said softly.

'Disappointed? We went crazy with grief. My husband never recovered. He wasted away and died. But I had another son and we left our home together. We have been in England for many years. We have tried to forget. We try to live.'

Ariadne nodded. 'It must have been difficult to carry on with your lives, knowing your son's killer wasn't properly punished.' She realised she was leading Thalia on, but she needed to know the truth.

'He *was* punished,' Thalia whispered. 'That is why we left our beloved island of Skyros.'

Ariadne understood. It had taken time, but ten years after his death, Georgios's murder had been avenged.

Thalia raised her tearful face, her expression plaintive. 'You must not speak of this,' she whispered. 'I can see you are unhappy, but you must promise me you will not speak of this. I have said too much.' She began to cry again. 'It happened twenty years ago,' she went on, clutching Ariadne's hand in hers. 'I tell myself Yiannis is safe now. No one is looking for him any more. But I am afraid. Every day I am afraid, and every night I lie awake, waiting for *Astynomia* to knock at our door and take my son away. He is all I have.'

As though she was hearing someone else speak, Ariadne heard herself promise she would say nothing to her colleagues about what she had heard that day. She knew she was ignoring a crime, but who would benefit if she were to investigate this act of violent retribution twenty years after it took place? The demands of the English justice system she served were unambiguous, but people had lived on Skyros for over seven thousand years. The police from Athens had arrived too late.

36

JAYNE DROVE VERY SLOWLY out of her garage. She had already pranged her car once, manoeuvring in a narrow space to make a sharp turn on to the lane leading down to the road. It was particularly challenging getting her car out in the dark. Fortunately no one was around when she left in the mornings, because she set off so early, but that didn't mean there would never be another car driving down to the road. Even when the narrow track was empty, as it usually was, negotiating a change in direction was tricky. In spite of her care, she failed to spot an obstruction in the alley until she drove over it. Her car lurched and she slammed on the brakes, coming to a halt with a sickening jolt. Vexed, she opened her door and was about to step out of the car when she froze. A pair of black leather ankle boots with shiny silver toecaps was lying on the ground where she was about to tread. Peering down, she saw the boots were attached to a pair of legs sticking out from under the car.

Shocked, Jayne studied the boots, trying to make sense of what she was seeing, while a white fog seemed to cloud her thoughts. As it cleared, she realised that she must have run someone over. She had no idea how long she sat there, staring dumbly at the boots. It was probably no more than a few seconds, but it felt like hours. And all the time her car engine idled, purring softly. Finally she began to recover from her initial shock, but she struggled to reconstruct what had happened. She knew she had been driving very slowly. Try as she might, she couldn't remember seeing anyone stepping out in front of her. Perhaps she had lost her focus and looked away for a moment, but she had been driving so slowly, a pedestrian would easily have been able to leap out of the way. It was hard to believe that neither of them had been paying enough attention to notice each other before the collision. Jayne wondered whether the woman was deaf or, more likely, wearing noise-cancelling headphones. Finally, it occurred to her that the woman was probably not actually dead. Possibly she was just stunned from the collision, and Jayne was stressing unnecessarily. After all, she had been driving very slowly.

'Hello?' she called out softly. 'Hello? Are you all right?'

There was no answer. The silence started to feel claustrophobic, and she felt an overwhelming urge to get away. Being careful to avoid trampling on the feet that were lying in the lane, she climbed out of the driver's seat. Stepping down, she accidentally nudged one of the leather-clad ankles. The feet didn't move. Without warning, she sneezed. Wiping her nose on her sleeve, she studied the scene in front of her and saw that the boots were now dotted with pale flecks of snot. They were sticking out between the front and back wheels of her car. Whether she drove forwards or backwards, she would have to run over the body again.

Glancing around, she felt confident that no one could see her. The place was deserted, curtains closed behind the only two windows that overlooked this end of the lane. The fabric of her trousers provided little protection against the gritty surface of the asphalt when she knelt down. Sharp points of stone pricked her knees as she leaned forward to peer through the shadows under her car. Fumbling with her phone, she switched on the torch to study the body. She couldn't see any blood, but the woman still lay without moving, her head concealed in shadow beneath the car. It was difficult to see what she looked like. Only her nose poked out from the hair that had fallen across her face. Scared to touch her, Jayne called out softly. There was no response. Using the edge of her phone, she nudged the woman's leg. Again, there was no response. It was awkward reaching forwards into the small space beneath the car, but she managed to hit the woman's thigh more forcefully. Again the woman didn't stir or make a sound, and her leg felt unnaturally hard. Clearly she was dead. In a way, Jayne almost felt a sense of relief knowing there was nothing she could do to help the woman.

She scrambled to her feet, her instinct screaming at her to distance herself from the body before anyone else appeared. There was nothing she could do for the dead woman. She had to think about protecting herself. She walked around the car, hesitating, but there was really only one choice open to her. Pulling out her phone, she started dialling 999 but then stopped after keying in the first number and switched her phone off. If she reported finding a body under her car, the police would assume she had run someone over. At the very least, she risked being arrested for driving without due care and attention, if not for manslaughter or even murder. Slipping her phone back in her bag, she walked away quickly. She hadn't seen anyone, and at that early hour it was unlikely that anyone had witnessed what had just happened. The dead woman had nothing to do with her. She would report her car stolen and deny having seen the body.

Although she did her best to walk silently, the gravel seemed to crunch really noisily under her feet as she hurried back to her empty garage. Once again, she took out her phone. This time she dialled two 9s before stopping. If the police were to request a sample of her DNA, the specks of her snot on the dead woman's boots would expose her lies. She had some bleach at home, but it would take too long to fetch it and clean the boots. In any case, she wasn't sure if bleach was actually effective in removing DNA. Her only safe course of action would be to remove the boots, without touching the woman's feet, but she had to hurry; it would soon be light.

Careless of the noise of her footsteps, she raced back to the car and managed to unzip both boots. Pulling them off proved surprisingly easy, because the woman's ankles were rigid and the boots just slipped off. She ran back to her garage and shoved the boots under a pile of old clothes she had been meaning to take to the charity shop. Muttering a prayer of thanks that her unwanted clothes were still in the garage, she made sure the boots were completely hidden. Disposing of them would have to wait. Right now, she had to focus on her immediate concerns. Her hands shook as she pulled out her phone.

'Police? I want to report my car's been stolen. I just came down to my garage and it's not there.'

The woman on the line responded dispassionately, taking down Jayne's details. She wanted to give a false name but that would be daft. She had to behave as though she was innocent. Next she called her office to explain why she would be late. And then she went home, washed her hands and face, changed her clothes, and went to work. Leaving her building through the front door, she avoided walking down the lane at the back that led from the garages down to Gillygate.

37

On Saturday morning, Ariadne went into work early and was waiting to speak to the detective chief inspector as soon as she arrived in her office. Binita listened to what Ariadne had to say before agreeing that they ought to at least bring Lauren in for further questioning. Ariadne returned to her desk and was absorbed in checking Lauren's contacts while waiting for her to be brought to the police station when Binita summoned the team. The reason for the briefing was apparent as soon as they entered the incident room, where a new image was displayed on the board: a young woman, grey-faced and blue around the lips. Below eyelids spotted with blood, her eyes were horribly bloodshot. Despite her injuries, Ariadne recognised her straightaway.

'That's Lauren Shaw,' she blurted out.

'Yes,' Binita answered shortly.

Had Ariadne arrested her the previous day, Lauren would be sitting in a cell, waiting to be questioned about the death of her boyfriend. It had been Ariadne's decision to delay the arrest, but she quickly dismissed the idea that she was in any way responsible for Lauren's death. She had acted rationally, and with good intentions. It was Lauren herself, with the support of her lawyer, who had insisted on leaving the police station.

'She wasn't wearing shoes when she was found, but her socks were clean, so her shoes might have been removed after she was killed. Alternatively, the killer could have carried her to St Giles Court, where the body was found lying under a car,' Binita said.

'Whose car?' Sam asked the obvious question.

'It belongs to a woman called Jayne Linden.'

'So she ran her over?' Naomi enquired.

'Surely it wasn't deliberate?' Sam asked.

Binita frowned. 'At first sight it appeared that Lauren had been run over, whether accidentally or deliberately. But that doesn't accord with her injuries, which suggest she was asphyxiated.'

'Are you saying the car crushed her windpipe?' Ariadne enquired, struggling to understand what Binita was saying.

'No,' Binita replied. 'The wheels ran over her chest and legs, after she was strangled.'

Ariadne studied the image, wondering if Lauren had been killed because of what she had seen. It seemed like the obvious conclusion. Jay had been suffocated after he had plummeted down the stairs and now Lauren had been run over after she was strangled. In both instances, someone had made a very clumsy attempt to disguise murder as an accident.

'What about the driver of the car?' Naomi asked. 'What did she have to say about it?'

'Jayne Linden phoned the police at six fifty this morning to report her car had been stolen. She's been questioned by a constable local to her place of work in Leeds. According to the report from Leeds, Jayne appeared genuinely shocked on hearing that a dead body had been discovered right outside her block of flats, underneath her car. She claims her car was stolen and she hasn't seen it since yesterday afternoon when she left it locked in her garage after returning home from work. She went to the garage this morning, at around six thirty, as usual, and found the garage door unlocked and her car missing. She was fairly sure she left the garage locked yesterday, as usual, although she admitted it was possible she had left it unlocked. Her account is perfectly plausible, and there's nothing as yet to connect her to the victim. She was happy to supply a DNA sample so she could be eliminated from the enquiry. So far, we're accepting her story that her car was stolen and she knows nothing about Lauren's murder, but we're looking into her background, just in case.'

After rereading all her notes on the victim, Ariadne went to look at the site where Lauren's body had been discovered. St Giles Court led around the back of a block of flats on the opposite side of Gillygate to Lauren's apartment. It was a dead end, leading to rows of garages belonging to the flats. The front entrance of the block of flats opened on to Gillygate, but the garages were tucked away out of sight behind the building. It looked as though Lauren had been killed out of sight, just over the road from the flat she had shared with Natalie.

The alleyway leading to the garages was cordoned off with a forensic tent in place, and a team of white-coated scene of crime officers was busily hunting for evidence. Ariadne pulled on her protective clothing and overshoes and logged her arrival before entering the tent. Recalling how her former inspector had been keen to view a crime scene before the victim was removed, Ariadne wondered what she had missed by arriving after Lauren's body had already been taken to the mortuary.

'There's no bag, and she didn't have her keys or phone or purse on her, so it could have been a mugging that went wrong,' a scene of crime officer told her. He pointed to the ground. 'It looks like she was dragged here from the street. You can't see the marks without magnification,' he added, seeing Ariadne's puzzled frown. 'We suspect she was brought into the alleyway from the street and killed here, where the attack was less likely to attract attention.'

Ariadne nodded. 'She lived just across the road, above the hardware shop. We're checking CCTV from all the shops along Gillygate. And we know who she is. She was at the police station yesterday, helping us with an investigation.' She paused. 'Can you tell whether she was wearing shoes when she was pulled off the street?'

The scene of crime officer grunted. 'Impossible to say for certain, although we don't think she was walking along the street in her socks because they're not soiled underneath. Maybe the CCTV will show something?'

Ariadne nodded. 'Yes, we're on it. Can you tell me anything about who was driving the car?'

The scene of crime officer shook his head. 'We've only found one set of prints so far, and probably only one person's DNA, which we're assuming was the owner's. She reported the car stolen, didn't she? If she didn't drive over the body herself, then whoever did was very careful not to leave any trace behind. But we'll keep looking. If there was someone else behind the wheel, we'll find something. Every contact leaves a trace.'

'We've collected a sample of the owner's DNA,' Ariadne told him. 'She reported the car stolen early this morning. Her garage is round the corner so she didn't see her car from there, and assumed it had been stolen and driven away.'

'Car thieves usually drive more than a few yards before abandoning a stolen car,' the scene of crime officer added. 'It looks as though the car thief ran the victim over and then scarpered. Leaving it on top of a dead body,' he added, with what sounded like a faint chuckle. 'Not exactly a joy ride.'

'Who found her?'

'A young man who lives in one of the flats here. He was taking his rubbish out to the bins and saw the car parked here, right on top of the body. He saw the feet sticking out and called us.'

'He didn't call an ambulance?'

The scene of crime officer shrugged. 'He said it was obvious she was dead.'

38

THE MAN WHO HAD stumbled upon Lauren's corpse arrived at the police station midmorning to make a formal statement. Ariadne took him to an interview room to question him. Numerous freckles showed up against the pallor of his face and straw-coloured hair flopped over his eyes whenever he lowered his head, which he did frequently. When he did look up, his green eyes seemed to be fixed on a distant horizon, as though he was looking at something invisible to anyone else. He looked very young.

'I was just taking the rubbish out and I saw these feet sticking out from under a Mini. It had been left at the entrance to the lane, blocking everyone else's access,' he added indignantly, as though parking selfishly was a worse crime than running over a pedestrian.

He shuddered. 'I'm not particularly squeamish as a rule, but it gave me quite a turn. I mean, it was like something out of a horror movie. I could tell she was dead,' he added sombrely, flicking his hair off his forehead.

'How could you tell that?' Ariadne asked.

'I looked under the car and she never moved. I shouted and—' He broke off, shaking his head. 'I pulled her hair, just to see if she was really dead. It was a stupid thing to do, I know, because now you'll find my fingerprints all over her head and think I killed her, but I didn't know what else to do to see if she was dead. And then I called 999. I didn't move her. I didn't even really touch her, apart from her hair.'

Gently Ariadne pointed out that it was probably impossible to leave fingerprints when touching someone's hair, but he would certainly have left traces of his DNA. The police would need to take a sample of his DNA to prevent any confusion when the body was examined. The young man nodded and said he understood and was keen to do what he could to help the investigation.

'How did you know the body was that of a woman?' Ariadne asked.

He shrugged. 'Her feet,' he said lamely. 'They looked like a woman's feet. They were too small to be a man's, and her socks were kind of pink with red stripes,' he added, as though that clinched the matter.

Ariadne didn't point out that men might wear stripy pink and red socks. Instead, she enquired whether he had recognised the dead woman.

He shook his head and his straw-coloured hair flopped from one side to the other.

'No. I'm afraid not. I've never seen her before. Do you know who she was? And why – why would anyone do that? Run someone over and then just make off, I mean. I guess it can't have been the owner of the car, or you'd have arrested them by now. Whose car was it, anyway?'

Ariadne explained that she was unable to share any information pertaining to an ongoing investigation, before sending him to make a formal statement, after which he would be free to leave. He seemed to have no connection to Lauren or her murder, but his background would be thoroughly checked all the same. The case seemed to be growing by the hour, with more and more leads to investigate, all of which would probably go nowhere. But until they had tracked down the killer, no one even vaguely associated with the case could be overlooked.

Having spoken to the witness who found the body, Ariadne reluctantly acknowledged it was time to share the terrible news with the family. Lauren's mother stared warily at her, as she stood on the doorstep waiting to be let in. Only a week had passed since they had last spoken, but Jennifer looked older and more careworn than Ariadne remembered her.

'I need to speak to you about Lauren,' Ariadne said. 'You might want to hear what I have to say without your son present, to begin with.'

Jennifer let out a faint rasping sigh, recognising that Ariadne had come with bad news, but her expression remained unnaturally impassive. 'Dylan's not here,' she replied in a voice devoid of emotion. 'He's out playing football. But he'll be home soon.'

'Can I come in? I think you should sit down before we go any further.'

Ariadne noticed that the BMX bike was no longer in the hall, as she followed Jennifer into a square lounge, where a patterned crimson carpet and crimson velveteen curtains overwhelmed the small room. Four armchairs, which were far too big for the space, added to the stifling atmosphere.

'What sort of trouble is she in?' she asked in a flat voice.

'Lauren's not broken the law—' Ariadne began, but Jennifer interrupted her.

'She's dead, isn't she? My daughter's dead. That's what you've come here to tell me. Isn't it? Isn't it?' Her voice rose suddenly, and her cheeks flushed. 'Please, tell me what happened.'

'I'm afraid her body was found this morning.' Ariadne paused. 'She wouldn't have suffered—'

'What happened?'

'We're investigating the circumstances of your daughter's death.' Ariadne paused. 'We believe it may have been deliberate.'

'I always said that boyfriend of hers was no good,' Jennifer snarled. 'He should have been locked up—'

'Jay didn't kill her. He was already dead when Lauren lost her life.'

'Well, he was no good,' Jennifer muttered darkly. 'He was a

drug addict, I know he was. She said he wasn't, but you could tell. She could have done so much better for herself. She was a beautiful girl, beautiful—' She fell silent, her voice broken by sobs. Suddenly her head jerked up and she looked at Ariadne, distraught. 'What am I going to say to Dylan?'

'A family liaison officer is on her way. She'll be here soon to help you with everything, as long as you need support,' Ariadne replied miserably, aware how inadequate that sounded. 'I'm sorry. It's the best we can do.'

Outside the house she met the family liaison officer, Susan, who was assigned to the Shaws. Ariadne smiled weakly at her. Susan was slightly plump and amiable, with soft eyes and a sympathetic air. She returned Ariadne's smile with a quietly confident nod, before going up to Jennifer's front door. Susan raised her hand to ring the bell, and they heard a dog bark inside the house. Ariadne admired her colleague; she didn't envy her, looking after the bereaved. It was difficult enough dealing with the dead.

39

AFTER A DELAY OF several hours, due to the pathologist's schedule, Ariadne went to the mortuary to discuss the results of Lauren's post mortem. Avril seemed subdued and started complaining about her mother-in-law's unreasonable demands.

'I mean, it's not like I'm no one. I'm his wife,' she said. 'She acts as though I'm not even part of his family, but I am his family now. He's told her as much, but she won't listen. And I can't say anything, can I? Not unless I want to fall out with her. And it might come to that,' she added darkly.

Impatient to find out more about Lauren's death, Ariadne didn't have time to chat.

'I need to speak to Jonah as soon as possible,' she blurted out, breaking into Avril's tirade.

Seeing Avril look crestfallen, she apologised hurriedly. 'I'm sorry to be so abrupt, but I'm on a deadline and I really need to crack on. I'm sure you understand?'

With a disconsolate nod, Avril ushered her along to the examination room where Jonah was busy with his grisly work. He raised a bloody gloved hand in greeting and Ariadne wondered fleetingly how his wife could bear for him to touch her. Dismissing such distractions, she voiced a cursory greeting before starting on her questions.

'So how did she die? Can you confirm whether it was murder?'

'Well, we can rule out suicide,' Jonah replied cheerfully. 'Unless she hit herself on the back of the head with sufficient power to cause significant damage to the skull, probably knocking herself out, and then strangled herself with her bare hands before driving a car over her own dead body.' He laughed, as though he had just told a joke.

His amusement was infectious and Ariadne couldn't help smiling. But the faint hope that Lauren might have killed Jay in a moment of passion, before guilt had driven her to suicide, was crushed.

'So it wasn't suicide, but do you think she was murdered, or could she have been run over and somehow accidentally strangled?'

Jonah shook his head. 'This was no accident. For a start, it wasn't the car that killed her. She was run over post mortem. She was already dead when the wheels crushed her here and here.' He pointed at the dead woman's legs and chest.

Ariadne stared at the contusions on Lauren's face and chest, and her crushed legs. It was hard to reconcile this battered and broken corpse with the young woman she had been talking to a day earlier. Although she had clearly been stressed, Lauren had nevertheless been vibrant and attractive, with her whole life stretching out ahead of her.

'What else can you tell us?' she asked.

'She suffered blunt force trauma to the back of her head, which would probably have caused her to lose consciousness.'

'So you're saying someone hit her.'

'Exactly. And with some force. We have no way of ascertaining whether that was an accident or deliberate.'

'Do you think it could have been accidental?'

Jonah shrugged. 'I'm not the detective here.'

'So you think it was deliberate?'

'Did I say that?' Jonah smiled.

'Well, let's stick to what we do know. What was she hit with?'

'Ah, the murder weapon. I'm afraid I can't help you with that either. It was something solid, and sharp, like the edge of a brick, perhaps. But in any case, the head injury didn't quite kill her, although it very well might have done so, and quite quickly.

Only before that injury had a chance to finish her off, someone made sure they finished the job by strangling her. You can see the petechiae to her eyelids and sclera.' He pointed at her bloodshot eyes. 'The contusions around her lips, added to signs of bleeding in her ears, all indicate that she was breathing when she was strangled to death, possibly unconscious but nevertheless still alive. So the final cause of death was asphyxiation by strangling, but I think the blow to her skull might have proved fatal if she hadn't died from strangulation first.'

'So she suffered two serious injuries. One was probably going to prove fatal and the other one killed her. And, after all that, she was run over,' Ariadne said.

'Indeed. She was damaged by the car, but that was after she was already dead.'

'So that could have been the killer himself – or herself – or perhaps it was someone who just happened to drive by and failed to notice a body lying in their path.' Ariadne sighed. 'This seems like a rather complicated death. We should call her Rasputin.'

Jonah chuckled. 'She was rather better looking than the mad Russian monk, I suspect.'

'And someone removed her shoes,' Ariadne said. 'Which doesn't make any sense. Were they removed after she was killed?'

Jonah raised his eyebrows in a comical expression of bewilderment. 'I can't comment on that as I haven't seen the shoes. Were they worth stealing, do you suppose?'

'Who knows?' Ariadne replied. 'We searched the area but we haven't found them yet.'

'Well, she looks more like Cinderella than Rasputin,' Jonah commented, brushing the dead girl's hair off her face with a delicate touch. 'She was young, wasn't she?'

'Twenty-four.'

They both sighed, momentarily caught off guard by an emotional response to the pitiful figure lying in front of them.

'Maybe the killer drove the car across the body in an attempt to hide her,' Ariadne suggested.

Jonah shook his head. 'If that was the intention, they didn't do a very good job of it.'

'No. More likely they were hoping to make the murder look like an accident. What else can you tell me about her?' Ariadne asked, focusing on what hard evidence the pathologist was able provide.

'She was killed some time on Friday evening. That much you know. She hadn't eaten much during the day, some pizza and chips, and she'd been drinking alcohol in the evening, not excessively,' he added, 'but a few glasses, without food. We'll have to wait for the tox report, but there are traces of what appears to be cocaine in her nostrils.'

'She was probably out having a good time,' Ariadne said sadly. 'We're showing her picture to staff in all the local bars and clubs and pubs, and if that doesn't throw up any results, we'll spread the net. But the more time passes, the less likely it is that we'll discover who she was with on Friday evening.'

Jonah nodded. 'She hadn't engaged in sexual activity before she died, although she wasn't a virgin.'

'We know she was in a relationship recently.'

'Ah yes, Jay, the other recent murder victim. You've got your work cut out with this case, inspector. I'm glad I don't have to do any of the thinking needed to find the murderer.'

'But if you had to come up with a hypothesis about this particular body,' Ariadne replied, 'what would you say?'

Jonah laughed. 'Your friend, Geraldine, used to do everything she could to wheedle answers out of me. But really, all I can do is report my findings. It's not my job to explain them. How is our ex-colleague, by the way? Have you heard from her at all?'

Ariadne told him she had been out with Geraldine the previous week, and she had looked well. 'She seems to be enjoying being a mother,' she added, not quite truthfully, since Geraldine had clearly been more interested in talking about Ariadne's work than about her baby.

'Yes, that's right, she's a mother now,' Jonah sighed. 'I can tell you from experience that being a parent can be a bloody business.'

Given the nature of Jonah's work, Ariadne thought that was a surprising description. Jonah continued, apparently oblivious to the irony.

'Give me a dead body over a live teenager any day. They're far less trouble. They don't answer back, for a start.' He grinned. 'Not that I don't love my kids, of course. They mean the world to me, but they can be a handful. Whereas this one,' he gestured at Lauren's corpse, 'she won't be nagging her father for a raise, or a new phone, or a car, or anything at all for that matter. Poor girl. Twenty-four with all her life ahead of her.' He raised troubled eyes to Ariadne. 'Make sure you find the animal who did this, and see him put behind bars for the rest of his life. Prison's too good for some people.'

'We'll do our best,' Ariadne replied.

She hoped it would be enough, but she was painfully conscious that she was murmuring a meaningless platitude. No doubt Lauren had believed she was doing her best, and where had that got her?

40

'YOU DON'T UNDERSTAND,' JAYNE grumbled.

She plonked herself down on the bed beside him and twisted round to look at Bob, doing her best to control her exasperation. Her boyfriend was kind to her, but there was no denying he was a bit dim.

'You're not listening to me. This is serious. I could be in real trouble. I need you to do exactly what I say.'

Bob raised himself up on one elbow and gazed up at her. He didn't look happy.

'Look, I wouldn't ask you to do this if it wasn't important,' she persisted, 'but I really need your help. You know the police interviewed me. They said they might want to ask me more questions. They told me not to leave York! I'm scared, Bob. What if they don't believe me?'

'They wouldn't have let you go if they weren't satisfied with what you told them,' he answered, not unreasonably. 'They haven't locked you in a cell, have they? You're getting yourself all worked up over nothing.'

She tried not to be annoyed at him for dismissing her fears so lightly. 'Maybe you're right, but the point I'm trying to make is that they might want to speak to you. They might not, but just in case they do, we have to be prepared.'

'Prepared? What do you mean, we have to be prepared?'

'We have to make sure our stories match.'

Bob clambered out of bed and began pacing up and down. 'What "stories"? What are you talking about? I'm not going to lie to the police. If that's what you've got in mind, you can forget it. In fact, you can forget about all of this.' He gestured towards her. 'You and me. If you think I'm going to stick my neck out for you, then we're finished. I'm sorry, babe, this isn't how I wanted things to turn out, but it's more than my life's worth to get involved in this mess. You know about my run-in with the police. I've been completely upfront with you about what happened when I was younger. I know it was a long time ago, but these bastards never let go. They'll have me on record somewhere, and I can't afford to get on the wrong side of the law again. Not for anything. Not even for you.'

Jayne drew in a deep breath. 'You don't understand,' she said, struggling to keep her voice steady. 'I'm not asking you to lie. When did I ever ask you to lie for me? That's the last thing I want.'

'What *are* you saying then?'

'I just want you to tell the police that I was with you on Friday night, that's all. I told them I came straight here after work. I left my car in the garage and walked here, like I always do. Shit, if I hadn't agreed to go into work on Saturday, none of this would be happening now. Anyhow, it can all go away, if you just tell the police I was with you on Friday night. That's all I'm asking you to do.'

'Why is all this so important?'

'Because I may need an alibi for Friday night, that's why. Listen, and please, please pay attention, for once. This is what I told them. I came here as usual after work on Friday. I stayed here, with you, all night. On Saturday I left here early, before six, and walked back to my flat. After going inside to collect my things, I went down to get the car and found my garage was empty. The door was unlocked. I reported my car stolen straightaway, and that was the end of it, as far as I was concerned. I called work to say I'd be late and went to get the bus to the station. Only then I was told that my car had been abandoned just outside the flat, in

St Giles Court, with a dead body underneath it.' She paused. 'Do you get it? Someone stole my car, and before they even reached the road, they ran over a woman. So they abandoned the car and ran off. That's what happened. None of it had anything to do with me, except that it was my car they were driving at the time. I haven't done anything wrong.'

She wasn't happy about lying to Bob, but it seemed best to keep to the story she had told the police. She hadn't known Bob very long, and wasn't entirely sure she could trust him with the truth. After his misspent youth, he was terrified of the police. Burdening him with an honest account that didn't quite coincide with what she had told the police might prove too difficult for him. Unless she was prepared to risk him caving in and telling the police what had really happened, she needed to keep him in the dark about the circumstances leading up to the fatal accident. It wasn't as though it had been her fault. She genuinely hadn't seen the woman dart out in front of the car, or she would certainly have swerved and slammed on the brakes, anything to avoid running her over. As it was, she had driven straight into her. It was sickening, but Jayne was as much a victim of the situation as the woman who had been knocked down and killed. At least she was dead and couldn't suffer any longer. Jayne might end up behind bars as a result of a stranger's carelessness, which would hardly be fair. Whatever happened, she had to make sure the truth never came out, and to protect herself she had to persuade Bob to back her up.

'It wasn't my fault,' she insisted. 'My car was stolen. I wasn't even driving it when the woman was knocked down.'

'The police will be able to tell that someone else was driving,' Bob pointed out. 'They can tell anything from DNA.'

'Not if the car thief was wearing gloves,' Jayne replied, with a jolt of unease.

'No, they can still tell,' he assured her. 'They can pick up DNA if someone just breathed in the car.'

'What if the driver was wearing gloves and had the window open?'

Bob shrugged. 'Who knows? The police have incredible resources. They know everything. You can't fool them. I should know,' he added sourly.

'I'm not trying to fool anyone,' Jayne snapped. 'I just want you to tell the police I was here all night on Friday. Is that so much to ask?'

41

THEY HAD TO ABANDON the hypothesis that Lauren had killed herself from grief or guilt following Jay's murder. It was a pity, but they now knew there had been another murder. Either they were looking for a second killer, or else someone had been prepared to kill twice, in which case they might kill again. Reluctant as they were to acknowledge what had happened, the evidence was clear. The pathologist's findings were unequivocal. The next issue to clear up was whether Jayne was implicated in Lauren's murder, since her car had crushed Lauren's dead body in what could have been a clumsy attempt to cover up how she had died. A forensic examination of the car had revealed no evidence to indicate that anyone else had been driving her car, so the likelihood was that Jayne herself had been behind the wheel. Her motive for driving over the body was obscure, but as a working hypothesis they assumed she had been persuaded to drive over the body in an attempt to disguise the murder as an accident. If that was the case, then even if Jayne herself wasn't guilty, she must know the identity of the murderer.

'They must be really stupid if they think we wouldn't discover she'd been hit on the head and strangled before the car ran over her,' Naomi said.

She and Ariadne were walking along the corridor together to the incident room, where Ariadne had summoned the team for a briefing.

'You can't assume a murderer is intelligent,' Ariadne pointed out. 'If it was a random assault that went too far, her attacker might well have panicked and behaved stupidly.'

'Really stupidly.'

'Haven't you ever done anything stupid when you were flustered?' Ariadne challenged her and Naomi looked faintly embarrassed.

'Not that stupid,' she muttered.

Ariadne recalled an occasion where Naomi had exposed herself to danger. If Geraldine hadn't saved her life, Naomi would probably have been killed by a violent psychopath.

'Well,' Ariadne conceded kindly, 'we've all done stupid things. I'm just saying, it's possible the killer panicked.'

'Yes, but if you follow that line of reasoning, then anyone might behave completely irrationally at any time, and we'd never be able to solve any case because there would never be any theory to test. We have to believe there's some sense in the way Lauren's killer behaved, some twisted motive we can pursue, or everything descends into chaos and we'll be grasping at random straws without any logic to the investigation. If that's what happens, we might as well give up trying to find out the truth.'

Naomi seemed to be warming to her subject, and Ariadne was quite pleased to reach the incident room and interrupt her colleague's diatribe. She informed her colleagues there was no forensic evidence found in the car to suggest that Lauren had been transported in it. If Jayne had run over the body, she had done so after Lauren was dead, which seemed to suggest that Jayne might know the killer.

'Granted Lauren and Jayne lived near one another,' Ariadne said, 'but there's no connection between them that we've been able to discover as yet. We'll keep looking, but we have to recognise the possibility that Jayne was telling the truth when she reported her car had been stolen at some point between six o'clock on Friday evening and six thirty the following morning when she went to her garage.'

'But you said there's no evidence anyone else drove her car,' Naomi pointed out.

Ariadne frowned. 'Exactly. Jayne's alibi for Friday night checks out, but you're right. Our problem with her alibi is that there's no evidence anyone else drove her car. '

She nodded at a constable who took up the account. 'Jayne was out in York on Friday evening, and she went home with her boyfriend who lives in Portland Street, less than ten minutes' walk from her flat. She stayed with him overnight. His CCTV confirms that she didn't leave until just before six the next morning, when she returned to her own flat and allegedly discovered her car was gone.'

'If Jayne didn't hit and strangle Lauren,' Ariadne said, 'and we can't find any evidence that anyone else drove her car, then Jayne must have accidentally run over Lauren after her body had been left in St Giles Court by her killer,' Ariadne suggested. 'And she lied about it to avoid being accused of killing Lauren.'

'If she lied about that,' Naomi said, 'don't you think she knows more than she's admitting?'

'Possibly,' Ariadne agreed. 'We need to question her again, and find out exactly what she knows. Something about this doesn't add up. She has an alibi that seems to prove she wasn't driving her car when Lauren was run over. But we can't find any evidence that anyone else was driving it either.' She frowned.

Sam muttered darkly about the problems that driverless cars were going to cause. 'Even if there's legislation to ensure they are all fitted with cameras, those could malfunction or be deliberately disabled, as could the sensors that prevent them driving into something. How reliable are they going to be?'

'Whatever else she may have done, let's assume for now that Jayne didn't kill Lauren, but lied about running over the body to avoid being accused of murdering her,' Ariadne said, ignoring Sam's interjection. 'So, who else is in the frame?'

Barely an hour after the meeting closed, Ariadne and Naomi were facing Jayne across a table. Jayne smiled anxiously and asked whether she needed a lawyer. Her voice was hoarse and she looked as though she hadn't slept since Lauren's body had been found. Her eyes had a misty haunted look and her face was pasty. She sat fidgeting with her chipped red nail varnish as she waited for Ariadne to speak.

'You're not suspected of any serious crime,' Ariadne replied. She leaned forward in her chair and spoke softly. 'But we know you were behind the wheel when your car drove over the body.' She raised her hand as Jayne began to protest. 'You didn't kill her. The victim was dead by the time you ran over her body. And now you need to tell us the truth about what happened on Saturday morning.'

Jayne's eyes opened wide with surprise. 'So I didn't kill her?' she asked in hushed tones.

'She was already dead when the car drove over her body,' Ariadne confirmed.

Jayne winced at the word 'body' and burst into tears.

'Tell me what happened,' Ariadne said when Jayne's crying had petered out into hiccups.

Jayne nodded. 'It's true. It was me. I ran over her, but I didn't know she was there. I didn't see her. The first I knew about it was when my car drove over something. There was a bump and when I looked out to see what was happening, I saw feet sticking out from under the car.'

Jayne described her alarm and her panic as she tried to work out what to do, before she finally called the police.

'Did you remove her shoes?' Ariadne asked when Jayne had finished her account.

Jayne nodded and explained that she had sneezed, splashing the dead girl's boots with snot.

'I knew that if I left her shoes, you would search for the person who had been sick, and you would find proof I was there.'

'Do you know who killed the woman whose body you ran over?' Naomi asked.

Jayne shook her head. 'I don't even know who she is. I mean, I know her name now, because they told me when they first questioned me, but I'd never heard of her until all of this happened. I'm sorry, but I didn't see her.' She confirmed that she had seen no one else in St Giles Court when she had run over the body. 'Can I go home now?'

'You'll be charged with concealing evidence and obstructing us in our enquiries,' Naomi said. 'Now we need a formal statement from you.'

One mystery had been solved, but they still didn't know who had killed Lauren.

42

On Monday evening Ian was out playing football. Geraldine knew he would be home late, so she invited Ariadne over for supper.

'I'm super excited about meeting Tom,' Ariadne said, sitting down in the kitchen. 'Is he asleep?'

Geraldine bent down to open the oven. She took a dish out and placed it on the hob.

'He's only a baby,' she replied, as she opened a bottle and filled two large glasses with red wine.

Ariadne felt a fleeting awkwardness, as though a shutter had come down between them.

'I don't know what you mean by that,' she challenged her friend. 'He's not just any baby. He's your son.'

Geraldine looked abashed. 'Yes, you're right, of course,' she agreed. 'I shouldn't be so negative.'

'Are you feeling negative?' Ariadne asked quickly. 'You know you can talk to me if you want. I mean, I don't know anything about being a mother. All I know about is work.' She laughed awkwardly. 'I dare say you've had your fill of that.'

Geraldine's expression grew animated. 'Listen, I love Tom, of course I do, but there's really not a great deal to say about him while he's still so little. What I mean is, he doesn't do anything that all babies don't do. I'd much rather hear about the case you're working on. Let me dish up, and then you can tell me about it. I've made lasagne. I hope that's okay with you? I think it's turned out all right but the proof of the pudding and all that.'

Ariadne smiled. 'It smells delicious.'

While they were eating, she told Geraldine about the interview with Jayne.

'That was unlucky,' Geraldine commented, pulling a comical grimace.

'I know. For a while there we actually believed we'd had a breakthrough.'

'I meant it was unlucky for Jayne,' Geraldine said. 'Running over a body and being terrified because you think you're going to be arrested for murder must be a frightening situation to find yourself in. It's easy to imagine she might have panicked and lied about what happened. If it was me, I might well want to avoid being charged with manslaughter as a result of driving without due care and attention.'

'Well, her alibi checks out, unless her boyfriend's lying. Of course, he's her boyfriend, and hardly objective, but his security camera seems to confirm her story. So all we can do is charge her for not reporting the incident. She'll get off with a suspended sentence, at most. This is delicious, by the way. Go on then, just half a glass.'

'So what's the thinking? Was it the same person who killed both Jay and Lauren?'

Ariadne described the two murders. Jay had been suffocated after falling down the stairs. Lauren had been struck on the head and strangled.

'On the face of it, they were completely different and there's nothing to suggest it was the same killer for both.'

Geraldine nodded. 'But there are obvious similarities between the two. For a start, both victims were effectively knocked out, stunned or somehow incapacitated, before they were killed, which suggests the killer or killers might have been relatively weak, possibly old, or female.'

'That's just supposition,' Ariadne murmured, and then waited, interested to hear what else Geraldine had to say. 'And that's not all that links the two,' she added, when Geraldine remained silent. 'There's still the fact that they were in a relationship until recently. Is it coincidence they were killed within two weeks of each other?'

'Why don't we start by going through your list of suspects?' Geraldine suggested as Ariadne finished her supper.

'That really was lovely.'

Ariadne refused a second helping, insisting she didn't have room for more. Geraldine was about to insist when they heard Tom cry, and she went to fetch him. They went and sat on armchairs in the living room while she fed him.

'He's gorgeous,' Ariadne said.

Geraldine looked down at Tom. 'He's a good baby,' she admitted.

'Well, you must be doing something right then,' Ariadne said.

Geraldine smiled, acknowledging the compliment, and Ariadne was pleased to see her looking relaxed.

'Now,' Geraldine said, as Tom closed his eyes. 'We were about to go through the list of suspects.'

'Are you sure you want to talk about it?'

'Absolutely. To be honest, I'm thinking of coming back to work soon, so it would be good for me to start getting back into it.'

'What does Ian think about it?'

'He's keen for me to stay at home, but honestly, I'm not sure how much longer I can carry on like this.' She heaved a sigh and the baby stirred in her arms without waking up. 'It's a terrible thing to say, I know, but I'm going out of my mind with boredom. Hearing about the case you're working on gives me something to think about.'

'Well,' Ariadne hesitated. 'If you're sure. It might help to talk through things. We seem to be going round in circles. Just when it seemed that Lauren killed Jay, she went and got killed herself, so that put the lid on that theory.'

'Not necessarily,' Geraldine pointed out. 'It's possible L killed Jay and then someone else killed her.'

Ariadne frowned. 'It's possible,' she conceded, 'but, like you pointed out, the two murders do have similarities.'

'You don't think Lauren could have been killed by someone who wanted to punish her for what she did to Jay – assuming she was responsible for his death, and her killer knew that.' She frowned. 'What about his other girlfriend? Could she have found out what happened to him?'

'It's a possibility we're considering,' Ariadne replied. 'We need to talk to her again.'

'Let's hope *she* doesn't end up being murdered too,' Geraldine said with a grim smile. 'And there's still the question of Mary's shopping trolley.'

'Mary's shopping trolley?' Ariadne repeated. 'I'm not sure what you mean.'

'Oh, it's probably nothing,' Geraldine admitted. 'I'm not even sure I know what I'm talking about.' She laughed. 'I've got babies on the brain and I'm not thinking straight.'

Ariadne smiled. 'That's understandable. And after all, taking care of life is more important than investigating death.'

Geraldine looked at Tom and smiled.

43

Avril greeted Ariadne like an old friend. The apparent return of her usual good humour prompted Ariadne to ask how everything was. She regretted asking as soon as the words were out of her mouth, but there was no going back. Avril explained that she had sorted out a problem with her mother-in-law.

'I thought she was having me on when she told me she couldn't remember what my cousin said to her. Of course, she knew exactly what I was talking about, but she must have decided she doesn't want to stir up trouble after all. I can't tell you how relieved I am. But really, what a fuss over nothing.'

Ariadne wasn't sure what Avril was on about, but she let her talk for a moment. Only half listening, Ariadne recalled the ructions surrounding her own wedding. Most of the disagreements had emanated from Nico's family, who seemed to thrive on confrontation. One cousin had refused to sit next to an uncle, and an aunt had threatened to miss the ceremony if she were to be seated on the same table as one of her sisters. At one point what had started out as a joyful occasion threatened to be reduced to an arena for airing family grievances. Ariadne's family had treated the approaching wedding with cheerful expectation, and she had kept away from the squabbles in Nico's family. Somehow, at the last minute, all the disagreements had seemed to melt away and the wedding had gone off without a hitch. Nico had laughed at Ariadne when she admitted she had been worried.

'They just like to make a fuss,' he had told her. 'They behave like children, because they're self-important and crave attention, that's all. There was never any doubt they'd be at the wedding, having a good time.'

'Family members don't always see eye to eye,' Ariadne now said evasively, hoping Avril wouldn't realise that she hadn't been listening.

Avril's eyes narrowed, calculating. 'Actually,' she said, 'it means we have a spare ticket now. I'll need to check, but would you like to come? It's going to be brilliant. And that way, if she changes her mind, I can genuinely tell her we've given her ticket away.' She giggled. 'I really need to find someone else to come with us as soon as I can. I mean, it shouldn't be a problem, it's months away. What do you think?'

Reluctant to admit that she had no idea what Avril was talking about, Ariadne smiled as warmly as she could. 'Now you've put me on the spot,' she said, forcing a laugh. 'When is it again?'

Mumbling that she would have to see what plans her husband had, and whether she would be able to take the time off work, she was relieved when Lauren's mother arrived. Harrowing though the meeting would be, it had rescued Ariadne from the indignity of having to confess to Avril that she had no idea what her spare ticket was for. Mumbling her thanks, she turned away.

Jennifer Shaw looked paler than Ariadne remembered, the strain of grief etched on her face: small vertical lines between her eyebrows, and her cheeks, already gaunt, even more sunken than before. Ariadne was pleased to see that she was accompanied by Susan, her family liaison officer. Her presence meant that Ariadne could leave after she had greeted Jennifer.

'How's Dylan coping?' Ariadne enquired.

Jennifer shrugged without speaking.

'He's doing well,' Susan replied decisively. 'He's a good kid.'

Jennifer let out a faint whimper and mumbled incoherently.

'Come along,' Susan said to her. 'Are you sure you want to go ahead? It's not necessary. We have the DNA confirmation of her identity so you don't have to view her.'

'I want to see my daughter,' Jennifer whispered softly, as though she couldn't bear to hear her own voice. 'I want to see her body.' She muttered something else, and her speech ended in a curious whimper, like an animal in pain.

After settling Jennifer in the waiting room with Avril, Ariadne had a brief exchange with Susan, who confirmed that Jennifer had not remembered anything that might further the enquiry into her daughter's death.

'She's as mystified as we are,' she said. 'All she can suggest is that it must have been an unlucky encounter with a mugger. Dylan seems convinced it was her boyfriend; he doesn't seem to grasp the fact that Jay was already dead when Lauren was killed.' She sighed. 'They're brokenhearted, both of them. It's no wonder they're desperate to see someone caught and punished. If Jay was still alive, I suspect Dylan would try to go after him.'

Ariadne felt a frisson of dismay. Dylan had not witnessed Lauren's death, but he was around the same age as Yiannis had been when his brother was murdered. Ten years later, Yiannis had avenged his brother's death.

'I'm being as encouraging as I can, but the truth is, he's taking it badly,' Susan added.

Leaving Jennifer to view the body with Susan, Ariadne left. Following Geraldine's example of leaving no stone unturned, she had gone to the mortuary to meet Jennifer in the vain hope of discovering something new about Lauren. In the event, Jennifer had been too wretched to talk, and all Ariadne had gained from her visit was a possible invitation to an unknown event she had no intention of attending. She had nothing against Avril, but her free time was precious. She would have to come up with an excuse, so as not to waste the limited time she could spend with her husband. It was hard to believe that she had once been unsure whether she wanted to marry Nico. When he had first proposed, she had considered refusing. Now, she was more content than she had ever been before. For her and Nico, having a child would complete their happiness. She thought about her friend, Geraldine, and sighed.

'I wish everyone was as happy as we are,' she told Nico when he phoned her at lunchtime.

He laughed, his voice light with happiness. 'Well, that would put you out of a job.'

44

As they had lunch together in the canteen, Ariadne and Naomi reviewed their suspects.

'And don't forget about Carly's ex,' Naomi said. 'The one who put her in hospital.'

'I wonder whether that was Jay himself,' Ariadne replied. 'In any case, we need to follow it up. If there was another violent man involved with her, we need to find him and check what he was up to at the time of the murder.'

Naomi frowned. 'It makes sense that he might be jealous of Jay, if he even exists, but there was no evidence of another man at the crime scene other than the landlord. And anyway, what motive could a jealous ex-boyfriend of Carly's have had for killing Lauren?'

They sighed in unison and ate in silence for a moment.

'This is pretty good, actually,' Naomi commented, poking her dinner with a fork.

Ariadne grunted. Since her marriage, she had cut down on what she allowed herself for lunch because Nico liked to enjoy a full supper. To be fair, he usually cooked as he often worked from home. Even when he went into the office, he had more free time than Ariadne when she was busy on a case.

'This is the only time I have to sit down every day with my beautiful wife and enjoy a good glass of wine and a proper meal,' he would say, raising his glass to her.

Ariadne did her best to get home in time for dinner every day.

Sometimes she was late, but Nico never complained. He knew she did her best.

'I knew how difficult it would be, this business of being married to a detective,' he assured her. 'I went into this with my eyes open. You have an important job to do and you know I'll support you in any way I can.'

She was grateful for his understanding. She knew many of her colleagues struggled to keep relationships going in the face of the long hours and stress they faced at work. All the same, knowing the trouble Nico took to cook for her, she felt a twinge of guilt whenever she was home late. She sometimes wondered if that was why he was so keen to make dinner, but she never challenged him about his motives.

'Yes,' Ariadne said, as she picked at a cold egg salad and watched Naomi finishing off a portion of hot casserole. 'We need to speak to Carly again. And this time she's going to give us some answers.'

It was late afternoon by the time Ariadne went to question Carly. There was no point in going to The Blue Cat before it opened. It was too early for customers, but the door was open and two hefty bouncers were already lounging outside. One was leaning back against the wall, his eyes closed as he took long drags on a cigarette. The other stood upright in the doorway, watching her. She walked straight past him and entered without exchanging a word with him. Inside the dimly lit club room, muted music was playing. A few girls were going through pole dancing routines, gyrating to a loud beat which drummed painfully inside Ariadne's ears. A couple of women in short skirts and sequined tops watched them idly. Ariadne went over to them and asked to see Carly.

'Oh, yeah, you're the cop,' one of the women said. She turned to her companion and said something, her voice lost in the surrounding noise.

'Filth,' the other woman mouthed silently, scowling at Ariadne.

'Where's Carly?' Ariadne said, when neither of the women moved to fetch her. She raised her voice. 'I need to speak to Carly.'

'Carly!' the first woman bellowed. 'Carly! Over here!'

One of the dancers stopped and turned to see who was calling out, and Ariadne recognised Carly. She was naked apart from a red thong and high-heeled red shoes with stiletto heels.

'What?' she yelled.

'Hey!' a man's voice called out. 'Shut up and dance. You're not paid to talk.'

Carly caught sight of Ariadne and came over to see what she wanted. Reaching the edge of the dais, she snatched up a bright green pashmina and wrapped herself in it.

'Hey!' the man called out again.

Carly ignored him and led Ariadne to a table in a dark corner of the room where they sat down together. The other women watched them as they walked away.

'Tell me about your last boyfriend,' Ariadne said.

'Boyfriend?' Carly scoffed, adjusting her pashmina.

'Man friend, then. The man you were seeing.'

Carly gazed around the room and heaved an exaggerated sigh. 'Will this take long? Only I'm supposed to be getting ready.'

'The sooner you answer my questions, the sooner we'll be done. Now, tell me the name of your last boyfriend.'

'Are you talking about Jay?'

'What we want to know is who you were seeing before you started seeing Jay.'

'What man in particular are you asking about?' Carly asked. She didn't look at Ariadne, but instead gazed at her left hand, checking each painted fingernail in turn. 'I'm not monogamous. I already told you, Jay and me, we weren't exclusive.'

Patiently, Ariadne explained that she wanted to know about any man Carly had been seeing a lot of before Jay died.

'Last time we spoke, you mentioned five names.' She checked her phone. 'Their names are Bobby, Len, Mike, Dave and Steve.'

Predictably, Carly screwed up her nose in an expression that suggested bewilderment. 'Who the fuck are Bobby, Len, Mike, Dave and Steve?' she asked with convincing nonchalance.

Ariadne concealed her irritation. 'Those are the names you gave me. You said they were the names of men you were seeing. I need their full names, and anything else you can tell me about them, like where they live, or where they work.'

Carly shook her head. 'Give it a rest, will you? I've already told you I don't know their other names, and I've no idea where any of them live. I met them here and there in different bars. That's all. And before you ask, I didn't make a note of their details.'

Other than repeating everything she had already told Ariadne, Carly had nothing to say. Ariadne persisted for a while, but it became obvious the interview was going nowhere. After a few more questions, Ariadne accepted that Carly was not going to divulge any details about any past lovers. She turned her attention to Carly's hospital records. Holding out her phone so Carly could see an image displayed on the screen, she watched her reaction.

'That's you, isn't it?'

Carly glanced down and shrugged. 'Could be.' She looked away.

'You don't look quite so pretty there,' Ariadne commented.

The face in the picture was recognisable as Carly, in spite of the bruised and blackened eye and the swollen lip.

'What you can see here is just the tip of the iceberg, isn't it? But you must remember the broken ribs and arm. I noticed your arms weren't moving together just now,' she added untruthfully.

'Had a good look, did you? I didn't clock you as a dyke. Is that why you keep coming back?'

Ariadne sighed gently. 'Carly, I'm trying to help you.'

'Bollocks. And there's nothing wrong with my arms.' As if to prove her point, she flexed her fingers.

'Doesn't it bother you that whoever did this is still out there, probably beating up other women? Or did you make sure he can't hurt anyone ever again?'

But Carly neither broke down nor let slip that she had put a stop to her assailant's activities. As she had told Ariadne, she was discreet.

'Look,' Carly said, 'if you were in my line of work, you'd know this happens. No one likes it, but some blokes become violent when they're drunk. That's why we have those big guys on the door looking out for us.'

'They didn't do a very good job of looking after you here.' Ariadne gestured at the photo on the table.

'I know, I know, it's all so shocking, isn't it? Listen, you can bang on about it all you like, and good for you, and I hope your middle-class virtue signalling makes you feel better about yourself and your privileged life. But if you lived my life, you'd accept this as an occupational hazard.'

'No one should put up with this.'

'Well, that's my decision, not yours. And as long as I'm earning as much in a night as you earn in a week, I'll be happy with my choice.'

'Carly, he could have killed you.'

Carly shrugged. 'We're all living on borrowed time, aren't we? You think you're untouchable, but how do you know you're not about to drop dead from a heart attack? You should see what some of the girls here get up to.' She mimed injecting herself, and then shooting herself in the head, and laughed. 'You think you're so much better off, living your safe life, but where does that get you? The best you can hope for is an old age wetting your pants and dribbling on your bib. No one wins in the end, not even you. So why don't you piss off and stop bothering me. I can look after myself.'

Ariadne put her phone away and stood up. There was no point in trying to persuade Carly that she might improve her chances of living longer if she paid more attention to her own safety. As for trying to extract any information from her, that was clearly a waste of time. Carly was too astute to give anything away.

45

It was nearly the end of the day, but Ariadne still had one more visit to make before going home. Recalling Sam Cullen's complaint about how much time he spent behind a desk, she told him to accompany her. Even though his role was restricted to driving the car, he was happy to be out of the police station, and working on a murder investigation. Jayne's boyfriend, Bob, worked in a small Italian restaurant on the Holgate Road. A sign in the window offered pizza and pasta dishes, and good wine. Sam drew up outside and followed Ariadne into the restaurant. Leaving him posted just inside the door, she went over to a tubby middle-aged man who was stacking mustard-coloured menus on a narrow side table. He spun round when Ariadne asked to speak to the manager.

'I am he,' the man replied self-importantly, throwing out his chest and speaking in ringing tones. He put the menus down and gave her a welcoming grin. 'Would you like to book a table, madam?'

'I haven't come here as a customer. I'd like to speak to Bob Quantrill,' she replied.

'He's busy in the kitchen,' the manager told her, sounding miffed. 'He's working until ten. You can catch him if you come back just before his shift finishes.'

He turned away to indicate the conversation was over.

'I don't think you understand. I'd like to speak to him now.'

The manager was about to reply, when Sam took a step forward. Catching sight of a policeman in uniform, the manager hesitated and stopped fussing with the menus.

Ariadne took out her identity card and nodded in Sam's direction. 'He's with me.'

'I'll go and fetch Bob right away, inspector,' the manager said, squinting anxiously at Ariadne's card. 'He's not in any trouble is he? I hope you're not going to keep him long. We're short-staffed as it is. He's the only chef in this afternoon and I've got a party of eight coming in this evening. There's a lot of prepping to do.'

Ariadne didn't answer, and the manager disappeared through a swing door marked 'Staff Only', to reappear a moment later with a lanky tow-haired figure at his heels. Bob was wearing a long apron that had once been white but was now stained with faded splashes of red and brown. His hair looked greasy and he stared at Ariadne through his straggly fringe, shaking his head with a baffled expression, as though he had no idea why she wanted to see him. But there was something wary in his eyes that suggested he knew exactly why she was there, and his lips trembled slightly as though he was frightened.

'What's this about?' he demanded, 'only I'm really up against it out there. Rocky's let us down again.'

The manager groaned.

'This won't take long,' Ariadne assured him.

Like the manager, Bob had focused his attention on Ariadne to begin with, and only now did he catch sight of Sam hovering near the door.

'Oh, you're cops,' he muttered, his shoulders drooping with an air of resignation. 'I thought as much. Well, you're wasting your time. I've got nothing to tell you.'

'There you are, then,' the manager interjected. 'Now perhaps he can get back to work.' He nodded at Bob, as though to dismiss him back to the kitchen.

'I'm afraid I need a few words with you, Bob,' Ariadne said firmly. 'We'll sit over in the far corner. Please give us some privacy.'

The manager looked as though he was about to object. Sam took a few steps closer and the little man scurried away, muttering audibly about living in a police state where honest law-abiding citizens were not allowed to get on with their work uninterrupted.

'Bob, I think you know what this is about,' Ariadne began.

The chef nodded, smoothing down his apron as he took a seat. On the far side of the restaurant, the manager was watching them. He tapped his foot impatiently, but there was not much he could do about it, with Sam positioned between him and the table where Ariadne was questioning Bob.

Perhaps aware that the manager was keen to hear what he said, at first Bob seemed more concerned about his work in the kitchen than Ariadne's questions.

'I don't see why this can't wait,' he said, quite loudly. 'I'm in the middle of my prep.'

Ignoring his protest, Ariadne questioned him quietly. 'Tell me what happened on Friday night.'

'Jayne was with me all night,' he replied in a low voice. 'She was pretty upset about what happened to her car. When is she getting it back?'

'When we've finished with it.'

'Yes, but when will that be?'

'I'm afraid I can't say.'

'No one seems to know anything.' He sniffed. 'Anyway, what is it you want from me? I can't drive so you can't pin this on me.'

'Tell me exactly what happened on Friday night.'

Bob shrugged and recited what sounded like a carefully prepared account, which tallied in every detail with what Jayne had told them. Ariadne was convinced he had been coached in his response, although that in itself was no proof that Jayne had been involved in Lauren's murder.

'You can check the ring doorbell if you want. I think the film is stored?'

Geraldine didn't tell him that all the available CCTV in his street had already been collected and checked, along with film from any cameras along Gillygate. All the footage showed Jayne driving home on Friday afternoon and walking in the direction of Portland Street an hour or so later. There was nothing to indicate that she had returned to St Giles Court, or walked along Gillygate to the front entrance to her block, before Saturday morning, after Lauren had been killed. It was possible that Jayne had returned back to St Giles Court and encountered Lauren and killed her, driving over the body in a clumsy attempt to pass her death off as an accident. The two women might even have arranged to meet there. But for that to be true, not only would both she and Bob have to be lying, but she would have had to avoid being picked up by any camera on the way. It seemed unlikely. They had to accept Jayne's alibi. With a sigh, Ariadne left. This had been another frustrating dead end. Both disappointed, she and Sam drove back to the police station in silence.

46

Ariadne wrote up her decision log and was about to go home, when Binita summoned the team to discuss a possible new development.

'What's going on?' Ariadne asked Naomi as they made their way to the incident room.

Naomi shrugged and said she had heard a rumour that there was a serious question mark over Jay's Greek landlord. Apparently a young man answering to Yiannis's description had fled from the small Greek island of Skyros not long before Yiannis had arrived in England. No one knew whether the fugitive was Yiannis, or what crime he was supposed to have committed, but it had clearly been serious. What made this old case potentially interesting was that the fugitive's surname was Karalis.

'Karalis is a common name in Greece,' Ariadne muttered, as they waited for Binita to arrive.

'You should know,' Naomi replied.

There was nothing accusatory in her colleague's remark, but Ariadne felt a frisson of unease, knowing she was concealing information about Yiannis's past. She wondered why Binita had been looking into Yiannis's background herself. Although she maintained a blank expression, Ariadne was apprehensive, not only for Yiannis and Thalia, but for her own reputation. She hoped Thalia would be discreet. If it ever came out that Ariadne had known about the revenge killing, and had failed to share her information with her colleagues, her career would be over.

There could be no excuse for concealing evidence relevant to a murder enquiry out of loyalty to a fellow countryman. It wasn't as though Ariadne was really Greek. She wasn't sure why she had been so rash.

'Yiannis Karalis has been living here for twenty years,' Naomi said. 'Surely, if there was a case against him, it would have come to light before this.'

'He said he owed money to someone,' Ariadne agreed cautiously. She shook her head. 'How long do people usually wait before writing off a bad debt?'

'It must have been a tidy sum to make him flee the country,' Naomi said. 'Perhaps he ripped off the Mafia.' It wasn't clear if she was joking, but Ariadne bristled.

'This is Greece we're talking about, not Italy,' she said, anxious to dispel the suspicion hanging over Yiannis like a cloudburst threatening to break.

'So you're telling us there's no organised crime in Greece?' Naomi asked her, with a sceptical smile.

'On a tiny island like that?' Ariadne gave her colleague what she hoped was a withering glare. 'Do you know anything about Skyros where Yiannis comes from? It's a tenth the size of Wales, for goodness' sake. Hardly a hub for international crime.'

'It sounds like a perfect hideout for anyone who wants to stay off the radar,' Naomi countered.

Binita entered the room and the discussion ended. Ariadne wasn't sorry her contretemps with Naomi had been interrupted. Although the wish to be friends with her colleague stemmed partly from their shared admiration for Geraldine, she genuinely liked Naomi. But more compelling than her liking for Naomi was her fear that she had been oversensitive to the suspicion that had fallen on a Greek man. She herself was only half Greek. Her mother had come to England from Athens on a gap year and had met Ariadne's father, a bluff Northerner. Despite their contrasting backgrounds – or perhaps because of the difference

– they had fallen in love and married. Ariadne had grown up in Yorkshire, from where she had made annual visits to Athens with her mother. Over the years, they had observed the beautiful city deteriorate, its modern buildings become dilapidated, its streets poorly maintained and increasingly strewn with litter, as unemployment rose and increasing numbers of young people became disaffected with their society. It was hard to believe Western civilisation had originated in Greece. But despite her physical distance from her mother's country of birth, Ariadne remained half Greek, and she couldn't deny a faint sense of kinship with Yiannis. Not only had he come to her for help, but she had given Thalia her word she would try to protect her son. She had been a fool to put her own career at risk for the sake of a stranger who had killed a man, but it was too late to change her mind now. All she could do was stick to her decision and hope that Thalia would keep quiet.

Binita looked more harassed than usual as she announced that they were under severe pressure to make an arrest soon. It was only just over a fortnight since Jay had been murdered, yet the media were already beginning to raise questions about what they referred to as 'police inactivity'. '*Is this the start of a drug war here on the streets of York?*' one headline had screamed, even though Jay's body had been discovered indoors, and there was no evidence to suggest a rival drug dealer had been responsible for his death. The way some journalists seemed determined to undermine the reputation of the police was a common concern among Ariadne's colleagues; they depended on the support of the public to give them information. Fortunately the reporters had not yet seen a connection between Jay and Lauren, with the suspicious death of a young blonde woman predictably regarded as more newsworthy than that of a drug dealer. '*Young Blonde Battered to Death*' the headlines ran, and '*Hit and Run – Blonde Beauty Left to Die*'.

'You probably all know by now that a wanted criminal,

Georgios Karalis, is known to have escaped from the Greek island of Skyros some twenty years ago. Georgios had a brother, Yiannis, who was eight years older than him. Yiannis Karalis was knifed to death in a street fight thirty years ago, when Georgios was just ten.' She paused. 'Ten years after Yiannis was killed, the man who knifed him was released from prison, having served his sentence. After his release, Yiannis's killer was fatally wounded and left to bleed to death. It could be a coincidence, Georgios's older brother being called Yiannis Karalis. What is certain is that Georgios disappeared from Skyros with his mother, and neither of them have been located since then.' She paused and looked around. With an effort, Ariadne held her gaze. 'It's possible the man who escaped from Skyros and arrived in England, calling himself Yiannis Karalis, is in fact Georgios Karalis. It seems Georgios may have adopted his brother's name after avenging his death and fleeing from Greece.'

'It's hard to believe he could have got away with it,' Naomi said.

'It's true he just disappeared, but that was twenty years ago,' Binita replied. 'It was easier to slip away back then. But the case was never closed. And now we're just waiting for confirmation of a DNA match with Jay's landlord. We're collecting a sample of his DNA right now and then we'll see what happens.'

Ariadne was silent. It looked as though Yiannis's past had finally caught up with him and his savage crime had been discovered. That was as it should be. Yiannis would be convicted of the murder he had carried out to avenge his brother. Ariadne could only hope a jury would not find him guilty of claiming a second victim, twenty years later. But they just had to wait and let justice take its course. There was nothing more she could do to protect Thalia and her son. She had already risked her own future with her complicity, keeping their secret from her colleagues. In spite of her pity for Thalia, and her conviction that Yiannis was innocent of Jay's murder, she felt a wave of relief wash over her that the secret of his past had been discovered. Soon she would no longer have to worry about keeping Yiannis's secret. She just had to hope that Thalia would keep hers.

47

AFTER WRITING UP HER report, Ariadne decided to have a coffee to clear her head. Somehow the more they found out, the less sense the investigation made, and she was feeling not only perplexed but exhausted. She invited Naomi to join her in the canteen for a short break.

'So what's going on?' Naomi enquired cheerfully, as they sat down. Ariadne had a mug of coffee, while Naomi had treated herself to a large doughnut, which she was gazing at with obvious relish. 'I'm a sucker for these,' she added, as she picked it up. 'Is Carly our murderer? Surely she might have been tempted to kill Jay if he was abusing her.' She took a bite out of her doughnut and swore as jam oozed out over her fingers.

Ariadne chuckled at her sergeant's dismay and told her it was time she learned how to eat like a grown-up.

'Murder never makes sense,' Ariadne added, as she handed Naomi a serviette. 'But Carly didn't strike me as a violent type.'

'Is there a violent type?' Naomi countered. 'Surely anyone could snap, given sufficient provocation.'

'Could you?' Ariadne asked. 'After all your training?'

Naomi shrugged. 'I could happily murder another one of these.' She grinned at her half-eaten doughnut.

'But seriously,' Ariadne continued, 'do you think she killed them both? Are you suggesting she snapped twice?'

'She could have killed Jay in a fit of temper, or jealousy, or something like that, a kind of crime of passion, and then felt she had to kill Lauren because she had become suspicious.'

Ariadne considered. 'It's possible, I suppose, in the sense that right now anything is possible because we're casting around in the dark. She would have had to be pretty clever about it to avoid being spotted on the street when she attacked Lauren.'

'She could have killed her somewhere else and just left her body in St Giles Court.'

'True, but then she would have had the problem of transporting the body, which would have taken some planning and determination. No, I'm not sure that really stacks up. We can't rule it out, and we certainly need to check out Carly's alibi for the time of both murders, but I'd be surprised if she killed anyone.'

'You thought Jay had been beating her up,' Naomi reminded her. 'Who knows what went on between them?'

'I know. It's not that it didn't seem to bother her, but she didn't seem upset about it.' She sighed. 'Of course, these things can build up.'

Naomi took a gulp of tea. 'That's really sad,' she agreed, before cramming the remainder of her doughnut in her mouth. This time, she didn't spill any jam. 'I can't imagine putting up with someone giving me a shiner like she had,' Naomi went on, when she had finished eating. 'Not to mention the broken bones. If it was me, I wouldn't let anyone get away with that, no matter how much they paid me, or threatened me.'

'You'd be more likely to knock them out,' Ariadne grinned.

'I don't know whether to be flattered or insulted by that,' Naomi replied.

As she was speaking, their colleague, Bert, joined them. 'What's all this I'm hearing?' he asked, as he sat down. He must have overheard the tail end of the conversation, because he asked Naomi who she was planning to knock out. 'Not me, I hope,' he added, laughing and eyeing the streaks of jam on Naomi's plate.

Ariadne smiled. 'We were just talking about one of our suspects, and discussing how she's suffered physical abuse in the past, even though she denies it. It's frustrating, but there's nothing we can do, as long as she refuses to report whoever's responsible for these attacks on her. We don't even know if it's one man, or more than one.'

'Or a woman?' Bert hazarded.

Naomi took a sip of her tea and wrinkled her nose. 'I don't know what they do to this tea, it always tastes stewed. Anyway, if Carly chooses to protect her abusers, rather than help us put them behind bars where they belong, like you say, there's nothing we can do about it. As for her lack of self-worth, there's nothing we can do about that either. I agree it seems insane to let someone get away with it. Is she a masochist, or scared out of her wits, or desperate for money? Who knows. But she's not the only woman to suffer physical abuse. And there's no knowing how many more are victims of mental abuse and coercive control.'

'It doesn't only happen to women,' Bert insisted. 'People seem to ignore the fact that a lot of men are abused too, and some abusers are women.'

'You're right,' Naomi said. 'And that's just as appalling. All I'm saying is, if people are prepared to put up with it instead of coming forward, then it's not our problem, it's theirs.'

'That's harsh,' Ariadne said, 'coming from someone who's supposed to be working to support members of the public.'

'I'm just being realistic,' Naomi insisted. 'We're police officers, not miracle workers. If I wanted to try and help people who won't help themselves, I'd have been a social worker.'

Ariadne didn't try to argue with her. She knew Naomi was right. It was a depressing thought. She did her best to hide her despondency when she arrived home that evening, but Nico asked her what was wrong almost as soon as she sat down.

'It's nothing,' she blustered. 'I'm just tired, that's all. It's been a long day, and this is a difficult case.' She smiled at him.

It was kind of Nico to take an interest in everything she did, but there were times when she wished he wasn't quite so attentive to her moods. He wanted her to be happy and carefree all the time, but that was as unrealistic as wishing that all victims of abuse would be keen to help bring their sadistic partners to justice. Sometimes she needed a little space to mull over a case without interruption from anyone. Sympathetic though he was, Nico would never completely understand the demands of her job. There were times, like now, when solving a case seemed impossible. Not for the first time, she wished she was still working alongside Geraldine. Ariadne didn't know how her former colleague had managed it, but somehow she seemed to have had an instinct for finding out who was guilty. With a sigh, she shrugged off her regrets. It was time for her to step out of Geraldine's shadow and lead the investigation in her own way. She couldn't rely on her every time she faced a challenge. Geraldine might be a first-rate detective, but she was on maternity leave. It was up to Ariadne to discover the truth, and that was exactly what she intended to do.

48

NATALIE WAS ASLEEP WHEN something disturbed her and she woke up with a start. It was still dark. Glancing at her phone she saw that it was one in the morning. She had been in bed for less than two hours. She closed her eyes again, hoping to go straight back to sleep, but she couldn't settle. Grief over Lauren's death, combined with the stress of having to pay the rent on her own, was making her jumpy. She knew she couldn't put off finding another flatmate for long, but somehow she didn't have the energy to look for someone else. Everything seemed to be falling apart around her and, although she tried to relax, she could feel tears tickling her eyelids. Her parents had invited her to go and stay with them for a few weeks, but that wouldn't solve anything and her mother would only get on her nerves, fussing. As she struggled to dismiss her stressful thoughts and relax, she heard it again.

This time there could be no mistaking the sound of footsteps.

Natalie felt her whole body go rigid with fear. Since Lauren's death she had been living alone, but now someone else was in the flat with her. There had been no noise from someone breaking in, just footsteps that sounded as though they were right outside her door. The only other person who had a key was the landlady, but she wouldn't enter the flat without giving notice, let alone be creeping around at one in the morning. Cautiously Natalie raised herself on to one elbow, trying to decide what to do. If she called the police the intruder might hear her talking on the phone. She would have betrayed her whereabouts and, by the time help arrived, she might have been raped, or killed. Her safest course of action would be to hide under the covers until the intruder had gone. If necessary, she would defend herself in any way she could. She made a mental inventory of everything in her bedroom – slippers, clothes, shoes, her phone – but could think of nothing she could use as a weapon to protect herself against a physical attack.

Whoever it was, they didn't seem to be making much effort to hide their presence, which was surprising given that they had broken in. Too scared to move, Natalie listened to the sound of feet shuffling, followed by a thud which was accompanied by a voice letting out a curse. The intruder had whacked themselves on something. Struggling against a fog of panic, Natalie registered hearing what sounded like a woman's voice. At the same time, a bright line appeared under her door. The intruder must have turned a light on. Although she was still frightened, somehow Natalie felt less threatened. At least she wouldn't have to worry about being raped and, if it came to a physical altercation, she might even win. Knowing the layout of the flat, she would be better able to find her way around in the dark. If she could turn out the light quickly enough, she might even be able to run past the intruder and down the stairs to the relative safety of the street where she could hide in a shop doorway and call the police. In addition, the intruder probably didn't know Natalie was there, which gave her the advantage of surprise.

A sudden eruption of anger drove her to defiance. Instead of hiding under the covers, trembling with fear as she waited to be discovered, she decided to seize the initiative, and catch the intruder by surprise. Silently, she sat up and reached for her phone. Even with the advantage of superior knowledge, she had no intention of behaving recklessly. The instant the stranger became aware of her presence, Natalie would call the police. Perhaps the other person would scarper as soon as they heard her talking on the phone, but with any luck the police would respond to the call promptly. It would give Natalie intense satisfaction to know the intruder had been caught as they fled, but her priority remained her own safety.

Swinging round to place her bare feet on the carpet, she pulled herself out of bed, feeling vulnerable wearing only a nightie that barely reached her knees. She wished she was at least wearing pyjamas. Moving slowly, she felt her way along the side of the bed towards the line of light underneath the door. Reaching it, with her phone firmly clasped in her hand, she flung the door open, at the same time reaching for the light switch, hoping darkness would give her an advantage over the intruder. Before she flicked the light off, she caught a fleeting glimpse of a hooded figure standing bent over in the middle of her living room, rubbing one knee which had presumably knocked the edge of the coffee table. Natalie hoped the intruder was badly hurt. It would serve them right. Her plan had not gone exactly as she had intended, as light still reached them through the curtained window, but it wasn't easy to see what was around. In the semi-darkness, the figure straightened up and Natalie realised she would have no chance of slipping past and escaping unseen. She had been stupid to think she could evade her intruder so easily. Once again, she felt her temper rise.

'Who the hell are you?' she demanded angrily. 'If you think you're going to get away with this, you're wrong. The police are on their way,' she added, although that was blatantly a lie. The intruder would have heard the phone call.

'I thought the flat was empty.' The rasping tone sounded unnatural. The intruder was probably attempting to disguise their voice.

'So you thought you'd just come in and help yourself?'

'I'm not a thief,' the hoarse voice replied. 'I came here to look for something.'

Natalie was curious in spite of herself. The whole incident had taken on a surreal feeling; she thought she must be dreaming.

'Who are you?' she repeated. 'What are you doing here?'

'I know what happened. I'm looking for evidence.'

'I don't know what you're talking about.'

'There has to be evidence.'

'Evidence of what?'

'Of what they did.'

'What who did?'

The intruder muttered something inaudible about sheets, and there was a flurry of movement as she abruptly spun round and made a dash for the door. An instant later, Natalie was alone in her living room, with nothing to show that she had just scared away a stranger. Her heart pounding now the immediate danger appeared to be over, she called 999 and reported that she had just surprised an intruder in her flat. Then she ran back to her bedroom and pulled on jeans and a sweatshirt over her nightie, before sitting down to wait in a daze for the police to arrive.

49

NEARLY THREE WEEKS HAD passed since Jay's murder, and Ariadne was at work early, reviewing all the evidence they had accumulated so far. By the time the medical examiner had arrived at the crime scene at midday, rigor mortis had already been affecting Jay's facial muscles, but had not yet reached his limbs. This had given the doctor a rough indication of the time of death around some two hours earlier. Ariadne turned her attention to Carly's statement concerning her whereabouts at the time of Jay's death. Carly had insisted she was at home at the time of Jay's death. While that was plausible, it was also possible she had been out visiting him.

With a sigh, Ariadne moved on to scan the documents relating to Lauren's death, which had occurred at an indeterminate time on Friday night. 'Somewhere between six pm and midnight,' was the closest the medical examiner had been able to determine. No one at The Blue Cat had been quite sure what time Carly had arrived there for work on Friday evening, but the team studying CCTV had spotted her walking in just before nine. St Giles Court where Lauren's body had been found was off Gillygate, on Carly's route from her home in Union Terrace to the club in Toft Green. That meant it was possible Carly had met Natalie between six and eight thirty, whether by chance or by arrangement. When questioned, only one witness had reported noticing anything unusual about Carly that evening. A dancer named Paula claimed that Carly had seemed jumpy, which was possibly an indication that something had happened to upset her on her way to work. There was often little point in recording vague hearsay, and Ariadne appreciated that the constable who questioned Paula had been thorough enough to note down everything she had said. But Paula's impression was too imprecise to be accepted as evidence.

Ariadne decided to question Mary again, since she claimed to have overheard the fracas preceding Jay's death. It wasn't long since Jay's murder, but Mary had been allowed to return home. Once again Ariadne drove to Penley's Grove and rang the bell. After a few moments, Mary came to the door.

'You're from the police, aren't you?' she greeted Ariadne, gazing crossly up at her. 'Can't a poor old woman be left in peace for five minutes? It's go here, go there, answer the door, answer the questions, pack up and move out of your home into some stinking hotel, move back home again. I've had enough of the lot of you. Go away and leave me alone.'

Her gnarled hand tightened on the door handle, but she was too slow. Before she could close it, Ariadne pushed the door further open.

'I'd like to talk to you,' she said firmly. 'This needn't take long. The sooner we get started, the sooner we'll be done.'

'I haven't had a chance to unpack my things,' the old woman grumbled. 'Go away. I'm not answering any more of your questions.'

'I need to ask you about your neighbour's girlfriends,' Ariadne said. 'You're the only one who can help us.'

Mary's eyes glittered and her hand gave an involuntary jerk.

'We'll show our appreciation for your time,' Ariadne added, and Mary grinned.

'Well, I'm always happy to help the police, you know that.'

She turned and shuffled slowly back to her own front door, where she led Ariadne through a dusty hall into a sitting room stuffed with faded furniture. Ariadne was aware of a stale smell that mingled with a faint scent of lavender as she followed Mary into her flat.

'I told you, it was those shoes that made me recognise her,' Mary said, before Ariadne had even sat down. 'It was that thin one. Lucy, was it? Laura? Something like that. Not that he ever introduced her. Not him. But I heard him calling out to her. Always shouting and thumping up and down the stairs to the street door at all hours. I never had any peace while he was up there.'

'Tell me again what happened on the day he died.'

'I heard the bell. He had it ringing and ringing, day and night, and I heard it as clear as if it was my own. So I looked out and saw her going up and heard them shouting.' She grunted. 'I heard it all, everything that went on up there. He was never quiet. If it wasn't one of his fancy women up there, it was the television or his music.' She shuddered. 'Horrible. Not what any normal person would call music.' She flung her withered hands in the air in a gesture of despair. 'We live in a horrible world, and it's not getting any better.'

'And you were sure it was Lauren?'

'I don't know what she called herself, but I recognised the shoes,' Mary replied. 'I told you, I saw her shoes. Those black boots with the shiny toes. They didn't look very comfortable. I don't know what these young women are thinking of. It's not how it was in my day. When we had to walk everywhere, we wore proper shoes, nothing fancy. But nowadays it's all cars and no one knows how to walk any more.' She shook her head, mumbling under her breath.

'What were they arguing about?'

Mary stared at Ariadne, looking affronted. 'Do you think I would eavesdrop on other people's business?' she asked indignantly. 'Get away with you. As if I can remember anything anyway, a poor old woman like me.' A sly grin crossed her wrinkled face and she held out a hand. 'You said you'd make it worth my while, taking up my time like this. As if I haven't got enough to do, packing to move out and packing up again to move back in.'

It had been another wasted day. With a sigh, Ariadne stood up. 'You were put up in a hotel, all expenses paid, for over two weeks,' she said. 'That's enough.'

Waving Mary's protests away, she was walking to the door when her phone buzzed. A couple of uniformed officers had answered an emergency call from a property in Gillygate earlier that day. Lauren's flatmate, Natalie, had reported a break-in at her flat.

'Why wasn't I informed about this straightaway?' Ariadne demanded, as she hurried back to her car.

While she had been running round in circles, repeating questions that had already been answered, uniform had come up with a development that might throw up a valuable new lead.

'We only just made the connection with your case,' the officer on the phone informed her dispassionately, her tone a reminder to Ariadne to maintain a professional façade, regardless of how she was feeling.

'Thank you for letting me know,' she replied formally. 'I'm going round there now to speak to Natalie. Please send me your report right away. This can't wait.'

She was aware she was sounding slightly melodramatic, but in such a perplexing case, any snippet of information might provide a crucial piece of evidence. She put her foot down as she drove to Gillygate.

50

Natalie called out, wanting to know who was there before she opened the street door. When Ariadne announced herself, there was a slight delay before the door opened a crack to allow Natalie to peer out.

'I suggest you get your landlord to put a chain on the door,' Ariadne said, examining the door frame. 'It's the simplest way to see who's calling before you let them in, and it doesn't cost much. It would be easy enough to fit on a frame like this.'

'I know,' Natalie replied as she opened the door. 'I've already asked her, but they take forever to respond to anything. Still, after what happened, I think she'll probably get on to it. It's in her interest to protect their property, never mind looking after me.' She smiled ruefully.

'I was sorry to hear about what happened,' Ariadne said. 'I'd like to ask you a few questions.'

'I've already spoken to a constable,' Natalie replied. 'Someone was here just a little while ago. But if it helps, I'm happy to tell you whatever you want to know. Would you like to come on up?'

A steep carpeted staircase led up to the flat above a hardware shop in Gillygate, opposite St Giles Court where Lauren's body had been discovered. The top of the stairs led directly into a living area, comfortably furnished but as untidy as when Ariadne had first been there. Below the window which looked out on the road was an old wooden desk with a battered swivel chair. Natalie walked over to the desk and stood staring out of the window.

'If I'd been standing right here when it happened, I might have seen the attack and been able to shout out, or run down, or call for help,' she said mournfully. 'I might have been able to intervene and it wouldn't – she wouldn't—'

She broke off and heaved a sigh. Ariadne was relieved that she didn't start crying. Natalie had been through a difficult time lately, but Ariadne really wanted her to remain calm so they could focus on talking about the recent break-in. It was hard to believe it was a complete coincidence that an intruder had turned up so soon after Lauren was murdered.

'I can't believe she's never coming back,' Natalie said, crossing the room to join Ariadne who was sitting in an armchair.

Natalie took the other armchair and sat, gazing miserably at Ariadne and picking at the frayed edge of her sleeve.

'We'll find whoever did this,' Ariadne assured her, trying to sound more confident than she felt.

'I know you're doing what you can. They came and took fingerprints and everything, and left an awful mess. Shouldn't they clean up afterwards? Anyway, I suppose you've all got more than enough to do, trying to find out what happened.' Natalie hesitated. 'Do you think whoever broke in was the person who killed Lauren?' Her voice wobbled when she uttered her friend's name, but she didn't break down.

'That's what we're going to find out,' Ariadne said. *If we possibly can*, she thought. 'Now, please tell me exactly what happened last night. I know you've been through it with us already, but maybe, on reflection, you'll remember some detail that slipped your mind just after it happened. You must have been extremely upset. Please, start at the beginning.'

Natalie nodded and described how she had been woken by a noise.

'What kind of noise?'

'I'm not sure, but then I heard footsteps in here. My bedroom's just over there.' She pointed to one of the doors leading off the living room. 'I knew it wouldn't be my landlady at one in the morning. In any case, she can't come in without letting me know in advance, so it had to be an intruder. I figured an intruder would be at a disadvantage in the dark, because they wouldn't know the layout of the furniture. Anyway, it didn't totally work out like that, because there was still just about enough light to see by.'

Hearing that, Ariadne held her breath and felt a tingling excitement. 'What did you see?'

'All I saw was a figure, in a hood. She turned away before I could see her face.'

'She?'

Natalie nodded. 'I think it was a woman,' she said uncertainly. 'I'm not positive, because I didn't really see anything. Not clearly anyway.'

'Let's assume for the moment you were right and it was a woman. What made you think that?'

'Before I came in here, from my bedroom, I thought I heard someone cursing and it sounded like a woman's voice. I had the impression it was a woman, anyway. But the next time she spoke, the words came out in this really forced grating kind of sound, as though she wanted to disguise her voice.'

'What did she say?'

'That was where it got really weird. I asked her what she was doing here, and she said she wanted to see the place. She said she thought no one was in and she had come to look for evidence.'

'Evidence of what?' Ariadne enquired.

'That's exactly what I asked, but she just mumbled something about sheets and left.'

'Sheets?' Ariadne assumed the intruder had been referring to the DNA found in Jay's bed.

'I don't know what she meant,' Natalie said. 'I didn't catch it. And then she ran off.'

'Can you remember anything about her appearance?'

Natalie frowned. 'It was difficult to tell because I didn't really see her.'

'Was she taller or shorter than you? Could you make out anything of her build?'

Natalie shook her head. 'I'm sorry, but I really couldn't say. It's not only that I can't remember, I just didn't see much. It all happened so quickly, I only saw her for a few seconds.'

'Did you see anything else? Anything at all? You said you thought the intruder was a woman. Was that only because of her voice? Did you notice her perfume? Or see her shoes?'

Once again, Natalie shook her head. 'It was pretty dark, and the whole thing was over in seconds. That's all I can tell you, really. I'm sorry.'

'There's no need to apologise. This has all been very helpful, and I'm sure the forensic team will come up with something useful. If you think of anything else, let me know, and make sure you get that chain fitted as soon as possible. I doubt your intruder will return, but it's always sensible to pay attention to security.'

Natalie nodded. 'We always thought that as long as the door was shut we'd be safe up here.' She sniffed and Ariadne wondered if she was crying. 'Safe. That's a joke, isn't it? Are any of us safe? Having a chain on the door up here wouldn't have kept Lauren safe, would it?'

51

On Friday evening, Ariadne arranged to meet Geraldine for a drink.

'If you're sure you don't mind coming out for such a short time,' Ariadne said when they spoke over the phone.

Geraldine laughed. 'I'd be happy to see you, even if it was only for five minutes. It's just nice to catch up.'

'Are you sure Ian doesn't mind being left holding the baby?'

'Oh, please. He sometimes goes out in the evening, so he can hardly complain if I do. Anyway, he loves being at home with Tom. They'll be fine.'

They met in the lounge bar of a hotel, where they had a wide view of the river through a wall of high windows. It was a spacious area with comfortable chairs, and fairly quiet. Only one other table was occupied that early in the evening. A couple of middle-aged women were conversing in low voices. After Ariadne had gone to the bar to order coffees, she sat down and asked how Tom was doing.

'Tom's great,' Geraldine replied.

Ariadne was pleased to hear her friend talking so cheerfully about the baby, and to see how well she looked.

'Motherhood suits you,' she said.

Geraldine shrugged. 'It has its moments,' she said, before she enquired about the investigation. Ariadne pulled a face and admitted that progress was slow.

'I've been mulling it over,' Geraldine admitted. 'Is it possible

Carly was convinced Lauren killed Jay, and so she killed Lauren in revenge?'

'It's possible. To be honest, we're still at the stage of thinking anything's possible,' Ariadne replied helplessly.

'Let's approach it from another angle,' Geraldine said. 'Who stood to gain by Lauren's death?'

'No one, as far as we can tell. She was virtually broke, with her earnings barely covering her regular outgoings. Jay used to help her out from time to time. He was not ungenerous with his money. Other than that, she got on well with her flatmate, with whom she'd been friends since they were at school together, and her manager where she worked was happy with her. As far as we can tell, she had no enemies. It's hopeless trying to find anyone who had an issue with her serious enough to want to kill her. The worst she's ever done is get a customer's flower order wrong.'

'Was it a coincidence, Lauren being killed so soon after Jay?' Geraldine asked. 'Don't you think the two murders must be connected?'

'Yes, that's a theory we're looking into, that someone who believed Lauren killed Jay might have killed her as retribution.' Even as she spoke, Ariadne could hear how unlikely that sounded, but Geraldine looked serious.

'Yes, that's what I've been wondering about. Didn't you say Jay's neighbour thought two women visited him regularly? What if the other woman believed Lauren killed him?'

Ariadne told her the team had been harbouring the same suspicion, but they had taken a statement from Carly, and so far they had found nothing to indicate she was responsible for Lauren's death. Ariadne had questioned her, and didn't think she was guilty.

'She seemed fairly laid-back about her relationship with Jay. I'm not sure she was even particularly bothered by his death, unless she's been lying to us about her feelings for him.'

Geraldine looked thoughtful. 'That's possible,' she said. 'And what about the old woman, Mary? Have you considered her as a potential suspect?'

Ariadne gave a dismissive shake of her head. 'She's too feeble to have overpowered a man like Jay.'

'Even after he'd fallen down the stairs and knocked himself out?'

Ariadne shook her head again. 'If you saw how frail she is, you wouldn't be thinking along those lines. She can barely walk unaided.'

Geraldine frowned. 'You mentioned she'd been shopping that morning,' she began, but Ariadne interrupted her.

'She's got a shopping trolley that doubles up as a walking aid. It's a bag attached to a tripod on wheels that she can lean on when she walks. She needs it to help her walk.'

'I'm sure she does,' Geraldine replied. 'All I'm saying is that it's easy to be blinkered by appearances, and it's dangerous to jump to conclusions without testing every possibility.'

'I don't know what you mean,' Ariadne retorted, stung by the accusation that she was being careless. 'I know what I'm doing and believe me, I consider everything extremely thoroughly.'

'Ignore me,' Geraldine said, smiling. 'I'm not even involved in the case. I'm telling you not to jump to conclusions, and here I am doing just that, only in my case I'm speculating from incomplete information.'

'Anyway, there's been a development,' Ariadne added. Keen to move the conversation into more comfortable territory, she brought Geraldine up to speed about the recent break-in at Natalie's flat.

Like Ariadne and the rest of the team, Geraldine thought it was probably no coincidence the two murders had been carried out within two weeks of each other, or that the break-in had happened just days after Lauren was killed.

'How did Natalie take it?' she asked.

'Well, naturally she was scared that an intruder had entered the flat, and she was still shocked about the death of her friend, almost on her doorstep. But she handled it well. She didn't break down and she was perfectly lucid in telling me what she knew, which wasn't much. The encounter was over so quickly, and the burglar was wearing a hood, so she saw nothing, and they disguised their voice. She did say she had the impression it was a woman and the intruder said she was looking for something, but she didn't say what.'

Geraldine grunted, frowning. Ariadne wondered if her friend had spotted something in what she had heard, but it was difficult to see what it could be.

'Natalie told me they'd thought they were safe up on the first floor,' Ariadne went on. 'Ironic, isn't it?' Almost in passing, she added, 'Naturally I advised her to put a chain on her front door.'

'Why didn't they do that when the lock was fixed?' Geraldine asked.

'They didn't need to fix it, as such,' Ariadne replied. 'But she did get the lock changed straightaway.'

Geraldine's expression grew curiously intense, and Ariadne felt a flicker of excitement seeing her friend's eyes brighten as they used to do whenever she spotted a potential lead.

'What do you mean, they didn't need to fix it?' Geraldine asked, sitting forward in her chair and staring intently at Ariadne.

'Only that there was no evidence the lock had been picked or tampered with. Why? What are you thinking?'

Geraldine shook her head, muttering that it was nothing. 'It's not my place to say anything. I'm not even involved in the investigation.'

Ariadne was disappointed. 'You can still tell me what you're thinking,' she insisted.

'I'm thinking that this is an interesting development.'

Ariadne stared at her friend. 'Wait,' she cried out, and glanced around, realising she had raised her voice in her astonishment. 'What do you mean? What development?'

Geraldine took a sip of her coffee.

'What have you seen that I've missed?' Ariadne pressed her impatiently. 'Tell me.'

'It's just that you said the lock hadn't been picked.'

'What I said was, we haven't found any signs the lock was picked. This might have been a relatively easy lock to pick, or we could be looking for an experienced house burglar. That narrows down our search but, even so, we still have to find them, and we can only speculate that finding the intruder will take us nearer to finding Lauren's killer.'

'There is another possibility,' Geraldine said softly.

She paused before asking whether a forensic examination of Natalie's flat had yielded any leads to the identity of the intruder.

Ariadne shook her head. 'We searched for fingerprints, but haven't found any that are unaccounted for. The intruder must have been wearing gloves.'

'What about DNA?'

'For a burglary where nothing was taken, and there was no damage? It's not really part of the murder investigation, so we can't justify putting in an urgent request for this. We might get something back further down the line, but that's going to take months to get the results. You know how it is.'

'There was no sign of a break-in,' Geraldine reminded her.

Ariadne frowned, unsure what Geraldine was suggesting.

'Wasn't Lauren mugged last week?' Geraldine prompted her.

Ariadne had the impression Geraldine was hinting at something, but she couldn't work out what it was.

'Yes.'

'Her bag wasn't recovered, was it?'

'Oh my God!' Ariadne burst out, finally realising what Geraldine was hinting at.

The two women seated nearby broke off their muted conversation to look over at them. One of them tutted loudly.

Ariadne leaned forward and spoke very quietly. 'You think whoever broke in could have been using Lauren's key.'

'It's possible.'

'Which means whoever broke in could have killed Lauren, or at least been present when it happened.'

'That's a bit of a jump, but it's possible,' Geraldine replied. 'At any rate, it might be interesting to find out what happened to Lauren's keys.'

Ariadne stared at Geraldine. 'That's what I was wondering. This might show us the killer's motive.' All at once she reached a decision and jumped up. 'I need to put this to Binita.' She hesitated. 'I'm not sure I can tell her we've been discussing this. I ought to credit you for the theory about the bag and the key and, of course, I want to, but like you said, you're not officially involved in the investigation—' She broke off feeling awkward.

'This isn't about getting credit for anything,' Geraldine replied. 'It's about tracking down whoever killed Lauren. I'm not involved, and it's best if you keep my name out if it. In fact, I insist you don't mention to anyone that we've discussed your case.'

Ariadne nodded and hurried away. At the door she halted and looked back over her shoulder. Geraldine was leaning back in her chair, smiling to herself.

52

Ariadne fell asleep, puzzling over what an intruder had been doing in Lauren's flat. When she woke up, she was still thinking about what Natalie had said. Back at her desk, she was reading through Carly's statements when it struck her that Natalie had misunderstood what the intruder had said. With renewed determination, she went to the detective chief inspector's office and knocked on the door.

'What is it?' Binita called out.

Ariadne opened the door and peered in. 'I need to speak to you.'

Binita glanced up from her screen. 'Can you come back later? I'm busy.'

'I want to run something past you.'

'Can't it wait? I'm in the middle of something.'

'That's the thing. I'm not sure it can wait. I think we may need to get on to it straightaway.'

'You'd better come in, then, but make it quick.'

Binita's dark eyes narrowed as Ariadne suggested that Carly might have broken into Natalie's flat. 'What gives you that idea?'

'Natalie thought the intruder mentioned "sheets", but she could have said "cheats". Carly had already told us Jay was seeing another woman. She told me he wasn't cheating as such, because they had an open relationship, but she might not have been completely honest when she said she didn't care that he had started seeing someone else on a regular basis.'

Binita looked thoughtful. 'It's possible,' she conceded.

'There's more,' Ariadne said. 'We never found Lauren's bag, and there was no sign of a break-in at Natalie's flat, so it's possible the intruder was using Lauren's key. And that means the intruder might have also been the person who attacked Lauren in the street.'

'And killed her,' Binita murmured.

'It makes sense,' Ariadne said. 'Carly denied that Jay was cheating on her, but she admitted he was seeing other women. What if Carly didn't mind him seeing other women on a casual basis, but was unhappy about him having a serious relationship with another woman? What if she killed Lauren in a jealous rage?'

Although the detective chief inspector was sympathetic to Ariadne's demands, she couldn't commit to doing everything Ariadne wanted straightaway.

'For now, you'll have to do your best to find proof,' she said. 'I'll do what I can.'

Ariadne left the detective chief inspector's office feeling more determined than ever to find the truth.

'I'm thinking Carly could be Natalie's intruder,' Ariadne told Naomi after she had spoken to the detective chief inspector. 'But it may not be easy to prove it.'

'Why would Carly have broken into Lauren's home?'

'Jealousy,' Ariadne replied promptly.

Naomi frowned. 'But why would she have wanted to go to Lauren's flat? Wouldn't she want to keep away from anything to do with Lauren, not go to her flat to steal her things?'

Ariadne frowned. 'This doesn't sound like an attempted burglary. There could be a connection between Jay's murder and the break-in. I think Carly might have attacked Lauren and stolen her bag, and then used her key to enter the flat.'

Naomi frowned. 'Okay, supposing for a moment that Carly killed Lauren, is it likely she would steal her bag and go to her flat? Surely that would be the last place she'd want to go. Why would she put herself at risk of discovery like that?'

'We should be able to look into it as a possibility. If there's a chance Carly broke into the flat using Lauren's key, you'd think it would be worth checking for traces of her DNA there,' Ariadne grumbled.

'There's no point,' Naomi replied. 'Finding evidence that Carly visited Lauren's flat wouldn't prove anything. Carly could claim she'd visited Lauren while she was alive, and no one could disprove it.'

'Well, in any case, there's no guarantee we can get another DNA sample processed straightaway. You know how urgent requests are strictly rationed these days, and we've already reached our limit. I told Binita how important this is, and she said she'd do her best, but her hands are tied. In the meantime, we'll look for prints in Natalie's flat, and send a search team to Carly's lodgings. They might come across something useful, Lauren's keys, if not her bag itself. I'll set that in motion and bring Carly in for further questioning.'

Later that morning, Ariadne gazed at Carly across the table as she announced her name and that of her colleague, Detective Sergeant Naomi Arnold. An elderly lawyer was sitting beside Carly. His hunched shoulders and round black-framed glasses added to his owl-like appearance, as he sat blinking at Ariadne. Carly looked pasty-faced without her usual heavy make-up. Her skin had an unhealthy sheen, and there were grey smudges under her eyes. In leggings and a baggy jumper, she bore little resemblance to the svelte woman Ariadne had met at The Blue Cat.

'What is all this?' Carly snapped. 'Can't you people back off? You're like a dog with a bone. I need to be at work early today and I've got a million and one things to do first.' She looked down at her hands, fingers splayed out, before patting her hair with a grimace. 'You might not care what you look like, but I have to make an effort to look good for punters. It doesn't happen just like that, you know, and I've got my living to make, same as anyone else. Can you imagine what would happen if I turned up at work looking like this?'

'You seem angry today,' Ariadne said quietly.

'Is that any surprise? I've answered all your questions, over and over, and now this.'

Carly waved one hand in the direction of the two detectives, before turning to face the duty lawyer sitting patiently beside her. 'They can't keep me here, can they? I want you to get me out of here right now. If I don't leave here soon, I'm going to miss my appointment at the nail bar. You're my lawyer, aren't you?' she snapped, as he began to remonstrate. 'So tell me, what's all that shit I've been hearing about strangers searching my place?' she went on, her face twisting into an awkward scowl. 'They're way out of line on that, aren't they? I need you to stop them harassing me. Isn't there a complaints procedure against the police?' She began to stand up, but the lawyer murmured to her and she sat down again.

'We just want to ask you a few questions,' Ariadne said in a reassuring tone.

'Questions, questions.' Exasperated, Carly turned to the lawyer. 'How can you just sit there while they hound me like this? I'm not even a suspect and they're treating me like a bloody criminal. I have better things to do than sit here listening to this shit.'

'Let's hear what they have to say,' the lawyer replied in an even tone.

'Some help you are,' Carly fumed, but Ariadne could see she was scared.

Pale and slightly sweaty, Carly licked her lips nervously and stared doggedly over Ariadne's shoulder, refusing to look directly at her.

'You told us you were at home on the Saturday night your boyfriend, Jay, was killed. We have reason to believe you were with him that morning.'

'Oh Jesus, not this again,' Carly wailed. 'How many times do I have to tell you, I never saw Jay at the weekend. Yes, I sometimes went home with him, but only during the week. Weekends are my busy time at work. I didn't kill him. He was good to me. Why would I want him dead?'

For an instant, Carly's pretence at insouciance slipped and she looked fraught. Within seconds, she regained her composure. The contortion in her expression was so fleeting, Ariadne wondered if she had imagined it.

'Tell us about Lauren.'

'Who?' Carly's face was now a mask of detachment.

Naomi slid a picture across the table. 'Carly is being shown an image of Lauren Shaw,' she said.

She put a second picture in front of Carly, this one showing Lauren's face after she had been strangled. The whites of her eyes were bright red, and there was bruising on her neck. Carly's eyes narrowed as she took in the second of the two images, before enquiring coldly who the women were and why Ariadne was showing them to her.

'That's two pictures of one woman, before and after she was murdered,' Naomi replied. 'She was Jay's girlfriend.'

'Yes, well, like I told you already, I knew he was seeing other people. We both were. But I don't see what that woman's got to do with me. So we were both seeing the same guy. So what? Some of my regulars are married, some have girlfriends. I dare say some have boyfriends. Not everyone appreciates being restricted to one partner. Can I go home now?' She turned once more to the lawyer and snapped at him to do something.

'My client hasn't been charged,' he said quietly. 'She has answered all your questions and now she would like to go home.'

Ariadne was convinced that Carly had been in Lauren's flat, but they couldn't hold her indefinitely without any evidence. 'Not just yet,' she said.

53

Ariadne had Carly held in a cell while they waited for the outcome of the search. She was beginning to lose hope of finding anything that would help the investigation when, at last, she heard from the sergeant in charge of the search team. With a grim smile, Ariadne summoned Naomi and had the suspect brought back to an interview room.

'My client has finished here,' the lawyer said. 'She is ready to leave.'

'I'm afraid we can't let her go just yet,' Ariadne replied.

'You can't keep me here,' Carly said. 'The lawyer said so.'

'Unless you charge my client, I insist you release her.'

'Very well,' Ariadne replied, trying not to sound pleased. 'Carly Fox, I'm arresting you on suspicion of the murders of Jay Roper and Lauren Shaw.' She proceeded to read Carly her rights.

'What are you on about?' Carly cried out indignantly. 'You can't pin those murders on me. You look down on my job, so you think I'm an easy target.' She turned to the lawyer once again. 'Do something. You said they couldn't keep me here. This is bullshit. They think because of what I do, they can get away with this, but I've got rights, the same as anyone else.'

Naomi held up a bag containing a shiny pink purse.

'Do you recognise this purse?' Ariadne asked. 'For the tape, DS Arnold is showing the suspect a purse found in the bins outside her home at 13.15 today. The purse contains a credit card belonging to Lauren Shaw.'

'What?' Carly screeched. Her cheeks flushed with indignation, or alarm. 'You went poking around the bins at my flat? You can't do that. They can't do that, can they? That's not legal, is it?'

'We had a warrant to search your flat.'

Carly started to remonstrate and then fell silent, scowling and biting her lip.

'Can you explain how Lauren's purse came to be in a bag of rubbish in the bins outside your flat?'

'I don't know,' Carly muttered. 'She must have dropped it there. How should I know how it got there?'

'If the purse was found outside my client's property, anyone could have deposited it there,' the lawyer pointed out.

'It was discovered at the bottom of a bag of rubbish, which contained a circular addressed to your client, and the purse has her fingerprints on it.'

'All right, all right,' Carly said. 'So I met Lauren and she lent me her purse before she was killed. I'd – I'd lost mine and she let me borrow hers. She said I could use whatever cash she had, as long as I paid her back. But I didn't know her well. When I heard she'd been mugged, I panicked and threw her purse away so no one could accuse me of mugging her. Anyone would have done the same. I was scared.'

The lawyer spoke up. 'I need to speak with my client alone.'

Sensing the suspect was growing desperate, Ariadne pressed on. 'We know what you did. Tell us why you attacked her. It will be much easier for you if you cooperate with us now.'

Carly shook her head. 'I told you, we were both seeing other people. It's ridiculous to accuse him of cheating. We were never serious about each other.'

'That might be how he was feeling, but it's not how you felt, was it? There's no point in denying it any longer.'

Ariadne didn't point out that it was possible to be convinced of the truth without being able to prove it, and as long as Carly refused to talk, she might yet evade arrest. Somehow, Ariadne had to persuade her to confess.

'Tell us why you did it,' Ariadne continued. 'I'm sure Lauren must have provoked you. Carly, we already have enough evidence to convict you. This is your opportunity to tell your side of the story. We know what you did.'

Carly's shoulders slumped and her expression of alarm gave way to one of resignation. The lawyer cleared his throat loudly and repeated that he wanted to confer with his client in private, but Carly ignored him and began talking very rapidly.

'Look, you've got this all wrong. I never meant to hurt her. You can't say it was my fault. I was on my way to work when I noticed her walking across Lendal Bridge, so I followed her. I'd seen her with Jay and I recognised her. I knew it was her because of these shoes she was wearing. I'd spoken to Jay's neighbour and she told me what happened. That bitch pushed him down the stairs. You weren't doing anything about it and, well—' She shrugged. 'I admit it, I let my temper get the better of me. All I could think of was how unfair it was. She'd killed him and the least she could do was apologise for what she'd done.'

'I'm not sure I understand. Who did you want her to apologise to?'

'To me, of course.'

'Why did she owe you an apology?'

'Jay was generous to me, and she took him away from me. She had no right to do that. It was only fair she should compensate me for what she'd taken.'

'So you killed her?' Ariadne prompted her.

The lawyer interrupted her to insist he speak to her alone, but Carly shook her head and continued with her account.

'It wasn't like that.'

'What was it like? If you don't tell us what happened, we're going to assume the worst of you.'

'I followed her to Gillygate. When she stopped to cross the road, I told her I knew what she'd done. I wanted to hear her admit it, but she denied it. That's when I understood that she didn't care what she'd done to me, and she was never going to accept that she owed me. Then she said Jay had asked her to marry him, and she laughed at me for thinking he had ever cared about me. "You can't seriously think he'd want anything more than a meaningless screw from a whore like you," was what she said. I hated her more than I'd ever hated anyone and when she turned to walk away, I lashed out. I wanted to make her suffer for what she said to me.' Tears spilled out of her eyes, but her expression remained cold. 'People are always sneering at me. People like you.'

'What did you hit her with?' Ariadne asked quietly.

'My client isn't going to say another word until she's had a chance to talk with me,' the lawyer interrupted.

'I didn't hit her. I told you, it wasn't my fault. I grabbed her hair and she lost her balance and fell backwards into the lane. She must have hit her head on the edge of a low wall there because she let out this kind of sigh and after that she just lay there.'

'What happened next?'

'I was scared. I thought I'd killed her.'

'You just said you wanted to kill her.'

'My client never said that she wanted to kill anyone,' the lawyer corrected her quickly.

'I may have hated her, in the heat of the moment, but I never intended to hurt her.' Carly turned and looked at the lawyer who was watching her in silence. 'It was an accident. You have to tell them.'

The lawyer began agitating for a break, but Ariadne had one more question for Carly.

'Was it an accident when you strangled her?'

'Yes, yes, that was an accident too. You have to believe me. I was trying to pull her into the lane, to get her off the road, out of sight. I didn't want anyone to see me with her. Then I was going to scarper and make an anonymous call for an ambulance. I never meant to hurt her.'

'Tell us how you came to strangle her.'

'I don't know, I don't know. I can't remember. I was panicking. I think I pulled her too hard. Maybe the strap of her bag got caught round her neck.'

'You seemed to recover very quickly. After you killed her, you went straight to work,' Ariadne said. 'And you forgot to call for an ambulance.'

'I didn't know what to do. I didn't want to get in trouble. I thought someone would find her and send for help and everyone would think she'd been mugged. So I took her bag to make it look like she'd been robbed, and ran away.'

'You attacked her and left her dying in the street,' Naomi said coldly.

'No, no, it wasn't like that.'

'What was it like?' Ariadne asked.

'I never meant for her to die. You have to believe me.'

'You killed Jay and Lauren because you were jealous of their relationship. You were jealous of their relationship and afraid he would leave you for her. You always wanted her out of the way so he would pay more attention to you. You never forgave her for having a relationship with him. Even after she was dead, you were determined to get your revenge.'

'No, no,' Carly sobbed. 'I didn't know she was dead. I never meant to kill her. I just wanted to – to punish her for what she did to Jay.' Her eyes gleamed, momentarily betraying her fury, and she hissed, 'I'm not sorry for what I did. She deserved to die.'

'Was it an accident when you killed Jay?'

Carly's eyes widened in surprise. 'I never hurt Jay. Not Jay. I would never have hurt him. I would have done anything for him. Jay meant everything to me. I don't know how I'm going to manage without his support.'

'Well, it's just as well you won't have to worry about paying your bills where you're going,' Naomi said.

54

THERE WAS A MUTED cheer when Ariadne announced that Carly had confessed to killing Lauren.

'We found Lauren's purse in with her rubbish so she couldn't really deny it,' Ariadne said. 'She's confessed and it all checks out.'

'No doubt she'll plead extenuating circumstances,' Naomi muttered, with a sour expression.

'Revenge is hardly extenuating circumstances,' Binita said.

Ariadne thought about Thalia's son avenging his brother's death and she shivered, thinking about the terrible secret she had agreed to conceal.

'Well done, everyone,' she said. 'And now, let's crack on. We still have another murder to work on.'

'A double murder is always tricky,' Binita said.

'It's just one now,' Ariadne pointed out. 'With Carly's confession, Lauren's death is accounted for. Unless we can find evidence someone else was there at the time Jay was killed, then it's looking like Carly killed him as well. We already know she's capable of murder, which makes her an obvious suspect. And we know she had motive and opportunity to kill Jay.'

'She killed Lauren in a jealous rage, so why not Jay as well?' Naomi asked.

'The other possibility is that Lauren killed him.' Ariadne sighed. 'One of our suspects has confessed to a different murder, and the other one is dead.'

'What about Yiannis?' Naomi asked. 'And Mary?'

'I can't see that either of them would have a motive to kill him,' Ariadne replied. 'Apart from her obvious physical frailty, Mary has a strong religious belief and that alone makes her an unlikely suspect. But we can't rule out anyone who could have been there.'

A sigh seemed to hover in the air before everyone returned to their allotted tasks. After reading reports and checking in with her colleagues studying CCTV, Ariadne met Naomi for lunch in the canteen.

'The VIIDO team spotted a hooded figure that could be Carly coming off Lendal Bridge and walking along the pavement towards Gillygate. The only clear shot they found was at the traffic lights at the junction of Bootham and Gillygate but even there the target's face was hidden under a hood. There's not enough to establish a definite identity, but it's given us enough to back up what we already know.'

'If she hadn't confessed…' Naomi said.

'I know, it was touch and go for a while back there.'

They smiled at one another.

'One down, one to go,' Naomi muttered. 'Did you believe her about Jay?'

Ariadne shrugged. 'She broke down and admitted to killing Lauren. She's already signed a statement. But she's still insisting she didn't harm Jay. She must have realised we'd nailed her for Lauren's murder, once she knew we'd found Lauren's purse in her trash. But she might still get away with killing Jay. Going down for one murder is better than going down for two. With a sharp enough defence, she might even get off with manslaughter. Then again, who killed Jay if it wasn't Lauren or Carly? It must have been one of them. We know Lauren was there, because Mary recognised her shoes.'

'Unless Mary was confused,' Naomi said.

'Or lying,' Ariadne said thoughtfully. 'I might question her again.'

'We've already questioned her two or three times. What more is she going to tell us?'

'I'm not sure,' Ariadne admitted.

She didn't add it was Geraldine's suggestion that Mary might know more than she had admitted. It was hard to see what else Mary could tell them, but a hint from Geraldine was enough for Ariadne to view the old woman as a person of interest. She decided to speak to Binita who asked the same question as Naomi.

'She had access to the hall before Jay was killed,' Ariadne said, attempting to put forward a justification for her interest. 'It's possible she might remember something else, something that might place Carly at the scene on the morning Jay was killed. It's even possible she was involved in some way.'

'Who? Mary? The old woman?'

'Don't you think she could have suffocated him? I mean, it's possible, isn't it?'

Binita gave Ariadne a sceptical look. 'Let's not start clutching at straws yet, especially such improbable ones. I grant you Mary had access to the hall, but why would she want to kill Jay? Maybe she had opportunity, but she had no motive and, in any case, she was hardly in a position to overpower a strong man.'

Ariadne thought about the frail old woman and had to agree. But Jay had no doubt been dazed by his fall, and the truth was that Geraldine's words were bothering her.

'I'd just like to bring her in tomorrow and question her.'

'Very well, let me think about it. We don't want to find ourselves facing charges of harassment. The media would love a story about us pestering some poor, helpless, old woman. You know how they love to sensationalise anything that puts us in a bad light. I can imagine the headlines and, to be honest, I'm not convinced it's worth the risk. What exactly are you hoping to gain from questioning her again? I appreciate you're trying to leave no stone unturned in pursuing every possible avenue, and even some that are implausible, but I have to keep in mind all the possible consequences of every action we take. We need to be constantly vigilant, Ariadne.'

It sounded like a warning. Ariadne wondered if the detective chief inspector had found out that she was concealing relevant information. She told herself Thalia would never have revealed Ariadne's complicity in keeping Yiannis's guilty secret. To do so would have betrayed her son to the police. Besides, Yiannis's crime from twenty years ago had no bearing on their investigation into Jay's death. But she felt uneasy. One false remark and everything would come crashing down.

Seeing her looking worried that evening Nico enquired what was wrong. Ariadne told him how reluctant Binita had been for her to question Mary again.

'She banged on about our public image, and how she has to consider the wider picture, and how bad it might look if there was any suggestion of us browbeating a poor old woman.'

'Maybe you should just forget about seeing this witness again. She's already been questioned, hasn't she?'

Ariadne nodded miserably, but she had made up her mind. She tried to respond to Nico's attempts at conversation over supper, but her responses were forced. After a while, he gave up and left her to her thoughts which remained fixed on the investigation. Geraldine had expressed surprise that they hadn't considered Mary a possible suspect. Geraldine was in no position to comment at all, since she was not involved in the investigation and had never even spoken to Mary, but nevertheless her comment was unsettling.

'What is it?' Nico asked again when she had finished clearing the table and stacking the dishwasher.

'It was Geraldine who suggested I look into this old woman who lives downstairs in Yiannis's rental,' she said.

'Geraldine?'

Ariadne nodded.

'I thought she was on maternity leave?'

'She is, but I've been discussing the case with her.'

'Is that allowed?'

Ariadne shrugged. 'No one else knows. We've just been talking, in confidence.' She sighed, thinking this was another secret she was keeping from Binita. 'That's not the issue. The thing is, should I trust Geraldine's opinion?'

'It's not about trusting or not trusting her,' Nico replied. 'She's not working on the case and isn't in a position to voice any sort of opinion on it. She only knows what she's heard from you, and what she's read in the papers.'

Wondering whether she was paying too much attention to her former colleague's ideas, Ariadne passed a restless night and had still not decided what to do when she woke up.

55

As soon as Ariadne entered Binita's office the next morning, she knew something was wrong. Binita seemed unusually sombre as she looked up and told Ariadne she had just received sad news.

'Is this about Mary?' Ariadne asked, without stopping to consider whether that was likely.

There was no reason why Binita would have come to the same conclusion about the downstairs tenant as Geraldine appeared to have reached. But at her advanced age, Mary might have fallen ill, and there were still questions for her to answer. If she was unable to speak, for whatever reason, that would put an end to Ariadne's latest line of questioning, and Geraldine's theory might never be fully examined.

'Mary? Are you talking about Yiannis's downstairs tenant, Mary Jones?' Binita repeated in surprise. 'No. It's nothing to do with Yiannis's tenant. It's Yiannis himself. The fact is, I've just heard that Yiannis Karalis is dead.'

'What?' Ariadne didn't try to conceal her shock. 'What happened? I spoke to his mother only a week ago and she didn't say anything about him being ill. How did he die?'

'Apparently it was very sudden,' Binita replied. 'I thought, as you're connected with the Greek community, that you might go and visit his mother, find out what you can from her.'

'But – but – you haven't told me what happened. It wasn't another murder?'

She wondered vaguely whether his past had caught up with

him, and he had been traced to York, not by the police as his mother had feared, but by relatives of the man he had killed all those years ago.

Binita gave a helpless shrug. 'It's not clear,' she said. 'Can you talk to his family, talk to his mother, and find out what happened to him? No one is telling us anything.' It sounded like an order.

Dismissing her suspicions of Mary for the time being, Ariadne hurried to Hope Street to speak to Thalia. There were a few cars outside the house, and she had to park further away than she wanted. The front door was open and she walked in, passing a couple of dark-haired men standing in the hall who watched her as she entered the living room. There she found several women dressed in black, standing around Thalia. She was seated on an upright chair, staring straight ahead, seemingly oblivious to the people who had gathered around her. The room was stuffy and there was a stale smell, as though the windows had never been opened. Hearing voices muttering in Greek, Ariadne felt like an interloper and, at the same time, a friend to Thalia. None of the other women probably knew her harrowing secret, the reason why she and her son had fled Greece twenty years earlier. In some ways, Ariadne had a more intimate relationship with the grieving widow than anyone else, even though she and Thalia had spent very little time together.

It wasn't going to be easy to force her way through the women who formed a group around the grieving woman, as though guarding her from intruders. Even if Ariadne managed to get close to her, it didn't look as though Thalia would be able to speak freely. Backing out of the room, she returned to the hall, where the two men stared openly at her, perhaps wondering who she was. One of them looked little more than twenty, the other was middle-aged. Ariadne approached the older of the two men and asked him what had happened to Yiannis.

'He's dead,' the man said dispassionately, looking coldly at her.

'Yes, I know that,' Ariadne replied. 'But what happened to him? I saw him recently and he said nothing about being ill. Can you tell me how he died?'

'What difference does it make?' the young man burst out. 'He's dead, however it happened.' He paused and stared angrily at Ariadne. 'Who are you, anyway? What do you know about Yiannis?'

'More perhaps than you do,' she said quietly. 'Tell me what happened. Did he die from natural causes? Or did someone kill him?'

'No one killed him,' the young man snapped. 'It wasn't like that. Now leave. You're not family. You have no business asking questions here in a house of mourning.'

'He wasn't physically ill,' the older man replied heavily. 'Not ill in the sense I think you mean. But he was sick.'

'Sick in the head,' the younger man said, scowling. 'What kind of a man does that to an old woman? He's broken his mother's heart, the coward. We all have problems, but we don't—' He broke off, seemingly unable to express his thought aloud.

For a second Ariadne stared at the two men in disbelief. 'Are you saying he took his own life?' she asked at last. 'Why? What happened?'

But the men refused to answer her questions. Feeling wretched, she returned to the police station without making any further attempt to speak to Thalia. Back at her desk, she phoned around the local undertakers until she found the one who was taking care of the funeral arrangements. Still shocked, she drove straight there and, once she had introduced herself to him, the undertaker declared himself happy to answer her questions. A gaunt man, nearly bald, he peered at her through rimless glasses with a professional expression of sympathy.

'The family are desperate to have him buried in consecrated ground, but there's not much I can do about it. The church is unyielding.' He sighed heavily. 'It's a sad case when a man takes his own life, but it's all too common. He hung himself,' he added. 'It was his mother who found him in his bedroom. Poor woman, she was distraught.'

'She must have been. How terrible.'

Having found out as much as she could, Ariadne returned to the police station to file her report. Yiannis might have killed a man, but he was beyond punishment now.

56

On Sunday morning, Ariadne went to speak to Binita again to request permission to bring Mary in for questioning, but the detective chief inspector was away at a meeting. Ariadne was already nervous, knowing she had concealed information, and she was reluctant to act without Binita's clear instruction. There was a risk attached to acting independently. Geraldine had sometimes been in trouble with their senior officer for going off on her own, but Geraldine's ideas had always produced results. Ariadne was fairly confident Mary had useful information to share, but she knew she might be reprimanded or even face disciplinary measures, if Mary made a fuss. But how badly wrong could it go? All she wanted to do was bring Mary to the police station and ask her a few questions. Anxious about trying to persuade Mary to accompany her, she drove slowly. Loath to provoke accusations of bullying or intimidation, she parked outside the house and sat for a moment, procrastinating.

She had almost made up her mind to abandon her plan and leave, when the front door of Yiannis's property opened and Mary appeared, dragging her grey and black shopping trolley. Had Ariadne been waiting for help in guiding her decision, she couldn't have asked for a clearer sign. Without pausing to think any longer, she jumped out of her car and hurried up the steps, calling out a greeting.

Seeing who was there, Mary drew back, looking vexed. 'What do you want? I told you before. Go away.' She fluttered her gnarled hand dismissively, and swung round to go back indoors.

Ariadne ran up the steps and placed one foot across the threshold to prevent the door closing. 'Are you going shopping? Can I give you a lift? I was just passing.'

Mary glared at her suspiciously.

'You look like you could do with some help.'

The old crone hesitated. In that instant of indecision, Ariadne took hold of the handle of the shopping trolley and began lifting it down the steps. Mary followed her, muttering to herself. With the trolley safely stowed in the back of the car, Ariadne opened the front passenger door and Mary clambered in. Ariadne was wondering how she was going to set about questioning her passenger, when Mary twisted round to look at her.

'I think you're the one in need of help, not me,' the old woman said. She coughed and began to wheeze.

'What do you mean, I need help?' Ariadne asked her, when the old woman had recovered her breath.

'I could tell you things.'

'What things?'

'I know what went on upstairs.'

'Go on.'

'You don't expect me to tell you everything for free,' Mary said. 'You people pay for information, don't you?'

'That depends,' Ariadne replied thoughtfully, as she turned the key in the ignition.

Mary leaned back in her seat and closed her eyes. She appeared to fall asleep, but after a moment she sat up quite suddenly and gazed around in bewilderment, demanding to know where Ariadne was taking her.

'We're going to the police station.'

'What? The police station? Why? I don't want to go there. You said you were helping me with my shopping.'

'And *you* said you had some information for us,' Ariadne replied cheerily. 'We can't pay you for anything you tell us unless it's registered through the official channels. So we're just going to the police station to record what you have to say.'

She hoped Mary would believe the story, but the old woman was not so easily fooled.

'That's not how they do it on the telly,' she said. 'They sit in their cars where no one can see them, and pay the informers whenever they have anything to share.'

'Well, that might be how they do things on the television, but it's not what we do here, in the real world. I'll take you to the police station where you'll be given a nice cup of tea and a biscuit.'

'I don't want a cup of tea and a biscuit,' Mary replied testily. 'I want to go home.'

'And then we'll just have a quiet chat and you can tell us what you know,' Ariadne went on.

Mary continued protesting feebly and Ariadne was beginning to think she might have to drop her unwilling passenger home, when greed overcame the old woman's reticence.

'You haven't told me how much you're paying me yet,' she said.

'That depends on you,' Ariadne repeated. 'We can't pay you much if you don't tell us much.'

Arriving at the police station, Ariadne left Mary with a female constable and went to find Naomi.

'You've brought Mary here?' Naomi repeated in surprise. 'Whatever for?'

Quickly Ariadne explained that she suspected Mary knew a lot more about the murder than she had yet admitted. She might know more than could easily be elicited from questioning her informally at her home.

'I'm going to tape her and I'd like you to be present,' she added.

'Does she need a lawyer?'

Ariadne shrugged. 'We're not arresting her, we've just invited her here to answer a few questions. She came in quite willingly.'

Naomi laughed. 'How did you manage that?'

'I said we would pay her for her information and she couldn't resist the offer of what she saw as easy money. But if she knows what I think she knows, then the deal might not turn out to be as easy as she thinks.' She smiled grimly and Naomi nodded uneasily.

'What did Binita say about it?'

Ariadne hesitated. 'She's not in today. She's out at a meeting, and I haven't had a chance to ask her yet. So, come on, let's do this.'

57

'I FINISHED MY TEA,' Mary was saying in her reedy voice as Ariadne and Naomi entered the room. 'Can you get me another one? And make it hot this time.'

Under the bright light of the interview room, slivers of pale scalp were visible among her wispy strands of grey hair.

'That will be all,' Ariadne told the constable who had been sitting with Mary, before dismissing her with a quiet word of thanks. 'The tea can wait.'

Ariadne and Naomi took their seats without responding to the old woman's request.

'It wasn't even hot,' Mary went on fussily. 'Can you please make sure the next one is hot. Not too hot, mind. You wouldn't want me suing you for burning myself.' She glanced at Ariadne from under lowered lids to check that her implied threat had been noted. 'I know my rights,' she added, in a pitiful attempt to demonstrate she wasn't intimidated by the situation. 'And then I'll be off home,' she added, with an air of finality.

'We'd like to ask you a few questions first,' Ariadne replied, ignoring Mary's facile attempt to take control of the situation. 'Then we'll consider your request.'

Mary scowled, mumbling disingenuously that she only wanted a cup of tea, and was that so much for a poor old woman to ask.

'Tell us what you heard on the morning your neighbour died,' Ariadne said.

Mary snorted and folded her arms across her skinny chest. 'I know why you keep asking me to tell you the same thing over and over and over again. You think you can catch me out. You're just waiting for me to change my story, however slightly, so you can accuse me of bearing false witness with a pack of lies. Do you think I'm stupid? Well, you got that wrong, because I'm not saying another word. So go on, do your worst. Take me to court and let the world see how you persecute a poor old woman. I'll go to the papers. Oh yes, I know a thing or two, and I have a powerful friend. You won't get away with this. The Lord looks after His own.'

She sat hunched in her chair, her beady eyes glaring, her lips working silently, a picture of indignation.

'Tell us about your neighbour,' Naomi said.

The old woman shrugged. 'What about him? He's dead, isn't he?'

'Did you get on well with him?' Naomi asked.

Mary's answer was petulant. 'You can mind your own business. I have no dealings with the devil.'

Ariadne sighed. Mary seemed a little crazy. She might have useful information she could share with them, but she was going to be a difficult witness to question. It looked as though the interview would turn out to be another waste of time. As for putting Mary in the witness stand in court, that would be pointless.

'I'm afraid your neighbour was murdered, so this *is* our business,' she tried again. 'Mary, you're not stupid. You know you can get in a lot of serious trouble if you hinder us in our enquiries. So why don't you just answer our questions? We need to know about your relationship with Jay.'

The crafty old woman's eyebrows rose in genuine surprise and she stared balefully at Ariadne.

'What are you talking about?' she retorted at last. 'As if I'd be having relations with a man like that. Your mind is corrupted by sin to think such a wicked idea. I'm a God-fearing woman, I'll have you know, and that man was possessed by Satan. No decent person would have anything to do with him. I shunned him. Do you think I would go anywhere near him and risk corrupting my soul?' She let out a low hiss. 'No, thank you very much.'

Ariadne glanced at Naomi. This was possibly a new development.

'What made you think he might corrupt your soul?' Ariadne asked.

'He had women up there, different ones,' Mary replied. 'But I already told you that. Don't you remember anything? No wife, no holy sacrament, just loose women, enemies of the Lord. And their carcasses shall be as dung.' She sniffed. 'Anyway, he'll burn in hell for all eternity, and good riddance. I didn't want him living anywhere near me. I'm a God-fearing woman. Those who follow Satan deserve to be punished for their evil ways.'

'What did your neighbour do that was so evil?' Ariadne asked.

'Didn't I just tell you he had women going up those stairs, tramps the lot of them, all walking past my door with their clattering feet and foul perfume. And I heard them through my ceiling, having carnal relations.' Her wrinkled face contorted with disgust and she muttered incoherently about the sins of the flesh.

Ariadne drew in a breath before enquiring very gently, 'You say you believed he should be punished for his sins, Mary? Was that what happened to him?'

Mary suddenly gave a start and shook her head. 'I won't say another word. He was an evil man, and noisy, and I'm not sorry he's dead. There! Now you know. I want to go home. You can't keep me here. I've done nothing wrong. I admit I was glad when I knew he was dead, but God forgives those who truly repent.'

Ariadne wasn't ready to give up yet. She asked Mary to remain where she was and said a constable would be back with the cup of tea she had asked for.

'And then can I go home?'

Ariadne didn't answer. The truth was, she didn't yet know whether she would be able to keep Mary in custody or not. It seemed almost unbelievable that the old woman could have been involved in Jay's murder, yet she had the opportunity and it seemed she might have had a motive as well. Mary believed Jay had deserved to be punished for his sins, and what greater punishment could be meted out than death? Leaving Mary in the care of a constable, Ariadne went to find out whether the detective chief inspector had returned.

'Very well,' Binita agreed, when Ariadne found her sitting at her desk. 'If you think it's possible she had some crazy motive for wanting Jay dead, maybe you're right, but do you really think she would have had the strength to kill him? I saw her, and she struggles to walk.'

Ariadne shrugged. 'I know, but she was there, and appearances can sometimes be deceptive.'

Binita looked thoughtful. 'It would explain how the killer managed to escape without being seen.'

Ariadne said she would go ahead and arrange to search Mary's apartment.

'I'll pass the request for a search warrant through as urgent,' Binita agreed.

While a search warrant was being obtained, Ariadne and Sam drove Mary home. They watched her shuffle with difficulty up the steps to her front door, fumble with her key, and pull her empty shopping trolley inside. Then they waited outside in the car for the search team to arrive.

'What are we hoping to find in there?' Sam enquired. 'Some kind of murder weapon?' He laughed. 'Perhaps she clubbed him to death. Or was she wielding an axe?' He grinned. 'Of course, she could be Superwoman in disguise.'

'The search team know what to look for,' Ariadne replied tersely.

58

A SIGH RIPPLED ROUND the room as the team heard that Mary had been brought back for further questioning. Someone muttered that they were going round in circles. Ariadne listened to a faint buzz of voices, all objecting to the latest development, but she kept silent. If her hunch was wrong, it would soon become apparent that she had been mistaken in wanting to treat Mary as a suspect. She tried to ignore the muttering as she walked past her colleagues.

'We've already had her in.'

'How on earth could that doddery old woman have had anything to do with it?'

'You know she's religious? It's in her notes.'

'I don't know what the DI thinks she's doing.'

'She's grasping at straws.'

'You tell me how that old woman could have killed a man like Jay.'

Ariadne made her way straight to the interview room where Mary was seated, waiting. The old woman's face was red, and she was panting as though she had been exerting herself.

'What is all this?' she demanded breathlessly, as Ariadne and Naomi sat down opposite her and switched the tape on. 'I insist on being taken home.' She rapped on the table with her knuckles. 'At once! They said I had to answer more questions but I know what's going on. You've brought me here to get me out of the way while your colleagues plant incriminating evidence at my flat. The world has gone mad, quite mad. They can't keep me here, can they?' she added, turning to the lawyer.

The duty brief that day was a young man who looked as though he had not long ago left school. He gazed straight ahead without moving a muscle as Ariadne explained she just wanted to ask Mary a few questions.

'I know, I know, they gave me all that mumbo jumbo when they came to collect me, but I don't know what you're talking about,' Mary replied. 'I've already answered all your questions and now I want to go home. You can't keep me here. Why does the Lord allow this persecution?' she demanded, turning once again to the young man seated beside her. 'You need to tell them I've done nothing wrong,' she said, glaring furiously at him. 'I'm innocent. Innocent!' Giving up on her lawyer, she turned back to Ariadne. 'You can't treat me like I'm a criminal. You have no right to harass me like this. I'm an old woman. You're going to give me a heart attack.' She drew in a wheezy breath. 'I can't breathe, I can't breathe.'

Hoping she was right in assuming that Mary's distress was a sham, Ariadne pressed on. 'We need to talk about your neighbour, Jay Roper,' she said.

'Yes, yes, I know who my neighbour was.' Mary's lips trembled slightly and she turned pale, but at least she seemed to be breathing normally.

'According to your statement, you heard your neighbour fall down the stairs in the property where you both lived. Then you told us you heard him moaning. Surely a religious woman like you didn't ignore him when he obviously needed help?'

At first Mary refused to respond. Then she denied having gone anywhere near Jay on the morning he died.

'I was afraid to go out,' she said, with a faint air of belligerence. 'So you know I had nothing to do with it. I was nowhere near him, shut up in my flat. I could have died in there and no one would have known.'

Ariadne was convinced that the old woman was hiding something, but Mary insisted that she had not left her flat that morning.

'You heard him, didn't you?' Ariadne persisted.

'Yes, there was a noise. He was always making a racket, that one. No one knows how I suffered, listening to the din he made with his music, and the shouting, and the thumping up and down the stairs, all day up and down. The Lord knows how I suffered.'

'What did you hear after he fell down the stairs?'

'I told you he was moaning and calling for help.'

'So you heard him moaning and went out to see what was wrong?' Ariadne asked again, hoping Mary would admit she had gone to see if Jay was still alive after his fall. But the old woman wasn't so easily caught out.

It looked as though they would have to release her, yet again, but Ariadne decided to keep her at the police station for a few more hours. In deference to her age, and since there was no proof she had been involved in a crime, she was allowed to sit in a small meeting room in the company of a young female police constable who reported that Mary never stopped complaining and demanding to be driven home.

'Has she said anything other than that she wants to go home?' Ariadne asked after an hour.

'Only that the tea is shit, and she's innocent,' the constable replied. 'Her lawyer is advising her to say nothing.'

Ariadne was having a break in the canteen with Naomi. Once she had finished her mug of tea, she was going to give up and send Mary home. Until her phone buzzed.

'Check this out,' she cried out, looking at the message.

The forensic team had just informed Ariadne that significant traces of Jay's DNA had been found on one of Mary's cushions.

'It seems he breathed and dribbled on it, consistent with it having been used to suffocate him,' Ariadne said. 'They'll send the full report in the morning, but they thought we would want to know straightaway. Too bloody right we want to know,' she added.

'So the murder weapon was a cushion,' Naomi said, and she laughed.

Together they returned to the interview room. A moment later, the constable brought Mary in, accompanied by the young lawyer.

'We know you suffocated Jay, and we know how you did it,' Ariadne began. 'So let's stop messing about, shall we?'

'May the Lord strike you down for saying such a thing,' Mary stuttered.

Quietly, Naomi explained the result of the forensic examination of Mary's cushions, and the old woman's expression altered as she listened. No longer crafty or cross, she looked frightened.

'It was a mercy killing,' she whispered.

Ariadne relaxed. They had their confession. But she still wanted to hear what Mary had to say.

'What do you mean, a mercy killing? Tell us what happened, Mary. You can confess now.'

She wondered whether the invitation to confess would act as a trigger to the religious woman, although they hadn't ascertained whether she was Catholic or Protestant, or followed some other religion. But that no longer mattered, because she was talking.

'I could hear he was in pain,' she said. 'I couldn't listen to that. Have you ever heard a grown man crying in pain? I suppose you have, in your line of work. I suppose it means nothing to you. But the Lord moved me to pity the man for his suffering. I knew it was the right thing to do, to put him out of his misery.' She fell silent, remembering, or possibly calculating whether she would be believed.

'You fetched a cushion, didn't you?' Ariadne prompted her.

'I told you, it was a kindness to save him from his earthly pain.'

'Even though you were sending him to burn in hell?' Ariadne murmured. 'So you suffocated your neighbour Jay?'

'Yes, I put a cushion over his face and pressed down on his nose and mouth until he stopped moving. He struggled at first, but it didn't last long. Then I went home and closed the door.' She looked up at Ariadne. 'I'm not sorry. It served him right. He was a sinful man and he kept me awake at night with all his noise. Many a time I wished he would go to the devil and now he has. The Lord is my witness, I was doing His will.'

Ariadne switched off the tape before pointing out that she doubted the Lord would appear as a witness in Mary's trial. 'God knows whether you feel any remorse for killing a fellow human being, but from where I'm sitting, I'd say you haven't repented at all. Still, you'll have plenty of time to reflect on your own sin when you're locked up in prison.'

The old woman seemed to crumple and she began to cry.

59

Not only was the investigation into the murders of Jay and Lauren over, but the team had also solved a third case from twenty years ago. Binita congratulated each member of the team individually as well as jointly. 'That's three murder cases we've successfully closed,' she crowed. Not only was the result of their hard work gratifying in itself, the outcome of the investigation would obviously not harm her career, and she was understandably pleased.

The officers involved were finishing their reports in an atmosphere of subdued jubilation. One of the three killers had ended his own life. Of the two remaining, one was in her eighties and increasingly frail. The sentencing judge might be lenient in view of the defendant's age and presumed confusion, but she would nevertheless stand trial. As for Carly, who had murdered Lauren with no extenuating circumstances, she would be found guilty and serve an appropriate custodial sentence. The investigating team had done well in arresting her. She had killed once, without any serious provocation, and there was no guarantee she would not do so again. They all felt the streets would be safer with her behind bars.

For once, the local media were full of praise for the police. '*Cold Case Solved by Hot Team*' one headline announced. '*York police keep the streets safe*' another said. The local television reporters were equally approving. Where recently they had been hypercritical, they were now positively sycophantic. Binita appeared on the Yorkshire news, wearing a dignified smile, and stressing how the successful outcome had involved many hours of dedicated work by a team of diligent officers.

'A team which you led,' the reporter added.

'Look at her, so smug now we've done all the work,' Naomi muttered.

'Let her enjoy her moment,' Ariadne replied. 'It was her career on the line, not yours, if we messed up.'

But there was still one person Ariadne wanted to speak to before she could feel satisfied the case was closed. Summoning her courage, she drove back to Walmgate and turned into Hope Street, on a journey that had become familiar to her. Approaching the front door, she hesitated, but it was now nearly two weeks since they had received news of Yiannis's death, and the initial period of mourning was over. Thalia might not have recovered sufficiently to want to talk to anyone, but Ariadne felt she had to try and speak to her once more, if only to express her condolences. An innocent bystander, Thalia had been witness to a series of devastating tragedies in her immediate family. With the death of her husband following the murder of their firstborn son, and now the suicide of her only other son, Thalia's story was as shocking as the Greek tragedies of ancient times.

The front door was opened by a woman wearing the customary black dress, black cardigan, thick black woollen stockings and stout black shoes. She smiled grimly at Ariadne as she let her in and accompanied her into the living room where Thalia was seated by herself.

'I've come to pay my respects,' Ariadne said.

Thalia looked up and mumbled her thanks.

'I'll be off then,' the woman who had opened the door said, as though she had been waiting for another visitor to arrive before she could leave.

Raising her eyes, Thalia nodded at the woman, and thanked her for visiting. Ariadne was relieved to find the grieving mother seemed to have recovered herself enough to function normally.

She was dressed in black, her hair was tidy and she appeared to be neatly turned out. Ariadne took a seat and expressed her condolences in a low voice.

'I only met Yiannis – I should say Georgios – recently,' she said, 'but he seemed to be a good man. Apart from—' She hesitated to mention the murder Georgios had committed, but Thalia understood at once what she meant.

'It was twenty years ago,' she protested feebly. 'That monster killed my son in front of his little brother. Georgios was only ten years old.' She let out a sob and pressed her fingers to her lips.

Ariadne felt sympathy for the other woman but, as a police officer, she could not condone what Georgios had done. 'He wasn't a child when he took the law into his own hands and carried out a revenge killing,' she responded gently.

'Who are you to judge my son?' Thalia cried out in a sudden burst of passion. 'Our pain was always raw. What difference can the passing of years make after such a loss? When we heard the monster had been freed from prison, Georgios was angry. He drank cheap wine to try and dull the pain, but pain like that never goes away. He was too drunk to know what he was doing when he ended the life of a monster who deserved only to die.' She paused for a second, remembering. 'My son, Georgios, was the hand of justice. Not for one moment did he regret his vengeance. He told me he had no choice, and I believed him.' She let out a pent-up sob. 'I still agree with him, but in the end he couldn't live with the knowledge of what he had done. "Where will it end?" he used to ask me. "Should I now be killed in my turn for what I did?" I tried to comfort him. I told him he had killed a monster. "But he was also a man," he would reply.' She sighed. 'I always knew this day would come. My Georgios was a good man. And perhaps it is for the best.'

'What do you mean?'

Thalia seemed terribly calm as she went on speaking, but tears streamed down her lined cheeks. 'We are island people.

Georgios could never have survived locked in a cell, day after day. And now, what is there left for me here?' She looked at Ariadne in mute appeal.

'What will you do?'

'I will return to Skyros, to my husband and my firstborn, and I will take Georgios with me,' she added fiercely. 'He will be reunited at last with his beloved brother and father, and I will tend their graves, and wait to join them.'

Ariadne was shaken by a renewed wave of pity for the grieving woman.

'Nico will take care of your affairs here,' she said. 'He can sell your properties and send you the money.'

Thalia let out a bark of laughter. 'What can I do with money now but buy fresh flowers for the graves of my loved ones?'

Muttering her condolences once more, Ariadne stood up. She saw no need to wait for the next visitor to arrive before leaving. Whoever sat by her side now, Thalia would always be alone.

'I still don't understand what made you suspect it was Mary who suffocated him,' Naomi said to Ariadne, as they were having a celebratory drink in the pub at the end of the day.

'I was wondering that as well,' one of their colleagues chimed in. 'She seemed so frail. It never occurred to anyone else that she could have been responsible for killing a man like Jay. What made you think it was her?'

Ariadne hesitated. 'Her legs seem frail and she's generally doddery, but the steps up to her front door are quite steep. If she's able to drag her shopping trolley up those steps, I thought it was possible she might have enough strength to suffocate Jay, especially after he'd been knocked out and dazed. It was just an idea, until the evidence confirmed it.'

It had actually been Geraldine who had first prompted Ariadne to consider whether Mary might have had sufficient strength to drag a full shopping trolley up the steps. Geraldine's observation had prompted Ariadne to question whether Mary might be guilty, which had led to the discovery of the unusual murder weapon. So, in a way, Geraldine was responsible for the successful outcome of the investigation. Nevertheless, Ariadne wasn't sure Geraldine would want anyone to know about her involvement. Added to that, Ariadne might acquire a reputation for being indiscreet if her colleagues found out she had been talking about the case to someone who was not technically a serving police officer. On balance, it seemed best to say nothing. As Geraldine had said, it wasn't about getting credit for solving the case, it was about serving justice.

60

'HOW DID YOU KNOW about the steps outside Mary's front door being so steep?' Ariadne asked Geraldine, the next time they met for their regular Chinese meal.

Geraldine looked embarrassed. 'I know I shouldn't have been poking around in a case that I wasn't working on, but one of the local papers mentioned that the victim lived in Penley's Grove. When I chanced to go for a walk along there, it wasn't difficult to spot the address where the murder had taken place. Police activity isn't exactly discreet.' She gave a shamefaced grin.

'Once those forensic tents go up, they're hard to miss,' Ariadne agreed, smiling. 'So, it was pure chance you happened to go for a walk in Penley's Grove?'

'Yes, well, anyway, I walked past the house and noticed the steps up to the front door and somehow that didn't quite tally with your description of the ground-floor tenant as physically frail. I just took a quick look in passing,' she added. 'Nothing more than that.'

Ariadne drew in a breath. 'But it was enough for you to notice those steps.'

'And that started me thinking.'

'It's lucky you did or we might never have searched Mary's flat.'

'Don't give me that. I didn't do anything. You're the one who kept investigating until you found the truth.'

'I never would have gone back there if you hadn't hinted at your suspicions about Mary,' Ariadne said. 'If you hadn't put me on to it, her cushions could have been binned before we checked them.'

Geraldine nodded. 'Cushions,' she murmured. 'I guessed it was something like corduroy, but I never would have thought of cushions. That was all down to you.'

Ariadne laughed. 'You'd have spotted them as soon as you set foot in her flat.'

Geraldine smiled. 'I suppose so. Anyway, what matters is that justice has been done, as far as it can be.'

Ariadne gazed at her friend. 'Not much justice for Jay or Lauren,' she said. Her thoughts drifted to a murder that had been carried out twenty years earlier, another revenge killing, and she thought about Lauren's nine-year-old brother, Dylan. 'When are people going to understand that taking the law into their own hands never works? I mean, where does it all end? What if someone had killed Carly as a punishment for Lauren's death? Would they have been killed in their turn?' She broke off with an exasperated sigh.

Geraldine nodded. 'The best we can hope for is that solving the case might deter someone else from trying their hand at murder. At least we have that. And maybe the bereaved families will feel that justice has been served.' She shrugged. 'I agree, it's not much, but it's all we can do.'

'So,' Ariadne said, sounding more cheerful, 'tell me about that little rascal of yours.'

'Who? Ian?'

They both laughed, and Ariadne felt her spirits lift.

'I miss you,' she said. 'When are you coming back?'

'That's assuming I want to come back.'

'Of course you do. Being a detective is what you are. You know that as well as I do. And you can tell Ian from me that there might be another murder if he thinks he can stop you returning to work.'

'I suppose,' Geraldine said, and she spoke very slowly, as though she was formulating the thought while she was speaking,

'I suppose life goes on in more ways than one when you have a baby.'

'Listen, I'm sorry if I've overstepped the mark, talking like this,' Ariadne said quickly. 'What you do is up to you, and it's none of my business. And if you're not happy about returning to work, that's between you and Ian and nothing to do with me.'

'There's nothing to apologise for,' Geraldine assured her. 'Quite the opposite, in fact. Discussing your investigation helped clarify my feelings, and I've decided to come back just as soon as I can finalise the arrangements for Tom.'

Ariadne grinned. 'It's not been the same without you. Although I was never really without you, was I? It was you mentioning Mary's shopping trolley that got me thinking.'

Geraldine raised her glass. 'We always did make a good team,' she said, smiling.

Acknowledgements

My thanks as ever go to the team at No Exit Press, Bedford Square Publishers: Polly Halsey for her invaluable help in production, Jem Butcher for his brilliant covers, Anastasia Boama-Aboagye and Abi Walton for all their enthusiastic marketing and PR, Jayne Lewis for her highly skilled copy editing and Nick Rennison for his eagle-eyed proofreading.

I am indebted to Jamie Hodder-Williams and Laura Fletcher at No Exit Press, Bedford Square Publishers, for their continuing faith in Geraldine Steel. It is a privilege to work with you and the team.

It's been quite a journey so far, and Geraldine Steel is not finished yet!

It amazes me that Geraldine and I have been together for fifteen years! My editor, Keshini Naidoo, has been with us from the beginning of the series, and I am very fortunate that her support for Geraldine remains as enthusiastic as ever.

My thanks go to all the bloggers and interviewers who have supported Geraldine Steel: and to everyone who has been kind enough to review my books. Your support is sincerely appreciated.

I am grateful to readers around the world for showing interest in Geraldine's career. I really hope you continue to enjoy reading about my detective.

Last but by no means least, my thanks go to Michael, who is always with me.

A LETTER FROM LEIGH

Dear Reader,

I hope you enjoyed reading this book in my Geraldine Steel series. Readers are the key to the writing process, so I'm thrilled that you've joined me on my writing journey.

You might not want to meet some of my characters on a dark night – I know I wouldn't! – but hopefully you want to read about Geraldine's other investigations. Her work is always her priority because she cares deeply about justice, but she also has her own life. Many readers care about what happens to her. I hope you join them, and become a fan of Geraldine Steel, and her colleague Ian Peterson.

If you follow me on Facebook or Twitter, you'll know that I love to hear from readers. I always respond to comments from fans, and hope you will follow me on **@LeighRussell** and **fb.me/leigh.russell.50** or drop me an email via my website **leighrussell.co.uk**.

To get exclusive news, competitions, offers, early sneak-peaks for upcoming titles and more, sign-up to my free monthly newsletter: **leighrussell.co.uk/news**. You can also find out more about me and the Geraldine Steel series on the No Exit Press website: **noexit.co.uk/leighrussellbooks**.

Finally, if you enjoyed this story, I'd be really grateful if you would post a brief review on Amazon or Goodreads. A few sentences to say you enjoyed the book would be wonderful. And of course it would be brilliant if you would consider recommending my books to anyone who is a fan of crime fiction.

I hope to meet you at a literary festival or a book signing soon!

Thank you again for choosing to read my book.

With very best wishes,

Leigh Russell

noexit.co.uk/leighrussell

About the author

Leigh Russell is the author of the internationally bestselling Geraldine Steel series, which has sold over a million copies worldwide. Her books have been #1 on Amazon Kindle and iTunes with *Stop Dead* and *Murder Ring* selected as finalists for The People's Book Prize.

www.leighrussell.co.uk

@LeighRussell

CREOLE SKETCHES

by

Lafcadio Hearn

Edited by Charles Woodward Hutson

With Illustrations by the Author

Zea Books
Lincoln, Nebraska
2022

ISBN 978-1-60962-223-7 paperback
ISBN 978-1-60962-224-4 ebook
doi: 10.32873/unl.dc.zea.1312

Zea Books are published by the
University of Nebraska-Lincoln Libraries.

Electronic (pdf) edition available online at
https://digitalcommons.unl.edu/zeabook/

Print edition available from Lulu.com at
http://www.lulu.com/spotlight/unllib

Contents

Introduction

Until the publication of his "Fantastics and Other Fancies" the work done by Lafcadio Hearn for the *Item* was utterly unknown. But those weird or dreamy sketches constituted but a small part of his work on that little journal. As assistant editor during the earlier years of his stay in New Orleans, he produced an immense number of editorials, translations, book reviews, dramatic criticisms, and sketches of all sorts, writing as he did for the paper every day, and not merely on Sundays, as was for the most part his custom in the case of his work with the *Times-Democrat* in the later years of his sojourn in this city.

The present volume contains a selection from his "Creole Sketches," together with a few other fanciful papers in a similar vein.

Partly because he was always deeply immersed in work or in study, partly on account of his natural shyness, he led in New Orleans the life of a recluse. Yet he had some friends, whom he greatly valued, and who still speak warmly of their intercourse with him. In one of his letters to Basil Hall Chamberlain, many years afterwards, he speaks of Charles Gayarré, the historian, as a "charming friend" of his. And in another letter to Chamberlain, in his remarks on modern Provençal, he says, "Some of my New Orleans friends used to speak it well." George W. Cable, the novelist, whose works he reviewed in the *Item* with enthusiastic praise, says that Hearn was a frequent visitor at his house, and that they profited by mutual frank criticism of each other's writings. Dr. Rudolph

Matas, the renowned surgeon, tells of intimate companionship with him during his stay in this city. Dr. Lucien Salomon, a physician of long-established reputation, states that he was introduced to him by Dr. Matas, and that, despite his eccentricities, he found him a "lovable fellow." We know that Hearn's lifelong friendship with Miss Elizabeth Bisland, now Mrs. C. W. Wetmore, began when they were workers together in the office of the *Times-Democrat*. During these later years, too, he was befriended by the Bakers, both Page and Marion, and the wife of the latter, known to literature as Julia K. Wetherell. He had friends, too, who were not so intellectual, but for whom his affection was great. One of these was Mrs. Courtney, his landlady through the later years of his sojourn in this city, to whom he wrote from time to time, during temporary absences, letters that prove how much he valued her kindness, and with whom he left that notebook which enables us largely to supplement his bibliography, hitherto confined to the lists set down in Dr. Gould's book.

It is true that many of these friendships date from a period subsequent to his connection with the *Item*. But during those earlier years he resided wholly in the Creole quarter of the city, and there he had large opportunities for studying Creole character and Creole customs. At this time Colonel John W. Fairfax, then owner of the *Item,* was, with the exception of George W. Cable, perhaps his only friend in the city. But he evidently soon made other friends, and those chiefly among persons more familiar with the Creole, than with the American, side of the city.

There are many marks by which his unsigned articles can be identified, among which not the least striking are certain peculiarities in punctuation. But the most noteworthy of all is the higher note, sometimes philosophic, sometimes romantic, to which he soars in every paper, whatever the subject. With him the touch artistic is always there: Journalism becomes Literature.

It should be noted, as a curious addendum to "La Douane," that the niches of the New Orleans Custom House are still empty of the figures that were destined in the original design to fill them. Can it be that they are still hidden away in some locked, and perhaps forgotten, room of that vast building?

"Eleusis" is an exquisite trifle, an accurate and detailed description of the toilet and dress of the ballet dancer, a fit companion-piece to "Les Coulisses" as an evidence of his intimacy with the inner secrets of the stage during his service as dramatic critic; — French in its lightness of touch, and dainty as the apparel of which it treats.

In "Some Positive Opinions" we have another and very different token of his experience when accorded the freedom of the greenroom.

The review of "The Grandissimes" — it is only one of several — is included as holding a close relationship with the sketches that are professedly Creole.

"The City of Dreams" depicts the result of the fateful yellow-fever epidemic of 1878 upon the smitten souls of the people. Fortunately science has forever rendered impossible the return of that heavy weight of woe that hung over the city in the year of which this

and many others of Hearn's more poignant sketches are memorials.

The Cartoons, done by his own hand, of which a few have been introduced, have been placed out of their chronological order for the purpose of distributing them through the book.

They were found in the *Item* files for 1880, and our suspicion that they, with the verses and, brief paragraphs accompanying them, were Hearn's was confirmed by a statement from Colonel Fairfax made to my daughter, Ethel Hutson, in 1913, and since corroborated by him. I append her account of his statements.

CHARLES WOODWARD HUTSON

Lafcadio Hearn's Cartoons

Lafcadio Hearn's first employer in New Orleans is still living— an active old gentleman of eighty-two, who may be found at his desk in the bank any day during business hours. He is Colonel John W. Fairfax, a veteran of the Confederate army, having gone into the war at the age of twenty; and he was a newspaperman of the sixties and seventies.

He was the owner of the *Daily City Item* when that paper gave Hearn his first employment in the city to which he came so enthusiastically in the winter of 1877-78, and where he so nearly starved before he got that job, in the summer of 1878.

"I remember Hearn very well, indeed," says Colonel Fairfax, "even that first day when he came to us for work. I am not sure whether he came to me in my office on Gravier Street, or whether Bigney — Mark F. Bigney, then managing editor of the *Item* — sent for me to come and see if we wanted to take him on.

"You see, Hearn was a most unprepossessing object at first sight. That odd rolling eye of his was the only thing you could see at first — enormous, protruding. After you got used to that eye, you saw that his other features were very good, and his face refined. But in addition, when he first presented himself here he was miserably dressed, and even his hands were grimy and his nails black.

"He had had a hard time, you see, since he had come down from Cincinnati; and one reason why Bigney hesitated about taking him on was that we had

heard that he had had to leave Memphis on account of his violent Republican ideas. Perhaps I oughtn't to tell that even now — but surely the war is over by this time. In those days, however, it was a serious thing in this part of the world, and it worked against Hearn.

"We took him on, though, and I had such a sort of sympathy for the poor fellow, who looked as if he hadn't had a good meal in months, and who seemed to feel keenly the way the boys treated him, on account of his Republican ideas, and his queer appearance and all that, that I asked him to come up to our house to dinner — not once, but again and again — twice a week, for a good while.

"Just the other day, my wife was recalling the time he first came. Dressed in a blue coat, linen trousers, his coat buttoned up to the throat to hide his shirt — 'wasn't he an odd sight?' said my wife. And shy? Why, that first meal he just sat and crumbled his bread — would scarcely eat a mouthful. Ours was a big family, and there were almost always guests; and until he got over his shyness we used almost to ignore him, going on with the family routine as if he were not there, to avoid embarrassing him.

"But when he got over that shyness, he was a charming talker; and we grew attached to him. My daughter used to tease him.

"He wrote editorials for the *Item*, but most of the political editorials were written by Bigney or by me. When, in the winter of 1881, the *Times-Democrat* offered him a place on its staff, we had to let him go, because we could not meet the offer. The *Item* then was only a two-page sheet."

Besides these editorials, and the occasional "Fantastics" which Hearn contributed to the *Item* between the summer of 1878 and the winter of 1881, a column of book reviews, called "Our Book Table," and a column of advice to young people, somewhat on the order of those of "Ruth Ashmore," "Dorothy Dix," and "Beatrice Fairfax," were conducted for many months by the pen which afterward wrote " Chita"! No wonder Hearn hated journalism.

Strangest of all, the young Irishman who was finding his *metier* through so many incongruous and distasteful tasks, drew a series of cartoons which appeared daily for more than half a year. They are quaint, grotesque, and crude, but many of them show the same weird suggestiveness to be seen in the odd little sketches with which he illustrated his letters to certain friends, and, like these, remind one of the drawings of Victor Hugo and of that artist whom Hearn so greatly admired, Gustave Doré.

Colonel Fairfax is authority for Hearn's authorship of these cartoons and the verses or prose sketches which accompanied them. In reply to queries about the articles to be ascribed to his queer protégé, the former owner of the *Item* said: "Hearn did not write the 'Wayside Notes' — that was my column. But I'll tell you what he did write — those verses illustrated with woodcuts. They were all Hearn's — his ideas, his verses, his drawings. He drew those cartoons — the first newspaper cartoons in this part of the country — and he cut them with his penknife on woodblocks — on the backs of old wooden types, which had been used for advertisements. They were just the

right height, you see, to fit into the bed — we used the old-fashioned flat-bed press, of course — and every day he would whittle out one of those drawings. Some of them were right interesting, too. You remember those about the old 'Magazine Market gang'? That was a gang of hoodlums that ruled all that part of the city, and the police were powerless. Hearn held them up to ridicule, in these cartoons — the hoodlums and the police — till something had to be done, and the police finally took hold and broke up the gang."

Many of the cartoons were political, a few on phases of national politics, for a Presidential campaign was at its height during the summer and fall of 1880, when this series appeared. Some were about the follies of the municipal officials, especially the Board of Health, whose futile efforts to control the yellow fever and other epidemics were bitterly attacked by the *Item* in those days.

But the majority of the cuts pictured quaint local customs, or else certain foibles of human nature which have neither season nor place. A dozen or so were devoted to the delineation of special public nuisances, under the head of "Illustrated Letters from the People," and anathematized the churl, the bore, the boy on "The Unspeakable Velocipede," and others whom the letter-writers objected to, as hostile to civic welfare or private comfort.

Some of these "letters" may have been contributed, though the drawings which illustrated them were Hearn's. Others must have been written by Hearn himself, for they are in his most extravagant style.

Colonel Fairfax says that it is possible some of the drawings may have been made by others, but he has no recollection of any one else but Hearn doing this: and he does remember him very distinctly, at work "with a penknife that had two blades, using first the large one and then the small one, to get the effect he wanted on the block."

The woodcuts we have chosen, out of the nearly two hundred which appeared between May 24 and December 10, 1880, have been selected because they illustrate the Creole life which fascinated Hearn in all its features — the "ultra-Canal" life which he ever preferred to the conventional uptown Americanized districts; the humble life of landladies and booksellers, of washerwomen and darkies selling clothes-poles; of queer old men haunted by "ghosteses," of flower-sellers and cemeteries, quacks and hoodlums.

ETHEL HUTSON

New Orleans
October 27, 1923

CREOLE SKETCHES

* *
*

The Glamour of New Orleans

Item, November 26, 1878

The season has come at last when strangers may visit us without fear, and experience with unalloyed pleasure the first delicious impression of the most beautiful and picturesque old city in North America. For in this season is the glamour of New Orleans strongest upon those whom she attracts to her from less hospitable climates, and fascinates by her nights of magical moonlight, and her days of dreamy languors and perfumes. There are few who can visit her for the first time without delight; and few who can ever leave her without regret; and none who can forget her strange charm when they have once felt its influence. To a native of the bleaker Northern clime — if he have any poetical sense of the beautiful in nature, any love of bright verdure and luxuriance of landscape — the approach to the city by river must be in itself something indescribably pleasant. The white steamer gliding through an unfamiliar world of blue and green — blue above and blue below, with a long strip of low green land alone to break the ethereal azure; the waving cane; the ever-green fringe of groves weird with moss; the tepid breezes and golden sunlight — all deepening in their charm as the city is neared, make the voyage

seem beautiful as though one were sailing to some far-off glimmering Eden, into the garden of Paradise itself. And then, the first impression of the old Creole city slumbering under the glorious sun; of its quaint houses; its shaded streets; its suggestions of a hundred years ago; its contrasts of agreeable color; its streets reechoing the tongues of many nations; its general look of somnolent contentment; its verdant antiquity; its venerable memorials and monuments; its eccentricities of architecture; its tropical gardens; its picturesque surprises; its warm atmosphere, drowsy perhaps with the perfume of orange flowers, and thrilled with the fantastic music of mocking-birds — cannot ever be wholly forgotten. For a hundred years and more has New Orleans been drawing hither wandering souls from all the ends of the earth. The natives of India and of Japan have walked upon her pavements; Chinese and swarthy natives of Manila; children of the Antilles and of South America; subjects of the Sultan and sailors of the Ionian Sea have sought homes here. All civilized nations have sent wandering children hither. All cities of the North, East, and West have yielded up some restless souls to the far-off Southern city, whose spell is so mystic, so sweet, so universal. And to these wondering and wandering ones, this sleepy, beautiful, quaint old city murmurs: "Rest with me. I am old; but thou hast never met with a younger more beautiful than I. I dwell in eternal summer; I dream in perennial sunshine; I sleep in magical moonlight. My streets are flecked with strange sharp shadows; and sometimes also the Shadow of Death falleth upon them; but if thou wilt not fear, thou art safe. My charms are not the

charms of much gold and great riches; but thou mayst feel with me such hope and content as thou hast never felt before. I offer thee eternal summer, and a sky divinely blue; sweet breezes and sweet perfumes, bright fruits, and flowers fairer than the rainbow. Rest with me. For if thou leavest me, thou must forever remember me with regret." And assuredly those who wander from her may never cease to behold her in their dreams — quaint, beautiful, and sunny as of old — and to feel at long intervals the return of the first charm — the first delicious fascination of the fairest city of the South.

La Douane

Item, December 2, 1878

That vast gray building on Canal Street, which seemeth ancient as Karnac, and upon which princely sums have vainly been expended in the foolish hope of completing it, has long troubled us with a strange impression difficult to analyze. A sense of weight and antiquity oppresses the beholder when he gazes upon it. Kinglake's nightmare of "solid immensity" may be realized by a careful study of it; and its loftiest portion affords an artistic effect of ruin — not the picturesque ruin of feudal remains, but ruin as of Egypt, vast and shadowy and dusty. It has been to the United States Treasury what the sieve was to the daughters of Danaüs. Rivers of gold have been poured into it; yet it remaineth as before. Its marble hall seems like the Pharaonic burial-chamber in the heart of the granite monument of Cheops; and its doors exhale in the most arid and burning weather a breath of damp chilliness, such as smites a mourner in the face when he opens the iron gates of a family vault. So weirdly does it seem to hint of Death and the Past that one cannot help wondering why its corridors are not hypogea and its offices filled with mummies. Without, in sooth, its very shape is ominous. It is, despite its windows and entrances, its pilasters and niches, a huge sarcophagus of granite. Its form is funereal; and against the dismal immensity of its exterior, the openings in its awful walls seem but as carvings upon some ancient stone coffin.

It is in very truth a sarcophagus, wherein repose the mummified remains of that which was once mighty, but not magnanimous; of that which was once rich, yet not honest; of that which once believed itself eternal and invulnerable, yet which expired like Herod of self-engendered corruption. Its corridors are indeed hypogea, filled with the mummies of Radical Pharaohs; and its marble hall a burial-chamber, empty, indeed, like that in the stony heart of the Great Pyramid, yet haunted by the ghost of that regime for which none are left to mourn.

But those empty niches in the great waste surfaces of the quadruple facade! Ah, those niches! — those niches! Why are they accursed with emptiness; why made hideous with vacuity? The statues of stone created to fill them were chiseled out a quarter of a century ago; and yet never have beheld the light of day. Their stone eyes have never gazed upon the glory of Canal Street; their marble ears have never hearkened to the gossip of politicians; their rigid forms have never left the enclosure of the wooden coffins into which they were first packed for importation. They sleep in the awful silence and darkness of the most dismal chamber in the whole gray building. They sleep, and the dust thickens upon their faces; and sometimes in the dead waste and middle of the night they do converse dismally together. They represent Faiths not worshiped under the old regime, Hopes that had failed, and Charities that would have been scorned; Virtues that had fled, or had hidden themselves in lonesome places; Saintly

Personages* who could not in those days have received respect; and Great Statesmen, perhaps, whose marble faces would have blushed into Egyptian granite, could they have seen that which was, but will never be again. And Radicalism, therefore, hid them away — not, indeed, out of consideration for their feelings, but out of consideration for its own. For it could not have endured the silent reproach of those eyes of marble, or dare to concoct plots within the reach of those ears of marble; and therefore the Faiths and the Virtues were cunningly hidden away where their presence could offend nobody. And now they ask, "When shall we be delivered from darkness and silence and oblivion? When shall the trumpet sound for our resurrection day? When shall we behold the great glory of the Southern sun and the splendor of Canal Street? Better even with broken noses to stand on our pedestals, better even to lose several of our Carrara limbs than this." But the silence and the darkness and the dampness remain; and echo answereth nothing.

* We might be mistaken, perhaps, in regard to the symbolic character of some of the Custom-House statues; for no living man of this generation hath a memory sufficiently strong to remember the day of their coming or the description which accompanied them.

Morning Calls — Very Early

Item, July 7, 1880

Pitis sans papa, pitis sans maman!
Qui ça ou z'aut' fé pou' gagnin l'arzan!
N'a couri l'aut'bord, pou' cerce pat sat,
N'a tournein bayou pou'pece patassa,
Et v'la comme ça n'a té pou' l'arzan.

Pitis sans papa, pitis sans maman,
Qui ça ou z'aut' fé pou' gagnin l'arzan!
N'a couri dans bois fouille latanie,
N'a ven so racin pou' fourbe planche,
Et v'la comme ça n'a te fé pou' l'arzan.

Pitis sans papa, pitis sans maman,
Qui ça vous z'aut' fé pou' gagnin l'arzan!
Pou' fé di té n'a fouille sassafras,
Pou' fe li l'encr' n'a porte grain salgras (chou-gras),
Et v'la comme ça ne te fé pou' l'arzan.

Pitis sans papa, pitis sans maman,
Qui ça ou z'aut' fé pou' gagnin l'arzan!
N'a couri dans bois ramasse caucos,
Avé non la caze n'a trapé zozos,
Et v'la comme ça n'a te fé pou' l'arzan.

Pitis sans papa, pitis sans maman,
Qui ça ou z'aut' fé pou' gagnin l'arzan!
N'a couri a soir chez Mamzell Maroto,
Dans la rie Ste Anne, ça n'a té sous leto,
Et v'la comme ça n'a te fé pou' l'arzan.

The above ancient Creole ditty contains some curious information about the occupations which some of our old-fashioned colored Creoles alone follow, and of which they alone know the Secrets. We are indebted therefor to a gentleman of this city who has made a rich collection of these songs.

The City of Dreams

Item, March 9,1879

Latterly it has been said that if New Orleans has any special mania which distinguishes it from other cities, it is the mania of "talking to one's self." It were useless to deny so widely recognized a fact as the propensity of people in New Orleans to perambulate their native streets conversing only with themselves. And strangers visiting us have said: "The people of New Orleans are inclined to madness; they converse continually with themselves, which is a sign of insanity." Is it that the people are being driven mad by stupid legislation and business losses and outrageous taxes? God only knows! But they do talk either to themselves or to viewless beings or to the sleepy shadows that fling jagged bits of darkness across the streets on sunny days.

They are comparatively many, these lovers of solitary musing; and usually seek the quiet of the most deserted streets — those streets to which the Secret Police of the East give the ominous name of *dead streets*. Perhaps one might say as well, *streets of the dead*.

At one time we took a special interest in watching those wandering and murmuring spirits. They are of various ages; but most generally advanced in years. The action of the younger men or women is usually quick and nervous; that of the older, slow and meditative. The former often speak angrily as if brooding over some wrong; the latter, rather in sorrow than in anger. All of which is quite natural and to be expected from those who talk to themselves.

What do they talk about?

That is a matter not always easy to find out. The hard echo of a brisk footstep on the pavement, even the sudden fluttering of a leafy shadow, seems often sufficient to break the reverie; the speaker looks about him like one awakened from a dream, gazes with a half-timid kind of suspicion at those who pass by, as if fearing to have been overheard; and walks off at a quicker gait. To study the character of these people perfectly, one must wear rubber shoes.

It would be cruel to wear india-rubber shoes for such a purpose; it would also be despicable. Therefore we cannot fully answer the question —

What are they talking about?

But occasionally the most innocent passer-by cannot fail to catch a word or two — sometimes strangely full of meaning, sometimes meaningless. We have heard such words. Occasionally vast sums of money were mentioned — billions, quintillions! — a sure sign that the speaker was financially stripped, and had little hope of favors from the goddess Fortuna. Sometimes we heard odd curses — men cursing themselves, and others, nameless places and nameless people, unknown memories and unknown misfortunes. Sometimes they spoke cheerfully, and laughed to themselves softly; — but this was seldom, very, very seldom.

Before the epidemic we fancied that the majority of these conversations with airy nothings were upon the subject of money. Indeed, most of the fragmentary mutterings which reached us seemed related to dreams of wealth — wild, vague, and fantastic — such dreams as are dreamed by those who have lost all and

hope for nothing, but who seek consolation in the splendor of dreams of the Impossible.

Then came the burning summer with its burning scourges of fever; — under the raw, merciless, dizzy sunlight, and the pitilessly clear infinite of warm blue above, the mutterers still wandered the silent streets, seeking out the bits of shadow, as Arabs oases in a world of yellow sand; — and they talked more than ever to themselves and to the shadows, to the vast void above and to the whispering trees that drooped in the mighty heat.

So the months rolled dryly and fiercely by; the sun rose each day with the same glory of angry heat; and the sky glowed each evening with the glare of molten brass. And the talkers became fewer; but they seemed to talk much more than they ever had before done. They talked to the black streamers that fluttered weirdly at the handles of muffled bells, and to ghostly white things hung to cottage doors and to the long processions that rumbled ominously toward the Places of Tombs.

Sometimes it seemed that one heard a sound of sobbing — stifled sobbing; as if a man were swallowing a bitter grief with bitter determination — but this was perhaps imaginary; for there were so many strange sounds in that strange summer that no one could well trust his ears.

The summer waned; and yet it seemed at last as though the number of those who talked to invisible things became greater. They *did* become greater in number. There was no doubt of it remaining before the first cold wind came from the far North, boisterous

and wild as though suddenly freed from some Arctic enchanter. And the numbers of the mysterious ones waxed greater.

Then at intervals their words fell upon our ears; and it seemed that the character of them had undergone a change — no longer expressing ideas of wealth. They had ceased to speak in our hearing of money. They spoke of the dead — and muttered remembered words uttered by other tongues — and asked information from waving shadows and white walls regarding people that God only knows anything about.

Perhaps they remembered that the only witnesses of some last interview were the same white walls and waving shadows. And the shadows lay there at just the same angle — well, perhaps, the angle was a little sharper — and they were waving just as dreamily as then. And perhaps a time might come in which all Shadows that have been must answer all questions put to them.

Seeing and hearing these things, we somehow ceased to marvel that some people dwelling in the city of New Orleans should speak mysteriously and hold audible converse with their own thoughts; forasmuch as we, also, dreaming among the shadows, spoke aloud to our own hearts, until awakened by an echo of unanswered words.

Ultra-Canal

Item, July 17, 1880

"Is the old man in?"

"Ah! de ole man! He not been live here since more as tree year. He have lef all his furnizer here; but I not know vat him become. I tink vat he lose himself."

"Lose himself?"

"Yes, I tink he lose to himself. Monsieur not speak Français? No? *Eh bien* I make try you explain, zough I not good English speak.

"You see, he have to him ze brain attack, I zink, of recent. He lose vat to him belong. Some time he lose coat, some time pant, some time shirt,— all time night-key. I vas oblige for him order more as tirteen night-key, for vat I make him to pay. He live in one kind of dream — *il s'embêtait* — he embeast himself much

— he seem all day like vat you call *sonambule*."

"Yes, yes! well?"

"*Eh bien!* — some time he put on tree pair pant. Some time on hot day he put him on ze overcoat. One day I see him try to put on to him ze pant for ze shirt. He have put to him ze arm in ze leg of ze pant; an' he swear *sacre roucht* for dat he not could put on —"

"Yes, I understand. But what has become of him?"

"*Attendez un peu.* I tell one. One oder day he not have any clothes on, an' he try to find his key, an' he swear at tailor for *sacre charogne* for dat he not have made him pocket vat he can easy find. He forget vat he not be dress. Den he lose to him money all time vat make him angry much. One time he take by mistake coat vat not to him belong, and take it to tailor for dat he put tail to it; an' he has to pay to de oder man, of wich he spoil de coat."

"Yes. But where is —"

"Vait — I explain you. He lose everyting — handchef, towl, pockbook, monee, key — all time. One domestique he employ only for find vat he los'; and domestique run himself away, for dat he not more can so hard work endure."

"But, for God's sake, what has become of him?"

"Monsieur, I not can you tell. He go out one morning, and I not have hear or see of him after. His furniser an' all be in my house. He have pay of advance. He owe me notings. He have not ever come back. No one have see or hear. I be satisfy vat himself he lose — like as he lose every oder ting — vat he lose never more find. Veil, he lose to himself. He never more himself find. *Que voulez-vous?*"

A Creole Type

Item, May 6, 1879.

It is a little curious how the old Creole element preserves its ancient customs and manners in the very heart of the changes that are going on about it. At half-past nine or ten o'clock the American city is all alive — a blaze of gas and a whirl of pleasure. The old French town is asleep; the streets are deserted; and the shadow of a pedestrian makes a moving black speck against the moonlight on the pavement only at long intervals. Creoledom wakes up as slowly and cautiously as possible; and has not fairly begun to enter upon the business of the day until the sun has warmed the streets. The comparatively new generation of American citizens, when brought into contact with this older population, is utterly unable to understand the difference of character; and shuns as much as possible the transaction of business with it — which contents the Creoles perfectly well. They seem to tolerate those who understand them, and to abominate those who do not, and propose to live in the good old way as long as possible — marrying and giving in marriage, aiding one another in a good brotherly way, and keeping themselves to themselves. If there is one virtue they possess remarkably, it is the virtue of minding their own affairs — which, alas! cannot always be said of all other people who dwell in New Orleans.

Nothing, perhaps, can be funnier than the contrast of character brought out by the attempt of a stiff-mannered stranger to do business with a typical Creole,

especially if the latter be of the fair sex. Let us imagine, for example, the episode of renting a house to a foreigner — somebody whom chance or curiosity has prompted to seek quarters in the old-fashioned part of the city. The stranger is a little phlegmatic; the woman is as much the opposite as any human being could well be — a little dark, tropically dark, but quite attractive, with magnetic eyes, an electric tongue, and an utter indifference to those ordinary feelings which prompt landladies to play the agreeable; — proud as a queen, and quite as determined to show her own individuality as the stranger is to conceal his own. She has a nice little house; and the stranger would like to rent it. She would also like to rent it; but only according to her own original idea of conditions, and she would never think of concealing her inmost feelings on the subject. She is determined that nobody shall impose upon her, and that fact she proposes to explain very forcibly forthwith; the stranger appears to be a good sort of man, but appearances are so deceitful in this wicked world!

She — "Ah, yes, monsieur, I have a nice little house. Let me beg of you to wait a moment until I open the other door, so that you can enter my parlor."

He — "But what is the rent of the house?"

She (in a voice sweeter than the sweetest honey) — "One minute! — this way, monsieur — come in; be seated, if you please."

He — "But what is the rent of —"

She (shutting the door, and placing herself before it like a statue of animated bronze, and suddenly changing the sweet voice for a deep and extraordinarily

vibrant alto) — "Ah, now, monsieur, let us at once understand one another. I have a nice little house. Good! You want a nice little house. Good! Let us understand one another. In the first place, I do not rent my house to everybody, monsieur. Oh, no, no, No!!" (*crescendo*).

He — " But what is the rent of —"

She (imperiously, terrifying him into silence with a flash of her black eyes) — "Do not interrupt me, monsieur. Three things I require from a tenant. Do you know what the first is? No? — then I will tell you. Cash, Cash, CASH! (*crescendo*) — right here in my hand — in advance— ah, yes, all the time in advance."

He (very timidly) — "Yes, certainly — I know — of course! — I expected; — but what is —"

She (in a voice like the deepest tone of a passionately agitated harp) — "Attends, donc, monsieur. The second thing which I require from a tenant is a guarantee that he will stay. Ah, yes! I am not one of those who rent houses for a week, or a month, or six months. Mon Dieu, non! I must have people who STAY, STAY, STAY (pianissimo); and they must stay a long, long time. You must not come to me if you want a house only for —"

He (with a last and desperate effort, which happens to be partially successful) — "O madam, I want to stay for a number of years in the house, if I take it; but I cannot take it until I have seen it."

She — "You shall see it, monsieur, you shall see it (parenthetically). Now the third thing which I require from a tenant is absolute cleanliness, absolute, absolute! No spitting on the walls, no dirt upon the doors, no grease upon the planking, no cochonnerie in the

yard. You understand me, monsieur? Yes! — you shall see the house: these are the keys."

He —"But what is the rent of —"

She (frightening him into motionlessness by a sudden gypsy-like gesture) — "Ah, monsieur, but I cannot trust you with these keys. No; my servant shall go with you. I cannot have all the doors of my house left open. No; I have had too much experience. My servant shall go with you. She shall bring me back my keys. Marie! come here! Go, monsieur, see the house!"

He (resignedly) — "Thanks, but may I ask what is —"

She (with a superb gesture of withering disgust and another of terrible determination) — "Do you not know, sir, that I would rather shut the house up until the last day of the world than rent it to the canaille! Ah! the canaille! Monsieur! Ah! the canaille, the canaille!"

(These last words, with an inexpressible look of horror upon her face, which would make the stranger laugh if he were not afraid to laugh.)

He—"And the rent is —"

She (sweetly as a rose-fed nightingale) — "Twenty-five dollars to a responsible party, monsieur."

The stranger is by this time fairly mesmerized. He has listened to a sermon, heard an oration, received a reproof, watched a most marvelous piece of natural acting by a beautiful woman, and felt his own will and purpose completely crushed out of him by the superior vitality and will-power of this wonderful creature, whose gestures, graceful as a bayadère's, seemed to weave a spell of magnetism about him. He sees the house; pays faithfully in advance; gives proper

recommendations; and never forgets the three requisites which his landlady taught him as forcibly as though she had burned the words into his brain with a red-hot iron.

GHOSTESES

Item, August 18, 1880

Midnight in an Ultra-Canal Pension.

You not know vat be dat noise of foots up de stair. Dat be de ole man vat die in my house ago ten year.

I see him now in my t'ought, 'sleep in ze berceuse; afraid to go to his room for cause of vat you call *farfadet*— goblin and ghosteses.

He vas very, very old, and he see always of tings vat not exist. He be much torment by goblin and ghosteses vat valk all roun' de house in de night; an' he say it vas one curssed house and one curssed city. He tell me dat people dressed like vas dress since one hoondred year come in his room in de middle of de night;

dat he lock de door but not could dem keep out; dat dey sit silent and make at him face horrible and not speak and not make shadow on de door.

Den he commence to us avake. In de middle of de night he knock at mine door and say, — " Monsieur, mount to my room for dat dere be one man dead in my chamber." So I mount and look and not see no man dead. "He go himself away," say de ole man, "for dat he hear you on stair. But have made stop my clock and my vatch." And I see dat de clock and de vatch not more march, — I not know how.

After dat he often tell me vat dere be in his bed dead vomans; and dat dead beoples him look at trough de vindow. So he become afraid more to bed go, and ven he mount he not himself sleep, but valk all night on de gallery, one lantern in his hand, and shoes all vat be of mos' heavy for drive away ghosteses — ta-ta-tata-tatata — all de long of de night. Much also he sing in de night and swear for dat dis be one curssed country of ghosteses. Also he swear at proprietor of house; for dat he not chase ghosteses.

So it arrive at las' dat not person in de house could himself to sleep go, and dat all de vorld begin to dem-selves much fatigue. Den dey construct one goblin of vatermelon and inside one candle light; and dey it put on stick and one sheet of bed to make look like fan-tome. So it come to arrive dat ven de ole man march himself he see one goblin march more horrible dan he have before ever see. So he let fall his lantern — vat cost tirteen dollar —, and try to descend stair for me avake for dat I chase him de goblin. But he fall de top to bottom of stair, and make himself much of hurt.

Never again he not speak and soon he be dead, and no person much sorry himself. But it vas much vicked!

It ten year since he be dead; but all de night he march like he march oder time. No one afraid; de ghost of de ole man not make much hurt to personne!

A Visit To New Orleans

Item, May 10, 1879

The Devil arrived at New Orleans early yesterday morning, having left his winter residence in Chicago at midnight. There was little need, he thought, to bother himself further about Chicago during the present summer, as he holds a mortgage upon that city, which has at present no prospect of being able to prevent him from foreclosing.

Sensitive to the beauties of Nature, — a trait for which he has ever been famous since that primeval morning when, hiding in the leafy shadows of Paradise, be beheld fair Eve admiring the reflection of her snowy limbs in the crystal waters of Gehon, — the Devil could not suppress a sigh of regret as he gazed with far-reaching eyes along the old-fashioned streets of the city, whose gables were bronzed by the first yellow glow of sunrise. "Ah!" he exclaimed, "is this, indeed, the great City of Pleasure, the Sybaris of America, the fair capital which once seemed to slumber in enchanted sunlight, and to exhale a perfume of luxury even as the palaces of the old Caesars? Her streets are surely green with grass; her palaces are gray with mould; and her glory is departed from her. And perhaps her good old sins have also departed with her glory; for riches are a snare, and gold is a temptation." And the Devil frowned anxiously, and his deep eyes glowed under his brows even as smouldering charcoal glows in the shadows of night.

The Devil had not been in New Orleans since the period of Reconstruction — a period at which, our readers may remember, it was proverbially said that New Orleans was "going to the Devil." Such also appears to have been the Devil's own personal opinion. He found things in such a condition about that time that he had not been able to find room in his voluminous breast-pockets for all the mortgages which he had obtained upon men's souls; and believing, from the mad career of Radicalism, that the whole city must be made over to him in the course of a few years, he had departed elsewhere in search of employment. "They have no need of me," said the Devil, "in the State of Louisiana."

The history of the overthrow of Radicalism, however, which the Devil read in the *Chicago Times,* filled him with consternation. He had a gigantic job on his hands in Chicago, and could not just then afford to leave Illinois, for reasons which we have at the present writing no need to specify. But the rumor of a reform in politics in Louisiana, and a just government, pleased him not at all; and he felt exceedingly anxious to visit the Crescent City. It happened, however, that he could not get away until the midnight between the death of Thursday and the birth of Friday. And, moreover, the Devil has private reasons for objecting to travel on Friday.

The odor of the gutters displeased him as he walked down Saint Charles Street, and he stopped his nose with a handkerchief bearing a pattern border of green skeletons and red cupids intertwined upon a saffron ground. "Poverty and dirt are sometimes virtuous,"

said the Devil, as he proceeded on his way. At the next corner he bought all the papers of the previous day. He put the *Picayune* in his pistol-pocket; cursed the *New Orleans Bee* and the *City Item,* and, flinging them back upon the dealer's stand after a brief examination of their contents, he folded up the other papers in a bundle for future reference. "There is too much virtue in the press, I am afraid," said the Devil; "the *Picayune* is the only paper which suits me."

The police stations were next visited; and the Devil smiled a ghastly smile. "I have no fault to find with the police," he said; "and that reminds me that my own police force below is getting disorganized. I'll have to recruit in New Orleans."

An examination of the records in the Auditor's office tickled him, until he exploded in an abysmal laugh — a series of bass notes singularly like the famous laugh of Mephistopheles in *Faust*. "Why, this system is almost as good as Radicalism," he said. "Forty-five thousand dollars for running an Auditor's office!"

He next read the order of the Mayor to the colored churches, and nodded his head approvingly. "Good enough in its way," he said.

By twelve o'clock he had visited all the public institutions; — the Sanitary Association highly displeased him; but the Board of Health put him into an uproarious good humor. "I was a fool to come down here at all," he said; " this Board of Health can do my work better than I can do it myself, and the people seem to be just fools enough to let them do it. Instead of honest poverty, I find vicious poverty; instead of reform, demoralization; instead of law, I find lawyers; instead

of justice, oppression. What Carnival King ever found a city so well prepared for him? I guess I shall leave at once; for I have no work to do as yet in Louisiana."

But before leaving, the Devil took a notion to alight upon the top of the State House to watch the Convention. He listened for several hours to the proceedings, much to his own surprise; and it was nearly three o'clock before he knew it.

"Half-past two o'clock on Friday," muttered the Devil; "and I have to be in Pandemonium by a quarter to three. I don't quite like the state of affairs in that old hotel; but I doubt if the situation really demands my presence; I think I shall send a subaltern up to the Convention; for the Devil's interests are not sufficiently represented. But I shall not come back here for twenty years. What is the use of staying in a city that is going just where I am going? Besides, if anything serious happens, my representative can inform me. They have an embargo on reform here, it seems to me — just as they have on commerce. After all, New Orleans in 1879 is not very much holier than New Orleans in 1866. I guess I'll adjourn."

And he adjourned, after having copied the word "Choppinism" into his new *Dictionnaire Infernale.*

Quack! Quack!

Item, August 20, 1880

Quack! Quack! I am on the rack.
  You promised to end my pain;
For a little wealth you'd restore my health
  You said; yet here I've lain
For weary weeks and for mournful months,
  With pangs that are only known
To the tortured victim of the Quack,
  When his faith to the winds has flown.

Death's shadow falls on my barren walls,
  It sleeps on my chamber floor.
Its marrowless bones mock at my groans.
  And point to the shining shore,

While a jeering, mocking, ugly grin
  Spreads over its fleshless face
At a double triumph — the Quack's success,
  And the Quack's supreme disgrace.

Complaint of Creole Boarding-House-Keeper

Item, September 27, 1879

O la canaille! la canaille! All time after dis I will make dem to pay in advance.

De first dat I have, say he vas a capitaine. I know not if he vas a capitaine; but he vas a misérable. After he have eat and sleep here six week and not pay me, I tell him, " Monsieur, I must money have."

He say: "Madame, you take me for tief?"

I say: "Monsieur, it is right dat you pay; I have wait long time assez."

He den say: "I learn you how to speak me in a manner so much insolent. *Now,* I not pay you till when I be ready, and I not hurry myself."

"Go out from my house!" I say.

"I go out, madame, from your dirty house when it me please" — dat how he speak me. And I could not force him to part till when I had take all de furniture out from his room. He owe me not more as seventy dollaire!

... After, I have one Frenchman, I tink him well elevated — le coco. He nail his valise on de floor for make me tink heavy; and he dispar one night — owing me forty-nine dollaire! I find noting in his valise only one *syringe.*

... After, I have two married. Dey pay me enough well, until when de woman run away wit some oder man. Her husban' stay till when he owe me eighty dollaire, After, he go too; and write me letter as dis:

"Madame, I cheat you of eighty dollaire; and I not wish only I could cheat you of eighty thousand dollaire. It was for cause of you dat my wife have run away."

After, I find out she was not his wife.

... Den I have a sick man. He fall on de banquette in face of my house, and I take him in to nurse. When dat he get well he tell me he vas one professor of langedge. He eat and sleep here four mont; and first he pay a little. He complain much from noise. He vas what you call nerveux — so like I was oblige for to make my daughter walk witout shoes in naked foots; and we to speak in dumb and deaf langedge by fear of make him trouble. He smoke in de bed and burn de cover; also he break de pot and de cradle-chair, and after, de window, an' de armoire an' de — vat you call de pendule; — he let fall ink on de carpet, and he spit tobacc' on de wall, and he vomit in de bed. But I noting say, as he not 'ave baggage; — ainsi, wen he owe me forty dollaire I not want turn him out for dat I get my money more late. When at de end I tell him to go out, he tell me he have receive a checque and pay me on Monday. But I nevaire see him after. He owe me one hundred and sixty-seven dollaire — and seventy cent vat I lend him for medicine to buy.

... After, I have one woman, species of camel (espèce de chameau) and one doctor, her husband (tout ce qu'il y avait d'abominable). She pretend to be — and you call dat? — sage femme; and he is not so much doctor as my cat; but for all dey doctor me for two hundred and fifty dollaire, and I not ever obtain of it not one sou.

... After, I have tree familee — all vat vas of rough and ugly; for one mont I not receive of rent. So I serve to dem notice of quit. But dey tell me dey not me pay nevaire, and not quit until when I make law-suit. Eh bien, de rent of de house vas not more as fifty dollaire, and de law cost me perhaps one affair of more like one hundred dollaire. Ainsi, I quit de house, an' leave dem all dere to do like dey would please. But before dat I could leave, dey steal me two buckets, and one stove, and one broom, and one clock, and one iron, and one coffee-mill, and one hen, and one leetle cat vat I much vas fond of, and one plate, and some linen of womans vat to me not belong.

The Boarder's Reply

Item, September 28,1879

Est-ce que vous vous fichez de moi? 'cré nom! No: I not no more pay my rent in advance, because dat I have not of fait in permanence of businesses in Orleans.

Wen I am first come I take myself a room in de Rue Bourgoigne. Dey have in first floor one bear, one parrot, and two macacs and several of cats of Malta; and wen dat I enter myself to pay my rent, I see all dat to move itself about inside. De woman was of color — vat you call one mulatresse — and I pay in advance — like one animal!

After vat I have live in de house six week, I not to her owe noting, but she me owe one affaire of ten piastres more as my rent vat I ever pay in advance; — for dat she me come near every day for borrow one quarter of piastre or one half of dollaire, or two dollaire, and she smile and make so many funny bêtises dat I not could her noting refuse. After dat I be dere two mont, she owe me two mont of room in more as I have her pay in advance.

After a little of time I not see more de little beasts; — she have sell de macacs and de bear for herself obtain money. And I vas well content dat de parrots not dere vas more; — it vas true little demons vas not allow to nobody to repose himself.

One night I not come home until twelve past, and I not hear noting of noise. After I enter into my room, and I find noting inside — no bed, no chaise, no armoire — noting only my linen-dirty and my blue

trouser-old. All de house empty; all de rooms naked — personne in its inside. She not have not pay her rent — so, by consequence, dey seize demselves de furniture and have clean out de house — of such way as I find myself have to sleep on one floor much hard and all vat dere vas of dirty. And never again I not noting see of de woman of color vat owe to me near twenty of dollaire.

... But I stay in de house, for one oder woman of color enter in morning; and she have much of furnitures. I explique myself to her, and she tell me in Creole — "To s'ré resté 'vec moue, mo to donné belle chamb' garni asteur, pou' même prix."* And I myself dere install. She ask me dat I pay in advance; and I not like for refuse, like I not have time for look for more rooms. C'est égal, say to myself I.

Sometime she clean well my room; and sometime she not it clean not of all. Sometime she permit to strange mens of color dat dey enter my room; and dey permit demselves to lie upon my bed wen dat I was out in way to make a walk. I not was content; but could noting do, for dat I have pay in advance.

One day she desire to buy a miroir, and she ask me dat I pay, for dat she not have of money; and she tell me her husband me pay wen he have de Saturday next arrive. I so pay, like one kind of beast vat I be; and

---

* Editor's Note: The Gumbo, or Creole, given above may best be rendered into the Gullah of our English-speaking coast thus:

"You be stay wid me, me gib yo' fine fuhnish' room now-now, fuh same price."

before dat come de Saturday, one sheriff take all vat vas in all de house; and I not vas able, never already, to obtain vat she me owe. Also I since inform myself for as she had noting of one husband.

... I be myself disgusted; and I take myself room in house of one white woman, de vat me ask dat I pay in advance. After, she not me well treat. She take from out my room one cradle-chair and much more of furniture, de vat she say vas not put inside but for ornamente. She have children vat tear my book, and one locataire steal my trouser, and one steal tobacco, and one steal my soap. Never I could myself keep a little of soap. I have dere one essuiemains for more as two week.

I pay first of mont after. Second of mont I come home, and I see a — vat you call vente à l'encan; and one woman come to have take away my book — one affair of fifty book. Never can I arrive to procure again de money to me, nor even to find where live de woman vat have take my book.

... One time of more I pay in advance. De lady was of France, and she had de face beautiful and de heart good. She not me treat but too much well. I have rest in her house forever; but I not rest long. I pay my rent ever de fifteen of mont. I pay de fifteen of Avril. De sixteen, she die quick of vat you call mort subite. Never I see in it-not-matter-what-oder-country of tings pareille. Not again do I be so much beast for in advance to pay.

Coming Events Cast Their Shadows Before

Item, August 19, 1880

It will come sooner or later; but the parties who should be most interested in such matters do not pay any attention to the shadows of coming events. The Widow with Wooden Legs, as the Spaniards call the Gibbet, is waiting to celebrate her nuptials with some of our hoodlums; and yet the latter do not seem to know it. A long time has elapsed since the Widow was last married here, although the number of fellows who ought to have been married to her by force is legion. She is becoming tired of widowhood; and this is leap year. She is going to propose pretty soon; and when she proposes it will be no use to try backing out.

Why Crabs Are Boiled Alive

Item, October 5, 1879

And for why you not have of crab? Because one must dem boil 'live? It is all vat is of most beast to tell so. How you make for dem kill so you not dem boil? You not can cut dem de head off, for dat dey have not of head. You not can break to dem de back, for dat dey not be only all back. You not can dem bleed until dey die, for dat dey not have blood. You not can stick to dem troo de brain, for dat dey be same like you — dey not have of brain.

A Creole Journal

Item, October 5, 1879

I read to you of my journal-book — how he do:

Jan. 1 — Mon cher, lend to me one little affaire of ten dollaire, and I pay de 1st, wit good intress. Ah! you be good friend. I be possess of money; but for now I have of de expenses large.

Feb. 1 — Mon ami, I much sorry for dat I not can you pay to-day; but soon I you pay wit grand intress. One mus' not ever angry himself for ten dollaire.

March 1 — Mon bonhomme, I not can you pay, not wen as I have of money. You be too much of impatient. I much sorry for dat I ever ask of you money.

April 1 — Monsieur, I not have ever suppose dat you like more one miserable ten dollaire as my friendship. I not ever more ask of you one faveur. I not like you speak me so.

May 1 — For wat you lend me money like one Imbecile? I more like owe one tousand dollaire as ten — for dat I more be respected. I be tramped upon for dat I owe one dirty ten dollaire. You be pay some one day.

June 1 — You are one Insolent! If suppose for dat I do owe to you one miserable dollaire! Is it dat you are one beggar and have of hunger, for dat am I to be ask all time? You take me as one Imbecile? Not have I tell you I pay wen I can? I not will myself suffer more to be insult for one dirty dollaire.

July 1 — To-morrow I can you pay. I hope to ask dat you do me one little faveur — to ask dat friend to you

dat he give me one place like collecteur or secretaire.

August 1 — I not pay until wen I can one place obtain.

September 1 — I not pay until wen sugar come in de market.

December 1 — I not pay ever at all. I not you noting owe. I not suffer dat I be eternal ask for money. I not speak you not more. Go to devvel for you ten dollaire, for dat I not slap you de visage.

The Restless Boarder

Item, October 27,1879

He come to me fust of de mont, an' say, "Madame, I must another room; I not can live in dat for de noise abominable vat make dose infants." And I reply him, "Monsieur, choose yourself vat room mos' you like."

Den he tell me to get him arrange one room on t'ird floor. I get room right morning. Evening he say, "Madame, I not can take dat room; I take back oder." So I change him de tings well more.

Next week he say, "Madame, I must anoder room obtain; I not can suffer more de noise of devils vat dose infants make." So I arrange room on fourt floor. In de evening he tell me his mind be change — dat he not more want dat oder room. So I have all for to move back again.

After, he come to me de t'irte-et', and say, "Madame, you get to me one oder room, dat for I not leave de house. No more can I suffer de noise infernal and outrajeous vat make dose infants detestable." I say, " Monsieur, take vonce vat room you deseer, and leave me tranquille."

He den take room on front floor; but in middle night he go down gentle de stair and put all tings up-downside, and go back in ole room. Den in de morning he tell my domestique to him aid, an' for more as five hour dey walk up de stair an' down de stair carr'ing much of valise an' of trunk an' of ole pantalons an' of washing-basin an' of pillow — and of pot. De vat me disguss.

At de end all at sudden he take oder room, and dere install him well — vat I much surprise. But not more be I surprise ven dat I see him go out from de house, away, an' one negro vat carry him de valise. And much be I content for dat I see it.

But I not long content.

De morning after I see a procession vat enter de house one time more — de negro, de valise, and he, and one boy vat carry him de tobacco-pot and boots. So he go up de stair, and put back himself to his ole room. Not ever in-no-matter-vat-place see I such tings.

Den he come to me an' say, "Madame, so some one ask after me, tell dem dat I am one mad." "Certain-lee," I reply, "I will so dem tell, for dat it be true." But I not understand vat he mean precise until one hour more. Den come to house one man who ask if dat he vas not live here.

"Ah, oui," I say, "he live here, but he is one mad."

"So it is," he reply, "I tink; for as he come to pay me one mont advance, and never not again come back. So you give to him back his monis."

Den I be sorry for dat I tell he vas one mad; for dat I see he not one mad at all; — but only one devil vat desire torment all person vitout paying for his vickedness. So I give to him de money, but notice of quit he not take; and I not can yet guess how far dat I be get rid him.

Furnished Rooms

Item, November 2, 1879

I not understan' for vat some peoples ask of prizes so much elevate for dere garneesh room — I much mistruss myself of such, peoples; — I believe dey all be of vat mos' vicked.

Firs', I go for ask prize of room in my street of de ——, for dat I observe of sign "Room garneesh" at door. Dey to me show one room well garneesh on t'ird floor — one big more as one cell of monk, an' I ask of dem de prize. Dey tell me de prize be t'irty dollaire by week. So dat I find myself much astonish, and I ask for see one oder of room. So dey show to me one oder of room on second floor; an' I ask de prize — ven dey tell to me forty-tree dollaire by week. It be one room of behind; so I demand for dat I see one room of before for curiosité. Den dey tell me vat de room of before be fifty dollaire for me, but for any oder one seexty dollaire by week. So I begin to take dem for mads; and dey ask me if I not deseer to see one room of de firs' floor, an' I say, "No — deveel! Vat for I see one sacré room vat cos' one hoondred dollaire? — better as I buy to myself one hoondred dollaire of mustard!" "Not one hoondred of dollaire," dey tell — "not more as one seventy-five dollaire."

And ven dat I save myself from de house away, dey laugh like all vat be of mos' idiot. Seventy-five of dollaire! Seventy-five tousand of deveels!

After I go see again more of house, and I find myself all astound. For de room vat I see of mos' good

market dey ask seexteen dollaire by week — it be vat you call one attique. Oder rooms not be more as seventee, eightee, one hoondred dollaire by mont — always in advance to pay. Vat mos' I have not understan' be dat I not see one room rent in all of house — not even one. It make me to tink vat dey not ever be rent — even for dat dey have sign " Room garneesh." And I tink dey all vat be of mos' vicked — for dat how can dey make for pay rent vit room empties vitout as dey be not honeste? It is so as I tink, and I tink also dat de poleeses not ought — but de poleeses! de poleeses! — to vat good dat I talk of de poleeses!

CHAR-COAL

Item, August 2, 1880

Black: — coalee — coaly!
Coaly-coaly; coaly-coaly; coal-coal-coal.
Coaly-coaly!
Coal-ee! Nice!
Cha'coal!
Twenty-five! Whew!
O charco-oh-oh-oh-oh-oh-lee!
Oh-lee!
Oh-lee-e!

[You get some coal in your mout', young fellow, if you don't keep it shut.]

Pretty coalee-oh-ee!
Char-coal!
Cha-ah-ah-ahr-coal!
Coaly-coaly!
Charbon! du charbon, Madame! Bon charbon?
Point! Ai-ai! *Tonnerre de Dieu!*
Char-r-r-r-r-r-rbon!
A-a-a-a-w! High-ya-a-ah! High-yah!
Vingt-cinq! Nice coalee! Coalee!
Coaly-coal-coal!
Pretty coaly!
Charbon de Paris!
De Paris, Madame; de Paris!

Mexican Coins

Item, November 3, 1879

"Sit down, O sunburnt wanderer, sit down! — Well, well! And whence comest thou?"

"I come," he observed with grim solemnity, "from Mexico."

And he laid upon the table a striped blanket, a worn valise, and a heavy leathern bag whose contents clattered like castanets as it struck the mahogany — Mexican gold.

"Why, we thought you were dead — all these years, and not a word!"

"Dead!" he echoed; "yes, I was dead, dead to the century for which I was born, and to modern civilization — dead from 1870 to 1879. I feel like one of the Seven Sleepers awaking to find himself moving in a new age; I have been living in the seventeenth century, and suddenly I find myself in the nineteenth."

"In Mexico City?" we suggested.

"No: in Mexico City one hears at least some echoes from the outer world — no, in Matamoras and Sonora. Mexico City belongs in some respects to the present century; the life of the provinces does not. Time seems to have stood still there for two or three hundred years. The printing is certainly of the sixteenth century; many manufactures are even mediæval; and agriculture is antediluvian. I knew an American who was idiotic enough to attempt the introduction of steel ploughs — he would not have dared to speak of modern machinery."

"And he —"

"Became instantly an object of suspicion and detestation. Had they not their good wooden ploughs, such as were used in the time of Montezuma, and before him? — And why should a cursed Gringo come to them with ploughs of steel?"

"And the money?"

He took a yellow coin from the wallet and held it up. On one side the Mexican eagle strangled its serpent victim; upon the other a naked arm upheld the Cap of Liberty before the open pages of a book, whereon appeared the syllable "Ley."

"They say the coins of a country indicate to some extent its social condition," he said. "See how rude and coarse the milling is compared with that of the American coin. There is a suggestion of the barbaric in it. But I like the eagle better. There is a ferocious grace in its poise which makes the idealized American bird seem stiff and clumsy by comparison — I admire that savage eagle, tearing the serpent to shreds; — but it is a symbolic lie; there is nothing of the eagle in the Mexican and much of the serpent. The whole design is a lie. There is the Cap of Liberty; and yet there is no true liberty of thought and speech in Mexico; — there is the word 'law'; and they have no law; they are *sans foi ni loi ni roi*. The coin is a braggart like the Mexican. Truly free nations do not boast too much of law and liberty."

"And the Exposition?"

"Ah, bah! — the Exposition! What have they to exhibit? Knives and revolvers and wooden ploughs?"

"Nothing else?"

"Ah, yes! — one Thing! — the one Thing in which Mexico defies competition. I believe I have brought a few specimens in my serape — magnificent specimens — which defy rivalry."

But when he ceased to speak, no answer fell upon his ear, and, turning himself thrice about, he found himself alone.

Louisiana People Not Gay

Item, November 4, 1879

"It seems to me," said the Parisian, " that in spite of an exquisite climate, the people of Louisiana are one of the most solemn-faced I ever saw. There is no real gayety under this glorious sky. People seldom laugh here; when they do, the laugh is apt to be cynical. Workmen do not sing while they work; boys seldom whistle when they go along the street. The farther south I go, the more I find this to be the case. It is true, the negroes sing; but their melodies are the saddest and weirdest I ever heard. Why, in Paris the workshops are merry as birds' nests — it is one ceaseless caroling from morning till night; and in European countries the singing of laborers and farmers is proverbial; song appears to be a part of their existence. I fancy that there must be something sad in the very intensity of life near the tropics."

"In some respects I agree with you," said the Englishman; "but I think the difference is due to the nature of the country. People do not sing in low flat countries, nor do they give vent to much reckless merriment. They sing in the mountains, and laugh among the hills. The hilly countries are the musical countries. Man seems happier the nearer he lives to the stars. It is not in low plains watered by great rivers like the Nile, the Ganges, or the Mississippi, that we need look for merriment; but among the mountain districts of Europe and America."

A Creole Courtyard

Item, November 11, 1879

An atmosphere of tranquillity and quiet happiness seemed to envelop the old house, which had formerly belonged to a rich planter. Like many of the Creole houses, the facade presented a commonplace and unattractive aspect. The great green doors of the arched entrance were closed; and the green shutters of the balconied windows were half shut, like sleepy eyes lazily gazing upon the busy street below or the cottony patches of light clouds which floated slowly, slowly across the deep blue of the sky above. But beyond the gates lay a little Paradise. The great court, deep and broad, was framed in tropical green; vines embraced the white pillars of the piazza, and creeping plants climbed up the tinted walls to peer into the upper windows with their flower-eyes of flaming scarlet. Banana-trees nodded sleepily their plumes of emerald green at the farther end of the garden; vines smothered the windows of the dining-room, and formed a bower of cool green about the hospitable door; an aged fig-tree, whose gnarled arms trembled under the weight of honeyed fruit, shadowed the square of bright lawn which formed a natural carpet in the midst; and at intervals were stationed along the walks in large porcelain vases — like barbaric sentinels in sentry-boxes — gorgeous broad-leaved things, with leaves fantastic and barbed and flowers brilliant as hummingbirds. A fountain murmured faintly near the entrance of the western piazza; and there came from the

shadows of the fig-tree the sweet and plaintive cooing of amorous doves. Without, cotton-floats might rumble, and street-cars vulgarly jingle their bells; but these were mere echoes of the harsh outer world which disturbed not the delicious quiet within — where sat, in old-fashioned chairs, good old-fashioned people who spoke the tongue of other times, and observed many quaint and knightly courtesies forgotten in this material era. Without, roared the Iron Age, the angry waves of American traffic; within, one heard only the murmur of the languid fountain, the sound of deeply musical voices conversing in the languages of Paris and Madrid, the playful chatter of dark-haired children lisping in sweet and many-voweled Creole, and through it all, the soft, caressing coo of doves. Without, it was the year 1879; within, it was the epoch of the Spanish Domination. A guitar lay upon the rustic bench near the fountain, where it had evidently been forgotten, and a silk fan beside it; a European periodical, with graceful etchings, hung upon the back of a rocking-chair at the door, through which one caught glimpses of a snowy table bearing bottles of good Bordeaux, and inhaled the odor of rich West India tobacco. And yet some people wonder that some other people never care to cross Canal Street.

The Creole Character

Item, November 13, 1879

It was not a difficult job to put up a wooden awning about the corner grocery — two stout Irishmen would have done it in twenty-four hours; but the corner grocery man was a Creole, and he hired four Creole carpenters. So they took three weeks to do it, and they have not done it yet. Ce pas baptême katin, travail comme ça; and they did not propose to work themselves to death. Life was too short. We went round the corner to look at them. Beautifully did they saw the boards and with exquisite grace did they hammer the nails — vrais poseurs they were; and then they wiped their brows and sighed, and rolled up cigarettes and went into the grocery to get a light. There they met Aristide and Jules and Albert and Alcée and Alcibiade, and they all took a drink and cracked awful jokes together. Then the carpenters went out again, and climbed upon the half-finished awning, and grinned at a swarthy young woman passing, who had a graceful air of deportment and a complexion like a statue of bronze. Then they laughed at one another; and it began to rain, so they went down and smoked some cigarettes, until it was time for dinner. After dinner they worked very slowly, deliberately, and artistically for ten minutes, until a mad dog came running down the street, which they chased for half a mile with surprising energy and astounding strength of purpose. And when they came back they recounted their heroic deeds to an admiring crowd in the grocery, and to the

washerwoman round the corner, and the Italian fruit-woman over the way, and the wife of the rival grocery-keeper on the other side, and the two lazy policemen on the beat, and the cook of the neighboring boarding-house, and the confectioner at the southeast corner, and the shoemaker at the northwest corner, and the butcher at the southwest corner, and the coal woman just round the northeast corner. Then they got ready to work; and commenced to hammer away to the air —

"Madame Caba,
  Tiyon vous tombe;
Madame Caba,
  Tiyon vous tombe;
Ah, la reine,
  Piye la su' moi;
Madame Caba
  Piye la su' moi;
Madame Caba
  Chandelle 'te teigne," etc.

Then it got dark, and they took another drink and went home. And it was even so next day also, and the next, and so for twenty-three days; and that awning still remains in a wild and savage condition of incompleteness.

Des Perches

Item, August 30, 1880

Daily he goeth out beyond the limits of the city into lonesome and swampy places where copperheads and rattlesnakes abound.

And there he cutteth him clothes-poles, wherewith he marcheth through the city in the burning glare of the sun; singing a refrain simple in words but weird in music.

A long and lamentable sobbing cry, as of one in exceeding great pain and anguish.

So sorrowful in sooth that the sorrow of the city drowneth the sound and sense of the words, — the words chanted in ancient Creole patois —

And we, listening to the cry, gave ourselves up to solemn meditation;

Dreaming of the cries of anguish that arise when a clothes-line, heavily burdened with its snowy freight, falleth upon the mud;

And the poor little woman sitteth down and crieth till her eyes are red, ere she findeth courage to commence all over again, and mend the clothes-line.

It is to avoid these things that men should buy clothes-poles.

Des perches!

And hearing the ancient negro once more lifting up his voice, we also remembered

That often in the dead waste and middle of the night, while meandering about the black backyard,

We were suddenly and violently smitten on the nostrils by the treacherous clothes-pole, hidden between lines of white sheets and shirts that waved their empty arms like spectres.

Also, we remembered how the wet linen fell upon our sacred person; and how we tried to lift up the clothes-pole again but could not; —

For the cunning of the washerwoman was not given to us.

But notwithstanding these things we do bless the clothes-poles, and him that sells them, remembering the service they do to the indispensable washerwoman.

Des perches! — des perches!

A Kentucky Colonel Renting Rooms

Item, November 15, 1879

"AH, one ting more — de name of monsieur?"

"Colonel Zachariah Mart —"

"Alors, alors, it must dat monsieur pay to me of advance."

"But why in thunderation didn't you tell me at first?"

"Ah, because monsieur did not tell to me vat he be one Colonel. I not have, monsieur, of fait' in peoples military. Dere vas one Captain vat swindle me of sixty dollaire, one Major vat cheat me of fifty dollaire, one Doctor Military of t'irty-nine dollaire, one Colonel of one hoondred and elefen dollaire. And dere vas one General vat ask me de oder day—"

"Yes, ma'am; but that don't apply to the Kaintucky —"

"Attendez donc, monsieur, until I be finish! De General say he nevaire pay of advance, but only all de tree mont. And den I tell him I not can do. He go way; so after I hear vat he owe tree hundred and ninety-seven dol—"

"But d—! excuse me, ma'am! I'll shell out for a month in advance!"

"One mont! Den, monsieur, I not ever can believe dat you ever have be one Colonel!"

"Well! I'll be Jehovahly — ... !!!"

"Pauline! en haut-là! Descendez donc pour m'arranger cette affaire. Je suis tout embaralificotée!!!"

The Dawn of the Carnival

Item, February 2, 1880

The Night cometh in which we take no note of time, and forget that we are living in a practical age which mostly relegates romance to printed pages and merriment to the stage. Yet what is more romantic than the Night of the Masked Ball — the too brief hours of light, music, and fantastic merriment which seem to belong to no century and yet to all? Somehow or other, in spite of all the noisy frolic of such nights, the spectacle of a Mardi Gras Ball impresses one at moments as a ghastly and unreal scene. The apparitions of figures which belong to other ages; the Venetian mysteries of the domino; the witchery of beauty half-veiled; the tantalizing salutes from enigmatic figures you cannot recognize; the pretty mockeries whispered into your ear by some ruddy lips whose syllabling seems so strangely familiar and yet defies recognition; the King himself seated above the shifting rout impenetrable as a Sphinx; and the kaleidoscopic changing and flashing of colors as the merry crowd whirls and sways under the musical breath of the orchestra — seem hardly real, hardly possible to belong in any manner to the prosaic life of the century. Even the few unimpassional spectators who remain maskless and motionless form so strange a contrast that they seem like watchers in a haunted palace silently gazing upon a shadowy festival which occurs only once a year in the great hall exactly between the hours of twelve and three. While the most beautiful class of costumes

seem ghostly only in that they really do belong to past ages, the more grotesque and outlandish sort seem strangely suggestive of a goblin festival. And above all the charms of the domino! Does it not seem magical that a woman can, by a little bright velvet and shimmering silk, thus make herself a fairy? And the glorious Night is approaching — this quaint old-time night, star-jeweled, fantastically robed; and the blue river is bearing us fleets of white boats thronged with strangers who doubtless are dreaming of lights and music, the tepid, perfumed air of Rex's Palace, and the motley rout of merry ghosts, droll goblins, and sweet fairies, who will dance the dance of the Carnival until blue day puts out at once the trembling tapers of the stars and the lights of the great ball.

A Mexican's Gratitude

Item, April 12, 1880

A pretty little story comes to me from Algiers.*

Some years ago, during the spring months, a vessel sailing from Vera Cruz arrived at this port with a swarthy Mexican crew. While toiling under the hot sun, one of the men became seriously ill; and when the vessel was ready to sail, it was found necessary to leave him behind. The circumstances are not precisely known to us, beyond the fact that a young girl found him early in the morning lying in the shadow of a pile of timber, a prey to one of those strange fevers that make one shiver with cold even under a sky of fire. He asked for water in his broken English, and the girl procured assistance from her home, which was not far off. Pity prevailed over all other considerations, and the stranger soon found himself in a comfortable bed with good medical attendance. The girl and her mother watched by his bedside and nursed him until he got well again. As he was only a poor sailor, utterly penniless, he could not even offer to recompense them: and as he could not speak English beyond such few words as a stranger picks up in a foreign port, he could not even thank them by word of mouth. Before he had even fully recovered his health, he left the house in spite of the old lady's remonstrances, and, kissing her hand with every sign

* A suburb of New Orleans.

of gratitude, he went his way. As he was never seen there again, it was supposed that he had been able to ship upon some Spanish vessel.

... Long afterward, it happened, by some strange chance, that the young Algerine above referred to found herself in the City of Montezuma. She had been married and was accompanied by her husband. One morning, just as the two had turned from the Plaza into a side- street a small, swarthy man, with gold rings in his ears, and carrying a large basket on his back, approached them, fixed his black eyes for a moment on the young lady's face, and with the sole explanation, "Madre de Dios! es la senorita!" fell upon his knees in the dirty street, and, seizing her hands, covered them with kisses, while tears of gratitude streamed down his bronzed face. The husband, a Cuban, who had often heard the story of the sailor, naturally understood and accepted the situation; while the little Mexican poured out his soul in comparisons of the young wife to guardian angels and saints and virgins, and in those strangely beautiful Spanish compliments which, when sincerely uttered, caress the soul of the hearer. And then, unfastening the strap of his basket and exposing its tempting cargo of luscious fruits and rich flowers, he besought her, upon his knees, to permit him to bear it to her residence as a gift.

"Tell him," she said to her husband, who acted as interpreter, "that we cannot accept his present, and that the pleasure of having been able to help him when in need is more than sufficient compensation for the service."

He begged so hard, however, that she was obliged to accept a handsome bouquet of flowers, and, imploring all the saints of Heaven to bless her, he departed sadly with his basket.

But it seems that he followed her home unawares; for every morning afterward, during her stay in Mexico, just as the mountain-peaks commenced to flush in the rosiness of dawn, the servant was awakened by a knocking at the street-door, and opened it only to find there a basket of fair fruits and tropical flowers that exhaled a perfume as passionate as the gratitude of the giver.

Washerwomen

Item, August 31, 1880

The washerwoman is a creature of which there are various species.

There is the washerwoman who works very cheap; but who never gives you back your own socks or undershirts; and the exchange is invariably to your disadvantage.

There is the washerwoman who makes it a rule of life to wash off all the buttons of your shirts and pull all the strings off your drawers and never dreams of putting them on again. This washerwoman charges like sixty.

There is the washerwoman who puts the thinnest kind of starch in your shirts, so that they become limp

rags after being worn an hour. This kind of washerwoman gets rich fast. She has an eye to business.

Then there is the washerwoman who promises to bring your clothes at a certain hour, and never does so under any possible circumstance.

But there is also the good, honest, industrious, prompt, and motherly or sisterly washerwoman who puts buttons on your shirts and darns up your socks and does not charge extra therefor.

We looked for such a washerwoman for two years before we found her. Now we wouldn't give her up for a small fortune.

If washerwomen have their faults, it must be remembered they have their trials and afflictions. Many of them have been spoiled by bad treatment.

There is no sort of thieving so contemptible as to beat one's washerwoman; but we doubt if any other class of working-people are so much victimized.

It is pretty rough to labor hard all the week, working until one is ready to drop down with fatigue; obliged to watch changes of weather; obliged sometimes when a clothes-line breaks to do all the work over again; obliged to furnish one's own soap and starch and blueing; —

And then to carry the work to those who ordered it, — all nice and clean and pretty, — expecting to receive the just reward of one's labor; —

But, on the contrary, to receive nothing but lying promises and sometimes even hard words; —

And then to go home hungry; and to sit down and cry because there is not a cent in the house!

No wonder the poor women often say it is better to be a sieve than a washerwoman.

No wonder that washerwomen should sometimes feel disgusted with their work, and cease all effort to try and please, and tear off buttons and pull off drawer strings with rage and fury.

It isn't their fault if they are not always angels.

Attention! Azim!

Item, July 8, 1880

> Editor *City Item* — Your columns contained a few days ago a recipe for gombo which contained neither okra filé nor fine herbs. Please give one from a genuine Creole cook, omitting nothing of the delicious compound so dear to Crescent City gourmands, and made in perfection nowhere else.
>
> Azim

We have just been to see a "genuine Creole cook," and one of the best in the city, who gives us the following receipts:

GOMBO FÉVI

A whole chicken — if chicken cannot be had, veal will serve instead; a little ham; crabs, or shrimps, or both, according to the taste of the consumer; okra according to the quantity of soup needed; onions, garlic, parsley, red pepper, etc. Thicken with plenty of rice. The gombo févi is made with green and fresh gombo or okra cut up. It would be no use to attempt to lay down rules in regard to the proportion in which the above ingredients are to be used, as there are not, perhaps, two Creole cooks who follow the same recipe exactly. Everything depends on taste and experience.

GOMBO FILÉ

This is made exactly like the other, but with pulverized okra instead of fresh green okra, and oysters are also

used, in proportion to the quantity of soup needed. If Azim needs further information, he must inform us, and we shall send him to a first-class Creole cook, with whom he can converse at leisure.

We fear that the good old Creole lore is rapidly disappearing, not merely in regard to cooking, but also in regard to natural medicine. The herb medicines of the old Creole nurses were matchless; and doctors were seldom called into Creole homes in the old days except in desperate cases. There were family secrets in regard to tisanes and cataplasms and purgatifs which boasted a San Domingo or a Martinique origin, and which many good old black women averred had come from Africa in the first years of American slavery — the only heirlooms which aged obi-men could bequeath to their slave children. Many of these secrets are kept with something of religious awe. Neither love nor money nor menaces could extort them from the owners. If childless, it is more than likely the secret will die with their owners; if they have children, these generally inherit the mystical power, but hardly ever do they seem in this generation to obtain the success of their fathers and mothers. We have often suggested that all the extant knowledge in regard to Creole cookery and herb medicine, so far as it is possible to obtain it, should be collected and published. Such a publication would not only be a literary curiosity, but also a work of rare practical value, and we sincerely believe the editor of such a work might find the investment a paying one. It would be hopeless to attempt a complete work of such a description, for reasons which

we have often given; but here remains a great deal which can be obtained and which is of great value. With time and leisure we should wish for no better or more agreeable employment than the collection and arrangement of such curiosities.

An Ultra-Canal Talk

Item, July 13, 1880

(Stranger approaches an ancient Creole house, rings the bell, and beholds the landlady. Landlady says something. Stranger loquitur in surprise:)

"He is dead?"

"Oh, oui, monsieur; 'e ees det, and dere is not person sorry. 'E vas all vat vas of most troublesome. All ze time vat 'e liv, I have troubles vit peoples vat come to see 'im. For everybody know 'im to be one mad, who like to spend his money in foolishness and bêtises. After his son die he not have nobody for 'im look after. So dey come to sell to 'im litograph, vich dey make 'im to believe to be oil painting by great master; an' 'e pay one, two, tree hoondred dollaire for litograph vich cost no more as fifty cent. Ven I tell 'im not buy, 'e tell me I was one ignorant and one imbecile vich have not appreciation of art. After, ven'e fin' out not oil painting, 'e call zem cursssed camel – two-hump camel, an' heap of robber (tas de voleurs) and charogne; an' 'e wish dem all blast by ze feefty tousand flames of hell. So zat 'e not talk of oder tings — only of robbers and liars and assassinses.

"Ven zey could not more sell to 'im play-bills as oil-painting of great master, zey sell to 'im of daub as great water color picser. 'E pay seventee dollaire for vat cos' not more as tree cent each. Ze frames wort perhaps six dollaire! At las' 'e fine out how zey 'im swindle; an' 'e talk of robber an' murderer an' camel of two hump. And 'e say dis country ze most curssed

country vat exist — all vat be of mos' canaille and racaille and charogne.

"Ven as dey not could no more to 'im sell picser, zey sell to 'im vat you call céramique, old cup and saucer and dish vat wort not more as ten cent and vat dey tell 'im from China come. 'E pay t'irty dollaire, as dey tell 'im very 'ard for find. But 'e find one day undare bottom of cup one word like 'BIRMINGHAM'; and 'e swear so dreadful vat I have me de finger in de ear to put. After 'e not talk more but of tief and liar, and of assassin and of infames and infant of ze devill and children of 'ell — vich 'e wish open and swallow zis sacré charogne de pays. And 'e also say more vat I not you dare racount.

"Also dey sell to 'im boots vat sole vat of paper was made and coat vat was glueded together, an' I not ever could 'im prevent to pay fiftee dollaire for ze coat an' ten dollaire for ze boot. Sixtee dollaire! And ven zat ze boot go into pieces an' ze coat tomble into rag, 'e could not enough to swear in such manner zat people hear 'im more as tree block. Ze same night 'e swear all night so as no one could fall 'imself to sleep. 'E said tings so terrible zat I stuff to me de ears wit cotton; but all same I hear 'im swear until ze sun get 'imself up.

"After, dey sell 'im furnisser, armoire, table, bed, chair for mahogany — vat was pine covered wit sometings. 'E pay tree hoondred dollaire! Ze table was only glueded and one day it burst ven he dere put to 'im de elbow; and ze bed also only glueded together. 'E go to law, but ze oder peoples much vas rich, and 'e lose five hoondred dollaire wit lawyer an' 'e soon tire of law.

"After zey sell to 'im vine vat not vas vine and fisky vat not vas fisky an' 'e pay like one millionaire zough 'e not have much of money. Not ever could I prevent 'im to buy or to be swindle."

"Did he say anything before he died?"

"I tink so! 'E not sick — never sick at all. 'E die sitting in ze berceuse. For 'e vas very old, very, very much old. And some one came to sell to 'im sometings. 'E try to get up; but not could, and 'e not let me to help 'im. So I not help 'im; and 'e say, 'Mon bon Dieu, have me mercy — Oh, le tas de canaille! Pray you for me! Oh, les sacrés voleurs! Lord have me pity! — Charogne de pays! — I believe me in de heaven for ze good! Oh, de curssed wretch! — Holy angel 'elp me up! — Oh, ze camel of two hump! — Oh, mon Dieu, miséricorde! — zis be one infame country of assassin and robbaire!' So 'e pray an' so 'e swear. So 'e die wit — 'Charogne de pays!' And ven ve sell of 'im ze picsers for vat 'e pay one fortune, dey bring not more as tree dollaire an' t'irdeen cent. But 'e 'ave near one hoondred years ven dat 'e be dead. I tink 'e ought have to be det."

Sons of the Sea

Item, September 1, 1880

They come to us from the uttermost parts of the earth, with the winds that swell the white sails of their vessels. There is a sparkle in their eyes like the sparkle of a distant sea; and a faraway look acquired by the habit of gazing over the infinite expanse of rolling water. They walk with a swaying motion learned from the gait of their own ships, and there is a tone in their voices like the tone of sea-winds roaring through the rigging.

They have passed over all seas, and heard a hundred tongues spoken.

And coming into a city; leaving the rocking deck for the motionless earth, they still wear a quiet dreamy

look, as of men accustomed to the sight of Nature in her most infinite aspect, and not liable therefore to be impressed greatly by the sight of the handiwork of Man.

But at times human frailty asserts itself; — the stern discipline of the sea has made the sailors long for some wild frolic on land; — strong drink and women hold out siren-temptations.

What wonder is it? Was not even Ulysses, that wisest of sailors, once obliged to bind himself to the mast lest the song of an enchantress might lure him to destruction?

The old sea-dogs are usually wise, like Ulysses; but the young ones will have their day.

Then again we have swarthy sailors from sunny West Indian ports, who wander about seeking for those who speak their own tongue, in order to sell odorous packages of cigars concealed in their pockets — cigars in which all the soporific fragrance of the tropics seems concentrated.

And having performed their little work of *contrabandistas*, they depart to enjoy a little fun with the profits thereof.

So do they sail from port to port; — more wearied by their stay on shore than by mighty wrestling with the Giant of Storms; for the whisky is not good, and there are other things which are worse.

But the sea who loves her children braces their strength up once more with the elixir of her bright winds; and drives away the fumes of a night of orgy, as evil dreams are scattered by daylight.

And as the sailors call east and west and north and

south; buffeted by wild winds; struggling with raging waves; making brief visits to strange ports; collecting dreamy memories of foreign lands; — until the time, comes for them to sail into that weird sea which is waveless and shoreless and shadowless and forever silent, and from which no mariner ever returns.

A Creole Song

Item, July 26, 1880

The following has been brought to us by a charming lady, herself a Creole, who tells us that it was a popular song in Louisiana at the beginning of this century:

Moin pas conné qui quichose
  Qui appé tourmente moin là;
Moin pas conné qui la cause,
  Cœur a moin brulé comme çà.
Ah Die! Qui tourment, qui peine,
  Dipis longtemps quimbé moi;
C'est tourment la passé chaine,
  Plutôt moin mouri yonné fois.

Toi conné qui belle rigole
  Qui coulé dans bananiers.
Où toi té sé fé la folle
  La foi qui toi té baigné.
D'leau la pas coulé encore —
  Des fois il 'rète tout court —
Li semble regrette encore
  Li pas baigné toi toujours.

Here is a free translation:

I do not know what it is which torments me thus.
I cannot tell what it is that makes my heart beat so.
O God! what torture! what pains I have suffered so long!

It is worse than the pain of fetters; I had rather die at once.
Do you remember the pretty little brook that ran through the banana-trees —
Where you used to have such fun, when you used to bathe?
That water has ceased to run; —
Since the time it stopped all at once —
It seems to me it died of regret
That its wavelets could not embrace you forever.

This translation, as we have already observed, is very free, but contains the spirit of the little song. We shall be very grateful to any of our readers who will bring us some more of these curiosities.

The Grandissimes

Item, September 27, 1880

At last it has come out in book form, this strange, weird, powerful, and pathetic story, which is certainly the most remarkable work of fiction ever created in the South.

It is difficult to render any idea of what this book is without making copious extracts. It is a dream which is not all a dream, a tale which is but half a tale, a series of pictures which, although in a certain sense created by the pencil of an Impressionist, wear a terrible resemblance to terrible realities. There are chapters which affect the imagination like those evil dreams in which dead faces reappear with traits more accentuated than the living originals ever possessed.

Is this strange New Orleans which grows up under Mr. Cable's wand our own New Orleans? It is; and yet it is something more. It is such a city as a wanderer sees by night in his dreams, who has left the shores of the Father of Waters for the icy winds and snow-shrouded scenes of some far-Northern winter; — a Southern metropolis, her streets paved with the gold of summer suns, her shadowy trees whose leaves never fall, her flowers that never die, her streets quaintly constructed like the Latin cities of the older continent, and all the motley clamor of a semi-tropical land in which even the sharp accents of European tongues lose their firmness, and old languages obtain a new softness and sweetness and languor. And there

is all this inexpressible glamour, and yet more, in ,the familiar and yet unfamiliar New Orleans of "The Grandissimes."

If it be so with the scenes, with the characters it is also so. We have seen these characters, and yet we have not seen them. Or, to describe our own impression still more correctly, we believe that we have seen them somewhere, and yet are not quite sure — like one greeted by some stranger whose features are not unfamiliar but whose name is forgotten.

There is, therefore, a certain vagueness about the work. But it is an artistic vagueness, like the golden haze of an Indian summer softening outlines and beautifying all it touches. The old streets seemed clouded with a summer mist; the voices of the people speaking in many tongues came to the reader as from a great distance. Yet why not? Is he not looking back and listening to the speaking shadows of another era, when Claiborne first came to Louisiana?

Yet the vagueness is never too vague. Sometimes the scenes are dimmed, but it is when the reader's eyes are dimmed by that moisture which it is the artist's triumph to evoke. Sometimes the scenes become terribly vivid, however, as in the death of Bras-Coupé, or the tragic end of Clémence. There is no dreaminess in those powerful pictures. Nor is there any in that painful incident when the apothecary reads the letter to Palmyre. This scene, not even excepting the execution of Clémence, seems to us the most vividly truthful in the book. It is less tragic, less exciting, less terrible than others; but it is a genre study of inimitable verisimilitude.

If there be one special characteristic of Mr. Cable's style that is specially striking, we believe it is his power of concentrated description. What could be more pithily forcible, more briefly comprehensive, more intensely impressive than the following description of an interior furnished in the old-fashioned Creole style? One must have seen such, however, to appreciate the power of these few lines:

> ... the rooms were so sumptuously furnished: immovable largeness and heaviness, lofty sobriety, abundance of finely wrought brass mounting, motionless richness of upholstery; much silent twinkle of pendulous crystal, a soft semi-obscurity — such were the characteristics.

Or this:

> ... The plantation became an invalid camp. The words of the Voudoo found fulfillment on every side. The plough went not out; the herds wandered through broken hedges from field to field and came up with staring bones and shrunken sides; a frenzied mob of weeds and thorns wrestled and throttled each other in a desire for standing-room — rag-weed, smart-weed, sneeze-weed, bind-weed, iron-weed — until the burning skies of midsummer checked their growth and crowned their unshorn tops with rank and dingy flowers.

We doubt whether this book, in spite of its delicate merit, will become a favorite with residents of the Creole city; — its spirit has already been severely criticized by a contemporary; — its paintings are not

always flattering to native eyes; — its evocation of dead memories will not be found pleasing. We cannot perceive that the merit of the romance is at all marred, nevertheless, by Mr. Cable's own peculiar views; and if we were inclined to criticize anything unfavorably in it, we should only question the reality of Honoré Grandissime. Was there ever a Creole of Creoles, living in such an age, who could have entertained such ideas on social questions?

There are very curious chapters upon Voudooism in this book; and we cannot share the opinion of many that it is a mere "absurd superstition." We believe it to be, or at least to have been, a serious and horrible reality; and we know of most intelligent families among our French-speaking population who share this opinion. Those who have really given serious attention to the subject have doubtless found that the traditions of Voudooism in Louisiana and elsewhere have at least as much claim to belief as the history of the aqua Tofana or of the secret poisoners of the Middle Ages.

We must specially call the attention of our readers to the Creole songs and refrains, published with the music, throughout the work. They are very curious, and possess a special philologic value. One, in particular, an African chant, sung by the negroes in cutting down the cane, deserves special notice.

But we cannot attempt to criticize Mr. Cable's book further. It must be read to be appreciated. We have not even attempted to tell the public what it is. We have only undertaken to express in a few words the peculiar impression which, as a work of art, it produces upon the reader.

The Indignant Dead

Item, September 8, 1880

If they are not indignant as a certain worthy Administrator declared they were, they ought to be.

During the last ten years three hundred and three persons have been murdered in New Orleans or vicinity.

And yet only FIVE of the murderers have been hung.

Only five—although eleven were actually sentenced to death.

Consequently the chance of being hung for committing a murder in this community is as five to three hundred and three.

Almost as little danger of being hung for having committed murder as of being run over by a railroad

train or cut in two by a buzz saw or brained by a brick falling from a chimney.

It is really horrible to read the report made to Governor Wiltz.

Of perhaps more than three hundred murderers — for many of these murders were committed by several persons — only three escaped from justice. What became of the rest? Where are the three hundred?

One hundred and sixteen were declared NOT GUILTY.

A nolle prosequi was entered in fifty-nine cases.

In nine cases it was "not a true bill."

There were three mistrials.

Twelve cases were transferred to the dead docket.

Without going much further into particulars we need only remark that the rest mostly escaped with light sentences, or were pardoned out of the Penitentiary.

Only five murderers were punished by death.

And that was only because they were strangers, —

Because they had no money to pay lawyers, —

Because they had no political influence.

Two Italians, two negroes and a Malay — probably less guilty than some who are now walking the streets!

There are nearly three hundred unavenged dead, — the blood of nearly three hundred victims crying vainly to heaven for vengeance!

If the dead are not indignant, in the immortal words of our Administrator, they ought to be.

A Creole Mystery

Item, October 6, 1880

They came together from Havana, mistress and servant. The mistress had a strange and serpentine sort of beauty; — the litheness of a snake in every movement; — the fascination of an ophidian; — and great eyes that flamed like black opals. One felt on meeting her that the embraces of lianas and of ivy were less potent to fetter than hers — and to fetter forever. Her voice was remarkably sweet, but had strangely deep tones in it; — and her laugh caused a feeling of unpleasant surprise. It was a mocking, weird, deep laugh, uttered without any change of features; there was no smile, no movement of the facial muscles; the lips simply opened and the laugh came pealing from her white throat, while the eyes, large, brilliant, and sinister with mockery, fixed themselves with motionless lids upon the face of the person present. But she seldom laughed.

None knew who she was. She was a mystery to the French people of the quarter. Her rooms were luxuriously furnished and hung in blue satin. At long intervals strangers called upon her — men of olivaceous complexion and hair tropically black with dead-blue lights in it. They spoke only in Spanish; and their interviews lasted far into the night. Sometimes they seemed to be gay. Gossipy people said they heard the popping of champagne corks; and a perfume of Havana tobacco floated out of the windows and hung about the shrubbery that enshrouded the veranda.

Sometimes, however, there were sinister sounds as of men's voices raised in anger, and at intervals the deep laugh of the mysterious woman, long and loud and clear, and vibrant with mockery.

The servant was a mulattress, tall and solidly constructed as a caryatid of bronze. She was not less of a mystery than her mistress. She spoke French and Spanish with equal facility, but these only on rare occasions. Generally no mute in the seraglio of a Sultan could be more silent or more impassible. She never smiled. She never gossiped. She never seemed to hear or to see; yet she saw and heard all. Only a strange face could attract her attention — for a brief moment, during which she gazed upon it with an indescribable look that seemed potent enough to burn what it touched. It was a look that made its living object feel that his face was photographed in her brain and would be equally vivid there fifty years after. The foreigners who came were received by her in silence and without scrutiny. Their faces were doubtless familiar. None of them ever spoke to her. She seemed to be more than a Doppelgänger, and to appear in five or six different rooms at the same time. Nothing could transpire unperceived by her; though she seemed never to look at anything. Her feet were never heard. She moved like a phantom through the house, opening and closing doors noiselessly as a ghost. She always suddenly appeared when least expected. When looked for, she was never to be found. Her mistress never called her. When needed, she appeared to rise suddenly from the floor, like those Genii of Arabian fables summoned by a voiceless wish. She never played with the children; and these hushed their voices when

she glided by them in silence. With a subtle intelligence seemingly peculiar to her, she answered questions before they were fully asked. She never seemed to sleep. Persons who visited the house were as certain to meet her at the entrance three hours before sunrise as at any other hours. She appeared to be surprised at nothing, and to anticipate everything. She was even a greater mystery, if possible, than her mistress.

At last the swarthy foreigners called more frequently and the interviews grew stormier. It was said that sometimes the conversations were held in Catalan; and that when Catalan was spoken there were angrier words and wickeder laughing. And one night the interviews were so terrible that all the old-fashioned French folks in the quarter put their heads out of the windows to listen. There were sounds as of broken glass and passionate blows given to the mahogany table. And the strange laughter suddenly ceased.

Next morning the postman calling to deliver a registered letter found the rooms empty. The spectral servant was gone. The sinister mistress was gone. The furniture was all there; and the only records of the night's mystery were two broken glasses and stains of wine on the rich carpet. The bed had been undisturbed. The clock still ticked on its marble pedestal. The wind moved the blue silk hangings. A drowsy perfume of woman lingered in the rooms like incense. The wardrobes retained their wealth of silks and laces. The piano remained open. A little Angora cat was playing with a spool of silk under the table. A broken fan lay on the luxuriously padded rocking-chair; and a bouquet of camellias lay dying upon the mantelpiece.

The letter was never delivered. The rooms remained as they were, until mould and dust came to destroy the richness of their upholstery. The strangers never came back, nor did any ever hear what became of them. The mystery remains unexplained. The letter remains in the dead-letter office. But I would like to open it and find out what is in it; — wouldn't you?

Whited Sepulchres

Item, September 9, 1880

It is rather ghastly to have death in the midst of life as we have it in New Orleans; but ghastlier when it is presented without even the ordinary masks. The skeleton of our public closet is exposed to broad daylight. Are we becoming like the Orientals who never repair? — do we accept all things with the fatalistic *Kismet?* Our bat-haunted prisons and our ruined cemeteries seem to answer in the affirmative.

They are hideous Golgothas, these old intramural cemeteries of ours. In other cities the cemeteries are beautiful with all that the art of the gardener and the sculptor can give. They are often beautiful parks, in which shafts of rosy granite or pale marble rise in

pleasant relief against a background of ornamental shrubbery; — birds are singing in the trees; — flowers are growing upon the gently swelling eminences which mark the sleep of the dead. There horror is masked and hidden. Here it glares at us with empty sockets.

The tombs are fissured, or have caved in, or have crumbled down into shapeless masses of brick and mortar; — the plaster, falling away, betrays the hollow mockery of the frail monuments; — the vases are full of green water and foulness; — the flowers are dying in their coffins of glass; — the crawfish undermine the walls to fatten upon what is hidden within; — and instead of birds, the tombs are haunted by lizards.

If we must have intramural cemeteries, at least let them be worthy of a civilized people. As they are, they are nightmares.

Eleusis

Item, November 12, 1880

Cool, soft light broken by curtains of lace; antiquated and elegant upholstery; a four-columned Creole bed, generously wide and lofty, its lace-fringed pillows embroidered with a rosy monogram; matting checkered in light colors; a bronze clock bearing the nude figure of Ariadne riding upon her loving panther; a glimmer of satin flung carelessly over fauteuils and sofas; a mysterious perfume of woman; a sense of some one absent, and a consciousness of wicked intrusion on the part of the writer — feelings intensified by the merciless ticking of the French clock: — this was Eleusis!

And the Mysteries?

Ah! the pretty mysteries; the dainty, soft, delicate, fragile, feminine mysteries! Fairy gauze and butterfly-satin, and moth-velvet and foamy lace and frosted silk, and that white samite — mystic, wonderful —which invites the hand to touch it with a timid caress, and the name whereof is only known to Woman; — and over all a hovering perfume — the perfume of youth, the odor of all that is sweet and feminine, the ambrosia that haunts the presence of Loveliness and clings to her robes — the frankincense of the Shulamitess!

This was the shadowy nook where the human butterfly nightly prepared to issue from her pallid chrysalis; the chamber where the pretty witch spun her web of magical gold.

"My thread is slim, my thread is fine.
But he must be
A stronger than thee
Who can break this thread of mine."

And the reader murmureth, perchance, that he is yet no wiser than he was before.

Behold! the mystery into which we would initiate thee, o reader, is a mystery of bayadères, a mystery of dancing girls "robed only in a fleecy cloud of veils," that mystery of the daughter of Herodias which made the king swear a great oath that he should give her all that she desired, even unto the half of his kingdom.

When thou beholdest the dancing girl coming forth to dance before the bow-curving line of lights; — when thou beholdest her poised in air, shimmering in foamy laces and creamy satin like some splendid insect; — when thine eyes are dazzled by the witchery of her feet so that thou even wishest to be a Herod that thou mightest offer her, not the half, but in sooth the whole of thy kingdom — dost thou not often marvel at the mysteries of her garb? — enticing only to deceive coquettishly — seemingly light as a Coæ vesta or a ventus textilis such as Egyptian dancers wore, yet faithfully guarding its secrets — thin as a dragonfly's wings, yet subtle enough to withstand the long strain of a pas de séduction? Let us, then, abandon the romance of idealism and descend to the level prose of explanation.

In dressing for the ballet, the fair dancer must disrobe as completely as for the bath. A thin and very

short chemise is the first article put on. It is peculiarly shaped, cut low, and has pieces to support it from the shoulders. Then the ordinary corset is put on. Then come the tights.

The tights are of flesh-colored silk, and all in one piece. They take the place of stockings and drawers, and are brought up over the hips and fastened with soft but strong tape above the waist and even over the corset. The whole body up to the bosom is gloved in them. If nicely adjusted, and not too often worn, their own elasticity keeps them from wrinkling.

Over the tights a pair of muslin drawers are worn, about as narrow and short as a boy's bathing-drawers. These are of gossamer lightness, but exceedingly white. They are worn for moral reasons.

Over the drawers are six of the lightest petticoats of tulle or tarlatan, whereof it is possible to conceive. These are all attached together at the waistband, so as to form but one piece. Light as they are, their number and starchiness enable them to preserve the graceful shape which gives the ballet dancer the appearance of some beautiful white fly.

Over the six petticoats a seventh, often equally light, but of much more brilliant material, is worn. Sometimes it is decked with flowers, sometimes fringed with lace; sometimes it is white; sometimes it is pink, scarlet, purple, or other color, according to the character of the drama. In Spanish or Italian dances it is very brilliant.

A corset of soft white satin is next put on over the tights and under-corset. Over this is worn a bodice of lace, of silk, of velvet, or other material, according to

the character of the dance. In ordinary ballet dances, however, all is white, even the slippers.

O the pretty little slippers! They have no heel, and are of the lightest imaginable; — white or pink satin. The uppers are heavily stitched with cotton all about the sole, so as to protect the satin wherever the pressure of the foot flattens it to a level with the leather. At the toe, where the main pressure is, the stitching is so thick and heavy as to form a pad. The slipper catches the heel firmly and is further secured with strong tape.

And then the dancer is attired. The coiffure is a separate matter, and varies according to circumstances.

But, alas! the little slippers can be used only once or at most twice; the tights must be frequently renewed; the tulle petticoats must be incessantly replaced; nearly all this fragile fairy costume continually demands renovation. The laces and upper ornamental apparel alone endure. So that every dancer must carry with her quite a little shoe-store; for in one opera season many dozens of shoes are worn out, and then they are useless, except for rehearsals.

And now our Eleusis having been sufficiently explained, we do propose to say nothing more upon the subject, and leave the reader to dream of — whatever he pleases!

Latin and Anglo-Saxon

Item, November 24, 1880

The French papers in Canada have latterly warned their readers that the Canadian French are being slowly but surely absorbed by the Anglo-Saxon element, and have been advising them to push forward into the valley of the Ottawa and there found settlements. This may possibly be done; but the end will, no doubt, be the same. The Canadian French have, nevertheless, been among the most thrifty, energetic, and enterprising pioneers in the world; certainly no other men with Latin blood in their veins ever showed more endurance and daring than the famous coureurs des bois and chasseurs de loutre. If the French Canadian is to be absorbed by the Anglo-Saxon element, we cannot avoid asking ourselves what chance the French element of Louisiana can have to resist absorption when the flood of emigration begins to pour southward with the advancing lines of railway?

The chances, in our opinion, are rather in favor of the Canadian French resisting longer than our own Creoles — unless the French element should be kept up by a continuous immigration. Old manners and customs and dialects and families endure longer in a severe Northern climate than in a semi-tropical land like our own. As we near the tropics decay becomes more rapid — not only material decay of substance, but decay of social conditions and institutions as well. Our French element is not composed, however, of such stern stuff as the French people of Canada. They have

become semitropicalized here; — they have felt the enchantment of a climate of perennial mildness, and have lived for generations under very different conditions to those which have hardened and invigorated the French people of Canada. It must be remembered also that the French Canadians have had to resist the strongest absorbing influences possible — those of the English, Scotch, and Irish elements in all their purity and force. The geographical position of Louisiana, her climate, and her comparative isolation only recently broken by new railroad lines, have aided the Louisiana Creoles in maintaining their individuality and their pleasant old-fashioned manner of existence.

We have often attempted to analyze the cause of the undoubted predominance of the Anglo-Saxon race wherever it plants itself. Many causes have been adduced, but none seem to us satisfactory. The Latin races are not less hardy and enduring, though inferior in physical strength. They are not less intelligent, though less self-denying. They are not less patriotic, though more cosmopolitan. They possess a number of sterling qualities which are wholly foreign to Anglo-Saxon, Teutonic, or Scandinavian character. In our opinion the real secret of the predominance of Northern races lies in the same causes which may partly account for the conquest of the Western Empire by the Goths, after the Roman armies had been fairly worn out in repelling barbaric invasion. The Northern races are far more prolific than the Latin. The Germans of to-day, for example, are filling up America with emigrants. What Latin race can send out such armies of emigrants? Probably not all the Latin races together

could do so! The fact is not perhaps flattering to the Northern races of Europe; for it is said that the lower organizations propagate most rapidly in all the orders of nature. But history confirms the fact that the real strength of a people lies not in valor and endurance alone, but in its capacity of self-multiplication. Nor is this comforting to think of when we gaze toward China. Idea is stronger than force for a time only; force at length will carry all before it.

The Flower-Sellers

Item, September 11, 1880

They sit forever under the shadows — silver-tressed and ancient — calmly weaving their flowers into rainbow-tinted gifts for youth and beauty.

And I, gazing upon them impassibly weaving the bright blossoms together, dream of the ancient Norns of Scandinavian legends —

Weaving the warp and woof of human destinies; — measuring terms of life as the stems of flowers are measured; —

Mystically mingling Evil with Good; Joy with Sorrow; Love with Grief; — tints of Passion with tints of Melancholy, — even as in a bouquet the hues of a hundred flowers are blended into one rich design.

Evanescent as the beauty of Woman are the colors of the flowers; — volatile their drowsy-sweet odors as the perfume of youth.

And thou, O reader, when thou receivest, from the wrinkled hands of the Norns, who measure the lives of summer blossoms, an odorous gift for the ivory hand of thy living idol, —

Knowest thou that the gift is in itself a voiceless symbol of the fragility of all which thou worshippest?

Fair girl, a mightier Norn than that grey woman who silently weaves her flowers in the sun, has measured the golden thread of thy life: —

Though sweeter than the presence of Esther, bathed six months in palm-oil and rich odors before entering

the chamber of the King — thy youth will pass like the breath of a flower; —

Though thy lips be as those of the Shulamitess, they will wither and crisp and wrinkle like the petals of a scarlet blossom; —

And as a flower between the leaves of a book, thou shalt be pressed between the marble covers of that ponderous volume in which Death, who is, alas! strong as Love, keeps the weird record of his deeds.

A Visitor

Item, November 26, 1880

"Juan Guerrero y Marquez, su servidor de V."

There are voices which surprise by their sonority. The voice of the speaker, as he introduced himself, made us lift our eyes in surprise to his face; — it was a soft roll of thunder, the richest and deepest bass that had ever vibrated in the writer's ears. To have heard it without seeing the speaker would have compelled the idea that it came from a chest of prodigious depth, from the torso of a giant. Not so, however. The speaker was a young and rather slender man, firmly knit, but with more grace than apparent strength in his frame; not over tall, but with a bearing as proud as his Spanish name. He spoke with the refined accent of Madrid, and the words came from his lips with such a musical depth as when the longest strings of a great harp are touched by strong and skillful fingers. The face was characteristic — a true Latin face, with the strong keenness of the Roman eagle in its profile; eyes large and brilliant as a falcon's; eyebrows thick as mustaches, rising toward the temples, with a slightly sinister elevation; mustaches curling up toward the cheek-bones; and such a short black pointed beard as we see in the portraits of Velasquez. This handsome and daring face belonged to a beautifully formed head, covered with the blackest curls possible to conceive — the head of an antique Roman soldier set upon a columnar neck. With the clear bronze of his skin, no more striking

type of the finest of the Latin races could have been asked for by a painter.

Artista español de los primeros, he had been travelling with a Spanish opera company through the West Indies, and enchanting the señoritas of Havana with the magic of his marvelous voice. Now he wished to visit some distant relatives in one of the far South American republics — members of his own Spanish family and bearing his own name, but born under the Southern Cross. He had never seen them; but strangely enough the ancestral family in Spain had maintained relations with its tropical children for a hundred years.

"And there is really a consul of that republic in New Orleans?" we asked in bewilderment; for, alas! we had never heard of him.

"Ciertamente, señor!"

So we went to find the consul. It was necessary, first, to find out who he was, and where he lived. The directory refused to yield up the desired information. Then we went successively to see a Spanish tobacconist and a Spanish wine merchant and a Spanish doctor and a Spanish apothecary and a Spanish journalist — who was not at home — and a certain Spanish lady who lives upon a street bearing the name of an ancient Spanish Governor.

It proved easier, however, to find who the consul was than to find where he resided. At one time we began to fancy that he was an illusion or a phantom. Seven different places did we visit in which he had formerly resided, but resided no longer — so that we felt even as wayfarers who vainly pursue after a will-o'-the-wisp.

And a young woman passed by, graceful as a panther, carrying a basket upon her arm. Her eyes were very large and black; her skin the color of gold; and her figure owned those indescribable curves, that cambrure de taille for which there is no expression in the English tongue.

"Que es bonita!" exclaimed the singer, with a caressing accent in his deep voice. If the woman did not hear the compliment, she had at least heard the Spanish tongue; for she suddenly turned, and, poised in an attitude of supreme grace like a statue of bronze, addressed the artista in a voice clear as a silver bell: — "A quien busca V., señor?" And their black eyes met. It was a tropical look: the man fascinated by the serpent grace of the woman; the woman not seeking to conceal her admiration of the handsome youth before her. Yes: she knew where the consul — Señor Don Alejandro — lived. It was just at the corner. "Mil gracias, señorita!" Not a Spanish girl, no — from some strange town with an Aztec name in the heart of Mexico. "Yo estaba allá!" cried the artist joyfully: "I remember it well — the plaza, and the old house of Señor — on the corner, where I spent some very pleasant days when I was traveling through Mexico." And then recalling old memories, they forgot for a moment all about the distant South American republic and the phantom consul. Adios — a clasp of olive-skinned hands; and with the old-fashioned and tender commendation to God, they departed, never to meet again — as seabirds flying over the sea to opposite coasts look into each other's eyes a moment and pass on.

"I have been to your opera," he said, "I like it. But neither the French nor the Italians know what the Spanish theatre is. It is not merely music and drama. It is a school. It is a medium of national instruction. It teaches feeling, expression, deportment, dress, courtesy, taste, appreciation of the beautiful. And that is why Spanish audiences are so difficult to please."

"I wish I could hear you sing," we said.

"Lo me gustaria mucho," he returned; "but I leave to-night. And you could not judge of what I can do unless you should hear me in the theatre. Do you smoke?" And he presented us with a real "puro."

Suddenly an organ at the corner struck up a fragment of *Faust* – the Gloria chorus of the soldiers. "Ah! I love that," he murmured; and suddenly the martial air rolled from his lips in tones rich and deep, but golden-clear as the voice of a mighty organ. It was only for a moment; but in that moment the children ceased their dances, and people passing through the old-fashioned streets paused and turned and wondered at the witchcraft of that marvelous voice.

" Adios, señor!" And we parted forever.

Creole Servant Girls

Item, December 20, 1880

Creole colored servants are very peculiar. They are usually intelligent, active, shrewd, capable. They generally perform well whatever they undertake. They are too intelligent to be dishonest, knowing the probable consequences. They comprehend a look, an expression, as well as an order; they will fulfill a wish before it is expressed. They see everything, and hear everything, and say nothing. They are consummate actresses, and can deceive even the elect. They can ape humility, simulate affection, pretend ignorance, and feign sorrow so that the imitation is really better than the reality would be, and serves the same purpose. They can tell a lie with the prettiest grace imaginable, or tell a truth in such a manner that it appears to be a lie. They read character with astonishing quickness, and once acquainted with the disposition of their employer will always anticipate his humors and make themselves pliable to his least wish. They are the most admirable waiting-machines which ever existed; — absolutely heartless, without a particle of affection or real respect for an employer or his children, yet simulating love and respect so well that no possible fault can be found with them. Once initiated into the ways of a household, it is seldom necessary to give them an order. They know everything that is required, and everything is done. If regularly paid and well treated, they will remain in a family for a generation. They

demand a great deal of liberty when not actually employed, and will not remain in a house when they are not wholly free after working hours to go out or in as they please. They know everything that is going on, and a great deal more than they have any business to know. If they consider their employer discreet, they will furnish him unasked with the strangest secret news. They possess family histories capable of doing infinite mischief, but seldom make use of them, except among each other. To strangers they are absolutely deaf and blind — neither bribes nor promises will extort information from them when asked by persons they do not know. They can keep people at a distance without offending; and become familiar to any extent without making themselves disagreeable. They can be superlatively vicious, and yet appear to be supremely virtuous. They can also be dangerous enemies — and there is no denying the fact that their enmity is to be dreaded. They speak several languages, and sing weird songs. They will do anything that any imagination can conceive for money; and are very friendly, indeed, as long as the money holds out. They are actually very cleanly, oddly superstitious, and very diligent. They have a way of working very hard without appearing to work, and of doing little or no work while appearing to be working themselves to death. Their virtues are simply the result of a great natural shrewdness, which appears to have been handed down from old times, with the Latin blood that beats in the veins of French-speaking quadroons and mulattresses. They will not steal; but they have no moral scruples when the infringement of morality does not involve

public disgrace and legal punishment. They do not like American or English-speaking people; and it is probable that none but Creoles know how to manage them. The type is fast disappearing; but it certainly affords one of the most extraordinary studies of human nature possible to conceive.

The Alligators

Item, September 13, 1880

None discover aught of beauty in them; yet they were once worshiped as gods.

They were not of this world, in truth, but of another — the Antediluvian world of monsters and dragons and vast swamps broader than continents — where there were frogs larger than oxen, and alligators longer than the serpent slain by the army of Regulus.

The Ichthyosaurus, the Pterodactyl, the Megatherium, the Plesiosaurus — have passed away with the Antediluvian world.

This strange being, with its dull cuirass marked like the trunks of the primeval tree-ferns, still endures — although new strata have been formed since the birth

of his species — although the monstrous vegetation of the swamps in which his ancestors crawled has been transformed to beds of coal!

Alligator, crocodile, or cayman — it matters little— they alike belong to the age before which history began.

And looking upon them, must not one dream of the sacred Ganges and the most ancient Nile — of South American rivers that flow by dead palaces buried in the vegetation of virgin forests — of dead civilizations — of Karnac and Thebes and Crocodilopolis — of catacombs and broken-limbed colossi — of empires and of races that have been swallowed up by Time? The world has changed, but the Giant Lizard changes not.

Home

Item, January 8, 1881

We have all heard curious things said about the peculiarities of New Orleans; we have heard that it was a city where the sun rose in the west and water ran uphill; we have heard it spoken of as built upon a dunghill, and there is a Spanish proverbial expression about it still more uncomplimentary, often uttered by West India captains, which we dare not cite, even in the original. But yesterday we received a visit from an old resident of thirty years' standing, who in the course of a conversation summed up his opinion of New Orleans with the phrase: "New Orleans is a city where it is impossible to make a home for one's self without marrying. I have tried for thirty years to make a home here, and failed." And this observation set us to meditating whether this were, indeed, owing to any peculiarity of the city, or to that vague longing for the quiet comforts of a household which all bachelors feel as life creeps by and each succeeding winter adds its frost to their beards. To the latter, we trust; for we wish to think well of New Orleans.

There is one thing certain: a rich man who understands what the comforts of life are may make a home for himself anywhere without marrying. But rich men form exceptions to the general rule governing human lives, and we are constrained to consider the matter from the standpoint of those who are not rich, and who must expect for the greater part of their lives to work for others, however independent their capacity

as artisans or talent as professional men may render them. The more sensitive their disposition and the more artistic their ideas, the more difficult, of course, must it be for them to obtain a home conformable to their desires whether married or unmarried. If unmarried, they may expect to have a hard time of it in any city, if compelled to live there for a number of years. Luckily for themselves, many such men are of wandering dispositions. They soon tire of a city; pack up and go elsewhere, after refusing good offers or neglecting first-class chances of becoming wholly independent by remaining. Being rolling stones, they gather no golden moss; and change of scenery and climate, new places and new faces, new friends and strange experiences become for them almost a necessity of life. These are the world's Bohemians. They are a class apart. They enjoy life, too, in a peculiar fashion which the generality of quiet people of regular habits do not understand. But there are many who, desiring to continue single, and obliged to live where fortune has cast their lot or run the risk of losing all and beginning the struggle with the world over again, do forever pursue after the chimera of a home, and cannot understand, until they have tried all possible expedients and suffered all varieties of disappointments, why they cannot make a home for themselves. To such as these, of course, the idea of a home is coupled with memories of the home of one's youth — cozy rooms, quiet, good fare, kindly attention, liberty to act and think, something to regret leaving, and to delight returning to of evenings; — a pleasant greeting, a dog barking with joy, a cozy chair by the fire, and a cat purring on the rug. And

yet how one can obtain these things without a woman's ministry nobody has ever pretended to explain. A woman is the soul of home; and without her there is little more than furniture and brick walls there. She transforms and beautifies everything. You may pooh-pooh and hum-hum! — but you cannot explain how the comforts of a home — a home such as the term was explained to us in childhood — can possibly be obtained without the presence of woman. Without her one may be said to live at such and such a place; but to say that "he has his home there" is sheer humbug. He has no home!

Consequently many really marry just to obtain a home — which is foolish enough, although the natural consequence of social conditions. We remember one case in this city — a young Frenchman who was continually changing his quarters for years, never being able to find rest or comfort in any one house. At first he had quite a number of effects; but these he gradually disposed of, because they proved serious impediments to his nomadic life, until at last his baggage consisted of a newspaper bundle and a box of matches. His marriage proved unhappy enough in the end. He drew an unlucky number in this great life lottery of ours. But to return to the point under consideration: what home is there for men circumstanced like those we spoke of? Boarding-houses do not offer any. Boarding-houses are good and necessary institutions — but there is no home life about them. No man who longs for home comforts can live in any one boarding-house beyond a certain length of time, or in a hotel. There is no privacy, no seclusion; one is always being

brought into contact with persons whom one does not care to know, and obliged to endure things which one does not like to stomach. Life in a private family is better; but, of course, the private-family boarder is always made to feel that he is not one of the family, and the manner of making him feel it is not the most agreeable thing in the world. Renting furnished rooms and boarding in restaurants, or "boarding around" as they call it, is vanity and vexation of spirit, and costs about as much as hotel fare without rendering one any more independent. Furnished rooms! — Furnished rooms! It is an awful, awful subject — too awful to dilate upon! Neither is there any stability about such a method of living. If one does find just what suits him, he can never tell how long it will last; but of one thing he must always be sure — that the better it seems the sooner something dreadful and unexpected is going to happen. And then ?

Well, when you have become tired of boarding-houses and restaurants and furnished rooms, you may try renting or buying a house of your own and furnishing it. But a man must have something round the house, if it is only a dog, to keep him company. And he must also have somebody to take care of his rooms. If he gets a housekeeper, to avoid scandal he must get the oldest and ugliest woman he can find. And servants and others victimize the bachelors terribly. Moreover, everybody living near such a man will regard him as a lunatic or an original, and treat him accordingly. The hand of society is raised against the man who tries to live alone in a house of his own — unless he be very rich. Sometimes five or six bachelors

get together, as we have known them to do in the French quarter, furnish a house, hire a housekeeper, and live a sort of club-life by themselves. But if they should fall out, the whole arrangement would prove more disagreeable than all the combined afflictions common to furnished rooms and boarding-houses.

There is no consolation. To get a home, one must get rich or marry, and even then he may not be lucky enough to get it.

Old-Fashioned Houses

Item, January 12, 1881

Probably there are as fine residences in New Orleans as in any other city of equal population in the United States; and the almost tropical beauty of the grounds and gardens which surround them lends them a charm that cannot be found in many other cities of North America. Most of these fine residences are built upon designs entirely different from the prevailing architecture of New Orleans houses; and it is pleasant to observe that a new style of building even small houses is coming into fashion in different parts of the city. Few of us can afford to live in palaces; and excepting residences that are absolutely palatial, there are very few comfortable dwellings, comparatively speaking, in the Crescent City. There is much picturesqueness; but picturesqueness is not comfort: there is much of outward charm in old- fashioned places, in quaint rooms, in audacious balconies, in mediæval-looking dormers, in peaked roofs, in maisonettes tinted lemon-yellow, pale rose, or faint green; but all this does not give the coziness of a home. The New Orleans of half a century ago is not suited to the wants of the New Orleans of to-day. The population has increased; there are infinitely fewer rich people here than formerly; there are many more inhabitants to the square mile, and the great houses which formerly constituted the winter residences of wealthy planters and others must now be portioned out among many families or transformed

into boarding-houses in order to be made profitable to their owners. A change in the old style of building dwellings is becoming more and more imperative every succeeding year.

The causes of the old style of building are attributable to a wholly different social condition which still existed a generation ago; and there is really no reason why it should survive at present. Nevertheless, we frequently see new houses in process of erection, being constructed upon precisely the same uncomfortable and antiquated plans which should be abolished forever. We have nothing to say against the outward appearance of New Orleans houses. The general effect is very pleasing; — no one with an artistic eye can avoid loving the zigzag outline of peaked roofs with the pretty dormers; the iron arabesques of graceful balconies, the solid doors and burglar-proof shutters, so brightly green. The old-fashioned houses are by no means ugly. But their interior arrangement is altogether condemnable and renders them almost unfit for modern homes. Take, for example, the ordinary double cottages of which there are thousands upon thousands in New Orleans. Not only do all the rooms open into each other, either with large folding or sliding or the ordinary doors; but each room of each house often opens into each room of its twin on the other side. Thus there are from two to three doors to each room, besides windows; rendering it difficult to warm any apartment in a damp New Orleans winter. Privacy is impossible; seclusion a mockery. Even the attics of two houses open into one another. Suppose one is looking for a house, and expresses his dissatisfaction with

this plan, the proprietor will exclaim with astonishment: "Why! there is a door; and the door is closed!" A thin door does not ensure seclusion or even quiet. Every sound can be heard distinctly in both houses — the crying of children in the night; family quarrels; noises of household work; and many other things which should not be heard at all. And the doors are not even double. In nine cases out of ten daylight shows through them. The same thing renders it very difficult to obtain comfortable furnished rooms in the city. Every room opens into another; and every movement of one's neighbor or neighboress is distinctly audible. All this might be avoided by the construction of hallways; and certainly it is not for want or value of space that we have so few hallways in the city. Immense rooms, high and airy! — but cold and comfortless — opening into other immense rooms — all opening into other houses: of such there is no end.

Now if there is one thing more essential than any other to the comfort of a house, it is seclusion! The English understand this fact even better than the Americans, and their cottages are model homes. When a man enters his house he wishes to be able when he pleases to shut himself up from the rest of the world, to be alone with his family or with his thoughts, to rest himself after the day's anxieties without further turmoil or annoyance. But how is he to do this when he finds only a partition thin as the cover of a novel between himself and others who are not of his family, and who live practically on the same floor and almost in the same room? If he wishes to enjoy an hour in his private study, it is not pleasant to be obliged

all the time to listen to noises in the next room, even if made by his own servants or his own children. For members of a family themselves require at times to seclude themselves from other members of the family; — there are business matters to be talked of; there are projects which children or servants should not hear; there are numberless things which the heads of a household wish to discuss by themselves. And to warm such houses in winter there must be a fire in every room upon the same floor; otherwise one will find that folding doors are a mockery and sliding doors a vexation of spirit. The double cottage is an abomination; and even the single cottage without a hallway is an affliction. Is it agreeable to be unable to go to bed either without passing through somebody else's room or having somebody else passing though your room? It is not even a civilized way of living; and certainly a vast majority of New Orleans houses would appear to a stranger to have been constructed with little regard to common decency. The truth is simply that twenty-five years ago people here lived very differently from what they can afford to do now; — everything was on a larger and more generous scale; and perhaps the dwellings were excellently adapted at that time to the wants of their tenants. To-day all is changed. Picturesque and uncomfortable New Orleans must disappear to give place to one perhaps less outwardly attractive but less illusive and more substantial. The result will certainly be less consumption and less rheumatism.

The Vendor of Wisdom

Item, September 15, 1880

The Vendor of Wisdom selleth and also buyeth at a moderate price all the wisdom that hath been crystallized into the shape of books.

In his antiquated and darksome little shop, the thoughts of thirty centuries reside.

Every wave of civilization that has ebbed over the face of the earth, has drifted something into that little dusty bookstore.

Every great event in the history of the earth has contributed a something to those dusty shelves.

All nations and tongues are represented there; all the philosophers have riches there; and there all the poets have preserved their word-music.

As for the antiquarian, he thinketh much of these things; for he knoweth by heart the story of each book, and now rarely openeth any save new ones — works of this age of ours.

Then he saith—

"Pshaw! They call that new, and I have beheld the same in books that were written lo! three thousand years ago!

"The founders of the Semitic and Aryan religions knew these things; and forsooth these modern fools offer them to us as something novel!

"The Egyptians were versed in the very profoundest philosophy of all these questions; — they were taught also in Rome and in Greece.

"Nevertheless, there are people in these days who imagine they can write something new upon the subject."

And saying these things he putteth the new book aside, and he taketh a duster and dusteth tenderly the thoughts of Plato and Aristotle and Socrates, and patteth the good old books on the back.

Never doth he lose patience — not even when bibliophilists steal his books —

Nor when cockroaches devour the backs of Aristophanes and Pliny, and of Diodorus Siculus, of Athenseus and Sophocles and Petronius —

Nor when bookworms bore holes through the Elzevir text of the Fathers of the Church —

Nor when, having bought a book for a good price, he afterward discovereth that the person who sold it to him had previously torn out the engravings —

Nor even when having been told to "lay books

aside," the person for whom they are laid aside never cometh back — so that they lay there until all hope of selling them has departed.

He putteth works of godly piety in the waste-basket.

And books in the French language, robed in yellow like Roman courtesans — these he selleth for a good price.

"For such," he saith, "is the depravity of human nature."

Never have I been able to learn whether he saith this seriously or not — so much doth his eye twinkle when he saith it.

He is never absent from his post; — for twenty-five years he hath lived every day with his books from 7.30 A.M. to 7.30 P.M.

And there will he remain, let us hope, for many years more.

Until they take him from his books and file him away, even as a roll of MS. in the marble pigeon holes which are never dusted and whose contents are never looked at.

Some Positive Opinions

Item, April 27, 1881

In a curiously illustrated edition of Balzac's "Peau de Chagrin" there is a strange and terrible face which some of you may remember having seen: it is the face of the bric-à-brac dealer who sold the mysterious parchment — a forehead of immense breadth; a nose like that of Mephisto in Retsch's outlines; a mouth thin, straight, and passionless; eyes large and sinister, with brows knotted above the nose like adders and rising wickedly toward the temples — in short, a face most sinister, most infernal, but withal fascinating with a diabolic fascination. Now, can you imagine such a visage transformed and softened by youth and femininity, made beautiful without losing its strength of menacing wickedness; the nose a little less rugged, the eyes a little larger, the brows a little lighter? Then you have before you an idea of the dancer's face.

We sat and talked under the fig-tree. At least *she* talked; I listened under the steady gaze of her basilisk eyes. She seemed to speak all modern tongues fluently; had excited passion by her lithe grace and surpassing skill of limb-curving in half the capitals of Europe. She talked about Havana, Buenos Ayres, Valparaiso, Vera Cruz, Mexico City; described Spanish dances in a mocking way peculiar to herself, speaking all the while in a voice deep and sweet as the lower tone of some reed instrument. But the depth of the voice and its sweetness wrought an unpleasant effect

upon the listener — such an effect as a wizard's music might have, luring to danger.

"I hate men," she said, with Italian vehemence, and an indescribable gesture of disgust; — "oh, how I detest them! It amuses me when I am dancing to think of all those thousand eyes glaring upon me, as at something they are almost mad to touch and cannot reach, and dare not touch if they could. It gives me pleasure; and often when I smile on the stage the smile is not mechanical; it is prompted by a sense of amusement which is too strong for me to resist. I know that hundreds of young fools will leave the theatre devoured with a wish they cannot gratify. Ah! I hate men!

"Of course you know as well as I do that they pester and torment us. I am burdened with letters, presents — stuff! Love! Ah, bah! In a life such as mine one soon learns what love is worth! I used to read the letters I got. Now I seldom read more than the first line! Presents? Yes, all I want.

"Let me tell you my way of treating the fools. I never answer a letter unless it is accompanied by a present — and the present must have some value. Flowers! — I hate flowers! What good are flowers to me? What value have flowers twenty-four hours after being thrown at my feet? I would be as pleased to receive a jar of ashes or a box of sand. Do you imagine I would pick up their worthless flowers? Never! I can always find some way to avoid that.

"Then I never answer in writing — never! No woman who is not an idiot will do that. I let somebody else carry my message — always worded in such a way that the fool imagines it is the greatest privilege in

the world to be permitted to see me. When he does see me, he pays dearly for it, if he is worth anything; and if he is not — which I soon find out — he never sees me again — except on the stage. And then it amuses me to know how I can torture him.

"I never say a pleasant word to an admirer. Why, if I did, the fool would really think he had made an immense impression! I have my own special way of treating him; he always brings me a present, of course. I never thank him! Never! I look at it; find fault with it; laugh at it; mock the man; and finally when he does not know what to do, I condescend to lay it aside. That means acceptance. He buys a better present next time; every time he buys me something, I treat him worse than before. Much worse! I have tormented men until they cried — yes, cried: the ridiculous fools!

"No; the worse you treat men, the better they like you! And you know it is all passion — wind and foam and smoke — a fancy — a passing beat of the blood, for which a man would sacrifice my life and happiness if he could and dared! But I know them! I can play with them as an angler plays with a fish! I sometimes let them kiss me if they are not too nasty — or feel my arms and shoulders, smooth me down — you know the way men like to stroke a woman, as if a woman was a cat! But I have a certain respect for myself. I believe in nothing but myself — and my mother, yes! Now, do you suppose I will allow men to make me their puppet, their doll, their kitten, their lemon to be squeezed and thrown away? Bah! I can play salamander. I am a juggler that can handle fire without burning my fingers. I can touch pitch and not be defiled.

No man can boast of the contrary. There are liars who say such things about all stage characters; but what do I care? I have made men pay well for all that men have said about me.

"Afraid? Pooh! Of what? I know desperate men when I see them. I have not lived and traveled for nothing. And I calculate my time nicely. I know just what I can accomplish during my stay in a city. And do you know that no man has dared to insult my face? I mean coarsely and abusively. They are afraid of me. The secret of success in life is to make people afraid of you. Only fools remain on the defensive. I am always on the aggressive. Insult! — I would poniard a man if I saw a thought of insult in his eyes! Law! What do I care for law? I am a law unto myself. Why, a woman has always the advantage in such cases. Suppose I say: 'That man came to see me under some pretext. He attempted to take advantage; I know how to take care of myself; — I killed him!' Who will contradict me?

"Lover! Nonsense! Perhaps, when I leave the stage! But I shall be mistress. Do you think I would allow a man to say to me, Do this, Do that?

"I forgot what I was telling you— when I allow a man to kiss me, he begins to be elated. He thinks he has an easy road before him. He begins to look confident. He becomes airy. Then the day after I refuse to speak to him, or see him at all! He feels as if struck by lightning. He imagines all kinds of things — that he has been slandered or something. He wants to make an explanation. He becomes pathetically eloquent. He writes crazy letters. I pay no attention to him. He becomes feverish, furious, frantic, desperate. He would

sell his soul just to be able to say one little word to me; — one little word would be for him what one little drop of water would be to the tongue of the damned. And he cannot get the chance to speak. He thinks of killing somebody. Then is the time to step in and ask and receive. Finally they learn to hate me. That is just what I want, and this is how I rid myself of them. The Fools!"

Voices of Dawn

Item, July 22, 1881

A dreadful sound is in his ears. — Job xv, 21.

There have never been so many fruit-peddlers and viand-peddlers of all sorts as at the present time — an encouraging sign of prosperity and the active circulation of money.

With the first glow of sunlight the street resounds with their cries; and, really, the famous "Book of London Cries" contains nothing more curious than some of these vocal advertisements — these musical announcements, sung by Italians, negroes, Frenchmen, and Spaniards. The vendor of fowls pokes in his head at every open window with cries of "Chick-EN,

Ma-damma, Chick-EN!" and the seller of "Lem-ONS — fine Lem-ONS!" follows in his footsteps. The peddlers of "Ap-PULLS!" of "Straw-BARE-eries!" and " Black-Brees!" — all own sonorous voices. There is a handsome Italian with a somewhat ferocious pair of black eyes, who sells various oddities, and has adopted the word "lagniappe" for his war-cry — pronouncing it Italianwise.

He advances noiselessly to open windows and doors, plunges his blazing black glance into the interior, and suddenly queries in a deep bass, like a clap of thunder, "LAGNIAPPA, Madam-a! — la-gniap-PA!" Then there is the Cantelope Man, whose cry is being imitated by all the children:

"Cantel-lope-ah!
Fresh and fine,
Jus from the vine,
Only a dime!"

There are also two peddlers, the precise meaning of whose cries we have never been able to determine. One shouts, or seems to shout, "A-a-a-a-ah! SHE got." Just what "SHE got" we have not yet been able to determine; but we fancy it must be disagreeable, as the crier's rival always shouts — "I–I–I! — I want nothing!" with a tremendous emphasis on the I. There is another fellow who seems to shout something which is not exactly proper for modest ears to hear; but he is really only announcing that he has fine potatoes for sale. Then there is the Clothespole Man, whose musical, quavering cry is heard at the distance of miles

on a clear day, " Clo-ho-ho-ho-ho-ho-ho-ho-se-poles!" As a trilling tenor he is simply marvelous. The "Coaly-coaly" Man, a merry little Gascon, is too well known as a singer to need any criticism; but he is almost ubiquitous. There is also the fig-seller, who crieth in such a manner that his "Fresh figs!" seems to be "Ice crags!" And the fan-sellers, who intend to call, "Cheap fans!" but who really seem to yell "Jap-ans!" and "Chapped hands!" Then there is the seller of "Towwells" and the sellers of "Ochre-A" who appear to deal in but one first-class quality of paint, if we dare believe the mendacious sounds which reach our ears; neither must we forget the vendors of "Tom-ate-toes!" Whose toes? we should like to know.

These are new cries, with perhaps three exceptions; — with the old cries added to the list — the "calas" and the "plaisir" and other Creole calls, we might "spread out" over another column. If any one has a little leisure and a little turn for amusement, he can certainly have plenty of fun while listening to the voices of the peddlers entering his room together with the first liquid gold of sunrise.

THE END

Notes

Notes at the foot of the page are by the author or by Charles Woodward Hutson.

18.1 **La Douane**] customs house (French)

18.4 Karnac] temple complex in Egypt with portions dating from the 3rd millennium BCE.

27.1 **Ultra-Canal**] Canal Street followed the route of a proposed — but never built — canal linking the Mississippi River with Bayou St. John and Lake Pontchartrain. It marked a dividing line between the older Creole French Quarter and the newer Anglo-American neighborhoods to the west.

31.32 cochonnerie] trash (*cochon* — pig)

32.15 canaille] the lowest class of people, the vulgar

32.30 bayadère] professional female dancer in India

34.6 berceuse] rocker

34.8 *farfadet*] sprites or fairies of French folklore

37.14 Gehon] one of four rivers issuing from the Garden of Eden

40.24 Choppinism] Dr. Samuel Choppin was President of the Louisiana Board of Health. He was criticized for allowing commercial interests to limit efforts to control the yellow fever epidemic. See Dennis East II, "Health and Wealth: Goals of the New Orleans Public Health Movement, 1879-84," *Louisiana History: The Journal of the Louisiana Historical Association,* Vol. 9, No. 3 (Summer, 1968), pp. 245-275.

46.3 Est-ce que vous vous fichez de moi? 'cré nom!] Are you kidding me? holy name!

46.18 bêtises] foolery

48.11 locataire] tenant

48.13 essuiemains] hand towels

48.16 vente à l'encan] auction

60.26 *sans foi ni loi ni roi*] without faith, law, or king

69.29 embaralificotée] embarked, underway

81.5 loquitur] speaks (Latin stage direction)

81.11 bêtises] foolery

82.1-2 canaille and racaille and charogne] scoundrel, scum, and carrion

83.6 berceuse] rocking chair

83.12 les sacrés voleurs] holy thieves

83.12-13 Charogne de pays] country carrion

92.19 aqua Tofana] poisonous compound of arsenic, lead, and belladonna used in 17th-century Italy

93.25 nolle prosequi] decision not to prosecute

99.1 **Whited Sepulchres**] Mathew 23.27 "Woe unto you, scribes and Pharisees, hypocrites! for ye are like unto whited sepulchres, which indeed appear beautiful outward, but are within full of dead men's bones, and of all uncleanness."

99.8 *Kismet*] fate, destiny

101.1 Eleusis] site of the "Eleusinian Mysteries," the most famous of the secret religious rites of ancient Greece

101.24 Shulamitess] referring to the female protagonist in the Bible's Song of Songs

102.22 Coæ vesta] semi-transparent silk garments from the island of Cos (Kos) in antiquity

110.3 su servidor de V.] at your service

112.4-5 cambrure de taille] arch of the waist

112.7 "Que es bonita!"] How pretty!

112.13 "A quien busca V., señor?"] "Who are you looking for, sir?"

112.19 "Mil gracias] A thousand thanks

112.21 "Yo estaba allá!"] "I was there!"

113.9 "Lo me gustaria mucho,"] "I would like it very much,"

113.11 puro] cigar made exclusively of tobacco from a single country

117.9 the serpent slain by the army of Regulus] In 255 BCE, during the First Punic War, Roman general Marcus Atilius Regulus led an invasion of Carthage that was met by a giant serpent or reptile at the Bagradas River. The beast was finally killed by the army and its skin — reportedly 120 feet long — sent to Rome.

131.3-4 Balzac's "Peau de Chagrin"] 1831 novel known in English as *The Wild Ass's Skin*

131.8 Mephisto in Retsch's outlines] Friedrich August Moritz Retzsch (1779–1857), German painter, draughtsman, and etcher, was known for his etchings of Goethe's *Faust.*

134.13 poniard] small slim dagger

Abstract

New Orleans in 1878 was the most exotic and cosmopolitan city in North America. An international port, with more than 200,000 inhabitants, it was open to French, Spanish, Mexican, South American, and West Indian cultural influences, and home to a thriving population descended from free African Americans. It was also a battleground in the fight against yellow fever (malaria) and in the political upheavals that followed the end of Reconstruction. The continued influx of Anglo-Americans and the renewed ascendancy of white supremacists threatened to overwhelm the local blend of languages, races, and cultures that enlivened the unique Creole character of the city. Writing for an English-language newspaper, Lafcadio Hearn presented the speech, charm, and humor of the Creolized natives on the other side of Canal Street, and illustrated his sketches with woodcut cartoons — the first of their kind in any Southern paper. These vignettes, published in the New Orleans *Daily Item* during 1878-1880, capture a traditionalist urban world and its colorful characters with a delicate and sympathetic understanding.

About the Author

Lafcadio Hearn (1850–1904) was born on the Ionian island of Lefkada to a Greek mother and British Army father. His parents' separation and annullment left him, at age 7, the ward of a paternal great-aunt in Dublin. She sent him to Catholic schools in Ireland, France, and England, but family bankruptcy interrupted his education and led to his emigration to America in 1869. His promised contacts proved worthless, and he was left broke and alone in Cincinnati, Ohio. He found work there with the expatriot English printer and socialist Henry Watkin and later as a newspaper reporter for the *Daily Enquirer*. In 1874 he married Alethea Foley, a 20-year-old African American woman (in violation of Ohio's anti-miscegenation law). They divorced in 1877, and Hearn moved to New Orleans where he lived ten years and wrote for several newspapers, starting with the *Daily Item* in June 1878, and later for national publications *Harper's Weekly* and *Scribner's Magazine*. He went to the West Indies as a correspondent 1887-1890, and then to Japan. He married Koizumi Setsuko in 1891, became a Japanese citizen in 1896, adopting the name Koizumi Yakumo, and taught at high schools and universities. His published books on Japanese culture were instrumental in introducing Meiji Japan to an international audience. He was succeeded as professor of literature at Tokyo Imperial University by Natsume Sōseki.

Charles Woodward Hutson (1840-1936) was a Confederate veteran, lawyer, painter, author, and professor of Greek and modern languages at Southern colleges.

Made in the USA
Columbia, SC
05 September 2022